A Maze of Crime and Mystery.
A World Where Killing Is Easy,
and Power Is Absolute . . .

Mulvaney: He likes ballet and busting hoods. He proved himself in the Special Forces and on the streets of Chicago. When the Feds need a cop to go crashing into the Orient, he's chosen for the job—because the one thing he will never do is quit . . .

Osgood: A veteran CIA operative, he lost his wife and children in a tragic accident. Now he only lives for the field—and the thrill of the work he does better than anyone else . . .

Andy Oakwood: Her looks were all class, her moves strictly professional. She's been a cop in Detroit and an MP in the Army, but nothing could have prepared her for the savage violence of the Yakusa —or the love of a man named Mulvaney . . .

Tanaka: He's a public prosecutor in Tokyo, and an underworld operator making waves from Southeast Asia to Moscow. He wants the Yakusa to take over the drug business from the American mafia—and then he wants to cut them out . . .

Tsukiyama Koji: In the dark whirlpool of violence and greed that has sucked in the KGB, the CIA, the FBI and the most vicious criminals in the world, he is the man everyone fears and no one knows—the ninja, the dark key to . . .

YAKUS

THE YAKUSA TATTOO

Jerry and Sharon Ahern

POCKET BOOKS

New York London Toronto Sydney Tokyo

Another *Original* publication of POCKET BOOKS

 POCKET BOOKS, a division of Simon & Schuster, Inc.
1230 Avenue of the Americas, New York, N.Y. 10020

Copyright © 1988 by Jerry and Sharon Ahern
Cover artwork copyright © 1988 Peter Caras

ISBN: 0-671-62668-X

First Pocket Books printing May 1988

10 9 8 7 6 5 4 3 2 1

POCKET and colophon are trademarks of
Simon & Schuster, Inc.

Printed in the U.S.A.

To Jerry Buergel,
who knows Chicago like we do.
Best wishes, buddy.

THE
YAKUSA
TATTOO

1

Ice-Out

SHEET ICE WAS LAYERED over yellow-tinged snow, and layered over again with a crust of white where the snow hadn't yet picked up the pollution-frosted massive mounds of frozen slush erected like bastions against an enemy, a perimeter broken only by the entrances notched into the parking lot. The snow had been falling with unremitting regularity for the past ten days. Overnight, there would be a dusting of it, and by rush hour at five in the evening when the Ryan and the Kennedy and the Ike were already glutted beyond capacity and the entrance ramps were spilling back into the feeder streets, it would come again, huge flakes driven on a gusting lake wind. South Side blacks called the wind the Hawk because it had talons that gouged through your clothes and grabbed you by the short hair and didn't let go until you escaped it indoors. And if you were one of the street people who weren't lucky enough to find a flop with the Salvation Army or one of the missions, the talons would go in so deep you'd die. He'd seen them, the leavings of the Hawk, blue-veined yellowed faces or grayed ones, depending on what race they'd started out. The Hawk was egalitarian—race, creed and national origin didn't make any difference.

He wondered if a well-fed, healthy man huddled under a blanket and sheltered from the wind could freeze like that. "Lew, I can't feel the toes on my left foot."

"Stomp your foot."

He stomped his foot and Lewellyn Fields snarled, "Son of a bitch, Mulvaney!"

"What you say 'bout my momma, man!"

"Cut out the phony black shit—and next time you stomp your foot, don't do it on my foot."

Mulvaney looked out from under his corner of the blanket through the open driver's-side window of the Ford. Nothing in the parking lot but the same ice and snow and half-dozen or so snow-abandoned cars. He looked across the front seatback. Between the blue and frost-gray splotches where their breath had frozen, he could make out the hulking gray of the Field Museum of Natural History at the edge of the parking lot. He wondered if any of the specimens inside had been found frozen to death. The face of his wristwatch was frosted over and he rubbed it with the gloved knuckle of his right thumb to read it. He drew his wrist back under the storm sleeve and told his partner, "Almost six-thirty."

"Two fuckin' hours?"

"Time flies when you're havin' fun, huh?" Mulvaney tried finding his cigarettes with his gloves still on. "What the hell are we doin' here?"

"Waiting to make a bust."

"I know that—shit, but why us?"

"We're cops—don't make a bust every once in a while, they stop payin' us or transfer us to property recovery or records. What you squirmin' around like that for?"

"Lookin' for my cigarettes."

"They ain't in my pocket, fool!"

"Yeah, well . . ." Mulvaney kept digging. He found the cigarettes and shook one out of the pack and got his lips around it. "Wanta cigarette?"

"I quit—yeah, gimme one."

Mulvaney passed the pack over and Lew Fields shook one out for himself, then handed back the pack. "You got a light, Lew?"

"I told ya, I quit. Where's your lighter? I saw it a couple minutes ago."

"Hang on," and Mulvaney kept digging. "That's where it is!"

"The lighter?"

"Naw, that third speedloader I thought I'd left at home. In my coat pocket." He took out the speedloader and blew tobacco bits and lint out of it and put it under his winter coat, in the pocket of the sport coat where it belonged with the other two. He found the lighter. "Here." He rolled the Bic's striking wheel a couple of times and got a flame. "What about Harvey?"

Fields coughed through a cloud of exhaled gray smoke. But it was so cold it looked the same way when you exhaled only air. "Harvey?"

"Yeah, Harvey. That house musta cost him a hundred and seventy-five thousand bucks if it cost him a dime."

"Maybe his wife had money."

"My ass—or hers. I grew up with Carol. Her old man drove a taxicab. Harvey's on the take."

"Just 'cause a cop's got himself a nice house don't mean—"

"Nice house. A Cadillac. Vogue tires. You know what a set of Vogues runs for a full-size car?"

"Okay, so fine—Harvey's on the take for somebody. Cool for Harvey."

"I coulda been on the take."

Fields looked at him under the blanket. "Maybe that old Porsche of yours will make somebody think you're on the take too. Cheer up, Ed."

"'Old' is right, Lew."

"For ten years old and with all the salt and crap they throw on the streets, it's in pretty good shape."

Mulvaney only nodded his thanks. There was a cold spot by his right knee and he tucked the blanket closer to him. The Porsche had been what he'd bought with all the dough he'd saved while he was in Vietnam playing George of the Jungle. With the prices on Porsches now, he couldn't afford one in a million years. At least the "bathtub" design hadn't changed much with time. And all the meticulous care he gave it had made the car into a classic. He'd been offered almost thirty grand for it a year or so back and his wife's lawyer had tried to get him to sell it a couple of years before that so the money could be split in the divorce settlement. The car . . . He had the sudden realization that the white

3

Porsche was really kind of symbolic, like it told the story of his life or something. A war. A war to get through college without getting drafted out of it. A war in Vietnam that nobody except the people stuck fighting it had wanted to win. The girl of his dreams had turned into the kind of woman nightmares were built of. Another war in divorce court. Then keeping the car cherry. It had been a constant battle—Edgar Patrick Mulvaney versus the Forces of Nature and the City of Chicago.

In the spring they repaired potholes with temporary stuff that crumbled away by winter, and you banged into the potholes and threw the front end out and screwed up your tires. Then in the spring they filled the potholes again and the crap got thrown up on the rocker panels and you cleaned it off. In the winter they sprayed salt all over the streets and if you got the car washed the locks would freeze and then you crouched down beside the door and blew hot air into the lock and everybody who drove by thought you were slipping your car the tongue. Half of the time you still had to find boiling water or heat up the key with your cigarette lighter.

On your shift, and too many other times off-shift, you pursued armed and dangerous nutballs for the compensatory time it would earn you—if you ever got a day off when you didn't have to show up in court to watch your case get thrown out and the nutball you collared get put back on the street so you could collar him all over again. You fought the forces of lawlessness, not for some noble purpose, but because if you didn't, the paychecks would stop and the house you inherited from an aunt who couldn't stand you while she was alive would be lost.

He remembered to light his own cigarette, and as he exhaled smoke and moist steam, he said to Lew Fields, "You forgot to wish me happy anniversary. Hell of a best friend you are."

Fields grinned, a gold tooth gleaming amid the white ones in the upper row. "Two years—yeah—hey. Happy Anniversary, Ed." Fields reached his left hand under the right side of his leather coat. If it had been the right hand going under the left side, a gun would have come back out. Instead, it was the hip flask. Fields unscrewed the cap. "Have some Jack."

4

Mulvaney shrugged. If a machine needed antifreeze, well . . . He took a swallow of the Black Label. Fields started singing "The Anniversary Waltz."

"Up yours." Mulvaney shot Fields a bird, then shot him a grin and handed back the flask. Fields rubbed it off on his sleeve and took a swallow, tilting the flask high and back.

"To Stella." Fields grinned, corking the flask again.

"I'm so glad she found a fella." Mulvaney laughed. "Stella woulda liked it better if I'd been on the take." It had been two years ago that Stella had remarried and the alimony payments had stopped.

"You into that shit again, man?"

"No, I mean it. I had all the opportunities. And I blew 'em. Hell, I coulda been in organized crime! Coulda amounted to somethin'! After all, my dad was a cop in the thirties in Cicero. Talk about opportunity."

"Was your dad on the take?"

"Wash your mouth out with soap, my man."

"So, it runs in the family, then. You never could have been a successful criminal anyway. You got terminal honesty."

"Kick me."

"I'd have to get out from under this damn blanket and I'm not doing that until our friends show up with their illicit narcotics and whatever other shit they got. Anyway, don't blame yourself, man—a lot of people are honest. It's like V.D. Hard to shake. And I gotta tell ya this, Ed."

"What?" The cigarette was burned down low enough so that to keep smoking it he needed to take off his glove. He threw it out the window instead.

"Admittedly, there are not as many honest folks as there used to be, but those that are bear up under the condition with considerably more grace than you do. My wife's honest. I don't hear her grousin' about it all the time. I'm honest. Don't hear me complainin'—not most of the time, anyway."

Mulvaney just shivered and huddled into the blanket more. When they had pulled into the parking lot at the Field Museum two hours earlier, the whitecaps breaking off Lake Michigan just across the Drive had been crusty with ice. To keep their car from looking suspicious, Mulvaney had shut off the engine. Otherwise, the exhaust would have steamed out behind them. But so the windows wouldn't freeze over and they couldn't see out, and so it wouldn't look like somebody was hiding inside the car, they had rolled the windows down. After the first fifteen minutes they'd both crawled over into the back seat and huddled under the blanket together.

If Vincent Washington showed up like the snitch had said he would . . . "I hope Washington resists arrest."

"Why? You wanna try out a new gun like the last time?"

"No—if it wasn't for Washington we wouldn't be sittin' here freezin' to death. I'm gonna kick his black ass right into the damn lake."

"A racial slur? I always knew you were a racist. When my wife hadda go and be fool enough to invite you over for Thanksgiving again, you hadda ask if we were havin' chitlins."

"You did last year, dammit!"

"You want soul food, you take your white ass down to some fuckin' restaurant on the West Side next time. Greens and chitlins—shit."

"So? I like ethnic food."

"Hell, next thing you know, you'll quit the cops and buy you a plantation and try to buy my wife and me too so we can work in your fuckin' cotton fields. 'Oh, yessuh, massah.' Shit!"

He didn't know why he looked up, but he did. "Hey— goin' down, Lew." Mulvaney pushed away the blanket and rolled stiff-legged into the front seat, breaking the L-frame Smith .357 from between the lips of the Bianchi X-15 rig suspended under his left shoulder.

"Dammit," Fields hissed, a snapping sound as he rolled in on the passenger side beside him, the Detonics Scoremaster .45 out of the leather, cocked and locked in his right fist.

Mulvaney realized he still had his right glove in his teeth and he spit it out, steam still coming off his hand as he bunched it around the black checkered rubber Pachmayrs. The revolver, a 681, stainless steel with fixed sights, had been action-tuned buttery smooth and round-butted, then Metalifed over the stainless, giving the steel a gunmetal-gray cast. A red insert had been set into the ramp front sight. He

6

gave the speedloaders a pat through his winter coat. It wasn't just Washington and a seller. It was Washington and three of his badasses and the Colombian guy and the Anglo who looked like he liked boys who was always with the Colombian and three other guys Mulvaney didn't recognize.

"Who you think they are, Ed?"

"I don't know—nine guys."

"Two of us."

"Call for backup."

"They'll hear us."

"Fine—wait until the buy goes down, then call for backup. Okay?"

"Yeah, already," Fields snapped.

Mulvaney had his eyes just at the level of the doorframe so he could watch the guys in the parking lot without them seeing him if they looked toward the car. Washington's stretched Continental still had the engine running and the glass was tinted so darkly Mulvaney couldn't tell if there was a tenth man behind the wheel or not. But there was no one behind the wheel of the other car, the one the Colombian and his squeeze had come up in, the Cadillac's driver's-side doors open and the interior of the car clearly visible. The motor was still running. "Where's the shotgun, Lew?"

"It was . . . Aww, shit."

"Whatchya mean—"

"In the trunk."

"Wonderful. Then get your butt back in there and dig through the back seat until you reach the trunk. Then let me know."

"My—"

"Wait—" The Colombian guy—he was tall, thin-featured like a woman, and had enough oil on his black hair to give every car in the lot a lube job—was taking a briefcase from Vincent Washington—also tall, also thin, but with a face that looked like anything but a woman's. And Vincent Washington was taking a black bag that looked like a box with a handle on it from the Anglo guy. A salesman's sample case. Mulvaney knew what the samples were.

"Yeah, that coke really makes you smile," Fields whispered, echoing Mulvaney's thoughts.

"Skip the shotgun."

"White of you."

"Bite it." Mulvaney reached for the door handle.

"I'm sliding out on your side—both my hands gonna be full."

Mulvaney looked at Fields and grinned. "If we were crooks, we'd be safe at home in bed right now."

"Or, on the down side, standin' out there tryin' to look tough and about to get busted."

Mulvaney didn't say anything.

"Make the call?"

"Make the call."

"This is Chicago 4192. Harvey, you there?"

Harvey—the guy who was on the take—and two other uniform guys were in the assigned backup blue-and-white that was parked just south by Soldier Field. "Lew—that you?"

"No, it's Santa Claus."

"Man, we're stuck. Tires froze up in the ruts. Sludged in, Lew."

"Gimme that." Mulvaney ripped the microphone from Lew Fields's fist. "Harvey?"

"Yeah—hey, Ed. Cold out there, huh."

"Kiss my ass." Mulvaney threw down the microphone. "You cool?" He looked at Lew.

"Was I ever anything else?" The bright polished .45 was in Fields's right fist and a four-inch stainless Smith .44 Magnum was in his left.

"I guess that means I gotta show the badge, right?"

"'Less one of us got three hands, it does."

"Shit—" Mulvaney wrenched the door handle and grabbed for the badge case in his left outside pocket, flipping it open just like Jack Webb had done it and he'd practiced doing with his dad's badge when he'd been a kid. Suddenly he was standing wide open without cover beside the left-front fender of the Ford and wondering why he was being so stupid, shouting fast at the top of his lungs in the cold dawn air, "Chicago Police! Up with your hands!"

He thought he heard Lew Fields laughing as the Colombian guy and Vincent Washington, just as if they'd rehearsed it, drew guns in perfect unison from the pockets of their overcoats and started shooting toward Fields and himself.

8

But Mulvaney was already moving, rolling over the hood of the car, plopping down into the snowbank beside which the Ford was parked. And Fields was already returning fire, the .45 and the .44 Magnum alternating, deafening in the cold air.

Mulvaney had his badge case in his pocket as he threw his right arm up just high enough to shoot across the hood, dumping the first six rounds from the L-frame just to show his sincerity and to cover Fields, who was diving down behind the rear end of the Ford.

"Shit!" Fields shouted.

"What do we do?" Mulvaney called back, finding one of the speedloaders as his left thumb stroked back the Smith & Wesson's ejector rod. He rammed the Safariland loader against the ejector star and dumped six fresh 125-grain Federals into the cylinder.

"We? What you mean we, paleface?"

Mulvaney just looked at him for a second. There really wasn't much choice. "Into the car—we gotta block 'em." Mulvaney yanked open the passenger-side door and threw himself down across the seat. More gunfire now from the druggies, the windshield spiderwebbing as Mulvaney realized at least one of the bad guys had an automatic weapon. "I'm gonna kick Harvey's brains out!"

"Can't kick out somethin' the man don't have," Fields shouted, Mulvaney hearing the trunk lid slam down shut, Fields saying, "Roll!" in the next instant as he lunged into the back seat.

Mulvaney was cranking the ignition. "Damn Chicago P.D. batteries!" With the radios and the Kojak light and the constant exposure to the cold, half the time you got a car assigned to you and before you could get it out of the lot you had to have it jump-started.

"Want me to check if the bad guys got jumper cables?" Fields laughed, Mulvaney hearing the tromboning of the Remington 870's pump, then his ears popping as the twelve-gauge went off right behind his head. The Ford would start. Fields said, "Quiet is the sound of a—"

"Shut up!"

The pump fired again behind Mulvaney's head and simultaneously the engine turned over. "Keep down, Lew!" Mulvaney had the selector into Drive 1 and stomped the gas, the Ford fishtailing on the ice, moving ahead, already the Lincoln Continental moving for the gap in the wall of ice, the Cadillac taking off in the other direction. But it was Vincent Washington that Mulvaney wanted anyway. Mulvaney pushed the pedal to the floor and wrenched the selector into Drive, the wheels spinning, the Ford out of any real control, but sliding fast now as Mulvaney cut the wheel—right toward the Continental. "Watch out, Lew!" Mulvaney threw open the driver's side door and shouted, "Jump for it!" as he threw himself into the snow, the fishtailing rear end almost rolling over him, Fields hurtling himself out, coming down on his right shoulder and rolling.

Mulvaney was up, running. The Continental was almost to the gate in the ice wall, but the Ford was catching up to it, broadsiding the Lincoln backward across the passenger side, the Lincoln skidding now, half-climbing a hill of frozen slush, stalling out and skidding left on its undercarriage, slamming into the next hill and stopping dead.

Mulvaney threw himself behind another hill of ice and snow as the submachine gun opened up again, great chunks of ice exploding in every direction around him as he stabbed the Smith revolver toward the car and fired. The booming of the shotgun—Fields. Mulvaney rammed another speedloader full into the .357 as he tucked down, his eyes scanning across the ice to see where Fields was hiding. He spotted him about ten yards back and twenty yards left behind a salt-stained abandoned car somebody had pushed into the lot off the Drive.

Mulvaney transferred the Smith into his left fist and reached under his coat to the small of his back. He snatched the Beretta 92F military pistol from his belt and thumbed up the safety. Another short burst from the subgun. "Now, Lew!" Mulvaney shouted across the parking lot. And he was up, running, one pistol in each hand, at the far edge of his peripheral vision seeing Fields running, firing the shotgun.

All four doors of the marooned Lincoln Continental flew open simultaneously, the subgunner rolling down the hill of ice, firing wildly, Mulvaney skidding to his knees on the ice just like he'd done as a kid so many times. But it wasn't some macho game this time. Both pistols stabbed forward in his fists as he shouted, "Lay down your weapon!" He didn't wait for a reply, both handguns firing, the Smith emptied, a half-dozen rounds out of the Beretta, the subgunner's body rocking with the hits, slamming into the ice-covered parking-lot surface, the gun skidding away from him, his body just twitching.

The shotgun again—Mulvaney heard the blast and the shattering of glass almost simultaneously as he rolled right, two of Washington's men huddled behind the hood of the Lincoln, firing handguns intermittently. Mulvaney threw himself across the ice and rolled, snatching up the dead man's submachine gun in his left fist, the empty revolver stuffed into the left outside pocket of his coat. He flattened himself at the base of the little hill. It was one of the little H&Ks, an MP 5-K 9mm. He bounced the magazine out and hefted it—the stick had maybe a dozen rounds in it, he guessed—then rammed it back up the well.

"Over here!" Fields shouted. "Washington and one more at the back of the car by the wheel well!"

Mulvaney tracked the voice—Fields was hunkered down behind a mound of ice.

Mulvaney shouted up the little hill toward the Continental. "Hey, guys! Guess who? Throw down your weapons and stand up in full view with your hands nice and high and nobody gets hurt. Look at it this way—you can always buy more cocaine. And your lawyer will have you shitheads out on the street before I get the reports written up anyway, right? So, no big deal. Whatchya think, Vincent?"

Washington's voice came down the hill with no hesitation. "Your ass is mine, honky!"

"Vincent, you're a likable guy and all, but I'm not into the sort of social encounter you're suggesting."

"Fuck you!" Washington shrieked back.

"I already told you, man—I'm into girls, ya know?"

There was a volley of gunfire—from the rear of the Lincoln, as best Mulvaney could tell. Apparently Vincent Washington was feeling punk this morning, Mulvaney mused, shrugging. "Okay, guys, what can I say, huh?" Mulvaney had the last speedloader emptied into his revolver. Ten rounds still remained in the Beretta, the Beretta going back into his trouser band; the subgun, with maybe four three-round bursts left in it, was in his right.

Mulvaney looked back toward Fields, saw Fields loading both his pistols. Then Fields gave him a nod. Mulvaney started edging around the base of the little hill. It had always worked for the Lone Ranger and Tonto on television—you circled the bad guys and got the drop on them from behind. Usually the Masked Man did the circling while his Faithful Indian Companion kept them busy. As if Fields were reading his mind, the shotgun started up again, Mulvaney's ears ringing with it as he got another ninety degrees around the base and looked up. The front end of the Lincoln swayed a little, suspended in air over his head. Mulvaney smiled. The little hill of snow and ice was pretty narrow at the top.

Mulvaney waited for the next shotgun blast and made a dead run for what was left of the unmarked Ford he'd used like a ball bearing in a pinball machine, diving down behind the front end to keep the engine block between him and the guys behind the Continental, handguns blazing toward him from the top of the little hill. His back against the left-front wheel, he shouted across the ice to his partner. "Lew, follow my lead—use the shotgun."

"You got it, man!"

Mulvaney took the little subgun in both fists, his revolver back in his pocket, and popped up to the level of the hood. He fired into the snow at the top of the little hill, right where the Lincoln Continental was balanced, chunks of ice blowing out and away. The subgun empty, Mulvaney tossed it down, the .357 coming into his left fist, Fields's shotgun firing, Mulvaney emptying the Smith now. The Lincoln was moving, swaying, the front end dipping down, one of Washington's guys jumping up on the hood and screaming and shooting. The guy fell away when Fields fired the shotgun again, the hood of the Lincoln dipping violently now. And suddenly the car was skidding downhill, the other guy from the front end clinging to it like some kind of idiot, Mulvaney thought. Mulvaney had the Beretta back in his fist and pumped two into the guy, then two more, the .45 in the man's fist discharging once as the body fell away down the back of the hill.

Mulvaney could see Vincent Washington and the other guy now, running across the parking lot, and then Mulvaney couldn't see them at all. The Lincoln nose-dived to the parking lot and the hood shot upward, a fireball belching up after it. Mulvaney flattened himself against the ice, tucking his head beside the wheel, hands over his ears. But he could still hear the roar. There was a secondary explosion; he heard it, his eyes too tightly shut to see even the flash.

He felt things pelting his coat and the back of his head through his stocking cap. And he was up, slipping on the ice, catching his balance again, running, over the crackle of the flames from the burning Continental, shouting to Lew Fields, "Come on, Lew!"

Better than a hundred yards ahead now, running, half the time looking as if they were skating over the ice, were Vincent Washington and the other guy. It was the first time Mulvaney had looked toward the museum end of the lot since the thing had gone down, and he saw the Cadillac that the Colombian and the Anglo and their three guys had come in, the Cadillac stuck in a snowbank and the three flunkies trying to push it out. It was a chance to bag them all or lose them all. As he ran, Mulvaney buttoned out the nearly spent magazine from the Beretta, reaching to the double mag pouch on his belt under his sweater and drawing out one of the twenty-round extension magazines, finishing the tactical magazine change and dropping the almost empty one in an outside pocket. He kept running.

In the distance now, coming from the direction of the Loop, he could hear sirens. But nothing from the direction of Soldier Field. "Harvey, you asshole," he snarled through the steam of his exhalations. Lew Fields was almost up even with him, and without looking directly at him, he shouted to his partner as they ran. "Looks like . . . like we know who Harvey's on the take to, huh?"

"Vincent?"

"Hell, yes—or the Colombian Blue Fairy."

"Damn!"

Washington was shouting something unintelligible, but the three guys working to get the Cadillac unstuck apparently figured it out, turning away from their task and crouching behind the Cadillac's rear end. Mulvaney started to look for cover. Not finding anything too close, he tried to make himself run faster instead. Washington and his man were nearly up to the Cadillac.

There was a voice over a P.A. speaker. "This is the police. All of you, throw down your weapons."

Mulvaney looked back once and grabbed his badge as he did. A blue-and-white, no siren, another one about fifty yards behind it, was sliding across the parking lot toward them. Mulvaney shook the badge toward them and angled his run to intersect with the car, the passenger side swinging open as he neared it. "Mike, it's me, Mulvaney—Mulvaney and Fields."

Mike Makowski worked Central and had worked Central since Mulvaney had gone on the Eleventh Street Tac Squad, and before that. "You look like shit, Ed!"

"You look like shit, *Sergeant*," Mulvaney corrected. The blue-and-white skidded to a dead halt. Mulvaney dropped down behind the open door, Makowski laughing like a lunatic, the rookie behind the wheel looking pale. Black people looked pale when their skin got a grayish cast, and this guy's skin wasn't black anymore.

Fields joined Mulvaney beside Makowski on the passenger side, hissing through his teeth, "Who the fuck's in the other blue-and-white, Mike?" The second car was skidding toward the Cadillac and looked like it would smash it in about thirty seconds, gunfire coming from the driver's-side window, gunfire coming at it from beside the Cadillac. "I don't blame 'em shootin' at him—hell, he's gonna ram 'em!"

"It's Reggie—"

"Aww, shit," Mulvaney snarled, pushing up from behind the modest shelter of the passenger-side door and breaking into a dead run for the car. Reggie Saddler was the only black guy at Central who looked in the mirror and saw Sylvester Stallone staring back at him. As Mulvaney looked back, he saw two things—Fields running after him, feeding more shells into the extension magazine on the 870, and Makowski and his rookie wheelman cutting hard right to block the Cadillac if it got out of the snowbank and started for the nearest way out of the parking lot.

Mulvaney started shooting again—not at anything in particular, but toward the rear end of the Cadillac to keep the three gunmen back there from shooting at Reggie, behind the wheel of the second blue-and-white, and to keep Washington and his employee from reaching the Cadillac. Running at full speed and shooting worked great on television and in the movies, but not in real life; all he was hitting was the snowbank.

Then Reggie's blue-and-white hit the Cadillac, catching

14

the Caddie on the left-rear fender and peeling away most of the rear bumper, the Cadillac lurching violently away from the snowbank. Vincent Washington was firing into the blue-and-white's windshield, Reggie spilling from behind the wheel with a .357 in one hand and a stainless-steel Smith .45 auto in the other hand, both guns blazing. Vincent Washington's man was going down, and one of the druggies with the Colombian and the Anglo who'd stopped running after the Cadillac long enough to trade shots was going down too. Washington fired again, at Reggie. Mulvaney, still running, fired at Washington. Mulvaney missed. Washington didn't miss and Reggie was down. The ice on both sides of Washington was pulverized as Mulvaney heard the roar of Fields's shotgun twice more, but Washington was rabbiting toward the Cadillac and didn't look hit.

Mulvaney body-slammed into the blue-and-white; it was the only way to stop. He dropped to his knees beside Reggie. The kid was breathing, but that was about all. "Shit—hang in there, Sly. We gotcha covered." Washington was almost to the Cadillac. "Dammit!" Mulvaney dove through the open driver's-side door and grabbed the microphone, thumbing down the push-to-talk button. "Officer down with multiple gunshot injuries in parking lot north of Field Museum of Natural History. Need ambulance and assistance. Quick!" And he threw down the microphone. To try to drag Reggie someplace out of harm's way could have done more harm than good if one of Washington's bullets had lodged somewhere dangerous. So Mulvaney left him. Fields had ducked behind an ice hill and was firing at the Cadillac, the two remaining guys with the Colombian and his Anglo squeeze running for the car and throwing lead toward Fields as they ran. The Cadillac started moving under its own power, wheels spinning. For a half-second, through the open doorway of the blue-and-white, Mulvaney caught a glimpse of the face behind the wheel of the Cadillac. It was the face of Vincent Washington.

The blue-and-white's engine was still running.

It was starting to sleet.

Mulvaney popped the parking brake, rammed the selector into Drive, and started fighting the wheel as he stomped the gas, the rear wheels spinning, but the blue-and-white moving forward, picking up speed. The Cadillac was picking up speed too.

The blue-and-white Mike Makowski's rookie piloted was blocking the main exit onto the Drive, but the Cadillac was moving too fast to stop now. "Damn compact cars," Mulvaney snarled. The Cadillac was full-size and would punch aside the blue-and-white if Vincent Washington had the guts to try it. Makowski and the young black rookie were out of the car, their revolvers leveled toward the Cadillac, Makowski firing a shot into the air with his right hand, extending his left-hand palm outward toward the Caddie as if he were directing traffic and thought Vincent Washington would stop. The Cadillac picked up speed. Makowski and the rookie opened fire at it. Mulvaney stepped on the gas. He could see Fields nailing one of the two gunmen who worked for the Colombian. The guy went down on the ice, Fields using the butt of the shotgun to keep him down, then taking off in a dead run after the other guy. The second man threw his gun at Fields, just like some idiot in a movie, Mulvaney thought.

Mulvaney had the blue-and-white going so fast now that he could never stop it, the distance between it and the Cadillac less than ten yards. Makowski and the rookie were firing one instant, then running for their lives the next. The Cadillac was smashing the rear end of the police car, spinning it out of the way, the police car's rear bumper shaving off, the Cadillac hesitating for a second, then out of the parking lot and into the Drive.

Mulvaney punched through after it.

He looked to his right. A salt truck with a plow on the front end. The salt truck couldn't stop. Neither could Washington in the Colombian guy's Cadillac. The plow caught the Cadillac by the passenger door and the Cadillac was airborne, hitting the road surface on the driver's side, rolling over onto its roof, spinning wildly, Mulvaney trying to stop, the salt truck with the snowplow dead in front of him. Mulvaney cut the wheel sharp right fast, the rear end fishtailing and dragging the blue-and-white further into the Drive, Mulvaney cutting the wheel sharp left to get some control. The salt truck was in the far-right edge of his peripheral vision now, then a sound of metal tearing, his body shuddering with the impact, the blue-and-white skidding laterally, right for the Cadillac.

Mulvaney cut the wheel left, then right, finding the position of the wheels, then cut the steering wheel right again and stomped the gas pedal. The blue-and-white's left-front fender clipped into the Cadillac, the Cadillac spinning, Mulvaney shooting past it. There was a hill of ice straight ahead and Mulvaney started pumping the brakes. Nothing happened. "Shit!" He threw himself down across the front seat and buried his head under his forearms.

When the impact came he felt it, his body wrenching with it, thrown hard against the seat, then pitched forward over the drive-shaft hump and onto the floor. Then all motion stopped. "Damn! I'm alive! All right!" He was up, moving, his left arm aching a little. He grabbed the passenger-side door handle and wrenched it, half-falling into the frozen slush just outside, his right hand clutched tight on the butt of the Beretta.

Mulvaney shook his head, spitting slush off his lips, snow falling heavily now. The salt truck was stopped dead in the middle of the Drive, salt still spraying from it on both sides, the plow at the front bent all out of shape. The Cadillac had stopped spinning.

Mulvaney stretched his right arm, the Beretta getting full of slush. He shook it free. To his knees. To his feet. He lurched into the Drive, a Volkswagon Beetle skidding past him, trying to avoid the rear end of the Cadillac as it dodged the salt truck.

He wasn't walking right, he knew. He shook his head to clear it. He looked behind him. The blue-and-white had plowed through the mound of snow and stopped dead against a utility pole. He hoped he wouldn't get stuck paying for the pole.

There was somebody half-falling out of the Cadillac. It was the Anglo squeeze, tears streaming from his eyes and blood where his lips should be. Mulvaney lurched toward him and slammed him against the car. "Move and you're in deeper shit than you are now," Mulvaney snarled.

"He's—"

"Who? The Colombian? Where's Washington?"

"There!" The squeeze raised his right hand fast to point,

17

and Mulvaney almost shot him before he realized what the gesture was. Washington was running again, out onto the spit of land that was less than a city block wide, the lake on both sides of it, at the end the Planetarium. "Help Fernando. Please," the squeeze begged.

Mulvaney hauled the squeeze down to his knees in the slush and salt and put the muzzle of the Beretta to the guy's head as he peered inside.

Fernando had a shard of windshield about the size of a bowie knife going in through the Adam's apple and pinning him to the front seat. Mulvaney looked at the squeeze. The Anglo was crying big crocodile tears, the kind that weren't phony.

With his left hand Mulvaney reached under his coat for the Model 90s and slapped one bracelet over the squeeze's right wrist. "Sorry, man," Mulvaney said honestly, then hauled the Anglo up to his feet. The car didn't smell like it was on fire or about to blow up, so Mulvaney wrenched open the driver's-side door and put the other cuff on the doorframe, the window already rolled away. Mulvaney started a quick pat-down—anything more serious, and the Anglo would have thought he was proposing, he figured. "You have the right to remain silent. Anything you say can and will be used against you in a court of law—you know the rest," and Mulvaney broke into a loping run, after Washington. He looked back. Fields and Makowski were entering the street; the rookie was back where Mulvaney had left the black Sly Stallone. Mulvaney shouted to Fields, "Read the squeeze his rights—the Colombian doesn't need to know!"

Mulvaney ran, Washington limping ahead of him but making good time, halfway out along the spit of land. Mulvaney kept running, almost losing his balance, then angling to where there was grass under the ice and snow. It would be less slippery there. He kept running.

Washington was into the street where it curved in front of the Planetarium now, then across it. Washington's pace was picking up. All those toasters he'd stolen as a kid, Mulvaney thought. The practice had made Washington a good runner. Real good.

Mulvaney hit the street as Washington disappeared

around the far side of the Planetarium. There was nothing beyond it except more driveway, some snow-covered rocks and a steep drop into the ice water that was Lake Michigan.

Mulvaney stopped beside the lower level of the Planetarium, flat against a stone wall. With his left hand he searched his pockets and found what he was looking for. He lit a Pall Mall and dropped the pack and the lighter back into his pocket, inhaling hard. He coughed, leaned his head forward for a second. More sirens. By now Harvey would figure it was safe to show up, that Vincent Washington wouldn't blame him for anything that had gone down. Mulvaney realized he was smiling.

With his left hand, the cigarette back between his lips, he reached down to his left ankle. The ankle rig was ballistic nylon and would wash. The Model 60 Smith was stainless steel and would clean up okay.

A gun in each hand again, Mulvaney started after Washington, shouting as he edged around the Planetarium wall. "Hey, Washington! Yo! Vincent! What's happenin', baby?"

"Up your ass!"

Mulvaney smiled—Vincent Washington's ego could always be counted on. He sounded like he was just around the corner at the back of the building, or maybe a little further out, nearer to the nasty, slippery rocks. Mulvaney smiled again. "Gotta cut out all those sexual innuendos, Vincent. But look—you're into that, that's cool. 'We serve and protect' regardless of sexual orientation."

"Fuck you!"

"Hey, Vincent, lighten up, man. You want that kinda action, that's cool. Can get your ass reamed five, maybe six times a day up there in the joint, Vincent. I hear it's a favorite game they play—sorta pin the tail on the donkey, huh?"

Mulvaney saw him as Washington stepped from hiding and started blasting, a .45 in each hand, Mulvaney throwing himself into the snow, firing both handguns simultaneously, Washington falling back.

Mulvaney was up, running. Washington was sprawled on his back, rolling over, reaching for the .45s he'd dropped into the snow, the slides locked back, empty.

Mulvaney stopped running. He spit out the cigarette.

"Motherfucker!" Washington shouted the words like a curse.

Mulvaney laid the little .38 snubby alongside the black-head collection that formed Washington's nose. "Are you in need of medical assistance, sir? If you are not in need of immediate medical assistance, it is my duty to advise you of your rights. You have the right to remain silent." And Mulvaney thumbed back the little .38's hammer. "*Real* silent if you so much as twitch, asshole."

The bad thing about it, Mulvaney reflected, was that Vincent Marcel Washington, Jr., had made him shoot so fast that all he had done was wound him a couple of times, so Washington wasn't going to be dead anytime in the near future. There was a way of fixing that, of course, of keeping Washington off the street for good so he'd never sell more coke to kids, never use it to trap teenage girls into prostitution, never use the money it made to hire muscle to go out and kill his rivals.

There was a way of fixing all of that. Permanently.

"I'll be on the street, motherfucker. And your white ass is mine."

"Vincent. How many times I gotta tell you? I mean, it's very flattering and everything, ya know? But you just aren't my type."

Mulvaney pulled the trigger, but kept the hammer back with his thumb and let it down slow.

Fields had been right. Terminal honesty. And murder—even of a guy like Washington—was as dishonest as you could get. Then Mulvaney thought of Harvey. Murder was *almost* as dishonest as you could get.

He recited the rest of the Miranda litany off the card he carried behind his ID in the badge case. You always read it, even though you could say it in your sleep, so the collar couldn't accuse you of forgetting to tell him part of it. It was easy enough to get back on the street, and there was no sense making it easier. . . .

The guys from the ambulances and the wrecker trucks, the guys and the women who were tougher than the guys with the news crews from WLS and WGN and WBBM and all the rest of the radio and television stations, and the guys

20

from the *Trib* and the *Sun Times* were all tripping over each other.

Mulvaney sat on the hood of a blue-and-white, the box of 9mm and the box of .357 retrieved from the trunk of their trashed unmarked car open beside him. He was reloading magazines and speedloaders, smoking a cigarette, just watching it all and trying not to think about what Hymie Silvers and Lew Fields were arguing about ten or twelve yards away from him.

Hymie Silvers was the watch commander and had bad breath and a brown tongue from kissing ass, Mulvaney had always thought. That Hymie had even come down here was a bad sign.

And then Mulvaney saw Harvey strutting around, his florid choirboy face all chubby and his cheeks looking like he was storing nuts, holding a doughnut in one hand and a cup of coffee in a white Styrofoam cup in the other. Harvey saw him. Harvey looked around for a second, visibly shrugged, then walked over toward him. Before Harvey was even near enough for Mulvaney to smell the coffee, he started saying, "Look, Ed, the car really was stuck. Ask Bleeker, huh?"

"Gonna be tough makin' the mortgage payment if Vincent takes a fall on this?"

"Hey, I don't gotta take that shit!"

Mulvaney rammed the automatic into his belt under his sweater and slid off the hood of the blue-and-white. He walked up to Harvey and stood there for a second. "You real tough, Harvey?"

Harvey didn't answer him.

"You well-connected, man? Make big trouble for me? Huh?"

"Don't find out," Harvey said softly.

"Harvey. You scare me," Mulvaney told him. He reached out and his right hand covered Harvey's left hand, the hand that held the coffee. Harvey's eyes got hard. Mulvaney drew the hand closer to him, toward his mouth. Mulvaney let the cigarette fall from between his lips into the coffee. "Thanks for helping me keep Chicago the cleanest big city in the USA, Harv." Mulvaney started back to the blue-and-white.

"Bastard," Harvey whispered behind him.

Mulvaney stopped, looked over his shoulder and grinned. "You ever wind up assigned to work with me again, develop a sudden case of the shits or something. 'Cause if you show up, there just might be a real serious accident—fatal. Real fatal, Harvey."

Mulvaney lit another cigarette and went back to reloading.

2

Spook Trade

MULVANEY CLOSED THE DOOR. Outside was bedlam. Inside was Hymie Silvers. Loud lunacy. Quiet ineptitude. "You wanted to see me, Heinie?"

Silvers looked up from his desk. There was a copy of the *Sun Times* on it and nothing else except a can of Coca-Cola. "It's 'Hymie,' Mulvaney."

"Gee whiz—I always screw that up, don't I?"

"Sit down."

Silvers always wore a hat when he was outside and half the time when he was inside, but he wasn't wearing one now and the carefully arranged piece of hair that was wound over the top of his head, Mulvaney guessed, had to be maybe a foot long. "Whatsa matter? Lew and I shoot too many bad guys? They filin' a union grievance?"

Silvers looked up from reading the comics. "If it was up to me, you and Fields and all the trigger-happy shitheads like ya'd be workin' for the Sanitation Department."

"Give us a letter of recommendation to your old supervisor and maybe I'll consider it, man."

Silvers' hands were shaking. "Don't push it. I saw the report where you said Harvey refused to respond to your backup call."

"He refused."

"The fuckin' car was stuck. I suppose that never happened to you?"

"You should be reading the *Tribune*—they got Dick Tracy. You could learn a lot, Heinie."

"You're a real gung-ho crimebuster, huh? Well, what I got for you is right up your alley, wiseass. Special assignment."

"Don't tell me—you need lessons in how to tie your shoes. That's why ya always wear those slip-ons, right?"

The trouble with Hymie Silvers was that he was gutless, Mulvaney thought.

Silvers said, "Nice thing about this job we got for ya is that it's kinda dangerous, I hear. So maybe you'll die."

"Look, Hymie . . ." He said it right this time. "With Washington off the street for a little while, Lew and I can get out there and get some stuff done. The Colombian's dead. The Anglo'll sing, maybe. There isn't any time for some cockamamie—"

"Take this address"—Hymie Silvers smiled, his teeth yellow and uneven-looking and the veins in his neck standing out—"and fuck off." His hand shook as he held out the folded piece of paper.

Ed Mulvaney stood up, took the piece of paper, stuffed it in the pocket of his blue jeans and left, trying to slam the door so hard behind him that the glass would break. But it didn't.

Fields drove the blue-and-white north on Michigan Avenue and didn't say much aside from an occasional remark about the heavy traffic and too bad there wasn't an armed robbery in progress so he could cut on the siren and the Mars lights and make some time. The address was an apartment in the Hancock Building.

"I'd like to tell Silvers what to do with his special assignment. In fact, I more or less did."

"I know—he didn't realize it was anatomically possible." Lew Fields laughed. "Maybe you opened up whole new vistas for the little creep—improved his sex life, you know. I had a kid like Hymie in one of my music classes once, ya know?"

"Was that the kid you almost shot?" Mulvaney laughed. Fields had been a Chicago High School teacher for a half-dozen years before quitting and joining the cops. His wife was a principal now at one of the few high schools where you didn't need a whip and a chair and body armor. It was the only way they could afford the apartment on Lake Shore Drive, Mulvaney always figured.

"That was a different kid. But this kid that I had like Silvers. Ten different kinds of dumb. I bumped into him on the street a year or so back, ya know? And you'll never guess what."

"What?"

"Owns his own business, makes a bundle."

"Coulda been bullshittin' ya," Mulvaney remarked.

"Rolex—not like yours, but the kind that's all gold, ya know? Ring with a diamond in it some skinny dude coulda hid behind. We had some coffee, then he climbs into his—get this—Ferrari Testarosa."

"Probably a Miami cop who works vice up here on vacation."

"Yeah. The car . . . Look, ahh . . . what's this special assignment?"

Mulvaney shrugged and looked away. There was a really pretty girl wearing high heels instead of boots who was trying to cross the street and figure out how to get across the slush rolling by in the gutter. "Stop the car."

"You crazy?"

"Stop the car."

Fields stopped the car about six feet from the end of the block and the same distance out from the curb and Mulvaney climbed out into the blowing snow. He started toward the girl, flashing his badge at her. She looked blond under the woolen scarf wrapped around her head and she was about twenty-five, kind of on the tall side. "Need some help, miss?"

The girl looked away. Mulvaney guessed he'd embarrassed her.

"I said, need some help—you know. Chicago Police. 'We serve and protect.' How about a little service?"

Mulvaney stood in the slush in the gutter, his shoes and his clothes still wet through from the morning. "Miss? You all right, or . . . ?"

The head turned around and he saw the eyes, a pretty

25

blue, but the makeup was heavy. The voice was a trembling tenor. "Look, officer, I'm going to a masquerade party. I don't normally dress like this, and—"

Mulvaney pulled the scarf away. The lips were dark red and there was a fake beauty mark on the left cheek and a spot on the neck where the damsel in distress had forgotten to shave close enough. Mulvaney stood there and just shook his head. "I been livin' in this city too long. I knew that." He turned and walked back toward the car, Fields edging up to meet him as he slid in, snapping away the cigarette butt, then slamming the door.

Fields asked, "Whatsa matter? Didn't she come onto ya?"

"What? Ahh . . . no—waitin' for a bus. Didn't wanna cross the street."

"Ohh, she's doing it now. Got her in the rearview," Fields said as they coasted through the intersection on the amber.

"Musta got tired of waiting," Mulvaney said through his teeth.

"So, what's this special assignment? Like I asked before."

"Don't know, Lew. Silvers made some crack that he'd heard it was dangerous or somethin'. Probably means he didn't know zip about it and he was just the errand boy for somebody higher up."

"You want me to wait for you?"

"No . . . no—listen. After I get outta this meeting, whatever, I'll catch a cab or a blue-and-white and then take the el home. I just wanna relax with a pizza and a coupla drinks and get to sleep early tonight. If I don't rack up some Z's I'm gonna catch the flu or somethin'—you know, wear down my resistance."

"You need a wife, man—a real one this time—no offense."

There was the customary humming and rumbling, and without looking, Mulvaney knew they were crossing the bridge over the Chicago River. He was staring at his hands instead. He closed his eyes. "I know one thing, buddy—I'm gettin' damn tired of this."

"The cold weather? I thought you liked cold weather."

"No—this business." He opened his eyes and looked over at his partner. "Only an idiot'd do this for a living, ya know?"

"What about that guy that called ya last week—your old Special Forces buddy? Grimshaw?"

"Bill Grimshaw. Yeah."

"He offered you some kind of job, didn't he?"

"Runs an executive-protection outfit and he needs somebody to run the thing for him. It's a real moneymaker but if somebody who knows what he's doing doesn't head it up, it'll go under. He's worried about his wife and daughters."

"I don't follow ya, Ed."

Mulvaney lit a cigarette. "Agent Orange. Part of the jungle he was playin' war in got sprayed, and he's been sick for a coupla years now. The doctors finally told him he's got less than a year until he's gone."

"Man, I shouldn't have asked—I'm sorry."

Mulvaney nodded, exhaling, saying slowly, "So he . . . ahh, he wants me to join up with him, learn the business while he's still able to teach it to me, then take fifty percent of it for myself and pump the rest of it to his family after he's gone. Make about sixty or seventy grand a year, he tells me."

"You gonna take it?"

Fields eased the blue-and-white up next to a fire hydrant, the John Hancock Building's upper floors lost in the swirling snow and the low clouds as Mulvaney stepped out.

"Well, you gonna?"

"I don't think so; I don't know. Hell . . . "Mulvaney threw his cigarette into the gutter. "Look . . . " He leaned back inside and extended his right hand to Fields. "If, ahh . . . if I wind up with this special-assignment shit keepin' me out a few days or something, well . . . don't let Heinie hook you up with some amateur who's gonna get your head blown off or somethin'—right?"

"I value you too, Ed." Fields took his hand for a minute.

"Right. Hey!" Mulvaney jerked his thumb skyward and shot Lew Fields a grin. "Don't take any wooden bullets, huh?"

"Right. You look like you're wearing the clothes the Goodwill people throw out—so make sure the security in this big fancy building don't pitch your white ass back into the street, man."

Fields grinned. Mulvaney slammed the door, standing

there a minute as Fields blended the blue-and-white into traffic and tried jockeying into position for a U-turn.

Then Mulvaney turned away from the street and stared up to where the clouds started and the black hulk of the Hancock Building disappeared. The address was an apartment on the forty-third floor, and from there you couldn't even see the street, he guessed.

He started inside. The story at the time they'd built it was that they couldn't have gone much higher because there wasn't enough bedrock to support more of it; he didn't know if it was true or not. And maybe it wasn't as tall as the Sears Tower, but it was tall enough.

He walked across the sterile lobby, getting a funny look from the guy at the security desk. "Rest easy, man," Mulvaney called out, flashing his badge and taking off his stocking cap. He stuffed them both into his pockets, searching the elevator-bank indicators to discern which elevator would take him to the forty-third floor. He found it, stepped inside the waiting box and pushed the floor button, the lights in the elevator bright and yellow-tinged. He looked down at his clothes. The shoes were salt-stained and squished when he walked. The blue jeans were salt-stained and smeared with dried slush. The Navy pea coat he wore wasn't all that blue because it was covered with slush and salt stains too and was faded anyway. Beneath it—and he was warm in the elevator—he had an old tweed sport coat and beneath that a long-sleeved V-neck sweater, and beneath that just a sweatshirt. He could tell whoever it was he was meeting that it had been exceptionally cold when he left the house that morning. It wouldn't have been a lie, that he had wanted to blend in with people and not look like a cop. You wanted that if you worked undercover or in plainclothes. He smiled at the thought—what he was wearing was about as plain as clothes came, but they kept him warm and hid his guns. Life was a trade-off anyway.

The elevator stopped just as he made himself swallow to relieve the pressure in his ears.

Mulvaney stepped out and started looking for the right suite number—and realized he was thinking about the job Bill Grimshaw had offered him, and hadn't really stopped thinking about it since Grimshaw had called him. He found the right number and tried the door. It was locked. He knocked. He waited. . . .

John Trench Osgood studied Edgar Patrick Mulvaney in minute detail. He knew the face well, knew the file better. But this was the first time he had seen Mulvaney in the flesh. Mulvaney just stood in the doorway, looking a little awkward if anything at all, his hands thrust into the pockets of a dirty-looking Navy-surplus pea coat, his arms too long for it and his wrists hanging out below the cuffs. His dark brown curly hair seemed so disheveled that Osgood theorized this Sergeant Mulvaney saw the inside of a barbershop with considerably less frequency than most men saw their dentists.

Osgood lit a cigarette from his case. The case—silver— and the matching Dunhill lighter were on the shelflike protuberance beneath the bank of monitors. He punched up Mulvaney's personal habits out of the dossier already accessed on the computer as he inhaled. Mulvaney, indeed, didn't frequent any barbershop at all, but instead had his sister, a beautician, cut his hair. The last time Mulvaney had visited his sister had been at the end of August and it was now the beginning of December. The curls were natural, not supplied by the obliging sister. "Hmm," Osgood said.

He looked back to the monitor that covered the doorway leading into the suite of offices the Chicago Crime Commission people used for sensitive meetings. The man from the Crime Commission was the only one in the room who knew of the surveillance. And that was one too many, Osgood personally felt. But he had not arranged this. If he had, the cameras would have had better coverage, because as it was, there were a few dead spots.

Osgood turned up the volume controls. It was just small talk so he returned to the file again. Osgood let himself smile. He probably knew more about Edgar Patrick Mulvaney than the man knew about himself. Mulvaney's last chest X ray had been good. The liquor store Mulvaney had stopped at three days ago sold bootleg whiskey in recycled bottles with new counterfeit labels. It was to Mulvaney's credit that he had thrown the whiskey out the next morning with only two ounces missing from the bottle. Osgood had reported the violation to the Bureau of Alcohol, Tobacco and Firearms on condition they wouldn't move on it until Mulvaney had begun his assignment. At least Mulvaney knew his whiskey.

It appeared Mulvaney knew a great many things. Four years at De Paul University, mostly on the downtown campus, leading to a Bachelor of Arts with a major in history. Six years in the United States Army, four years in Vietnam in Special Forces. Two Purple Hearts, a Bronze Star, various other citations. Separated as a captain and joined the Chicago Police after spending six months in police-science courses at Triton Junior College. Passed the sergeant's examination the first time without attempting to bribe anyone. Various departmental citations—almost as many as departmental reprimands.

Mulvaney's only close friend since the divorce was his partner, Sergeant Lewellyn Fields, no middle name on record. Fields had represented a problem at first; Fields's wife's brother had been a black activist during the 1960s. But there had been no documentable contact between the brother and Fields or his wife for ten years.

Osgood looked back to the monitors. Mulvaney was taking off his pea coat and setting it on a chair. The rather tacky-looking food-stained tweed sport coat did a poor job of hiding the shoulder holster beneath it. But on the plus side, if he—Osgood—hadn't known Mulvaney carried an automatic in the small of his back and a small revolver in an ankle holster, he wouldn't have spotted them yet.

Osgood punched up the weapons stuff.

Mulvaney habitually carried a Smith & Wesson Model 681 .357 Magnum, which replaced the smaller K-frame he had carried prior to the introduction of the newer frame size. There had been a succession of 9mm automatics, Mulvaney switching to the Beretta 92F immediately after it was adopted by the United States as the M-9. The ankle-holstered Model 60 .38 Special was something Mulvaney had owned before enlisting in the Army, and reports indicated he had carried it throughout his years in Vietnam. Chicago police officers, as a collective entity, seemed fasci-

30

nated with the idea of carrying several handguns. Osgood imagined it was part of the *Weltanschauung* engendered by the Prohibition days of gun battles in the streets.

Mulvaney was not known to use a knife, and Osgood found that curious, since many of those who had served in Special Forces, and afterward remained in one violent profession or another, seemed wedded to the blade.

Mulvaney was six-foot-three, making him two inches taller than his own six-foot-one, Osgood reflected. Mulvaney was thirty-eight years old, making him ten years younger—curiously, almost to the day, both their birthdays being in July.

Osgood stubbed out his cigarette and watched Mulvaney intently as the Chicago police sergeant sat down and lit a cigarette. Pall Malls—Osgood verified the file. Mulvaney had an air of youth about him, a sort of rawboned young-punk toughness, his overall appearance vaguely resembling the look of an unmade bed. But then, the carelessness in appearance reflected the life-style, Osgood thought.

Osgood had never had boyish good looks. He had been offered his first drink in a restaurant when he had just turned thirteen. Appearance and chronological age had eventually blended and, if anything, an objective analysis of his own appearance would have placed his age lower now than it actually was. Mulvaney's build bespoke strength. Indeed Mulvaney frequented the YMCA, and data suggested he was quite fit. Osgood considered himself. He had never looked the brute-force, muscular type. Wiry, yes. He wagered with himself that he could take this Mulvaney fellow and another one or two just like him if the need arose.

Osgood smiled. A woman years ago had once told him that he was reminiscent of Edward Arlington Robinson's Richard Cory. Osgood had been dismayed, slightly shocked. But the woman had only smiled as she embraced him, saying that he just looked so "imperially slim." He'd found the comparison uncomfortable nonetheless.

The small talk was ending. It was obvious that Mulvaney recognized each face in the room, as Osgood had known that he would.

John Trench Osgood dialed up the volume and shifted his

shoulder holster a bit as he leaned back and listened and watched. . . .

Mulvaney's eyes moved from one face to another. He knew them all. The man who had met him at the door had introduced himself, but Mulvaney recognized him from the papers. Burton Randolph Wilkes, chief executive officer of Simtronic Enterprises, married to one of the wealthiest women in Chicago and one of the top three men in the Chicago Crime Commission, the citizens' task force that had been a prime force in the battle against organized crime and political corruption in Chicago and Cook County for decades.

Armand Batista, the head man of the local Federal Drug Enforcement Agency task force. Batista's right hand was short three fingers. As a field agent, the story went, his cover had been blown and the bad guys were whittling pieces off him when the calvary arrived. Mulvaney thought it was lucky they hadn't picked something of similar shape to a finger but only one in number to start with. Batista had eight kids. Maybe not so lucky for Mrs. Batista.

Thomas Kaminski, chief deputy to the Cook County sheriff. Kaminski was not a political appointee, but a county sheriff's policeman who had worked his way up. He had a reputation for being a hard guy to get along with, but an honest one.

Randall Lord, special agent-in-charge, Chicago office of the Federal Bureau of Investigation. Lord was new to the post and as yet unproven. The guy he had replaced had left him big shoes to fill.

The next two men, as far as logic and reason dictated, shouldn't have been in the room at all.

One was Colonel Deighton Calhoun, the head of Army Intelligence out of Fort Sheridan, and a hell of a good poker player, as Mulvaney had found out many years ago, before meeting Calhoun again stateside. It had been in the back room of a bar in that jewel of the Orient known as Saigon and had cost him three hundred bucks and a Randall bowie knife.

Sitting next to Calhoun was Timothy Dern, the guy who was the local employment counselor for the Central Intelligence Agency. Tim Dern was positively the happiest-looking man Mulvaney had ever seen. Always a smile, always a glad hand, always happy to sit down and buy you a cup of coffee and chat. Never carried a gun, he said, but Mulvaney had noticed the smell of Hoppe's Number 9 overpowering Tim's after-shave once, and thereafter had taken it as a personal challenge to discover just where the man carried his gun.

Mulvaney had spotted Dern picking up his dry cleaning a few weeks later, and backtracked him to the dry cleaner, gave the proprietor ten bucks and flashed his badge to get the guy to call the next time Dern brought in a suit. The call came, the citizen happy to be helping the cops with an investigation, however "just routine" it was. The suits were cut to hide a shoulder holster under the right armpit. Dern was right-handed, and Mulvaney kicked himself for never spotting it just because it was on the wrong side of the body.

The last man there was a man Mulvaney didn't like. Edward Hilliard, Central District commander for a while and now a deputy superintendent. Then, as now, not a nice man at all.

Wilkes said, "You know everyone in this room, I understand, Sergeant."

"Yes, sir—some more than others."

"Have you any idea why you were asked to meet with us here?"

"No, sir."

"Relax, Sergeant Mulvaney. This is a silly way to put this question, I guess, but—well, anyway—you've heard of Enrico Ajaccio?"

"Yes."

"Couldn't very well be a police officer in this town and not know him, could you?"

"There are a few officers, Mr. Wilkes, who probably don't know the name. They're the same ones we issue maps and flashlights to when it's time for them to find their rear ends."

Hilliard snapped, "That'll be enough of that crap, Sergeant!"

Mulvaney looked at Hilliard and smiled. Maybe he, as a sergeant, was the lowest-ranking guy in the room, but

33

Hilliard, for all his bluster and his five-hundred-dollar suits, was the second-lowest. "Just trying to keep the conversation lively, sir," Mulvaney told him.

Wilkes spoke fast. "So . . . all right. Enrico Ajaccio, one of the inner circle of the Chicago Crime Syndicate, one of the decision-makers, has decided to tell all. To us. Tell us everything we want to know that he knows. You appreciate, no doubt, what that could mean."

"A lot of cops are gonna be in deep shit for one thing."

"Dammit!" Hilliard was on his feet, his face livid with apparent rage—or was it that the truth hurt? Mulvaney wondered.

Wilkes spoke quickly again. "Mr. Ajaccio has the ear of everyone that matters in organized crime in Chicago and Cook County, is well-connected with Mafia interests in New York and Las Vegas and the West Coast. In short, he's potentially terrifically valuable to us."

Mulvaney was about to ask why Ajaccio was deciding to talk, when there was a knock at the door. Wilkes got up and walked across the room. The room was an office, but furnished like a living room, with overstuffed chairs and a sofa and a couple of coffee tables. Mulvaney wondered if this was the secret meeting place the Crime Commission supposedly had, where depositions could be taken and witnesses could rest in adjoining bedrooms. He guessed it probably was.

When Wilkes opened the door, the man who entered from the corridor had still another recognizable face. It was Harry Lorenze, with the state attorney's office. Lorenze nodded to Mulvaney, saying, "Sorry I'm late, gentlemen." Lorenze had been a Chicago cop for ten years, and a good one. Then he had finally gotten through with law school and the bar exam and joined the state attorney's office. As far as Mulvaney knew, Lorenze was a good man at his job.

Lorenze sat down, and Wilkes, standing this time, began to speak again. "Mr. Ajaccio has volunteered his cooperation in exchange for some assistance from all of us in this room."

"All of us?" Mulvaney repeated.

"More or less." Wilkes smiled. "A family matter has arisen for Mr. Ajaccio and he tells us he has exhausted all his own best efforts to resolve the matter, but to no avail. He'll talk in exchange for help. One of the carrots he's holding out in front of us is a rundown on all the Crime Syndicate involvement in Great Lakes area drug traffic, possibly on both sides of the border. He says he has information regarding Cuban government involvement in using drugs to finance arms for Communist-sympathetic revolutionaries in Latin America. He says he can provide us with names of various elected and appointed officials throughout the Midwest, Northeast and Southeast who are on the take, Sergeant. So we think it's worth helping Mr. Ajaccio. And it's the decent thing to do in any event, considering the circumstances."

Mulvaney choked back a laugh. Hilliard would be doing the same, Mulvaney realized, and the thought of sharing an emotion with the deputy police superintendent sobered him.

Wilkes was pacing the room now, his hands in his trouser pockets as he walked. "Ajaccio has a nephew. The young man's name is Peter Ellermann. Like you, Sergeant, he's a veteran of the Vietnam conflict. And it's from that this situation has arisen. Ellermann, according to Mr. Ajaccio and what we have collectively been able to confirm, was a prisoner of the Vietcong for some nine months. Ellermann and three other men were able to break free while they were on some sort of work detail . . . Let the colonel tell you. That's more his department, anyway."

Colonel Calhoun cleared his throat and stubbed out his cigarette. He was slightly built, looking more like an accountant than a professional military man and a spook type to boot. At the time of the poker game, Calhoun had just made captain and so had Mulvaney. But Calhoun had been Regular Army, and when the war was officially over, Calhoun hadn't found himself unemployed. "Peter Ellermann was a door gunner. He made a little rank but was never any great shakes as a soldier. But he did his job okay. After he got captured, escaped, and finally reached friendly forces, he insisted that he be allowed to go back and lead a rescue column to get the guys he and his two buddies had left behind. That wasn't possible at the time. Because of the injuries he sustained, he never returned to active duty and was honorably discharged with a couple of citations to his credit. Ellermann seemed to adjust pretty well to civilian life. Finished college and, as far as anyone can ascertain, he never went to work for his uncle. Never even saw his uncle, Mr. Ajaccio. Ellermann specialized in cartography, electronics. He went to work for one of the big defense aviation companies on the West Coast. Did brilliantly. Never married, but there was no reason to suppose he was . . . well, you know. Anyway, two and a half years ago, he cleaned out his savings account, his checking account, sold his house, put it all into traveler's checks and took off."

"Where?" Mulvaney asked softly. He felt he already knew. Sometimes he'd thought about it himself.

"Southeast Asia."

"Shit."

"More or less, Ed." Calhoun nodded. "More or less."

"He's . . . ahh—"

"No, Sergeant," Wilkes interjected. "We don't want you to go to Southeast Asia and find him. Tell him, Colonel."

Calhoun cleared his throat. "Peter Ellermann spent the last two and a half years ducking in and out of Southeast Asia, mostly Vietnam and Cambodia, looking for MIAs, trying to get definitive proof of MIA survival. He was involved in various abortive rescue attempts and the last time got so deep into Vietnam he almost never got out.

"Ellermann was in Japan," Calhoun continued, "following up another lead or something. And he disappeared. Vanished."

"That doesn't sound hard to do," Mulvaney said.

"Especially where Ellermann was hanging out," Calhoun agreed. "All the high-crime areas, trying to get information from smugglers, drug runners. He might be dead."

"Probably dead," Mulvaney said softly.

"Probably not," Dern, the CIA man, interrupted. "When Ellermann disappeared, his sister got worried. Tried the normal State Department routine, I'm told. Then finally she contacted Enrico Ajaccio. Told him that Peter had vanished in Japan somewhere and the government couldn't do jack shit to assist. So Ajaccio started pulling some strings and looking around to find out what he could. All his efforts were fruitless and . . . well, he'd given up."

"That's just before something happened that made him approach us," the FBI agent announced flatly. "Ajaccio was contacted by the Yakusa. It's the Japanese version of the Mafia, only a lot more institutionalized and sometimes a lot more deadly, as we understand it. The Yakusa informed Ajaccio that it wished to negotiate exclusive trading arrangements with the Chicago Crime Syndicate to provide it with opium-derivative narcotics the Yakusa smuggles out of the Golden Triangle."

"Burma and around there," Batista, the Drug Enforcement Agency man, said.

Mulvaney nodded.

Dern picked up the thread. "DEA intelligence people and our own guys had suspected something interesting was going to happen in the Golden Triangle because of some political stuff going on there. But we never expected this. I don't think anybody did."

Wilkes said, as though his words were running a race with his thoughts and barely keeping up, "Imagine what would happen if the Yakusa and the Chicago Crime Syndicate made such an exclusive arrangement. In order for it to work, the CCS people would have to shut down their Colombian connections and the free-lancers to keep a price war from beating the Yakusa-supplied drugs off the street. We'd be talking the bloodiest internecine crime warfare this country has ever seen. And it wouldn't just be in Chicago. Because the Yakusa already does some trading into the New York Five Families. We'd eventually have the Chicago Crime Syndicate at war with the Mafia, and whoever won would control so much money and so much street traffic that the price could be cut for a few months, even a year, and the number of addicts could increase by as much as fifty percent. The dabblers wouldn't be dabblers anymore. The schoolyard kids would be able to afford what they needed to get hooked. You'd see illegal drugs become the undisputed leading moneymaking industry in America. And the people who ran it all would have so much money they could insulate themselves against the law so well we'd never get them."

"They're offering to trade Ellermann back to Ajaccio for all of that? I mean—"

37

Calhoun spoke. "No—because obviously Mr. Ajaccio would agree and then tell the Japanese gangsters to fuck off and die once he had Ellermann back. No, it's much more imperative than that. The Japanese intend to keep Ellermann as a perpetual hostage to ensure Ajaccio's cooperation."

"One of Ellermann's fingers was sent to Ajaccio as proof of the Yakusa's sincerity," Wilkes almost whispered. "And what Ajaccio's really afraid of is that the Chicago Crime Syndicate hierarchy would go for the deal in a big way. They couldn't afford to refuse, because if they did—the hell with Ellermann—but if they refused, what if the Yakusa made an exclusive offer to the Five New York Families? We're talking billions in dollars and untold political and social power."

"All because of some guy who wanted to play Rambo," Mulvaney said under his breath.

Hilliard snapped, "Why don't you keep the cracks to yourself, Sergeant Mulvaney. Just shut up and listen."

Mulvaney looked at Hilliard. Calhoun laughed. Mulvaney said, "What Ellermann did, from what I understand, was what a whole heck of a lot of guys would like to do." He looked at Dern. "Are there MIAs in North Vietnam?"

"There is no North Vietnam anymore," Dern answered quietly.

Calhoun almost hissed the words at Dern. "Bullshit. Satellite data could confirm MIA sightings if anyone wanted to. I'm with Mulvaney. Was Ellermann just blowing smoke? Or don't we want to find—"

"I think that's enough, Colonel. Fort Sheridan isn't exactly the hub of the universe, but there are other posts—"

"Gentlemen!" Wilkes stopped his pacing. He lowered his voice as Dern and Calhoun stared toward opposing sides of the room. "The point is, if Ellermann remains in captivity, we could have a most serious new wrinkle in the scheme of organized crime. If, on the other hand, Ellermann can be found and freed—"

"Or verified dead," Dern interrupted.

"Yes." Wilkes nodded slowly. "Or verified dead, then Ajaccio will tell us all he knows. The situation is like this," Wilkes said, thrusting both hands into his pockets again and staring at Mulvaney, his dark eyes very intense, as though he were arguing a case in court rather than trying to hire a stooge. "The Japanese authorities cannot be alerted. Although the vast majority of Japanese officialdom is quite honest, I'm sure, it is possible that a Yakusa informant might become privy to some important detail, and the entire operation would be nipped in the bud."

"You want me to go to Japan and—"

"Yes, but let me finish, Sergeant," Wilkes said insistently. "Because of the potential for a leak, no matter how remote that possibility, whatever attempt is made to secure Mr. Ellermann's release must be made unofficially. Mr. Dern's superiors assure me that such operations have been undertaken in the past with mixed but generally favorable results. It was decided that a Chicago police officer would be the ideal candidate for the assignment."

Mulvaney looked at Hilliard as he said it, almost daring the deputy superintendent to say something. "I joined the department two weeks before the regulations requiring commando training and a detailed knowledge of Japanese language and culture went into effect. Sorry, guys."

Wilkes seemed undaunted. "You were picked out of all the personnel on the Chicago force—even over those with a knowledge of Japanese—because of your outstanding record in the United States Special Forces during your time in Vietnam and your outstanding record on the street—"

Hilliard laughed.

Wilkes continued. "Outstanding record on the street—and I mean that quite literally, Sergeant Mulvaney. In both cases, Army and Police Department, you seem to have an uncanny knack for getting the job done, no matter how difficult—"

"Violent, you mean," Hilliard growled. "Like a lot of these quick trigger artists who lost Southeast Asia for us, he thinks with a gun."

Mulvaney realized he didn't really have to sit there and listen to Hilliard. Unemployment would be better than this. "Fuck you, Hilliard."

Hilliard was up and moving across the room, a blackjack in his right fist.

Dern said, "Holy shit."

Calhoun laughed again.

Hilliard stopped short, the flat sap at shoulder height and ready to strike, his body suddenly trembling. Then he farted so loudly it sounded like someone had just sat down on one of those whoopie-cushion things from the gag shops.

Hilliard's eyes were riveted to the muzzle of the little snubby .38 Mulvaney had drawn from the ankle holster, his left leg crossed, left ankle and empty holster resting on his right knee. "Lay that sap on me, motherfucker. And I've got a room full of witnesses to justifiable lethal force. Come on—you got one free. Do it."

Wilkes, his voice very even, said, "Superintendent Hilliard, why don't you please sit down, sir? I think Sergeant Mulvaney may have overreacted, but you must admit that such a comment as you made could easily bring about such a result. The war in Vietnam is still a raw nerve with many of us. My older brother and my wife's cousin died over there."

Mulvaney didn't move the gun.

Hilliard lowered the blackjack, licked his lips, hunched his shoulders and stalked back toward his chair on the other side of the room.

"I have to finish this, Sergeant," Wilkes said.

"Go ahead, sir."

"The reason it had to be a Chicago police officer and not somebody else, Sergeant," Wilkes said slowly, "is we have to make you look dirty. We've already taken steps to do it, assuming you'd agree to cooperate."

"You what?"

"This is being financed with Ajaccio's money. We had to make it look like you were on Ajaccio's payroll if you got caught—either by the Yakusa or the Japanese authorities. We've already started adjusting some of your banking records. Ahh . . ." Wilkes looked away, walking toward the drawn drapes over the window. He kept talking, but the words came slowly, hard-sounding. "You have two new safe-deposit boxes. One in a bank in Oak Park and one in Milwaukee. You've got fifty thousand dollars in there. It's yours if you do this. The IRS can't trace it. Ajaccio's money will pick up all your expenses and—"

"You made me dirty. All of you."

Hilliard started to speak, but covered it by clearing his

throat. Dern said, "Ed, this is for your country. Sometimes certain things have to be done—"

"I never took a bribe. Not even when I was workin' traffic. I never helped myself to some poor joker's color TV set when I was workin' robbery. You know how much cash Fields and I recovered when we nailed those three guys who stuck up that bank in Arlington Heights?"

"No," Wilkes said softly.

"Two hundred and eighty grand. The Arlington Heights job, a bank job in Gary and another one in Indianapolis. Two hundred and eighty grand—and that's all there was. And we turned in every fuckin' dime of it. There musta been ten thousand just in singles."

"That's very commendable, and that's why we want—"

"You made me dirty for a lousy fifty grand so I could go after some gung-ho kid who belongs to Enrico Ajaccio?"

"I . . ." Wilkes breathed.

"You just change your damn records back the way they were and that money can sit in those safe-deposit boxes until it rots, I swear it."

"Hear me out," Wilkes said softly.

"Bullshit." Mulvaney holstered the little .38 and stood up to walk.

"Hear him out," Hilliard said easily. "Remember that shooting three months ago? Fields got stabbed and you went after the doper who did it, wiseass. The doper pulled a gun on you and you shot him twice in the pump. Remember?"

"Over on Forty-seventh and Green."

"That's the one, tough guy." Hilliard grinned. "You walk outta this room and all records of the suspect's gun and even the gun itself permanently disappear. Manslaughter. Maybe murder. How long you think you'd last with all the guys you've put inside, ass-wipe?"

Mulvaney just stood there.

Wilkes talked. "Sergeant, this can all have a happy ending. If you succeed, this will be the biggest single victory over the Chicago Crime Syndicate since Capone was put away almost sixty years ago."

Mulvaney's voice sounded to him as if he had lost his soul. "I don't know anything about Japan. I was never even in Japan when I went over to Nam. I wouldn't have the vaguest idea where to start looking for him."

"We planned for that too, Ed," Calhoun said. Mulvaney looked at his face. There was no help in Calhoun's eyes. "There's been a growing problem with drug abuse among armed-forces personnel in Japan and the others who breeze in and out for R and R. We had a team we pulled out of the MPs, working undercover to track the suppliers. One of 'em's gonna help you, Ed. You're going. You know you don't have any choice. I can't even say I'm sorry. Maybe you were dumb not to split that bank money with your partner and head for some sunshine."

Mulvaney sat down.

Inside the room on the next floor, John Osgood lit a cigarette. The bad thing about this business was the danger that you'd think you'd been told everything and then realize you hadn't. Mulvaney's face read like a book for the visually impaired. Anger. Desperation. Resignation.

And defeat. The defeat was the bad part. They had hooked Mulvaney for the job. Of that there was no question. But they might have destroyed the one necessary quality that Mulvaney had.

Osgood looked through the file again, scanning it by working through it eight lines at a time. In the Army. On the police force. Sloppy attention to detail. Unorthodox procedures.

The one positive quality had been the absolute unwillingness to give up.

They were talking about the MP detail working undercover narcotics. Osgood listened because he had nothing else to do. And he watched.

Colonel Calhoun was speaking. ". . . a friendly nation. But the higher-ups are the ones we aren't certain about, so it was determined that work should be undercover. Then, when the whole case is laid out, put in the laps of the Japanese authorities, by then it will be too late to screw it from the top if there is somebody big working with the Japanese criminal group. That's the same reason we're making you look like some kind of crooked cop, Ed. You'll be working with Sergeant Oakwood. Oakwood's got guts. Sergeant Oakwood's partner, a Corporal Tyler Koswalski . . ." Calhoun seemed to be reading notes off the ceiling. Either that or praying for inspiration. Perhaps calling for the Muse. "Koswalski was recently murdered. The killer used some sort of edged weapon and nearly severed the head from the body. Oakwood was offered out, but only went in deeper, after whoever it is in Japanese officialdom—if there is someone—who's playing both sides of the court.

"Oakwood's service record has been lost." Calhoun smiled. "Intentionally, of course. No verifiable connection to the U.S. government other than citizenship. Only one man in Japan knows what Oakwood's into. That's the provost marshal. When you get to Japan, there'll be two people who know Oakwood's working in deep cover. Oakwood will be your . . . your contact. Help you every way possible."

There was silence in the room for a long time. Osgood stood up, his eyes on the monitor that showed Mulvaney's face.

Mulvaney asked, "When do I leave? How do I find Oakwood? What about weapons?"

"Good!" Dern said.

Hilliard looked like an overweight cat about to belch up another canary.

Then Mulvaney said something John Osgood thought was most interesting. "One more question: How do you bastards sleep at night?"

Osgood usually slept quite well, he reflected—six hours was all he ever needed or wanted, and he could get along for weeks on four hours out of each twenty-four. But he wondered if he would sleep tonight. He thought about that very seriously for several minutes while he slipped into the jacket of his blue pinstripe suit, raised the blue silk crocheted tie from half-mast and squared it at his neck. He started shutting down the systems, still thinking about Mulvaney's remark.

All systems off, the disk with Mulvaney's file on it out of the computer and into the black leather attaché case, the case locked and the little booby trap inside the case set, he picked up the khaki Burberry trench coat and started for the door.

As he gave the room a quick glance to make certain

everything was in order, as it should be, nothing left behind, he hit the light switch.

John Trench Osgood had decided. He would sleep well tonight. He always slept well on overseas flights, and besides that, there was nothing on his conscience.

Not this time.

Not yet.

3

Things That Go in the Night

MULVANEY HAD KICKED three punks off the Lake Street el when they'd tried hustling an old lady for money. He hadn't buzzed them with the badge, which would have been the simple way. He hadn't opened his coats and let them see one of the guns. Another simple way.

Instead, he'd gotten out of his seat and grabbed one kid by the back of the neck and spun him around and slammed his face into the window of the connecting door leading to the gap between the cars. He'd backhanded the second one across the windpipe and the kid had dropped to his knees, holding his throat with both hands. The third kid came at him with a knife and Mulvaney had let him come, caught the forearm and smashed his right knee up into the kid's elbow, and if the elbow hadn't broken, it was the next best thing.

He'd thrown all three of them off the train at the next stop. The old lady was sitting in her seat clutching her purse with both hands and looking like she was going to have a heart attack. He had picked up the knife and closed it and handed it to her. "Here—next time some eighteen-year-old comes up to you, stick him with it." And he'd gone back to his seat and gotten off at Austin just before Chicago turned into Oak Park. He caught a CTA bus and rode to the stop just past North Avenue and walked the rest of the way west.

The mail was junk except for an early Christmas card from a guy he'd known in Vietnam. The guy's wife had a passion for avoiding the rush. He'd put the card on the living-room mantelpiece and walked through the house to make certain nobody had decided to come in and do some cleaning for him while he'd been gone. But the television and the VCR and the stereo were where he'd left them last, and nobody'd boosted the stove or the refrigerator. He'd stopped three twelve-year-olds once when they were trying to boost a 250-pound safe.

He poured himself a drink, a bar glass with three ice cubes filled to the rim with Seagram's Seven. His new "boss"—or maybe "capo" was a better word—Ajaccio, was supposed to contact him tonight about the rest of the details. Mulvaney drained half the glass and put in another ice cube, then filled the glass again.

Dinner.

He felt Italian and musical and flipped through the Rolodex on the kitchen counter until he hit P and started going through the cards. Some of the best pizza—in the entire world he was sure—was available for delivery to him, and the selection would be difficult. He checked his watch. Durante's had such slow delivery that on a cold night like tonight the pizza'd be cold, and somehow it never tasted quite the same rewarmed in the microwave he'd bought himself as a Christmas present at Sears last year. Enrico's— no. That was the same as Ajaccio's first name and the association would ruin his appetite. O'Hara's—the Chinese couple that had bought up O'Hara's after Ollie Centenelli had gotten shot trying to stop a B&E artist made good pizza and big pizza. It was eighteen inches in diameter.

Mulvaney took the phone off the kitchen wall and sipped at his drink as he dialed. He told Mrs. Fong he wanted a super-deluxe, but as usual, with no black olives and no anchovies. And as usual she told him she'd only charge him for a deluxe and did he need any Coca-Cola? He told her no and said good night and cut her off as she promised faithfully that he'd have the pizza in thirty minutes or less. Dinner accounted for, he left the kitchen. Stella had made such a big deal out of cooking—and had been lousy at it. He had tried teaching her, but she had no natural talent for it. As he walked into the living room and started stripping off

46

his coats and his guns, he reflected that Stella had little natural talent for anything—even *that*. It was still something that amazed him—that she'd found somebody to be unfaithful with. Which proved, he supposed, that a lot of people were harder-up than one might readily assume.

Right now, he was hard-up. There was this English teacher, a real knockout, that he'd met one time when Lew had asked him to pick up his wife at the high school. But Lew's wife refused to introduce them because she believed that mixed-race relationships only led to trouble. He'd wondered at the time if she spoke from personal experience. There was this girl who worked in records downtown. He'd bought her lunch, and after she'd ordered the most expensive thing on the menu she had gotten around to telling him that she never went out with police officers because her last boyfriend had been a cop and they always broke dates.

Then there was the AIDS thing. You had to be so careful who people had been with. Being single was enough to make you paranoid.

The tape he'd rented the night before last was already overdue and he decided to watch it. Baryshnikov dancing *The Nutcracker*. He loaded it into the VCR, pushed all the right buttons and threw his pea coat down on the floor and the rest of his stuff on the recliner. He kicked out of his shoes and pulled the Model 60 out of the ankle holster, not bothering to remove the holster. He set it on the little wine table beside the recliner. He left the L-frame in the shoulder holster and put it on top of his sport coat. He peeled off the sweater while the titles ran. He got the Beretta from the small of his back and set it beside the little .38 on the wine table. He pulled the two magazines for the Beretta out of the carrier, put them down. He got rid of his wallet and his money clip and his keys, and picked up the Beretta again and walked over to the couch and sat down, the Beretta on the coffee table.

He picked up his drink and started watching the tape. He didn't like *The Nutcracker*, really, but Baryshnikov had to be the greatest male dancer alive and Mulvaney had started thinking ballet was about the greatest art form there was when his mother's brother, a maintenance worker at the Civic Opera House, had gotten the family tickets to see *Swan Lake*. His father had announced halfway through the performance that ballet sucked, and spent the rest of the time in the lobby smoking. But Mulvaney had gotten hooked and caught it live whenever he could. He'd taken Stella to the ballet a couple of times and she'd gone out into the lobby to smoke too.

The pizza came in the middle of a *pas de deux,* Baryshnikov freeze-framed in the middle of an impossible-looking *grand jeté* as Mulvaney hit the pause button. He wondered if Baryshnikov had some magic way of conquering gravity for a split second at a time. The doorbell rang again. "Just a sec!" Mulvaney called out, grabbing up the Beretta and stuffing it in the back of his pants. Anybody who went to his door in Chicago after dark without a gun was either an optimist or an idiot.

The doorbell rang again.

Mulvaney caught up his money clip and reached for the doorknob.

As he pulled the door inward, he could see the pizza deliveryman standing just inside the open storm door, his face gray-looking and tired in the white wash of light from the streetlamp in front of the Perembski house next door. Mulvaney pulled the door open all the way and said, "You pizza delivery guys must feel like the guy on the dog sled bringing serum to the Eskimos—the unsung heroes of—"

The door started opening faster than it should have and the pizza was moving forward and the pizza man was lurching toward him and Mulvaney instinctively stepped back and away, bringing his left arm up to block, reaching his right hand back. The pizza man sprawled forward, shouting something in Polish. Behind the pizza man was a short, squat black guy Mulvaney recognized as a suspected West Side hit man named Abner Leech. Leech had a sawed-off shotgun. Mulvaney said "Shit!" and threw himself to the floor and rolled. The middle of the coffee table blew away. Suddenly Tchaikovsky was playing again, and as Mulvaney rolled, he caught a fleeting glimpse of the television set and the ballet that had resumed. "Son of a bitch!" Mulvaney fired a double tap, then another and another. Leech's shotgun, a pump, fired again. The pizza man screamed, still in Polish. The lamp on the wine table disintegrated and the top of the fireplace mantel was gone. Mulvaney rolled again.

48

Mulvaney did another double tap and Leech's shotgun discharged into the floor, blowing away half the pizza. But Leech was going down, multiple hits visible in the abdomen and chest and one in the left cheek. Mulvaney, on his knees, wheeled toward the door.

"Vincent." Mulvaney stood up slowly.

"I told you your ass was mine."

"Wait a minute, okay?" Mulvaney kept his pistol trained on Vincent, which was only fair, since Washington had a sawed-off just like Leech's trained on him. He reached across his body with his left and gave Leech, who was wobbling back and forth like a tree about to fall in the forest, a shove in the center of the chest. Leech fell backward across the already destroyed coffee table.

"What the hell you do that for, honky?"

"Didn't want him to fall on the pizza, Vincent. Now—you must heal quick, man. Wounds botherin' ya at all?"

"I'm touched, motherfucker."

Mulvaney grinned—Washington looked about ready to pass out. "I wasn't talkin' about your mental problems, Vincent. So, you sure you remembered the crossbolt safety on that Remington?"

"What?"

"Crossbolt safety, Vincent." Mulvaney shook his head. "Move your right thumb back toward the rear of the trigger guard and feel around. What do you feel?"

Vincent didn't answer for a second. Then, "It's like a button, man."

"You just might have the safety on. I betcha you do."

Washington's eyes flickered down toward the gun. Mulvaney punched the Beretta forward as he sidestepped left and his right first finger pumped the trigger twice. Vincent Washington's eyes imploded in the sockets and the shotgun fired and the television set exploded and Washington's body plopped back through the doorway onto the porch.

"Keep your head down, pizza man!" Mulvaney shouted as he picked himself up off the floor.

He approached the doorway, the Beretta tight in his right fist. He stepped onto Vincent's chest and looked down from the porch, then both ways on the street. Nobody else.

Mulvaney shrugged, worked the Beretta's safety and

dropped the hammer, then shoved the gun into his pants. He grabbed Vincent's ankles and dragged him back inside halfway, not enough to make it look odd but just enough to make it look indisputable that Vincent had been inside the house when his brains had been given an airing.

Mulvaney looked down at the pizza man. "You okay?"

The guy had his hands over his head and didn't look up. "Is it over, man?"

"Yeah—you're gonna have to hang around."

The pizza man looked up from the floor. "You gonna call the cops?"

"I *am* the cops—and this is simply a rapid-response test to see just how fast 'Chicago's Finest' can respond to a gunshots-fired call."

"Who called?"

"Somebody probably called. Or if they didn't, they will." Mulvaney reached down to the floor. The upper-right quadrant of the pizza, as it was oriented to him now, was shot away. Mulvaney picked up the pizza, tore off the "fifty-cents-off-next-time" coupon, walked across the room and set the pizza on top of the plastic lid over the stereo. He opened the wrapper and looked at it. Mrs. Fong, God bless her, had remembered to pull the anchovies and the black olives. He found a piece that looked unaffected by buckshot, using his left hand because his right hand had some of Leech's blood on it.

There were sirens in the distance. He figured the first blue-and-white would be at the door in maybe three minutes, plenty of time for a piece or two and to get over and fish his badge out of his pea coat and have a warm smile waiting.

"Hey, pizza man," Mulvaney said, his mouth full. It had not stayed very warm. "Ya want some?"

Mulvaney didn't look around, but he knew it was the wrong thing to say. But the carpet would have had to be cleaned anyway. . . .

The phone rang and he picked it up. "Yes."

"Mr. Osgood."

"To whom am I speaking?"

"Ahh . . . this is Lawrence Schuyler, Mr. Osgood . . . ahh . . ."

"I know—Dern's assistant."

"Yes, sir. I came for your, ahh . . ."

"My, ahh . . . yes. Well, my 'ahh' is up here waiting for you. Room 1903. I suppose I must speak with the night clerk."

"Yes, sir."

"Put the person on." Osgood lit a Pall Mall in the blue-yellow flame of the sterling-silver Dunhill. Cigarette brand was one of the few things—perhaps the only thing—he shared in common with the cop, Mulvaney. The night clerk came on, a woman. He imagined it was the girl with the auburn hair who had smiled at him when he had checked at the desk to see if there were any messages. "Yes. This is Mr. Osgood in room 1903. The gentleman at the desk. Is he black?"

"Yes, sir."

"About twenty-eight or thirty, would you say?"

"Yes, sir."

"Then that is indeed the gentleman I'm expecting. And I was wondering if you could do me a favor. I contacted room service about fifteen minutes ago to order a club sandwich. Could you please tell the room-service people to delay the sandwich about ten minutes? It would be most awkward to have food arrive for one."

"I understand, sir."

"Thank you. You're very sweet." Osgood hung up the phone and left his cigarette burning in the ashtray as he stood up. WTTW was one of the finest Public Broadcasting System affiliates to be had and, as had been the case in previous visits to Chicago, he had found their taste in programming to be impeccable. He turned off *Masterpiece Theater* as he passed the box and walked to the door. He moved the chair from beneath the knob (habitually, when staying in American hotels, he would arrange for a straight-backed chair to be placed in his room, complaining of a bad back) and placed it beside the door. He undid the security chain and then opened the door a sufficient distance for a knock on the door to open it fully.

That done, he returned to the bed where he had been sitting and took a drag from the cigarette and returned it to the ashtray, then reached under the pillow for the P-38 K. He had bought the last six Interarms had carried in inventory when he had learned the gun was to be discontinued. His friend there, Bob Magee, an old campaigner like himself, had arranged the purchase for him. The original Osgood had possessed was lost during an unfortunate incident in Afghanistan two years ago. Five more remained locked in various safe-deposit boxes, the last of the six in his right fist now.

He took another drag on the cigarette.

There was a light knock and the door swung inward. "Mr. Schuyler?" Osgood made his best smile as he leveled the 9mm at the good-looking young black man's thorax.

"Ahh . . . yes, sir." In the man's left hand was a black leather briefcase.

"Well, it's always a pleasure to meet a young fellow just starting out in this business. Come in and close the door, please."

"Yes, sir."

Osgood adjusted the position of the Walther's muzzle to match that of young Mr. Schuyler. "I believe there's a code phrase or some such silliness you're supposed to recite?"

"Yes, sir."

"Well, let's have the recitation and then I'll give you mine. All right?"

"Yes, sir. Ahh . . . wait a minute. Yeah . . . ahh . . . 'I am at a loss for words to describe the works of Bertol Brecht.'"

Osgood allowed himself a smile. "Let's see if I can remember mine. Ah! 'One of Shakespeare's simplest yet most eloquent lines from the history plays is "Yon gray lines which fret the clouds are messengers of the day."'"

Mr. Schuyler visibly relaxed.

Osgood set the pistol down on the nightstand and picked up his cigarette. "May I offer you a tumbler of Cutty, Mr. Schuyler?"

"Gee, thanks, sir, but my wife's expecting me and I've gotta drop your stuff off with Mr. Dern before I can go home. I mean . . . hell, yes. Just a little. Not too many junior men like me get the chance to share a drink with John Osgood."

Osgood could not argue with such crystal-clear logic and so stood up in order to pour the libation. "Ice?"

"No, sir. Straight, if you please, but only a little."

"Good man!" Osgood nodded, pouring a finger into the tumbler and holding it up for the young fellow to see. "Adequate?"

"Indeed, sir."

"Then a toast, if you'll indulge me. To friends well met."

Schuyler beamed his approval and they clinked glasses and Osgood drained very little from his already filled glass, then set it down. "I have two guns for you, and a knife. Make certain that Dern doesn't screw up. I'll need these delivered as arranged, as soon as I'm off the plane."

"Yes, sir. May I, ahh . . ."

"See them? Certainly."

Osgood crossed the room—he avoided suites because they made one conspicuous, and no matter how luxurious, were never as comfortable as one's own home—and opened the soft black leather flight bag's outside pouch. In a military flap holster that most of the time served as a pistol case rather than a holster was a well-worn full-size standard Walther P-38. "Just a plain, ordinary P-38, but as fine a backup gun as one could wish for. You'll take the gun, the holster and the accessories." He placed the unloaded gun back in the leather, then set it on the low triple dresser in front of the mirror. The silencer came next. It was eight inches long and about the size of a nice plump bratwurst— the kind found on crisp fall days in out-of-the-way villages in the mountains where there were restaurants frequented only by the locals and those who would travel far for good simple fare. The cleaning kit. The spare magazines for both guns—they used the same—and two plastic boxes of fifty rounds each, Federal 9mm BP 115-grain Jacketed Hollow Points.

Osgood reached in to his shirt pocket and withdrew the little penknife he habitually carried there. "What's that, sir?" Schuyler asked.

Osgood allowed himself another smile. "There's a story with these, a rather interesting one at that. Looks like a pen when carried in the shirt pocket, doesn't it?"

"Yes, it certainly does."

Schuyler was a clever young fellow. "Well, years ago, these were smuggled in from Brazil by everyone and his brother. You'd put them in the bell of a saxophone or in the side of your shoe or what-have-you. Stainless steel, sharp as a razor, hold an edge as well as an Ama pearl diver can hold her breath. Then this fellow named Rau began importing them legally, calls them the B&D Grande. As inconspicuous as anyone could want, and reliable too. Tell you what." Osgood grinned genuinely. "I'll try to remember to send you one. Just make certain Dern doesn't try to liberate it."

"I could pay—"

"Consider it a token of trust—I like your cut, Schuyler." Osgood meant it. The young man, despite the obvious politeness in the face of one of the Company's ranking case officers, seemed sharp.

"I don't know what—"

"Then take some advice. If you don't know what to say, don't say anything at all." Osgood walked over to the nightstand and picked up the Walther P-38 K. He worked the base-of-the-butt magazine release and placed the magazine on the table beside the ashtray, taking another drag from the cigarette and stubbing it out. He worked the slide, catching the chambered round in his palm as it ejected.

He worked the hammer drop, watching it as it returned to the horizontal position. "So that's a P-38 K," Schuyler said behind him.

"You know your guns, Schuyler."

"Not all that well, sir. But I grew up on James Bond movies and *The Man from U.N.C.L.E.* reruns on television. When I joined the Company, I found out there was one case officer who had a record that made fiction look pale, if you'll pardon the expression." Schuyler smiled as Osgood looked at him. "So I learned everything I could about you, sir. By the time I'd joined, they'd stopped making those. But can I show you mine?"

Osgood liked the young man—but he had never considered himself stupid. He braced himself to crush the larynx or drive the nose up through the ethmoid bone just in case Schuyler's offer to show his gun was anything other than what it appeared to be. "Of course."

Schuyler reached to his right kidney, where Osgood had spotted the gun the moment the younger man entered the room, and produced a Walther P-5. "Closest I could find to yours, sir."

Schuyler disarmed the weapon and passed it over for inspection. Osgood felt genuinely touched. "You flatter me, Mr. Schuyler. This is a fine weapon. May you never have to use it in anger, and if you must, may you always use it with honor." After inspecting the gun—there was nothing out of the ordinary about it, but he lingered over it nonetheless—he returned it to Schuyler, who turned away as he reloaded it, keeping the muzzle pointed at the bed.

"So, Mr. Schuyler. I imagine that wife of yours is going to be angry."

"She's a great girl, sir. I know sometimes the hours kind of get to her, but she never complains."

Sincerely—more so than Schuyler might ever know—Osgood told him, "You're a very lucky man." He helped Schuyler pack guns and ammunition and the little B&D Grande in the briefcase, then clasped hands with the younger man as he walked him to the door and said good-bye.

There was an empty feeling as Osgood shut the door. He disliked being without a gun. He intensely disliked the feeling. But Schuyler's remarks about his wife . . .

Osgood secured the chain, slid the chair under the knob and walked to the window, moving back the curtains. His own wife had been understanding of the missed holidays and birthdays and the calls in the middle of the night that meant he would be gone for weeks or months and never be able (at least officially) to tell her where.

She had loved him.

She had been taking the twins home from Easter Sunday dinner, having explained away his absence with the usual awkward-sounding lies. The man who had been drinking heavily because, as it was later learned, he had fought with his wife, had hit the car and Natalie and John Jr. had been killed instantly. John Jr.'s twin sister, Elizabeth, had died in the ambulance on the way to the hospital. John Trench Osgood had always told himself that his wife's soul and his son's soul had waited until little Elizabeth had been able to join them.

Snow was falling heavily and against the warmth of the window it melted and streaked and looked like tears.

There was a knock at the door. It would be the club

sandwich. But he would be careful lest it be something else. . . .

The telephone rang and the digital clock read two A.M. Mulvaney had just gotten to bed around one, the crime-lab people and the local district commander and the homicide detectives all finally gone. There hadn't been much left of the pizza and Mulvaney had gone to bed hungry. There were chalk marks and tape outlines on his carpet and bloodstains too, not to mention the stains from the pizza. His insurance man would have to be notified. He had been told that he would be leaving for Japan the next day, but it already was the next day. His sister had keys to the house and could let the insurance agent in.

Mulvaney picked up the phone, expecting one of Ajaccio's underbosses with travel arrangements. It was Lew Fields. "You okay, man?"

"Yeah." Mulvaney turned on the nightstand lamp.

"When I heard Washington was on the street—"

"Now he'll be under it," Mulvaney said, cutting him off. Mulvaney found his cigarettes and lit one. "Do me a favor?"

"Sure—what?"

"I'm leavin' town tomorrow—at least I think I am. That thing we were talkin' about isn't it."

"All right." Mulvaney figured at least someone from among the people at the meeting in the Hancock Building had a wire on his phone. Maybe they all did. "What you want me to do, Ed?"

"Find out how Washington could have gotten out so quick. That's quick even for that scumbag lawyer Washington used. Then save the information for me. And watch yourself, man. Call ya when I get back."

"Right—take it easy, man."

"I always do." Mulvaney hung up.

He stubbed out his cigarette and reached over to catch the light, but the phone rang again.

"Hello?"

"This is Phil Catania, Mulvaney." Phil Catania was Ajaccio's chief underboss. "Mr. Ajaccio wants to speak with you."

"Put him on."

56

"Mr. Ajaccio never conducts business on the telephone. In fact, he almost never uses it at all."

"Too many numbers and letters, huh? So—"

"So—you know Fiorelli's out on 147th?"

"In this snow—you're full of shit."

"The roads are clear enough, Mulvaney. Be there." Catania hung up.

Mulvaney hung up. He closed his eyes for a minute . . .

The garage Mulvaney kept the Porsche in was heated, the only way to ensure that a car could be washed and otherwise maintained in the Chicago winter. When the temperatures got really low—like in January—the air hoses at the gas stations didn't work and you couldn't even change your tire pressure. He had his own small compressor and did all of that himself. Oil changes, tune-ups, hand washes. And he'd have to wash the car tonight because the instant you took it out, the salt started eating at it.

Just keeping the garage heated to where the temperature stayed up above the freezing mark cost him a lot. But the car was gorgeous. The leather upholstery was supple, smelled good. The interior—the instruments on the dash, the dash itself—all of it sparkled and gleamed. His windshield wipers were fighting the snow and already the places where the wipers didn't reach were salt-stained and the white of the hood was grayed. When you hit a patch of road surface the salt trucks had just worked, you could hear the stuff pelting the undercarriage and the rocker panels.

Mulvaney looked at his watch as he took the off-ramp from the Tri-State and turned south on Cicero Avenue and kept driving. It was a little after three. He hadn't bothered with a shower. After this was done and after he washed the Porsche, he'd need to shower again anyway. He kept driving.

He'd been told Ajaccio would contact him, but hadn't assumed that actually meant a meet was coming. What did Ajaccio want to say anyway—"Bring backa my nephew, copper, please"?

Enrico Ajaccio had been big in the rackets when Mulvaney's father had been on the Cicero cops, so big he couldn't be touched by anybody. And now a bunch of Japanese gangsters who called themselves Yakusa were doing it. It was tough for Ellermann, being caught in the middle, especially if he'd stayed clear of the rackets all his life. Sins of the father or something like that, Mulvaney thought.

He hit 147th Street and turned east. Catania had shot him the straight dope about the streets. They were clear enough for driving.

Mulvaney saw the sign now: "Fiorelli's Italiano." The marquee lights were on, the parking-lot arc lamps. But the lot was empty except for a salt-splotched black Cadillac and a black Ford Crown Victoria, equally salt-stained.

Mulvaney pulled up beside the Cadillac. He put the stick in neutral and applied the parking brake, climbed out and locked.

He looked around the lot as he hunched his shoulders against the cold. He'd left the pea coat at home, wearing the lined raincoat instead, and the instant he stepped from the car, regretted it.

He started inside, the lot heavily salted with just an occasional slippery spot. The front door was open and he went in. There was a long, narrow alcove designed to accommodate lines of customers waiting until there was room in the bar where they could lap it up until their tables were ready. There was a small lectern at the head of the alcove and a reading lamp over it, the kind of thing used in funeral parlors over the visitors' register. Mulvaney glanced at the open reservation book. He spotted the names of two congressmen and a suburban chief of police.

He tried the door beyond it. Open. He went through.

Fiorelli's was usually a little too expensive and he hadn't been there in years. It looked like they had recently remodeled; the atmosphere was more plush, more expensive than he remembered it.

And there was Ajaccio, sitting in a booth along the wall. The booths were raised up three steps above the floor level, like you were ascending an alter.

Mulvaney saw Catania coming up on his right. "Sergeant Mulvaney. Good to see you again." Catania stuck out his hand. Mulvaney shrugged and shook it. "Can I take your coat?"

"You and the driver came with Ajaccio in the Cadillac. So

where's the driver and where are the guys who came in the Crown Vic?"

"Around. As a matter of fact, the driver, as you called him, is preparing some fresh coffee. Would you like some?"

"Sure—thanks." He fished his badge case out of the coat pocket and handed over the coat.

"You didn't really need to come armed, Mulvaney. We're all on the same team now, right?"

"Rah-rah; sis-boom-bah. A Chicago cop's gotta be armed twenty-four hours a day. And anyway . . . hell . . ." He left Catania and the raincoat and dropped his badge case in his right hip pocket with his handkerchief as he crossed the main room and started toward the steps.

Ajaccio stood up. "Sergeant Mulvaney. It's good of you to come so far on"—he gestured expansively—"on a night such as this. Driving in Chicago is bad enough with good road conditions."

"Right," Mulvaney nodded. He doubted Ajaccio had driven a car personally in forty years. For his middle seventies, though, Ajaccio looked pretty good. Expensive gray slacks, alligator-skin black loafers, an open-collared red sport shirt and a gray cashmere sweater that buttoned in the front. With a full head of white hair and wire-rimmed glasses and smiling eyes, he looked like a rich retiree who should have been in Florida.

"Sit down, Mulvaney."

Mulvaney sat down. "Catania knows about this?"

"He knows that I hired you to do a few things for me over the years and I'm hiring you to do this. Answer your question?"

"You on the level?"

"What do you mean, Mulvaney?" Mulvaney lit a cigarette. Ajaccio pushed an ashtray toward him. "Try not to blow smoke my way. Even though I quit twenty years ago, it still brings back a craving."

"Sure—what I mean is this whole deal with Peter Ellermann—and I emphasize the word 'deal.'"

Enrico Ajaccio smiled. He had a voice as smooth as Canadian whiskey. "Yeah. I learned one thing years ago that has helped me out a hell of a lot. You get what you pay for—and if you don't pay for it, one way or the other, you won't get it. Power. Women. Doesn't matter what." Ajaccio fell silent. A guy in a dark suit that looked like it cost more than Mulvaney earned in a week came up with a tray and a pot of coffee, two cups and saucers, a bowl of sugar and a container of cream. He was as broad-chested as Arnold Schwarzenegger, but taller.

The guy left.

Ajaccio resumed speaking. "I know what I need. I know it's the only thing I can pay that'll get me what I need. You're gonna get my boy back."

"What's he to you? I mean really?"

"They wouldn't let me fight in World War II because of my record. There was also some question about my citizenship at the time. Anyway, I respected the guys who fought. Peter was a hero in his war and he tried doing something this country should be doing—gettin' the rest of our boys back. And all this trouble he's in is because of me anyway. I owe it to him. That satisfy you?"

"Not really. I don't buy the patriotism stuff from you." Mulvaney poured himself a cup of coffee, offered, then poured one for Ajaccio.

Ajaccio pushed over the cream. "I never use it. Watchin' my cholesterol."

Mulvaney poured cream in his coffee and then sipped at it. "My compliments to the chef—good coffee."

"There's fifty grand in two safe-deposit boxes. That's yours no matter what happens. I can't ask for it back."

"Somehow I bet the feds'll find a way to screw me out of it."

"You bring Peter back alive, there's a hundred more where that came from. Already put away for ya. I'll just pass you the key and you walk with it."

"I like money as much as the next guy—but not yours. The only reason I'm doing this is that Hilliard threatened to pull the rug out from under me on a shooting."

"A bad shooting?"

"A good shooting," Mulvaney said.

"Some cops are bastards."

"So are some mob people." Mulvaney grinned. "You're important in the scheme of things, but you don't have the power to pull all the mob's business to these Yakusa assholes. I learned something a long time ago too. What you don't know can kill ya. So—what the hell's goin' on?"

Ajaccio laughed. "I don't understand. You want me to—"

"This is a scam. You know it. Or if you don't, you're not just old, you're dumb. If you're not in on it, we're both gettin' fucked over. But you can insulate yourself. I can't. So I gotta know."

"I told you the truth. I want Peter out, back here where those bastards can't touch him."

Mulvaney shrugged. "Let's say I buy that for a minute. You're really gonna tell everything?" He laughed. "Or just tell 'em stuff they already know and laugh about how they helped you pull off something you couldn't do yourself?"

"You think the government people are that naive? I already hung myself on tape to those guys. I'm on borrowed time. Whether you pull it off or not, I'm a dead man. What they want's the rest of it, the really good stuff. I'm a dead man whether you pull it off or not, so I'll tell 'em the rest whether you pull it off or not, just so I know you tried. For once in my life, I'm shootin' the straight shit to an honest cop. Will ya bring him back alive?"

Mulvaney drained the coffee cup. "I'll tell you the same thing I told them, Mr. Ajaccio. I know squat about Japan—the people, the streets, the language. How can a cop work the streets on a missing-person thing if he can't talk to anybody? I don't have any contacts over there. Nothin'."

"What about this MP of theirs?" Ajaccio looked angry. Was he thinking he'd bought the wrong man at the slave market? Mulvaney wondered.

"This MP's gonna help me. Supposedly knows the streets and the rackets and the whole nine yards. But still, why they picked me doesn't make any sense. You have anything to do with it?"

Ajaccio didn't answer for a second. Then, "I told them I wanted Peter back. Then they came to me and told me about you and how this hadda be set up. That's it. Nothin' more."

"What kinda connections you use over there when you tried on your own?"

"Some people. You wouldn't wanna know 'em."

"I wanna know 'em."

Ajaccio looked uncomfortable, cleared his throat, swallowed his coffee. Without cream in it, it had to be scalding hot. "How well you know what I'm into?"

Mulvaney held his left hand up, palm outward, and started lowering digits as he ticked off the list. "Numbers, drugs, prostitution, protection, fencing operations—shit, I ran outta fingers!"

"The people in Japan. I made a contact—I needed a contact. A guy in Vegas turned me onto a guy in Hawaii. The guy in Hawaii runs girls into Japan. White slavers. Like I said, you wouldn't wanna meet 'em. Didn't do shit for me anyway."

"You want Peter back? Names . . ."

An hour later, things memorized that could have bought him a lot of power or a lot of grief or maybe both, he left. Catania would give him the tickets, he was told. And in the parking lot, Catania handed him an envelope, shivering, no coat on, telling Mulvaney, "Don't fuck with Mr. Ajaccio, Mulvaney. Just don't."

Catania walked back inside. Mulvaney got into the Porsche and locked it, then started it up. He opened the envelope. Round-trip ticket to Japan. An American Express card in his name and a wallet of traveler's checks. He counted up. Fifteen thousand dollars.

He crammed it all into the pocket of his raincoat and started the drive home. The car had to be washed. There was a passport and other stuff to pick up. His sister had to be called so she could check on the house and the car for him. And the flight left O'Hare at noon.

With his luck, it'd be a bumpy flight and he wouldn't be able to sleep and all they'd serve would be sushi. He wondered if you could buy a decent pizza in Japan. He figured the chances of finding a good Chicago-style pizza in Japan were about as good as finding a guy with a missing finger named Peter Ellermann. About as good a chance as a snowball had in hell, the way Mulvaney figured it.

4

Groundwork

HE HAD SPECIFIED that his Shinkansen reservations would, of course, be for the Green Car, and made certain to sit on the right-hand side of the train. The *Bullet Train* was moving west with a punctuality he could have set his Rolex by. Precisely forty-five minutes out of Tokyo, John Osgood saw Mount Fuji. The view was always breathtaking. In exactly another two hours and fifteen minutes the Shinkansen would pull into the Kyoto station and he would fetch down his carry-on luggage and exit. He had learned years ago that to travel light was to travel efficiently.

A vendor interrupted his view, asking in poor English if he wished to purchase a bento or perhaps just a tangerine. Osgood waved the man away with a smile. Box lunches had never been his first choice in life. He had eaten aboard the overseas flight and would eat again after checking in at his hotel. He had taken a cab from Narita airport to the train station, getting in the shorter line for larger, more expensive taxis. That had served two purposes. First, he enjoyed a more comfortable ride. Second, the line for the more expensive surface transportation always moved more rapidly and his contact would be in the longer, slower-moving line for the less expensive transport.

Osgood had recognized the attaché case. It was identical to the one he carried. He recognized the man's face from a photo he had been shown. And the green shirt and red necktie, however theatrical, clinched it. As Osgood had come abreast of the contact, Osgood had set down his briefcase and the contact had made himself stumble. *"Gomen nasai!"*

Osgood had smiled, having caught the man's elbow as the fellow started to fall, dropping his attaché case to the pavement as he did so. Osgood released the elbow, then picked up the attaché case.

It was, of course, the identical duplicate the Japanese had carried.

In the Western-style men's room at the rail station, Osgood had entered a booth and quickly checked the contents. The latest edition of the *Wall Street Journal,* four packs of cigarettes, a paperback novel, an additional supply of business cards printed in both languages, the P-38 K, the standard P-38, the ammunition and spare magazines, the little Grande pen-shaped knife. He had slipped the knife into his shirt pocket, loaded the P-38 K and left it in the case, then closed the case. The rest room smelled of disinfectant.

The case was now beside his feet on the *Bullet Train's* floor.

There would be much to do after checking in at the Hilton (he always used American hotels whenever possible) and showering and changing. There were contacts to be reestablished in the Kyoto underworld. None too obviously, but quickly, he had to establish Edgar Patrick Mulvaney as an enforcer for the Chicago Crime Syndicate, a rogue cop who had come to Japan to "kick ass and take names," as the expression went, blood in his eye for the Yakusa leadership who had had the effrontery to kidnap Enrico Ajaccio's nephew and hold him for ransom, men who had had the pure audacity and unmitigated stupidity to cut off the nephew's finger and send it to Ajaccio.

The Japanese were wonderful people at spreading news, and by the time Mulvaney actually arrived, he would be a marked man.

All cars except the last were smoking cars. But his seatmate, a man of about fifty with nicotine stains between the first and second fingers of his right hand, had not yet smoked. Propriety demanded courtesy if he—Osgood—

was to smoke first. As he took his cigarette from his case, he murmured, *"O-saki ni,"* and lit up.

People kept smiling at him and saying things he didn't understand. He smiled back. Mulvaney remembered one time a few years back that he had been sent to handle an extradition warrant. The cops in some small town in Georgia had picked up a guy wanted for two rapes and a string of B&E's in Chicago. There'd been a foul-up in the paperwork—on his end—and he'd spent three days in the little town. It was just like that here. Everybody smiling at you as though you were a long-lost brother. It was enough to unnerve him.

Dern had met him at the airport in Chicago for a last-minute briefing. Sergeant Oakwood was to meet him just outside immigration, Dern had told him. And precious little else.

It hadn't been a bumpy flight, but he hadn't slept very much anyway. The food had been Japanese-style American —perfectly palatable, but he had never really eaten well on planes. And now he had been waiting in the Tokyo airport for twenty minutes. He knew enough about spook work from his days in Special Forces to know that late contacts were bad contacts. And even more on the minus side, he didn't know what Oakwood looked like, Dern simply telling him, "Oakwood will recognize you," then giving him passport and visa and a wish of good luck.

Mulvaney had been watching this knockout girl for about twenty minutes, realizing he had stared at her ever since he spotted her. And the good thing was that she was staring back at him. She was tall, had a figure that looked great—as much as he could see of it under the kind of woolen poncho thing she was wearing instead of a winter coat. Her hair was short, just to her shoulders, and rolled inside like women sometimes do it (he had never figured out what kept it that way and his ex-wife had never worn her hair that way so he'd never found the answer), the color a bright reddish brown. From the distance, it looked like she had a few freckles. She was wearing either a dress or a skirt that came down almost to her ankles, dark brown, and boots with high heels that disappeared under the hem of whatever-it-was.

She started walking toward him. "You're Mulvaney, aren't you?" she said.

"Yeah."

"What the hell's the matter with you? There's supposed to be a phrase, right?" She had a pretty voice, a nice, throaty alto.

"What phrase?" he asked her.

"A phrase."

"Dern didn't give me any damn phrase. What—you Oakwood's squeeze? Well, you got it wrong, honey." It was a shame if she belonged to this Sergeant Oakwood. He wished she could belong to him instead.

"You don't have the phrase. And you think I'm somebody's squeeze?"

"Well . . . what . . . You work with Oakwood?"

"They didn't tell you much, did they? How do I know you're Mulvaney and not just some guy in tacky clothes they sent in as a ringer?"

"You just called me that," he retorted. "So . . ." He wondered if Oakwood had his picture and had given it to her.

"Damn," she said, tapping the toe of her right boot on the floor.

"Look, did you know a guy named Koswalski too?"

She looked at him hard. Then, "What do you know about Koswalski?"

"He wasn't lucky."

"I'm Andy Oakwood."

He blinked.

She said it again, her voice lower than before. "Andrea Louise Oakwood, sergeant first class."

"Holy shit."

"Let's get the hell outta here. May as well stick with me, since we made the thing so damned obvious." He caught up his bags and fell in with her. The airport patrons seemed to part like a wave in front of her. Walking beside her now, he realized that with her high heels she was just about an inch shorter than he was in track shoes. He kept beside her. "I know your service record. You may have been a captain then, but don't go trying to pull rank on me now."

"No, I wouldn't think of doing that. Why the hell didn't they tell me you're a girl?"

"Maybe they figured you'd notice on your own—how the hell should I know? Nothing's been going right. Why should this go right?"

"You . . . ahh"—he lowered his voice—"got a piece for me?"

She stopped dead and turned around and hauled back her right arm, her palm outstretched for a slap, her green eyes cold as ice for an instant. Then she started to laugh and brought her arm down and put her arms around him and he dropped his luggage. Her lips were next to his ear and he felt a stirring in his crotch. "You meant a gun, didn't you?" she whispered, giggling a little and making the feeling in his crotch more pronounced.

She stepped away from him and picked up one of his bags as if it didn't weigh a thing.

"You thought . . . Well, I'm not that direct. But I wouldn't mind discussin' it."

She looked at him; she laughed; she resumed the forced march from the airport.

There had been a crazy taxi ride, then a train ride on the fastest train he'd ever seen in his life, and then another taxi ride until at last he reached some semblance of normalcy. It was a Hilton hotel. Not that he stayed in Hiltons very often back home, but in fewer than five hours since getting off the plane he had developed a terrific case of homesickness for America. Oakwood hadn't talked with him much on the train at all, just helped him order a box lunch when he'd said he was hungry, helped him use chopsticks, which he'd never been very good at, given him some touristy-sounding information on the *Bullet Train,* Mount Fuji, the traditionalism of Kyoto society (he hadn't even known they were going to Kyoto) and then told him how to find the bathroom.

The relationship was not developing along promising lines, Mulvaney decided.

The lobby of the Hilton looked Japanese yet reassuringly familiar. He registered, showed his passport and visa (he made a joke about being in a foreign country once and having his Visa revoked by just using his MasterCard; she didn't laugh) and went to his room, Oakwood still carrying one of his bags, using the key and going inside first.

Mulvaney stood in the hallway. "Can I come in, Mom?"

"Come in and close the door behind you."

Mulvaney came in, closed the door behind him and put down his other bag. It was pretty much a standard expensive hotel room; really not just a room, but a small suite with sitting room, bathroom and bedroom. He explored it briefly; the appointments were Western, the decor Japanese. When he returned to the sitting room, Andrea Oakwood had taken off her poncho. It was not a dress, but a skirt that she had worn underneath it, a blouse with a sweater over it, the blouse white and the sweater—a sleeveless round-necked pullover—camel-colored. She didn't wear much jewelry. Small pierced earrings, a single gold chain intertwined with the big floppy bow that formed the collar of the blouse, and a matching bracelet on her right wrist. All gold, but not super-expensive-looking. There were some advantages to working Burglary. On her right wrist—she was rolling up her sleeves and he didn't know for what—she wore a plain watch, some kind of digital that was all black and looked like somebody had taken a man's watch and shrunk it to fit.

"Now can we talk?" Mulvaney asked her.

She shook her head, saying nothing. She opened the saddlebag-size purse she'd been carrying—he'd seen it every once in a while under the poncho—and took out something that looked like a voltage meter. She started moving about the room, putting the gadget near each of the lamps, near the base of the telephone. She was looking for bugs.

He shrugged, sat down on the couch, kicked out of his track shoes and lit a cigarette. He glanced at his watch. People didn't just forget to give code phrases. Dern had intentionally never given it to him. Which meant that Dern personally or the CIA officially had wanted him to attract some attention when he arrived in Japan. Which didn't make any sense, of course, but official policy rarely did make much sense. The idea, as it had been explained to him, was that Oakwood would assist him in finding the missing nephew, then he would somehow (manner unspecified) rescue said nephew and get him to the American embassy. He'd seen something like that plot in the old Jimmy Cagney film *Blood on the Sun*. He hoped he'd have better luck than Cagney if it went that far. The bad guys had been waiting for him and nailed him. But he was only wounded and *Leave It to Beaver's* father had come out of the embassy just in the nick of time and Cagney had triumphed. But Andrea Oakwood didn't look a thing like Sylvia Sidney.

He looked at his watch again. It had been ten minutes. "Hell with it," he muttered, then raised his voice so she could hear him. "You into Cagney films much?"

He looked up and she was standing right next to the couch. "What the hell are you talking about?" With her sleeves rolled up and her little hands on her hips and a lock of her hair fallen across her forehead, she looked kind of cute.

"Cagney films."

She just shook her head. "The room's clean as far as this gadget can tell me. They could have parabolic microphones trained on the room, or fiber-optic stuff I can't find."

"They? You mean the Yakusa?"

"No, the Japanese Boy Scouts. Of course, the Yakusa— and you'd better watch where you drop that word now that you're in this country. You wanted a gun . . ."

She started to reach into the huge purse.

"The exact words had something to do with a piece."

She looked across the coffee table at him. "The gun you'll get—the other thing you gotta work for. And you're not doin' too well just yet."

He stood up.

Out of the purse there magically appeared a Beretta 92F just like the one he'd left with his sister back in Chicago. "What about the extension magazines and the ammo?"

"You rate good service." She was still fishing in her bag.

"I thought you didn't want to talk about the other thing yet?"

"Get your mind out of the gutter, huh?"

"That's not exactly what we call that part of the anatomy in Chicago where I come from, ma'am," he drawled.

She handed him the extension magazines. They were already loaded. He would unload them and check them, of course. The head stamp on the top cartridge in each read "Federal" and he was satisfied. She put a plastic box down on the table. He opened it. More of the same. He picked up the gun, bounced the magazine and cleared the chamber. He tried the trigger pull. It was factory and heavy but satisfactory. "You just watch it that nobody sees you with it. Or you're in deep shit. A Japanese citizen can't run around with a handgun, can't even own one unless it's a damn toy, so the cops aren't too happy when they spot a handgun on a foreigner."

"Speaking from personal experience?"

"No, and that's because I'm smart. Just see that you are."

"I'm real smart, Sarge. Now, tell me what's comin' down and then point me in the direction of some American food. That crap in the lunch box on the train didn't do it for me."

"You want it quick?"

"We talkin' about that again?"

She just shook her head and sat down on the edge of the coffee table, her legs spread apart like a man would do, the skirt reaching to the floor. "All right, let's put our cards on the table, Mulvaney. It was a good idea puttin' the word out on the streets that one of Ajaccio's enforcers was coming to town and that he was a crooked cop to boot. Good from the standpoint of getting fast action out of the bad guys, but not so good for you. You're a walking target and have been since last night. That layover time you spent in Hawaii may have been nice R&R time but if this wasn't intentional, then it was the crappiest timing I've ever seen."

"I spent the night in Hawaii because the reservations read that way. And nobody told me anybody was puttin' any word out on the streets about me. And this code-phrase shit. What was it supposed to be?"

"What—tryin' to see if you just missed it?" She looked up at him but he didn't answer her. She shrugged and said, "You were supposed to ask if I had the correct time. I was supposed to give it to you. You were supposed to say that this was your first trip to Japan. I was supposed to say that I'd been here many times. You were supposed to ask if I could give you the directions to someplace where you could see a tea ceremony. That was it."

"Nobody ever gave me any of that stuff to say. Somebody's settin' me up to attract attention. Put the word out I'm coming, then didn't give me the code phrase, so we drew enough attention to the meeting at the airport that nobody could miss me, just in case they had." He looked down at her, his hands going to her upper arms. He pulled her to her feet and she tossed her head to get the hair back off her forehead. She had good little biceps and triceps under the blouse. "What did they tell you?"

"The Army?"

"Yeah—they tell you to put the word out on the street? I mean, you're the dame with all the hot connections, workin'—"

Her hands found his face and for a second he was torn between thinking she was either going to kiss him or gouge his eyes out. She didn't do either one. "You mentioned Koswalski. It was the Yakusa that had him iced. And it was because there's some damn Japanese official who's tipping the Yakusa. Just like the mob back home, they've got their hooks into lots of people who have big ears. I follow orders, but not stupid ones."

"You really are a cop," Mulvaney said to her, his arms folding around her. "On the outside, or you just been at it so long for Uncle Sam?"

"My dad's in the FBI. I never wanted to go to college, just wanted to be a cop. Did junior college and took police science. I was a cop in Detroit for three years. I didn't like it. Didn't want to go back to school. I couldn't stand the crap. So I joined the Army after they promised me MPs. Figured if I didn't like it I wouldn't have to re-up. I liked it."

"Detroit's a rough town."

"That's not why I left. At least with the Army if I make a bust and I've got 'em nailed good enough, it sticks. I got tired of bein' a damn revolving doorman."

"You could never be a doorman. You'd flunk the physical," he said to her. It sounded lame but it was the best thing he could think of. Slowly—he was afraid she'd knee-slam him in the crotch—he lowered his face the slight distance toward hers, her body leaning in against his, like her body was kissing him. Gently he touched his mouth to hers. Then he kissed her harder and she started kissing him back and her hands were holding his face and her body went tight against him and his hands were in her hair and he was kissing her again. She pulled free. He looked at her.

"That wasn't so bad," she said, running her fingers back through her hair. "You've done it before."

"Once or twice, maybe."

"And I liked that—that you didn't try slippin' me the tongue. You know how many guys these days, the first time they kiss you they try slippin' you the—"

"Hey, how you feel about the second time?"

"It depends on the guy."

"Can I audition?"

She walked toward him again, her hands thrust into the pockets of the long skirt. Her hair needed combing. "So, audition," she said, smiling a little.

Mulvaney reached out his hands to her shoulders, his fingers touching at the skin of her neck above the collar of her blouse. Her hands came up and tugged at the bow, and the collar opened up. His hands moved inside the blouse, but not very far. He drew her toward him, still holding her that way. She raised her chin a little and he put his mouth over hers and, hesitantly, moved his tongue forward and into her mouth, feeling the tip of her tongue against his for an instant, feeling her hands touching at the fronts of his thighs, her body going limp against him.

He let her go. "Did I make out okay?" Mulvaney grinned.

She ran her tongue across her lips as she stepped back, and her hands went to the bow thing at the front of her blouse and she retied it quickly. "I'll have to let you know. Requires some more checkin' out, Mulvaney. You might have to audition some more."

"When?"

"When's it good for you?"

"Now."

"Not good for me. There's a place I gotta take you before dark. The job."

"How about after dark? I could audition pretty good then. Whatcha think?"

"You're gonna think I'm easy," Andy Oakwood whispered.

"I know I'm a fool, fallin' for a soldier like this. If it works out, you'll just leave your boots under my bed whenever you feel like it and be gone the next morning, leaving me to worry about whether or not you'll ever come back."

"You're full of shit." She laughed. "But I like you, Detective Sergeant Mulvaney. What do your friends call you? Edgar?"

"No, almost nobody calls me Edgar. Sometimes they call

me Superman or Spidey or 007. But they never call me Edgar."

"Ed?"

"Ed's cool. Andy?"

"Yeah. My grandfather was Andrew, so they figured Andrea was as close as they could get. Everybody that doesn't call me Sergeant Oakwood calls me Andy."

"Well, Sergeant—"

She came close to him again and he didn't want her to because if they really had to do something before it got dark and she got too close to him they'd never get out of the room until morning. "Go to the bathroom or somethin'." She smiled. "You're lookin' obvious."

He looked down at the front of his pants. She was right. He was looking obvious and it wasn't that he was wearing his heart on his sleeve. . . .

The car, a Honda Accord, handled pleasantly. With the traffic in the city it had been easy enough to keep up with the small Ford Sergeant Oakwood was driving, without ever being seen. Once out of the boundaries of Kyoto itself, he had lain back, using the homing device to monitor the Ford's movements, only rarely having visual contact with it.

After nearly an hour, much of it because of the traffic, the night coming quickly now like a purple veil being drawn back to reveal blackness, the Ford stopped. Osgood accelerated to get the car in sight again before Sergeant Oakwood and Sergeant Mulvaney got too far away from it. The countryside—pine trees and little else in the last ten minutes—would be easy enough to get lost in for an ex-Special Forces captain and a sergeant in the military police who had both airborne and ranger schools behind her. There was, of course, no reason for them to attempt to lose themselves—but to expect the unexpected was to be prepared. He saw the Ford pulled off at the side of the road and Mulvaney and Oakwood disappearing into the trees. Oakwood wasn't dressed for an expedition into the woods. Mulvaney appeared always to dress that way.

Osgood left the car, locking it and setting the alarm, then crossed the two-lane road onto the grassy area along the opposite side. He headed for the trees, the binoculars he had ordered to be placed in the car for his use swinging from around his neck, and in the left outside pocket of his leather sport coat a wildlife guide to Japan. The binoculars and the book would at least provide some props for the story he'd tell if his presence were detected.

He kept moving, realizing that Mulvaney and Oakwood hadn't gone off into the woods, but were following some sort of path. Osgood hesitated. But there was no choice. He took to the path, walking quickly, opening his sport coat to better reach the P-38 K under it. He was warm enough with the lightweight leather coat and the cotton sweater he wore beneath it, but as soon as the sun was fully down, that situation would change. He had brought his woolen sweater in the car just in case. He kept going. There was nothing up here that he could recall except some isolated houses belonging to the very rich and an old Zen Buddhist shrine. He had always admired the way of Zen.

Logic had always appealed to him.

Osgood heard a rustle of fabric ahead. Assuming it was Sergeant Oakwood's skirt getting caught in something, he slowed his pace, then stopped completely. Logic dictated that Sergeant Oakwood, if his first assumption were true, would have said something. If nothing else, some muted profanity. Why hadn't she spoken? he wondered.

He drew the P-38 K and waited.

Osgood heard what sounded like movement ahead. He moved as well, the pistol tight in his right fist, his pace quickening.

After several minutes he stopped abruptly. At the edge of the treeline where the path ended, he saw them, Mulvaney's right arm around her shoulders.

For some strange reason, the two of them were staring at the walls of the old Zen Buddhist shrine, talking in tones so thoroughly hushed he could only detect they were talking at all because of the way they moved their heads. He read lips and the binoculars were adequately powerful that even in the declining light he could have monitored their conversation. But they were looking away from him.

Why were they studying the shrine so intently?

"How very bizarre," Osgood said under his breath. And now he would have to return here to find out just how bizarre.

5

Night Moves

SHE CONSIDERED HER cover blown. He had never had one to get blown. So there was little point in hiding their relationship. At least he hoped they'd have a relationship not to hide.

They had gone back to the hotel because he had insisted on American food for dinner and the Hilton's restaurant featured a dual cuisine.

There was a choice of dining Japanese style on one's knees or Western style on one's posterior and he elected the latter.

They sat across from one another at a table for two and Andrea Oakwood sipped at her wine, smoked some of his cigarettes and told him what he had seen at the end of the path through the woods. "I told you it was a Zen Buddhist shrine. And it was that. You watch any karate flicks, Ed?"

"Chuck Norris stuff. I went through a Bruce Lee period like most guys. Why?"

"Tell me what you think a ninja is."

He laughed.

She repeated herself. "Tell me what you think a ninja is."

He sipped at his wine, wishing the steak he'd eaten hadn't gone so quickly, happy he was spending someone else's money to buy it. "Okay. Political assassins who dress in black clothes and are real good at martial arts and carry swords and shit. Was that a good answer?"

"You're partially right. There are ninja clans—"

"I know. They have karate schools and they fight in the streets and stuff like that."

"Be serious, Ed."

"Okay." He wiped his right palm over his face and lowered the corners of his mouth. "See? Serious as anything."

"They're criminals. The politically involved acts weren't politically motivated. At least not on their parts. They're criminal societies. A lot of people will tell you they don't even exist anymore. But they do. They have a lot of money and sometimes the Yakusa people hire one or another of the clans to work for them. Sort of like a New York mobster hiring a torpedo from Cleveland or something."

"Enforcers?"

"Killers. Let's say you're a Yakusa boss and there's a gang of thieves giving you some headaches and ripping off some of your profits. What do you do? Send your own boys? Maybe to talk to them once, but what if that doesn't work?"

"In Chicago, you'd get somebody to break some arms and legs, and if it were real serious you'd have 'em killed."

"They do the same thing here," Andy told him. "They hire the ninjas."

"You're bullshitting me."

"Then who the hell did I see meeting with Mizutani Hideo three nights ago? He was wearing a black ninja outfit—tabby boots and the whole shot. You think the head of the Yakusa himself was wasting his time with some nutball who just thought he was a ninja?"

Mulvaney sipped at his wine, reached for the bottle and refilled the glass. "Who's this Hideo character?"

"Mizutani Hideo—I told you," she insisted, taking another one of his cigarettes. He lit it for her and lit one for himself. There'd been apple pie on the menu and he'd ordered it, and the waiter, a Japanese who spoke perfect-sounding English, arrived with it then. Andy hadn't wanted a dessert. The waiter left. Andy started talking again. "He's an Ajaccio, but over here. Only he's bigger than an Ajaccio.

He's like whoever it is who's the real boss of all the New York Families. He doesn't meet people who aren't important, and he drove out to some old shrine at midnight and met this guy."

"How do you know that?"

"Mizutani likes white girls sometimes. I was one of his white girls once, just to get in there to his house and see what I could dig up on him."

"What'd you dig up?"

"Nothing. But I learned what his car looked like and got the plate number."

Mulvaney just looked at her. "You sold your body to get a look at the guy's car?"

Her eyes hardened. "He likes watching white girls dance. He likes drinking with them. He's seventy-three or seventy-four and I don't think he could get it up if his life depended on it, okay?"

"What kind of dances you do?"

"I took my clothes off so he could look at me."

"You're right—he must be outta gas. If you danced naked in front of me, I could be in a full body cast and I'd get it up somehow. So—you found out what his car looked like."

"After Koswalski died, I started following the car every time it left his place."

Mulvaney stubbed out his cigarette. "Musta been a lot of fun."

"You still on the dancing stuff?"

He smiled. "No—I meant following the guy's car. I mean, like to the grocery store and everything?"

"It's a 1954 Rolls-Royce, black. They don't take it to the grocery store, Mulvaney."

"So where do they take it?" He started eating the pie. "Want some? Pretty good—nice and tart. So where'd he go?"

"I followed the car for two weeks every time it left his place."

"And they never got wise to you?" Mulvaney asked her.

"I changed cars every day. Cost me an arm and a leg to rent 'em and I got myself a couple of wigs and wore different outfits so his people wouldn't catch on. This one time"—she laughed a little—"I dressed like a Japanese. Imagine that? Me—carrot top here?" She touched her hair. "One time I even dressed up like a guy."

"That's not so much fun. I do it all the time." He was finished with the pie. "Where'd he go?"

"One time he went to visit a private house about two hours away from his place and I was already tipped to the Ellermann thing and I thought, 'Hot shit! I found the Ajaccio brat.' But it wasn't that. He met with a bunch of guys. I had a real hard time checking the license plates without going official. That was why I couldn't just make the Rolls-Royce through channels. But I got a make on two out of three of them. One belonged to an executive with one of the big electronics companies. And the other one belonged to a guy from the Russian embassy."

Mulvaney swallowed too much wine too fast and almost choked on it. "What?"

"Just control your breathing for a sec and you'll be okay," Andy counseled him. He nodded, not saying anything. "I figured I was onto some good stuff and I kept at it. That's when the car left without him and came back with new tires on it. I figured something was up. Maybe a long trip, and this would lead me to the Ellermann kid or more Russians. So I hung around, kind of camped out when I wasn't swapping cars or clothes, alongside the road where the car hadda pass, right? The car goes by at nine-thirty and I follow it. I figured this might be the big one because there was never any night stuff before."

"What were you wearing this time?"

"That was the time I dressed up like a guy."

"Good thing nobody looked close." Mulvaney had learned he could make her blush a little if he worked at it hard enough. She looked pretty when she blushed.

She ignored him, but her cheeks flushed. He wondered if other parts of her blushed. He hoped he would find out soon. He hoped he would find out tonight. She was talking again. It was something else she seemed to do a lot. "I drove out along that same road you and I went on this afternoon, followed them to the shrine. Thank God I didn't get too close, or that guy in the black clothes, the ninja, woulda spotted me."

"Were you able to hear anything they said?"

"I caught one thing. One of them—I think it was Mizutani Hideo—said, 'Vietnam.'"

Mulvaney lit another cigarette.

Osgood had followed them back to the hotel, watching as they went into the restaurant, then hurriedly going up to his own rooms. He packed a few things in the attaché case—it was the expandable type—and left again, gassing up the Honda and driving out along the same road, back toward the same spot. He stopped the car along the roadside and climbed into the back seat to change quickly: a black woolen pullover sweater, the shoulder holster going on over the sweater, and over the holster a black cloth windbreaker. He pulled on the skintight black leather gloves he habitually carried and climbed back behind the wheel, resuming the drive.

He parked the Honda close to the spot where he had parked it earlier, but turned around so it would be facing the proper direction toward Kyoto, then locked it and set the alarm. No binoculars and no wildlife handbook this time. If someone spotted him near the Zen Buddhist shrine, he would cut and run or fight. Talking would be of little avail.

He reached the trees and followed along the edge of the treeline until he reached the path, looking behind him, then down along the path. He had a Mini-Maglite clipped inside the windbreaker, but to use it to navigate the path would be a dead giveaway. Instead, in almost total darkness except for the intermittent light of the moon when the clouds broke, he started down the path. His right hand slipped under the windbreaker and he broke the Walther from the holster, the pistol tight in his fist and close at his right side. In motion pictures and on television, people walked with guns in both hands extended at arm's length, as though witching for water with a dowsing stick. In reality, this not only looked stupid but was a superb way of setting oneself up to be disarmed. He kept moving, a brisk commando walk his chosen gait rather than a run.

Osgood reached the end of the path, the gray slate walls which surrounded the shrine rising up like black shadows darker against the night. Vines rose along the wall, and as he looked right and left, then ran the open expanse, he aimed himself at what looked to be some of the sturdiest of these, intending to climb them.

Osgood reached the wall, flattening himself against it for a moment. He was not out of breath. When circumstances permitted, he ran two miles per day five days each week, this in conjunction with a vigorous program of calisthenics of his own design, and weight training whenever equipment was available. He kept himself fit. Osgood reached the chosen portion of the wall and tugged at the vines. "Here goes nothing," he said under his breath, holstering the Walther and starting to climb.

He reached the height of the wall, twenty feet as he gauged it from the climb, and was met with a narrow slate tile roof. This could be dangerous he thought, the wrong step causing a tile to crack and dislodge. He spread-eagled himself and started along the up-angled uneven surface slowly, his weight distributed as evenly as possible.

He reached the crown of the roof, which was rounded, apparently made of the same materials.

He could now see down into the garden, and as the cloud cover broke he could see within the walls in some detail. There was a perfect "dry landscape," as it was called. He had expected the old shrine to be overgrown with weeds, much as the walls were overgrown with vines. But there was evidence of considerable care here because a dry landscape had to be constantly tended so nothing would grow except in the designated islandlike areas set about it. The sand which surrounded the islands was constantly raked to texture it evenly and in such a manner as to aid in contemplation.

The moon was very bright now. This dry landscape had been tended recently, perhaps within the last twenty-four hours.

The cloud cover returned and the interior of the garden was lost in shadow. But for a fleeting instant he saw a deeper shadow, moving. Osgood froze.

A chill wind was picking up. He looked skyward. In another few seconds the clouds would part again and the moon, almost full, would bathe the garden once again in light.

Osgood waited, realizing he was holding his breath.

The wind heightened and the clouds moved and there was

light. In the moonlight which illuminated the garden, he saw two shadows, but they were alive, had form, substance. And he knew what he was seeing, but didn't believe what he was seeing.

The two figures, blacker than the night surrounding them, their blackness having betrayed them, were moving in a counterclockwise circle at the center of the dry landscape garden. As his eyes adjusted to the light, he realized there were not just two of them. There was a rank on either of the two longest sides of the rectangularly shaped garden, one rank almost immediately below him, the other directly across from him. All these persons were black-clad like the two figures at the center.

There was a flash of steel, almost simultaneously, in the hands of both central figures. In the next instant it would begin, a duel with *daito* and *shuto*. The *daito* was the long sword, or *katana,* its blade, or *tachi,* when combined with sharkskin handle and the classic *tsuba,* or round guard, forming the samurai sword of legend. The *shuto* was the short sword, or *wakizashi,* the classic killing knife. Only in the most advanced Ni-To-Ryu were both blades used, and the two figures at the center of the garden held them presented now, crossed. Though there was no means by which he could measure the distance between his observation point and the two figures about to fight, Osgood knew the tips of the blades would be overlapping by no more than four inches, the classic *en garde* presentation.

What was unfolding before him was a centuries-old ritual of combat, a fight between two ninjas. Perhaps two separate clans, or perhaps one of the men had somehow dishonored the clan and was being given the honor of dying in combat.

Osgood realized that he too would be given such an honor if he were discovered.

He watched, daring not even to move a muscle lest some betraying sound bring the ninjas below him onto the roof en masse.

The two figures circled, the blades moving, but not carelessly, neither motion nor energy lost. Then one of the figures charged, the swords in his hands crisscrossing and slicing the air as he spun, twirled, vaulted. The other figure gave ground, but steadily, as though calculated, the attacker still whirling like the funnel of a hurricane, then suddenly

81

stopping as the second figure sidestepped and there was a flash of the longer blade, then the shorter blade. The attacker stood stock-still.

The attacker's blades twirled and vanished into their sheaths. Then the attacker's body crumpled. Osgood felt something shift beneath his right foot. He held his breath. There was an ear-splittingly loud crack as the clouds returned to mask the face of the moon once again. A tile fell. There was a shout from beneath him in the garden.

Osgood was already moving back the way he had come, but disregarding the possibility of some additionally betraying sound now in favor of speed, reaching the vines, grabbing hold, throwing himself over the edge, going down hand over hand for what he judged as perhaps six feet, then dropping, coming down on all fours like a cat would fall, throwing himself into the run before he was fully erect.

He looked up and back once—a ninja, *katana* held high over his head, the tip of the blade forward, edge up to the sky, was leaping down on him. Osgood's right hand flashed beneath his coat and he wheeled, the P-38 K in both fists, firing a double tap, catching the black-clad warrior in midair, the body crashing down. There was another shout, and Osgood, his pistol still in his fist, ran along the path, not looking back, afraid of what he might see, half-expecting to feel hot breath on the back of his neck in the next instant, and cold steel there the instant after that.

Another shout, but the words hard to distinguish and no time to ponder their meaning. Only one of the words stood out: "Chunin"—tactical leader or field commander. Osgood kept running, with his left hand finding his car keys and clenching them tightly.

Running.

He reached the edge of the path and wheeled, stabbing the Walther back along the funnel through which his pursuers must pour if they were to run at full speed, firing out the remaining seven rounds, hearing a scream of pain, a shout of anger, another scream, the rattle of a sword.

He turned and ran, no time to reload, the slide still locked back open, across the open expanse now where he knew a *shuriken* or an arrow could cut him down; but there was no time to waste dodging a possible missile. He had to reach the car.

He saw the Honda, parked as he had left it. He increased his pace, giving the run all the speed he could, because it would take critical seconds to unlock the car, then enter it and lock the door as he fired the engine, geared up and drove for his life, seconds in which the ninjas could be upon him. Once before in his life he had seen the work of blades such as these men would carry. Such steel could slash tires, cleave the roof of the vehicle, shatter the windshield, leave him trapped like an animal in a pen ready for slaughter.

Osgood collapsed against the car, stabbing the key into the lock, missing, trying again, getting it inside, twisting it, the alarm sounding because he hadn't switched it off, almost breaking the key as he tore it free of the lock and threw himself down behind the wheel, slamming the door, locking it.

He fumbled the first time he tried inserting the key into the ignition, cursing his loss of composure, the engine turning over. Something hit the car and he looked to his left. Three men in black, then a *katana* crashed across the windshield. It shattered as Osgood slammed the transmission into first and stomped the gas pedal to the floor. The car was being overturned, the left-rear wheel spinning clear, he realized. He double-clutched and upshifted into second, then into third, the right-rear wheel finally getting enough pulling power. There was a scream from one of the men trying to overturn the car and a fist hammered through the rear windshield as the car veered crazily right and left out of control for an instant. Then he was on the road, the rear end fishtailing maddeningly, Osgood's left forearm in front of his face to protect his eyes from the wind of the slipstream and the flying glass. He would have to trash the car and leave the hotel very quickly because, unlike their medieval counterparts, modern ninjas would very likely have Department of Motor Vehicle contacts and be able to trace a rented car's license plate within hours. He upshifted into fourth. Once he had placed several miles between them and himself, he would shake the glass from his gun on the seat beside him and reload it. Ninjas could die just like anyone else, he reminded himself, wanting a cigarette, wanting to be away from here, remembering at last to turn on his headlights.

Osgood just kept driving. . . .

* * *

Sergeant Oakwood pushed the sheet which had covered both of them all the way down and spread her legs for him and Ed Mulvaney slipped between her thighs, his lips touching at the brownish-red nipples of her marvelous breasts. "Why am I letting you do this?" Her voice was soft and he could feel her breath against his face. "I haven't asked you about your sexual contacts in the last couple of years. I didn't want you to use a rubber. I'm nuts."

"No you're not—you're gorgeous." He stopped kissing her breasts for a moment and said, "I didn't ask you anything either. Maybe we're both nuts."

"We're both gonna get killed here. Maybe that's what we're thinking," she whispered.

"The only danger now is a heart attack," Mulvaney told her, penetrating her, a little scream coming from her as she exhaled, her hands clutching at his back, at the bare skin of his behind.

Her body was moving under him, her long legs—impossibly long because she was so tall—entwining. His left hand moved under her back, arching her upward, his right hand on her left breast, his mouth smothering hers, their tongues touching, the movement of her body and his suddenly one movement. Her breath was coming hard and so was his and he felt the control going, all of his senses focused like they had never been focused before, Andy telling him she loved him, her lips beside his left ear.

For an instant he thought he was going to die inside her and he felt himself explode. Her body trembled and he felt her nails bite deep into the flesh of his back and her body molded against his. There was a wetness and the smell of his own substance and he sank into her arms and she held him more tightly than anyone had ever held him in his life. . . .

John Trench Osgood had his bags packed and his hotel bill paid, the taxicab pulling up at the front of the hotel for him, the doorman signaling him. Osgood waited for the cabdriver to leave his vehicle and open the trunk lid, Osgood keeping only the attaché case, the rest of the luggage going into the trunk. The cabdriver got the door. Osgood tipped the doorman, since it was an American hotel, then climbed inside, his right hand drifting under his coat.

The cabdriver spoke English. "Where do you wish to go, sir?"

"I'm not in a hurry, driver. Take me for a ride and I'll tell you later." The taxicab pulled out of the driveway. If he were being followed, he wanted to know for sure, and giving the chase car a nice long ride was the best way to find out. His eyes alternated from the driver to the rear window. He had learned years ago that the best way to stay alive was to trust no one.

6

The Mastery of Invisibility

GONROKU UMI'S WATERY dark eyes became suddenly hard.

"Gonroku-san. What troubles you? It is written in your eyes, but I have not the wisdom to read the inscription," John Trench Osgood said softly.

"Osgood-san. The words you bring to me are what trouble my spirit."

They sat at the exact center of the *zashiki*, tatamis covering it from end to end. The *fusumas* were slid shut on their tracks, affording what little privacy could be expected in a twelve-by-twelve-foot room with rice-paper walls and doors. The room was without adornment, except for the customary *tokonoma*—flower arrangement—which sat beneath a picture of Gonroku Umi's younger brother, who had been among the Divine Wind during World War II.

"It is common wisdom, Osgood-san, that those who claim much knowledge of my country claim also that the ninja is nine parts myth and one part antiquity. But as is so often the case, those who lay claim to knowledge rarely possess the same."

Gonroku Umi had been an agent in the Japanese Secret Service during World War II. He had helped with the organization of its postwar current-day counterpart, then retired to his family home to begin writing what Osgood considered, when completed, would be a work of monumental proportions. An encyclopedic reference, it would be the definitive history of World War II from the perspective of Japanese intelligence, as told by a man born to money and power who, because of the war, was the only surviving member of his family. It was said in some circles that Gonroku Umi had learned of the existence of the United States' ultimate weapon. But because of professional jealousy within his organization, this knowledge, which could have caused Japan to surrender prior to the atomic bombings of Hiroshima and Nagasaki, saving countless lives and preventing untold misery, was never revealed.

Gonroku Umi never spoke of it.

Osgood addressed the man. *"Oyabun,* would it be possible that somehow these secrets of the Yakusa which I seek are intertwined with the secrets of the ninja clans?"

Osgood had done honor to Gonroku Umi, calling him "master." Gonroku showed that he accepted the honor by addressing Osgood as his apprentice. *"Kobun,* would it be possible that the night should follow the day?"

"Then if this is so, would the ninjas also hold Peter Ellermann, whom I seek?"

"Osgood-san." Gonroku Umi allowed a smile to raise the corners of his mouth so fleetingly that as Osgood perceived it the smile was gone. "Where would one keep a thing of great value? Inside a fortified place or inside a house with rice-paper walls?"

"How do I find these ninjas, Gonroku-san?"

"I trust that they shall find you, Osgood-san. But this would prove your undoing, I think. For all the skills you possess might be as nothing against the humblest of their number if surprise, the ninja's greatest ally, were used against you. But during the war, I had occasion to deal with one of the oldest and greatest of the ninja clans. Truly, I doubt that such men as those would have soiled their hands with Yakusa business. I can compose an introduction for you. But should, by any chance, this clan be the one which you observed last evening, then my appeal that you be treated with consideration will be to no avail. And you will surely die, Osgood-san. We must have sake together for what perhaps will be the last time."

"Sumimasen, Gonroku-san." He lowered his head, telling the old man that his indebtedness to him was eternal.

It was a fish market, like Fulton Street used to have. Fish, vegetables, things that smelled like home, but strange too. Andy Oakwood, holding his hand, had only let go to show him things like lotus root. There were things that looked like tomato slices but had holes like Swiss cheese and were all the wrong color. There was live food and there was rice and there were people with woven shopping baskets on their arms, breath steaming as much as the warmed food some of the street vendors sold.

The morning was cold, colder-seeming still since the warmth of the night was behind them and the task which had brought them together was once again foremost in their minds. Or almost foremost. Because the task might take them apart.

She clutched his hand tighter and stopped them beneath a red-and-white vertical sign. It had a telephone number in happily recognizable arabic numerals.

They entered through a narrow glass-fronted door. Andy hissed, "Watch yourself in here."

"What is this place?" he asked. They passed through the smaller foyer and through an almost identical door, though because it was inside, the second door's appearance was less weathered. Had he waited the extra few seconds, he wouldn't have had to ask.

Andy told him what his short tour in vice had already confirmed. "This is called a *'tsurekomi hoteru.'* You'll love it."

There was a charge desk with a man with almost no hair and wrinkly skin and coke-bottle glasses standing behind it. He wore a flashy but nonetheless expensive-looking jacket. For the old guy's sake, Mulvaney hoped it was a sport jacket and not a suit.

Andy stopped at the charge desk and started speaking in Japanese. The man's face lit up and as he turned away for an instant to get a key from a rack just behind him on the wall, Mulvaney noticed the guy's trousers. It really was a suit.

Andy looked at Mulvaney for a minute, then reached into her purse and opened her wallet, handing over money. He said to her, "You want this guy to think I can't afford to pay?"

"Last night was your treat." She handed over the cash—what looked like a lot of yen—and the old guy handed over the key. Andy smiled and gave him a come-hither look. Mulvaney had heard guys in Vietnam who'd done R&R in Japan talking about places like these, "Love Hotels," prostitution houses without the prostitutes, although that could be arranged as well. But they were sort of institutionalized versions of the motels that dotted the far southwest side of Chicago, rooms rented by the hour, not the night. A place to crash with a girl and use a bed you never slept in. Places like that had a big laundry bill. Places like this too.

"In 'love hotels,'" Andy Oakwood told him as they walked along a long narrow corridor, "they try to cater to your fantasies. Sex is much more open here than it is back home. It's almost expected that a successful man will have a mistress. There's not much premarital dating and most of the marriages are still arranged by the parents. So there's a lot of repressed sexuality. There are some places I've heard about where guys go and put on diapers and get bottle-fed and changed and cuddled—but no sex."

"Sounds exciting to me," Mulvaney said as they climbed a flight of stairs.

"I picked a fantasy for you. The perfect thing for a cop."

He just looked at her, not saying anything. There was a job to do, and as much as he wanted to crawl back into bed with her, he had to find Peter Ellermann before Ellermann got more pieces cut off him and sent back to Uncle Enrico.

They reached the top of the stairs. Andy checked door numbers, stopped before one at the center of the upstairs hallway, put the key in the lock and turned it. The door opened.

She walked inside and he followed her. She was a girl of many parts, he decided. There were bars on all four walls and there was a set of theatrical-size jail keys on a hook beside the door. There was a second door just inside, this one all bars. She picked up the set of jail keys and went inside the cage.

There was a steel-looking gray plate, on the far wall, inset into the bars. The plate was about six by three feet. There were shackles at the top and bottom, and one in the center—he imagined for the neck. On a similar plate on the left-hand wall was an assortment of whips, handcuffs and thumbcuffs. There was even something that looked like a muzzle, but made for a human-size head.

He turned around; Andy Oakwood was laughing at him. "I mean, if you really wanna try some of this stuff, well, take off your clothes. But one of the girls I danced with when I went up to you-know-whose house brings guys here sometimes. She's a hooker. And she's supposed to meet us here." He guessed he was looking at her strangely because she laughed at him again. "I'm not into that either. She called me yesterday morning before I picked you up in Tokyo and told me to meet her here, that she had something for me—information, I mean."

He took Andy in his arms and kissed her hard on the mouth, then let her go. "You picked this room for me, huh?"

She laughed again. "Actually, I didn't. She told me to go to the desk clerk and tell him I wanted Mr. Anata's room."

Mulvaney crossed the room, his hands going to the bars and testing them. Real. "She a Japanese girl?"

"No—I told you. Our dirty old man likes white girls dancing for him."

Something clicked in his head. "Where's she from?"

"She never talked about it."

"Think."

"I think she spent some time in Hawaii. Why?"

"What kind of gun do you carry?"

"Detective Special. Why?"

"Unlimber your Colt, lady—you're gonna need it." He reached under his brown horsehide Indiana Jones jacket. A friend who ran an outfit called Adventure Supply in southern California sold the things. They were longer than a bomber jacket, just like the ones in the movies. Because of the added length, they were perfect for hiding a gun. The Beretta 92F was in his fist, his right thumb working up the safety as he crossed the room again and started for the door.

This was a death trap.

He reached the door and turned the knob. It fell away in his hand. "Ed?"

"You got us in deep caca, kid. Hang loose. Those boots

you're wearin'? They just good for walkin' or they good for runnin' too?"

"I run okay in 'em."

Mulvaney took a half-step back from the door and kicked forward, his right leg snapping up, his foot hitting the lock plate. The door which opened inward, sagged a little away from the jamb. He kicked it again: more sag. He took a few steps back. "Get ready to run. And have that Dick Special handy!" Mulvaney threw his body weight against the door and the center cracked under the force. His right shoulder ached. He pushed away from the door and started kicking at it, wheeling half-right and Tae-Kwan-Do-ing it. The door shattered after three blows. Mulvaney reached out and ripped it away from the jamb. The Beretta tight at his side in his right fist, he peered into the corridor. "Aww, shit—come on!" Mulvaney stepped through the doorway and opened fire at two men with M16 assault rifles who were running along the corridor from the stairwell. He kept firing, shouting to Andy, "Run for it—the other end of the hallway!" He didn't know what was down there, but it had to be better than this. One of the guys was down, the other one opening fire. Mulvaney wanted to duck back inside the room, but that would leave Andy the only target—and he suddenly realized that even though he'd known her less than twenty-four hours, he loved her. He honestly, really loved her. He almost forgot to shoot—almost—emptying the Beretta into the second man as the wall beside him ripped apart, the second guy going down.

Mulvaney ran toward the two gunmen, grabbing one of the assault rifles, his hands mechanically swapping magazines—pocketing the empty standard-length fifteen-shot magazine, inserting one of the two twenty-round spares. It was ten feet to the nearest M16—but then the stairwell vomitted men with handguns, and there was at least one more assault rifle. Mulvaney didn't even remember throwing himself to the floor, he just heard Andy shout at him, "Flat on the floor, Mulvaney!" He heard a familiar sound, a .38 Special emptying fast, and he looked up. The guy with the assault rifle who came up the stairs was down and so were two of the guys with him. Mulvaney started to his feet, reaching out his left hand and grabbing one of the two M16s by the flash hider. It wasn't even warm so he guessed he had the one with the full stick. He swung the rifle up, found the selector and touched the trigger, spraying death toward the end of the corridor—a full thirty-round magazine from the weight of it, half of it emptying in two long, ragged bursts.

Then he turned and ran. Oakwood fired her revolver again, stepping back, her long right leg snapping up and out as she turned half-left. The Tae-Kwan-Do kick looked awkward and stupid because she was wearing an ankle-length skirt, but the door slammed open and inward. Mulvaney was beside her in the next instant, holding the M16 in his right fist, the Beretta in his left. Oakwood held the little blue Dick Special in both hands and shouted something in Japanese that Mulvaney guessed translated into "Freeze your ass!" Under the circumstances this seemed reasonably appropriate, since there was a guy wearing a pink ballet tutu (he didn't look Japanese, but more Vietnamese) getting it in the rear end with a dildo from the hands of a Japanese girl who was wearing nothing but a smile. The room was decorated to look like a stage, with an audience of anonymous smiling faces painted on one wall. On the opposite wall were curtains, and hanging between these were small things that could have been maps—roll-downs—the one covering the center of the wall now a group of anonymous ballet dancers in tutus of the same color. The guy was standing perfectly erect, not to mention the part of his anatomy under the front of the tutu. He screamed in pain like a woman in labor. The girl was still working the dildo as if nothing had happened, as if she weren't even aware of the intrusion.

Mulvaney guessed maybe the angle was wrong that way. He shrugged his shoulders and shoved past the interrupted tableau, going toward the window. There was a drop of about ten feet to the roof next door, the distance between the two buildings something Mulvaney gauged as about six feet. It could have been an ankle-breaker or worse.

The window was nailed shut. Mulvaney fixed that with the butt of the M16. "Cover the door, kid!" He didn't look back to see if she did. She was a good trooper. That he'd learned. The window frame was the tough part but it wasn't his rifle anyway so he knocked it out. He stepped through, onto the sill outside, the wood feeling rotted underfoot. He got a handhold and reestimated the distance. Only eight feet down from the sill, but still about six feet from here to the next building. "Andy! Front and center now!"

She was coming, the Dick Special in her right hand, her skirts hitching up as she slid through the window.

"Can you jump this in those boots?"

"Try me!" The gun was into her purse and she was gone. Mulvaney watched as she hit the next roof and rolled onto her left shoulder, the poncho obscuring her face for a second, her panties showing. Then she was up, getting her clothes back under control. But he noticed she'd gotten her gun back in hand first.

Mulvaney hoped he'd survive the jump as well as she had.

He looked back through the window, toward the doorway. "Tutu" and his assistant were just standing there. Then suddenly three guys with handguns burst into the room. Mulvaney pumped the trigger of the M16 once in a short burst, sending all three of them back through the doorway and into the corridor.

Mulvaney safed the Beretta and rammed it into his belt.

And then he jumped, the selector on the M16 going to safe under his thumb, his arms wide away from his body, his knees coming up to take the spring. He hit the roof, rolled, fell, got up to his knees shouting to Andy, "Down!" He checked the M16, the selector coming to auto and his right first finger touching the trigger as the three guys with handguns hit the window and began firing. He emptied the assault rifle, driving them back, getting a couple of slugs into at least one of them. He threw the empty rifle toward the window and ran, grabbing Andy by the hand and running with her across the roofline.

Mulvaney heard a familiar sound, the pitch of it wrong, but the origin unmistakable. He held her hand tighter and started running faster. It was an elevated train.

They reached the end of the roof and Mulvaney looked down. There was a fire escape, and about six feet from that, rail ties. Another two feet in were tracks.

He looked back. Men were coming after them through the window, at least one assault rifle visible. Mulvaney snatched the Beretta from the trouser band of his blue jeans and opened fire, shouting to Andy, "Down the fire escape—to that first landing. We're gonna jump to the tracks. But this time I go first. Move!"

She went over the edge and Mulvaney went right after her, staying behind the ledge as he swapped more shots with the men coming through the window. He turned his eyes away just in time as a burst of assault-rifle fire sprayed concrete dust against his face and neck. He snapped off another two shots and started down the fire escape.

She was on the landing, Mulvaney not daring to jump the last few steps because the fire escape was old-looking and vibrated as he moved on it.

He was beside her, safing the Beretta, handing it to her. "Here—if they peek over the edge, use it. I'll go first. Stuff this in your purse when you jump. I'll catch you."

"I love you—don't ask me why, 'cause the hell if I know."

"I love you too—and ditto."

Mulvaney stepped over the railing, rust all over his hands, flaking off. It looked like a wider jump from where he stood, but there was no choice now. If they took the fire escape down into the street, there was no telling what was waiting for them. He jumped, reaching out, feeling he'd done something wrong as he made the jump, realizing he was coming up short, dropping too fast. His hands reached out and he caught the end of one of the ties, his body swinging past it, under it, his grip almost going. Andy screamed, "Ed!"

"I'm all right!" He wasn't all right at all, but that was the kind of macho thing guys were supposed to say to women. He moved his left hand, reaching out, getting a better grip. It was now or never. Strength would only fade, grip would only weaken. He moved his right hand to the next tie, got a firm grip and started pulling himself up. Andy screamed at him again. "I'm all right," he shouted. He could hear the train coming, figured he should hurry.

Mulvaney summoned all his strength and heaved.

He was up, his elbows locked. "Oh, shit!"—a train, the wind of the slipstream pummeling him, his grip going. He started falling, the train whizzing past him. They do things fast here in Japan, he thought fleetingly. But his left forearm was over one of the ties. He swung there, catching his breath, the train gone now, his ears ringing with the sound of it. And over the ringing sound he could hear Andy

94

screaming at him. He looked back. Two men were coming over the edge of the roofline, a third on the roofline leveling a pistol toward him.

There was a shot and involuntarily Mulvaney closed his eyes, expecting to feel the sudden heat and then the cold—just the opposite of the way it was when a knife got you. But he didn't feel anything and he looked behind him, across the gap. Andy stood poised with the Beretta in both fists, watching the Japanese with the handgun toppling over the edge of the roof.

Mulvaney pulled himself up, rolled onto the ties.

There was another shot, then another and another. He was on his knees on the ties. Andy was firing up at the guys on the roof, but they were back behind the roofline. "The gun! Gimme the gun!"

She looked at him, her green eyes focusing tight on him for an instant. Then he saw her work the safety and in one fluid motion the gun was airborne, Mulvaney reaching for it, feeling it, feeling it slipping through his fingers, trying to grab for it. He had it by the muzzle, between his first and second fingers, no grip on it at all. Slowly, Andy screaming, "Ed! Shoot!," he drew it toward him, his left hand catching the grip.

There wasn't time to shift it. He caught the safety with his left thumb and his left first finger snapped the trigger. The guy with the assault rifle was leveling it right at him. The Beretta fired first, the stock of the M16 shattering, the Japanese killer's hands going up to his eyes, a scream coming from his lips.

And then Andy was crawling over the rail, shouting to him, "Catch me, Ed!"

Mulvaney didn't have time to do anything with the pistol, just reached out his right arm, scooping her into it, throwing his weight back so she wouldn't pull them both over the edge and down to the street below.

He had her. He pulled her back against him, then shoved her behind him and fired the Beretta again. Another of the Japanese aimed a handgun, and the track behind him sang with the ricochet. Mulvaney fired again; the man went down.

"Come on!" he shouted, grabbing her by the left hand, the Detective Special in her right, jumping from tie to tie, away from the building. He didn't know where they'd go, but he knew what they'd do when they got there. . . .

John Trench Osgood told himself that it was impossible for Mulvaney and Oakwood to get into very much trouble if he stopped tailing them just for the morning. The thing with the ninjas he had stumbled onto last night had to be followed up. And to keep dogging Mulvaney and Oakwood in hopes they would lead him to Peter Ellermann, rather than following a direct lead that could get him there faster, would be stupidity.

Gonroku Umi had sent one of his granddaughters, a very pretty and oddly very Western-seeming girl, to rent a car in her own name as an added precaution for him. After girl and car—a Jaguar sedan—had returned, he had thanked her politely, reminded himself she was almost young enough to be his daughter—less ego-bruising than putting it the other way—then bid farewell to Gonroku Umi. He set out for the mountain community where he hoped to find the ninja clan leader, Tsukahira Ryoichi, with whom Gonroku Umi had dealt fifty years before.

Common sense had forced him to ask: "You are certain, Gonroku-san, that this ninja Jonin has survived the years?"

Gonroku Umi had replied, "Am I certain that you are a man to whom honor means much, Osgood-san?"

Osgood had asked no more; he went forth with confidence. Some things—precious few, but some—remained certainties in the world. The rising of the sun, the passing of the seasons, and the wisdom of his old friend.

He drove on.

The road wound steeply upward into the mountains, evergreens dotting the precariously inclined slopes. A boy on a bicycle seemed transfixed by the elegance of the Jaguar. A group of girls in blue skirts and white blouses stepped to the side of the narrow road as he drove on, smiling demurely, or perhaps even giggling.

Gonroku-san's granddaughter had left a sandwich for him in gold wrapping over ordinary wax paper, the sandwich very Western, a slice of thick roast beef between two thin pieces of bread. He ate it as he drove. The twins would have been young adults now, dating, preparing for their futures. He kept driving, passing through a small hamlet where he saw many old people in a central square seated on folding chairs, conversing among themselves. He went past a schoolyard which was empty and, as the little community gave way again to the natural environment, he saw a small factory. He couldn't tell what the factory produced but it seemed to be a reminder that while life there seemed unchanged by the course of time, change was really everywhere.

The turnoff Gonroku-san had told him of loomed ahead on his left. He geared down, taking the turn slowly, because the gravel road was all but hidden by the two-lane highway on which he had been driving.

He kept the pace slow because the gravel road was little wider than the car, and to have met another vehicle coming down the mountain, at any speed, would have been disastrous.

Osgood's thoughts turned to what Gonroku Umi had told him of this ninja Jonin. The interwoven fabric of history and legend had it that the ninja's origin was in the sixth century, arising from a conflict between two warring princes, the first "ninja" a spy. From this had sprung the martial art shrouded in mystery for better than a thousand years—men who could, as legend had it, cloud the minds of their opponents, whose life was consumed in the mastery of ninjitsu and the skills of Tonpo and Inpo, escaping and hiding.

The road rose sharply and leveled off. Osgood realized he had climbed to the height of a plateau, a flat table on a mountaintop. A village opened before him, but not an ordinary village. It was a place that made the little hamlet through which he had passed before seem as modern by contrast as New York City, or Kyoto itself.

Buildings of dark brown wood were ranked on both sides of a street little wider than a narrow path, the street made of flagstones or perhaps only polished river stones. He stopped the car at the edge of the village.

He got out, not bothering to lock the car. The trunk was locked and that was where he had stored his belongings. And he felt that these ninjas, if indeed they were one-tenth as clever as they were supposed to be, would not be impeded by something as elementary as a locked car door should they wish to enter the vehicle.

At the far end of the street, perhaps five hundred yards, was a walled enclave. The architecture which rose beyond the walls was clearly Buddhist, with slopingly curved peaked tile roofs, each corner decorated with some symbol. Beneath the roofline was what seemed to be an interior roofline.

Osgood left the button of his leather sport coat open, though he doubted getting to his gun faster would do him any good. He had been told by Gonroku Umi that this was a community of ninjas. They farmed, they gathered, they produced crafts which were taken down from the community and sold in order to buy that which they could not make or grow themselves. It was a community untouched by time. As he walked down the exact center of the jigsaw-patterned stone street, Osgood saw no telephone line, no electric-light poles, no hint of the world outside.

About a third of the way along the street he heard the hissing of a forge and looked to his left. To the side and rear of a house like all the others was a building smaller than the rest, one wall removed, it seemed. An old man in a white robe and black lacquered *eboshi* hat was heating steel over a charcoal fire. As if on cue, he rose, and two younger men in the enclosure of the forge took the billet of steel and began beating it, the ringing of their hammers loud in the cool midday air.

They were making a layered blade for a sword; how many folds, he wondered, would it have; would it be like the swords of Muramasa or those of the heroic craftsman Masamune? The story went that a man once wished to test the sharpness of a Muramasa blade and for that purpose placed it in a stream. Leaves fallen from the trees overlooking the stream floated in its current. As a leaf would touch the edge of the Muramasa blade, it was cleaved in two. But then the experimenter placed in the stream a blade crafted by Masamune. No leaf would touch this blade. Rather, all passed around it to one side or another.

It was always thought that the blade took on the character of the swordsmith who crafted it; Muramasa was of great skill, but deranged. His blades brought their owners to violence and bloody death. And it was said that on festival days the gods would sometimes inhabit a sword—these swords, and the greatest of swords enduring down through the ages, were said to be those of Masamune.

Osgood realized he was staring, then walked on.

Tsukahira Ryoichi—what kind of blade was his? Osgood wondered.

He reached the twin gates in the wall surrounding the enclosure, a bell set beside the gates at the right, a cord leading down from the clapper.

Osgood seriously doubted his presence was unknown, but for form's sake he struck the corded clapper and the bell sounded. His breath made steam as he exhaled.

The gate on his left opened, an old man in a robe of black silk like a priest might wear standing in the opening. Osgood spoke. *"Konnichi wa. Watashi wa Osgood John to moshi masu. Hajimemashite. Dozo yoroshiku. Shigoto de kite imasu."* Osgood placed his palms against his thighs and bowed politely.

"Konnichi wa, Osgood-san. O-shigoto wa nan desu ka?"

"Taisetsu desu. Tsukahira Ryoichi to ohanashi shitai no desu ga? Taisetsu desu."

The old man in priest's robes paused a moment, his eyes seemingly fascinated with Osgood's Adam's apple. But Osgood knew this was only a sign of respect, its genuineness of no concern.

"Osgood-san, o-hitori desu ka?"

"Hai."

"Doko no kuni kara korare mashitu ka?"

"Gonroku Umi kara," Osgood told him.

The old man seemed to take pause at the name, then merely said, *"Osgood-san, ohairi-nasai."*

Osgood bowed again, as did the old man, Osgood merely saying *"Arigato,"* then entering between the gates.

Beyond the walls there was a path wide enough for a dozen men to walk abreast, the path forming a rectangle surrounding the structures whose roofs he had viewed from above the level of the wall.

They crossed the path, toward low steps which rose to enter the structure. Osgood asked the old man, *"Toi desu ka?"*

"Iie, Osgood-san."

Osgood nodded. They were crossing beneath what

amounted to a multistory breezeway, building on either side of them and above as well. Beyond the breezeway, he saw a Shinto-influenced *torii* gateway, and just beyond that a clear pond with green lily pads on the gray surface at its center.

A man stood beside a gently curving tree. He was so tall that for a moment Osgood thought the fellow could not be Japanese; Chinese, perhaps. The man turned.

Osgood very slowly withdrew the letter, still in its envelope, from the left outside pocket of his coat. He began to address the man in Japanese, but the tall man spoke. His English was stiffly accented but syntactically perfect. "I speak English, Mr. Osgood. And in the case of this structure, the walls literally do have ears. You come from Gonroku Umi." It was a statement, not a question.

"Yes. This letter should explain." He offered it, dispensing, as Tsukahira Ryoichi had, with the customary formalities so intrinsic to Japanese conversation.

The envelope was opened and the note unfolded. Tsukahira's eyes moved along the page, glancing at Osgood once, then back to the ideographs. He placed the letter in the envelope with meticulous care, then folded the envelope exactly in half—not almost—and placed it within the folds of the black sash at his waist. Tsukahira said nothing for a few moments.

He was just as tall close up as he had seemed the first moment Osgood had seen him. He was dressed completely in black, the sash, the upper garment, and the ankle-length pleated samurai-style skirt. Black tabby boots showed beneath its hem.

"So . . ." He stretched the word so it sounded as if it had many more syllables than one. "Osgood-san wishes to learn about ninjas who work for the Yakusa." He said the last word as though it were vile in his mouth. Osgood found that encouraging.

"Gonroku-san assured me that Tsukahira-san would not soil his hands with such men."

"Gonroku-san spoke the truth, Osgood-san. Come, walk with me and we shall speak of this."

"Yes." Osgood nodded. He fell in at Tsukahira's left, as a junior officer would beside a higher-ranking man. Osgood found himself studying Tsukahira's face. Nobility. Purpose. Determination. All these words came to mind. He would have to be well into his eighties, but he looked not much more than fifty. The flesh of his spatulate-fingered hands and of his longish neck was tight. They walked beside a pond on a raked gravel path that circumscribed it. Another breezeway was visible on the opposite side.

"I have heard the term Yakusa, of course. But I have never dealt with such men. It would be a betrayal of all in which I believe and have striven to impart to those who serve me. During the war, in which I first met Gonroku-san, I and my ninjas fought to serve Japan. It is the *honsho* . . . What is your expression, Osgood-san?"

"Character, inner strength."

"Hai—it is the character of a man which makes him a ninja; the skills he must master arise from this alone. To serve those who prey upon the weak and the helpless, as do these Yakusa, would be in violent disagreement with true character."

"This is rude, I know, and the answer must be before my eyes, only I am too stupid to see it, but what do you do?" Osgood was aware of the potential in his question.

Tsukahira answered without hesitation, but with a question. "What do you do, Osgood-san?" He stopped walking, smiling fleetingly.

"I . . . ahh . . . I had imagined Gonroku-san had . . . ahh . . ."

"You are like us. That is enough for you to know." He began again to walk. The breeze crossed the pond there, cold but pleasantly so.

As they neared the opposite side of the pond, where the second breezeway was set, Osgood could hear sounds, as if men were fighting, but in the way of some bygone era—or in a way he had seen only the previous night. The clattering of steel on steel.

They walked on, Tsukahira saying to him, "You have come to me for help in the name of a man who is at once a former comrade and someone whom I greatly respect. And so I will speak with and answer you as truthfully as I would answer Gonroku-san. The ninjas of whom you speak do not exist."

"I saw them with my own eyes, Tsukahira-san."

They entered the breezeway. "Osgood-san. There are men who call themselves ninjas. One such man is Tsukiyama

Koji. He leads a criminal brotherhood which has adopted much of the ninja way, but is not ninja. There are always those who pervert what they seek to become. He is such a man. He sprang from a line of ninjas stretching back for many centuries. Tsukiyama was trained as any boy his age born to the ninja tradition would be trained. But after some time it was learned that he cared nothing for our ways, only our abilities. Is my meaning clear?"

They stood beneath the far side of the breezeway, a large open courtyard between them and the far wall. The scene was vaguely similar to what Osgood had witnessed the previous evening: men in black, ranked on either side of the rectangle, two men in the center, fighting. But rather than a *katana,* each man used a *shinai,* a sword comprising four pieces of bamboo held together by the *sakigawa,* a leather end cap at the tip, and a *tsuka-gawa,* or leather sheath, at the haft. These were joined by *tsura,* cord running the length of the *shinai* to form the spine of the blade. Leather was bound approximately two-thirds of the way up the "blade" to additionally reinforce it. A practice sword.

The two fighters, upon seeing Tsukahira, brought their swords to a sheathlike hold and bowed deeply. There was a sharply issued command and both ranks fell in to the center of the courtyard, bowing.

"My pupils, Osgood-san." Tsukahira bowed and snapped an order. The men returned to their positions on either side of the rectangle, the two fighters taking *chudan no kamae* positions. Tsukahira ordered them to continue, then resumed the conversation. Osgood watched as the men attacked, counterattacked, thrust and parried. "Tsukiyama was sent out." There was an air of finality to his words.

After several seconds Osgood spoke. "What happened to the boy?"

Tsukahira did not answer for a moment. Then, his voice low, he said, "He took what he had learned and, as I have said, perverted it. He is the man you seek, an assassin who sells his talents and those of the assassins under his command to the highest bidder, the Yakusa, or anyone else."

"His father was a ninja, you say?"

"And his father before him, and for centuries it was that way."

"Has no one made the attempt to stop him? I mean, with all due respect, Tsukahira-san, the rogue—"

Tsukahira interrupted him. "He is the son of my daughter, and when she died, she extracted from me a promise. I have kept that promise. When honor lies along two conflicting paths, the pilgrim is doomed."

"Can you tell me where to find him—before he finds me? Logic dictates that he holds a certain man prisoner, a man whose importance is unfathomably great. To your country and to mine." Osgood studied the chiseled granite face opposite him.

"It is possible to contact Osgood-san through Gonroku-san?"

"I will see that it is, Tsukahira-san."

"You must eat with me, and we can speak of more pleasant things on such a fine winter day."

"Tsukahira-san honors me greatly and I must accept." Osgood bowed, and Tsukahira did the same.

It was only standard police procedure. The girl who had told Andy Oakwood to come to the love hotel for a meeting had either acted directly as the agent for the Yakusa assassins—a trap from the beginning—or somehow divulged the information before she could keep the appointment herself.

Andy insisted that the girl would not have worked for the Yakusa voluntarily.

Ed Mulvaney reserved his judgment.

As they drove, having wisely parked the car several blocks from the love hotel where the meeting was to have been, Andy spoke almost frantically. "Jill wouldn't have screwed us like that."

"She ever tell you how she got into being an exotic dancer?"

"The usual stuff. Liked to sing and dance when she was a kid and decided that was the life for her. All of a sudden she was an adult and on her own and if she was ever gonna do it, it had to be then. You see a lot of women in the service who jumped into something. Because they figured it was do it or rot. Some of them jumped into the Army, some of them jumped out of something and went into the Army to start over again. Jill tried making it as a dancer stateside. She said that's what eventually led her here. I tried pumping her. Nothing more than that. It was almost like she hurt inside too much to talk about it. I mean, no girl grows up wanting to prance around naked in front of some slobbering dirty old man."

He didn't say anything, lit a cigarette.

"What are you thinking?" she asked, not looking at him.

"Ajaccio gave me a name. I think somethin's finally starting to come together. I got an address here in my wallet—hang on." He pulled his wallet out of his hip pocket and began searching through it. It took him a minute, and his wallet was half-empty, the contents all over the seat between them, but he found it. "Tell me when it's good for you."

After a second the traffic in front of them and around them broke and she said, "Give it to me." He watched her lips move as she read the card. "I know where this place is. Warehouse district. Bad part of town. More dangerous at night, but it might be easier to get in and out."

"Fine—then let's go look up Jill." He took the card back from her and started repacking his wallet. She turned the car into a narrow street with precariously balanced tall skinny row houses in shades of gray and brown flanking both sides. The car reached the end of the street and turned right into heavier traffic. His wallet packed away, Mulvaney began reloading the spent magazine for his pistol. He didn't know what they'd find when they found Jill Linton, but he already knew he wouldn't like it. . . .

If the lettering on the signs that stood out like a pox on the sides and fronts of the buildings hadn't been Japanese, Mulvaney would have placed the street somewhere on Chicago's West Side. Older homes and down-at-the-heel stores that spelled poverty in boldface caps were on both sides of the street, but the street and the sidewalks were so spotless he guessed he could have eaten off them. There was a challenging-looking parking slot that Andy squeezed them into, and Mulvaney, his gun back under his coat, climbed out on the curb side.

A strong ice-edged wind was whipping along the street and Mulvaney turned up the collar of his coat. Andy

104

Oakwood stepped out of the car, the poncho billowing around her and the wind catching her skirt. She had control of the skirt with her left hand as she reached the curb.

"That gray building," she announced, raising her voice over the keening of the wind.

He looked in the direction she had looked. A three-story structure that looked very Western, like all the buildings here. Not like a nice place to live.

They started along the sidewalk, Mulvaney keeping his coat open, Andy's right hand in the pocket of her skirt; he guessed she had her gun in her hand.

Clean-faced little kids too young for school, he guessed, or off for some reason were playing across the street. Their clothes were poor.

Andy stopped at the door on the right side of the building. Beyond it, through the glass, he could see a dimly lit staircase.

"Top floor," she said almost hesitantly.

"Top floor," he repeated. There would be no roof to jump to this time. The buildings on either side were taller by at least eight feet. Mulvaney had his gloves on and he twisted the knob and let them inside. "Prints—don't touch anything."

"A lady always has gloves." She smiled thinly.

"Right. Put 'em on." He started up the stairs, looking behind him once. She was pulling on little brown knit gloves with leather palms.

The stairs creaked under his feet. He took them two at a time and stayed beside the wall to minimize the noise.

He reached the first landing, looked up the well. Nothing. Then back down. No one appeared in the foyer. He started up again, still taking the stairs in twos, stopping at the head of each staircase, looking along the length of the bare-bulb-lit hallway.

"Last one on the end. I was here once, like I said in the car," Andy whispered.

Mulvaney walked along the length of the hallway, Andy taking the other side. Her right hand wasn't in the pocket of her skirt anymore, but under her poncho. He reached his right hand behind him, his fingers closing over the butt of his gun but not drawing it until he stopped beside the door.

Andy took the opposite side of the door. "Knock gently," he said in a stage whisper.

Andy knocked. She knocked three times. Mulvaney waited. Nothing. He signaled for her to do it again. He had the Beretta in both fists, beside his right shoulder, his back flattened against the wall. He reached out and tried the knob. The door was locked shut.

It was an old-style skeleton-key lock but he'd left that key ring at home. Andy whispered, "Cover me," dropping into a crouch in front of the lock plate, a PCS lock-pick set in her left hand, her gun on the floor beside her.

"No." He pushed her back. She had the gun again, the PCS set disappearing into her purse. If there were bad guys on the other side of the door and she wasted time picking the lock, all she'd get for her trouble was shot.

Mulvaney took a step away from the wall, then back-stepped into the center of the corridor. "Cover me," he told her. He took a long-strided step forward on his left foot, his right leg snapping up and out, the flat of his right shoe hitting the door where it met the jamb. The door shattered inward.

Andy was through the doorway first, something Mulvaney hadn't intended even though it was the correct thing procedurally. He was through the doorway right after her. Andy's breath came like a little scream, frightened-sounding and full of sadness.

It was a one-room apartment with a sink in the far corner and a pair of alcoves that he imagined concealed toilet facilities and a closet, both of them draped over. There was a Japanese-style mattress flat on the floor by the wall that had the only window.

Jill Linton's blond hair was matted with dried blood and her blue eyes were wide open. At least the face matched the description Andy had given him in the car.

It was odd seeing someone with her feet pressed against the back of her head.

Andy fell in his arms, her tiny right fist still holding the little .38, but the back of the hand tight against her wide-open mouth. She was breathing heavily. Tears rimmed her green eyes. She was trying to choke back the last of a scream she had already let out.

"Hang in there," Mulvaney whispered. The muzzle of his

gun moved across the room from side to side, his eyes back to the dead girl, her head, her headless naked torso. And for the first time Mulvaney noticed there was a finger missing, and part of another one. Perhaps she had held up a hand to protect her neck from whatever had severed her head.

"It's like . . . like . . . like when they killed . . ." Andy was crying now. She pushed herself away from him, rocking her body back and forth with her arms folded across her breasts, her gun still in her hand.

"Like when they killed your partner, Koswalski."

She only nodded, her throat making little heaving sounds as if she were going to throw up or wanted to but couldn't.

Mulvaney looked at the dead girl again. There was nothing one could tell from her body without the benefit of a medical examiner. He looked quickly around the room, never moving from the spot where he stood. There was a photograph slid into the frame of a mirror. He walked toward it, not touching it. The blond hair and blue eyes of the girl in the picture—it was a younger, happier Jill Linton, with some sort of ruffled dance costume on and a smile that could have lit up a dark night.

"We go see Shinoda, the white slaver. Tonight." He took Andy by the left hand and started back into the hallway, telling her, "Get rid of that gun; when we get into the car and away from here, then let it all out or you'll carry it inside you forever." The room was behind them and Mulvaney wouldn't look back even once.

The Vietnam reference still bugged him, the thing Andy had told him she overheard when the Yakusa head, Mizutani Hideo, had been talking with the guy in black at the midnight meeting in the Zen Buddhist shrine. And the thing she had told him about seeing a car she'd identified as belonging to a Soviet official. And the Yakusa people killing the girl just like Andy's partner had been killed. There was something that didn't make sense about it. The Yakusa guys who had come after them at the love hotel had been normal street-muscle types, hardcases with more guns than brains. But the killing of Oakwood's partner, Koswalski, and the killing of Jill Linton—there was a slickness about them that the Yakusa talent hadn't demonstrated at all.

He thought of Shinoda Akiro, the white slaver who

suckered girls into thinking they were getting big job offers in the Orient, then brought them to Japan and threatened them with everything from beatings to death to big trouble with the law. If Shinoda wasn't a key, he was a big step closer to finding the key. Ajaccio had told Mulvaney what Shinoda did for a living. Mulvaney's experience had filled in the details. There'd been a missing-persons case once that had turned into a double murder back when he'd worked homicide. Tracking it down had led him into the white-slave racket. It turned his stomach.

There were so many female teenage runaways that whoever compiled statistics on the numbers had to be doing it full-time. Some of them just ran away. Some of them never got that far. There were people all over who liked young girls, guys who only made it with virgins and paid big money for the chance. And a lot of girls got shipped overseas.

But Jill Linton had been the worst kind. The face and Andy's remarks afterward, when she had stopped crying, had put Jill's age at about nineteen. The Jill Lintons were the worst kind of cases because they walked into it with eyes wide open and full of stars. Nobody had to drug them, nobody had to ship them. Somebody just gave them airline tickets, passports and visas and told them they were going off to begin an exciting career. No one told them that the job description included getting slapped around or starved if they mouthed off, that the job description included all the dirty things their parents had never wanted them to hear about. And if they didn't do them and act like they enjoyed them, violent things even their parents hadn't heard about would happen.

Jill Linton's room had been a place to come and sleep, not to spend the night. It was one step up from a rat hole because she did all the stuff they told her and was trustworthy, so they let her out to live on her own but they never paid her enough money to do anything else—like go home. Girls like Jill didn't call Mom and Dad because if everything had been cool to begin with they wouldn't have left in the first place. So they just went down and when they thought they couldn't go down any farther they went down some more.

Shinoda was the career counselor.

Mulvaney had driven after leaving Jill's place because Andy couldn't see well enough through the tears. But Andy, quieter, had been all right after the talking and dinner. She drove them now. Going back to the hotel would have been suicidal, so they had driven out of the city, found a restaurant, and she had watched him eat. If he'd stopped eating every time he saw a body somebody had done something disgusting to, he figured he would have been the skinniest guy in Chicago. He put away a steak and potatoes and something that was supposed to be apple pie but was really apple cobbler, then coffee and a couple of glasses of blended whiskey (not his brand but okay). He'd smoked the last of the cigarettes he'd brought with him and had to pay an outrageous price for some more. Then they'd gotten back into the car and driven around until it was long after dark and long after business hours for anybody except a cabdriver, a cop or a guy like Shinoda. There weren't any cabdrivers around when Andy snugged the car against the curb. Mulvaney just sat there watching the street and trying to ignore the windshield wipers.

The wind that had cut through them more on the way out of Jill's than it had on the way in had blown in dark blue-gray cloud layers, one stacked on top of the other, that had followed them out of the city. It rumbled a few times when they had walked into the restaurant, then waited and finally attacked when they ran for the car. As they had driven back into the city, the rain had stopped falling as recognizable droplets and started coming in wind-driven sheets.

It was raining like that now and the windshield wipers didn't do much more for visibility with the car stopped. But he could see the sign for the "club" across the street. "What's the Japanese stuff mean?"

"It means 'The Happiest Ladies' or something like that."

"You stay in the car. I'll be able to make myself understood once I get inside the place." The gun was in his fist. "Some things are universal."

He started to get out of the car and he felt her hands on his neck and turned around. "Kiss me—hard," she breathed. Her hands were on his face. He shoved the Beretta under his thigh so both hands were free and he put his arms around her. He did as she had said—he kissed her hard. Then he shoved his gun under his jacket and stepped out into the rain.

Rain blew across the sidewalk in waves. It felt like ice water against the exposed portions of his flesh as he hunched his neck down and ran into the street. There were a few cars, windshield wipers waving frantically like the feelers of a frightened insect. But Mulvaney dodged them, hardly breaking stride until he reached the curb on the far side of the street. The sign that translated into "The Happiest Ladies" was hot pink, and the rain driving against it made it appear to go in and out of focus constantly. Mulvaney didn't run anymore, just walked toward it steadily, the rain inside his clothes, inside his shoes, his eyes blinking against it so he could see.

And then he was under the awning—pink and black stripes—and the rain was just a loud, hollow drumming sound. Water had accumulated in huge puddles in front of the doors. He opened the glass doors and almost threw the doorman to the floor. The man smiled, saying in English that sounded like he'd got it from a movie, "Welcome to the Happiest Ladies. Raining cats and dogs outside, huh?"

"Yeah—or cats at least." Mulvaney was inside the foyer. "I wanna see Shinoda."

The doorman's eyes got a little tight. "Shinoda-san is very busy. Maybe some other time."

Mulvaney made a grin. "You just a doorman or you a bouncer?"

The doorman's eyes lit with a smile. "Whatever I gotta be."

"That's fuckin' wonderful you're so versatile." Mulvaney slammed his left knee up into the guy's crotch and his right hand made the Beretta appear, the pistol's muzzle under the guy's left nostril as he doubled over and started to cough. "Take me to see Shinoda-san or you're up for the next nose job—capeesh?"

"Yeah, yeah, man!"

Mulvaney let the doorman/bouncer straighten up, the dark eyes hard and full of hate. "You'll never walk outta this place, man."

"The booze is so bad it gives ya the trots, huh? Thanks for the tip. Now, move, bouncer." The doorman opened the interior door—this was wood and Japanese-looking—and Mulvaney followed him through. Compared with the glitzy sign over the awning outside, the interior was almost subdued. The reds and blacks and golds were straight out of Las Vegas, the lighting early-cocktail-lounge. The doorman stood three feet from him and Mulvaney could barely see his face. There were some of the "Happiest Ladies" over by the bar, one of them behind it, more of them circulating. They were mostly white, a few black. Mulvaney had the gun under his coat as he gave the doorman a shove. The guy started walking around the perimeter of the main room, as if he weren't allowed on the floor. The clientele was exclusively male, almost exclusively Japanese, the rest other Asian nationalities. As they passed near one of the booths, Mulvaney noticed a balding guy with his right arm so far up under a dye-job redhead's dress that he could have been giving her an internal. Mulvaney kept walking, seeing three doors at the opposite end of the room.

As they neared the doors, the doorman turned around so suddenly Mulvaney almost drew his gun. "Look, man—he's gonna kick my ass."

"I'll blow it away—you choose."

The doorman shrugged and started for the center of the three doors, stopped in front of it and knocked. "What's behind the other two? A lady and a tiger?" That was the trouble with literary allusions these days, Mulvaney thought: nobody caught them.

The center door opened and a man about five-foot-eight filled the door laterally, his head shiny like a cue ball. His hands, folded almost gracefully in front of him like he'd broken the zipper on his fly and was trying to cover it up, were the size of Polish hams.

The doorman started talking fast in Japanese. Mulvaney pressed the muzzle of the Beretta against his right ear. The short muscleman in the door started to move. Mulvaney stepped back as he rapped the Beretta across the back of the doorman's neck, letting the guy go down as he leveled the 9mm at the muscleman. "Don't—understand 'don't,' sweetheart?"

The muscleman was still coming and there wouldn't be anything else to do but shoot him about a half-dozen times and hope he'd go down like the doorman had.

Then there was another face in the doorway. Older, but not by much, maybe late forties or early fifties. And the face seemed to say without any words: I've got power. The new guy in the doorway snapped out something in Japanese and the muscleman stopped in mid-stride as if somebody had just hit his remote-control button.

The muscleman eased into a more comfortable-looking standing position and the guy in the door started speaking English. "What the fuck you want comin' in here and musclin' my guys?"

Mulvaney controlled the impulse to laugh, but barely. "You Shinoda?"

"I'm Shinoda. So?"

"Ajaccio sent me. We gotta talk. Without the comedy twins."

Shinoda's face seemed to relax. "You the guy I been hearin' about?"

"If it's the guy who's gonna kick your face in, I might be him. I wanna talk now."

Shinoda nodded, firing something off in Japanese. The muscleman dragged the doorman out of the way. Mulvaney slipped the gun under his jacket and followed Shinoda inside. It was an office like any other, plastic-looking and modern. Nothing to write home about. Shinoda sat down in the high-backed swivel chair behind the paper-littered desk, the chair making him look smaller than he was. It almost seemed like part of the job description, because guys who were heavy into pimping were almost invariably on the short side, and pushing women around seemed to make them feel taller.

Mulvaney didn't take the chair opposite the desk; he'd seen too many spy movies where sneaky Oriental bad guys had the chairs opposite their desks rigged with something. He stood. "You know a girl going by the name Jill Linton? About five-six, blond hair all matted with blood? Pretty blue eyes and her head and her body can go in two different directions at once? Ever hear of her?"

Shinoda didn't answer for a second.

"I'm wet; I'm tired; I'm pissed. Talk to me."

"You're the Chicago cop who's on the take to Ajaccio, right?"

112

"And you're the scumbag who white-slaves American girls, right?"

Shinoda started to laugh, but the laugh didn't come. Mulvaney figured maybe Shinoda had seen his eyes. "Why'd you come here, cop?"

"Where'd you learn your English?"

"San Francisco. Born and raised there."

"You wanna go home in a body bag? Tell me about Jill Linton."

"I don't know no Jill what's-her-name, all right?"

Mulvaney fished out his cigarettes, found one that wasn't too wet and lit it. "She was one of your girls. Either that or Japan's got your twin brother hidden around someplace. Your M.O. is all over her, Shinoda. Young girl. Wanted to be an entertainer. Got suckered out to Hawaii and then over here, and all of a sudden she couldn't go back home. She danced for Mizutani Hideo. Ring a bell?"

"Man, you can get yourself fucked bad talkin' about him." Shinoda lit one of those cigarettes that looks like a cigar somebody left out in the rain to shrink.

"Who's the Yakusa usin' for specialized hits, Shinoda?"

Shinoda's eyes were pinpoints of light. "Why the hell you comin' to me, man?"

"'Cause you're a connected man, greaseball. This'd be a protected operation. And Ajaccio came to you for help gettin' the nephew back, Peter Ellermann. And you couldn't help for shit, which means you're tighter with the Yakusa than you are with the stateside guys. You don't supply women for fun and games to the head of the mob if you don't know him." Mulvaney leaned across Shinoda's desk, the cigarette hanging out of the right corner of his mouth. Shinoda's cigarette fell from his lips onto the desk. Mulvaney grabbed Shinoda's left ear and dragged his head down with it, slamming it into the pile of papers on his desk where the cigarette was smoldering. Shinoda shrieked with pain. Mulvaney let go of his head and was around the desk, the gun out and against Shinoda's right temple by the time the muscleman and the doorman were through the doorway. "Bouncer—tell Gargantua there to back off or Shinoda's brains are all over the desk! Got it?"

"Shit, man, you can't come—"

"Shinoda, curb the enthusiasm of your employees," Mulvaney said. He let Shinoda's head rise a little, the guy scraping the leavings of the cigarette off his left cheek. There was a faint burning-flesh smell, like when somebody uses an electric needle to take off a wart.

"Get outta here. This mother's crazy!"

The two guys backed out through the door and closed it. Mulvaney wheeled Shinoda around, the muzzle of the gun at the tip of his nose. "You're real good at character assessment, snotball. And I'm gettin' crazier by the minute. Tell me wonderful secret things or you buy the farm." The Beretta had double-action first-round capability, but Mulvaney thumbed back the hammer just for emphasis.

"Holy—"

"Tell me about Jill Linton. Tell me about Mizutani Hideo. Tell me about Peter Ellermann. Tell me who makes special hits for the Yakusa. And if anybody comes through that doorway, a bullet goes through your head."

Mulvaney smelled urine. Shinoda had wet his pants.

Shinoda started to talk. "You gotta promise me: you don't say nothin' to nobody about this. Or I'm dead anyway."

"I won't promise you shit. Let's see what you can tell me first."

"All right . . . all . . . Yeah." Shinoda sounded like he was hyperventilating. Mulvaney backed away a little and manually let down the hammer, then perched on a corner of the desk where he could keep one eye on Shinoda and one eye on the door.

"So speak to me," Mulvaney said.

"Jill—that ain't her real name. But I didn't have nothin' to do with nobody getting killed."

"Who chops off heads for the Yakusa?"

Shinoda licked his lips; his hands pulled his wet pants away from his crotch; he talked. "Word is that . . . You gotta promise you won't—"

Mulvaney interrupted. "Tell me what I wanna know or you won't have to worry about somebody else killin' ya."

"Word on the street—it's just like it is in the States, ya know?—word is that he's hired some ninja."

"A what?"

"Ninjas—ya know? The guys who run around in black and kill people with knives and shit. They're real, man! And

114

Mizutani-san hired this ninja to put the bag on Peter Ellermann and to do some other stuff for him, ya know? So it's this ninja dude that killed Jill what's-her-name and . . ."

"And who else?" Mulvaney asked.

Shinoda looked like he'd lost it, his eyes dead. "Some Army guy—that's what I heard. Some Army cop. This was a coupla weeks back. Mizutani-san's got some big deal goin' down, ya know? And he ain't got the talent to cover it. So he hired this ninja fucker."

"What's this ninja dude's name?"

Shinoda said something Mulvaney guessed was a name. "Tsukiyama Koji. You're fuckin' dead you mess with him, man. I hope he cuts your balls off."

"What's this big deal Mizutani's got goin' down? The Ellermann shakedown on Ajaccio?"

Shinoda looked him in the eye. "I think it's bigger than drugs, man. Now, get outta here, huh? Please?"

"Where do I find this Tsukiyama Koji fella?"

"You don't find him; he finds you."

"In case he's runnin' behind schedule or somethin', I don't wanna miss him. Where?"

Shinoda didn't answer for several seconds. Mulvaney said, "I gotta cock this pistol again, the hammer comes down when I put your lights out for good."

Shinoda licked his lips again. "He can do worse than kill me."

"So can I. Maybe put it on the street that you told me everything you know about the Yakusa—"

"Man!"

"Where can I find this ninja guy?"

The words came out like vomit. "He's got a squeeze he keeps that works at the Garden of Blissful Beauty. Her name's Ikuta Chie. You mess with her—"

"Fuck off and die." Mulvaney smiled, standing up, starting toward the doorway. "If your guys are outside waitin' for me with guns or stuff, you better hope they do their number good."

He opened the door. The muscleman and the doorman were there. Mulvaney looked back toward Shinoda, who shouted something at the two guys. Mulvaney glanced back at him again. "I told 'em to let you go. No sense them killin' ya when somebody else'll do it for me."

Mulvaney assumed Shinoda meant this ninja guy Tsukiyama Koji. His track shoes sounding squishy because they were still wet, he walked past the muscle and across the main floor of the Happiest Ladies toward the street. If this was happiness, he didn't want it.

John Trench Osgood awakened, his hand reaching for the Walther P-38 K beside the wooden pillow. Gonroku-san's daughter knelt beside the mattress. "Osgood-san. There is a messenger here from the friend of my father, Tsukahira-san." He felt embarrassment that he was holding the gun. He sat up. Tomiko's almond eyes were bright. Her lips were pursed and reminded him of a rosebud. For an instant he wondered what the flower would be like.

"Thank you, Tomiko." Osgood smiled. Gonroku had told him to call the girl by her given name, that he was considered a respected family friend, not a *gaijin* visitor. He had told Gonroku Umi that he was honored and had henceforth addressed the girl informally. "Where is he? This messenger."

"In the garden, Osgood-san." She bowed, hands folded in front of her.

"In the garden," Osgood repeated. He stood up, dropped the P-38 K into his right hip pocket and began to button his shirt. "One messenger only, Tomiko?"

"Yes, Osgood-san." The girl smiled. She had very pretty hair, black like the feathers of a raven and just as shiny. He started to bend over to pick up his shoes, but she dropped to her knees, saying, "May I, Osgood-san?" She held his right shoe in her hands.

"That's unnecessary, really." There was genuine disappointment in her eyes. "All right, then. Thank you."

She assisted him with first the right shoe, then the left. She stood, Osgood helping her to rise, and he opened the sliding door into the garden. He saw no one at first glance, but he wouldn't have assumed a messenger sent by a ninja Jonin to be the conspicuous type.

"I am here, Osgood-san," a voice said, coming from the darkness a few feet to his right. He turned toward the voice quickly, the gun in his hand automatically. "What is this?"

"Forgive me, please. Force of habit," Osgood said into the darkness.

116

He didn't know what he had expected, but the man who stepped out of the shadows was dressed more like a cat burglar than a ninja—ninja civvies, he theorized. Black suit, black turtleneck shirt, black shoes.

"You have a message for me, sir."

"Here." He handed over an envelope—the color, black. He bowed slightly.

Osgood returned the bow. He took a step back into the light from the open bedroom and tore open the envelope, which was lined in black foil. Here, clearly, was a message from a man who didn't wish his correspondence to be casually intercepted. The stationery was white, the Japanese symbols for Tsukahira's name in very small letters at the bottom of the plain writing paper, the note itself in English, perhaps a means of assuring it would not be read by the messenger.

Osgood-san:

I have weighed your words carefully. I have also weighed the promise of which I spoke. I learned that the pilgrim whom I mentioned was doomed solely because he saw but two paths and failed to see that along these lay only his perception of honor—whereas on yet a third path there was true honor. The man of whom we spoke may be found sometimes to frequent the Garden of Blissful Beauty in order to keep the company of a certain Ikuta Chie.

May you always walk the third path.

Tsukahira had named the place, named the bait. But to reel in a ninja might be exceedingly difficult. Osgood looked up to address the messenger, but the messenger had disappeared into the night.

They had gone to Andy's place, not the apartment where she lived, but an apartment she kept for emergencies. There was dry clothing there for her—she'd gotten out of the car and run through the rain to him as he'd left Shinoda's place and gotten herself soaked almost as badly as he was. There was dry clothing there for him as well—the late Koswalski's things.

He showered first while Andy made coffee. Afterward,

117

Koswalski's blue jeans proved a good fit, but the arms of Koswalski's shirts seemed too short, so Mulvaney just rolled them up. She poured herself coffee and him a glass of whiskey, then showered while he set about cleaning the Beretta.

The Garden of Blissful Beauty was a very exclusive club frequented by the elite of the elite. It was impossible to enter without an introduction from a member. Mizutani Hideo was a member. Andy doubted that Tsukiyama Koji, an assassin, held a membership. If his girl, Ikuta Chie, was there, she was probably a highly tipped and highly desirable hostess. Many such women were kept by wealthy men, and Tsukiyama might well be exceedingly wealthy.

Mulvaney was getting the Beretta's slide back onto the frame when Andy, hair wrapped in a yellow bath towel, body wrapped in a yellow bathrobe of the same material, exited the bathroom. "Got it all psyched out, Ed?"

"Yeah. We somehow make this Ikuta Chie broad, then follow her and stake her out until her boyfriend the ninja drops by."

"And then you just catch him, right? Bullshit."

"You fail to appreciate the finesse with which I will entrap the suspect, my dear," he laughed.

"Entrapment's illegal."

"Legal, my ass—anyway, I used the wrong word. I meant plain old 'trap.' This guy's in the sheets and we nail him. He's not gonna jump around yellin' 'karate' and makin' chicken noises much if I blow out his kneecaps."

"Yuck," she said. She leaned on his shoulder, her right arm around his neck as he reloaded the magazine he'd emptied for cleaning.

"This is the guy who made these blue jeans ownerless, kid."

"You sure he . . . ahh . . . he killed . . . ?"

"He killed Koswalski, near as I can figure. And Jill Linton. And he's probably the guy you saw talking with Mizutani Hideo in that Zen Buddhist garden. He's the key to the whole thing—to getting back Ellermann and maybe to finding out who it is the Yakusa's payin' off in the government to cushion their drug business. Solve your case and my case with this guy."

Her hand trailed along his shoulder. She took a sip from

his whiskey glass and then sat down at the small kitchen table just opposite him. "If he's a real ninja, he doesn't work alone. I mean, he'll have an organization. And if he's real, he's so good it's almost supernatural."

"Too many karate flicks, kid. And besides, the good guy always wins, just like Chuck Norris and Bruce Lee, huh?" He shot her a smile as he rammed the magazine up the butt, stripped the first round, then buttoned out the magazine to load another round, giving him sixteen.

"This isn't funny, Ed. A real ninja is death incarnate."

"You can say the same thing about Chicago cops, sweetheart."

"What if this pimp Shinoda called Tsukiyama Koji and tipped him?"

He lit a cigarette. They were mostly dried out now. "First place, I got it on good authority that ninjas never check their answering machines. And second, if Shinoda told this ninja he blew the whistle on him, Shinoda'd be as good as dead. Shinoda was scared to death. Like I told ya, he peed in his pants. Not because I had a rod up his nose, but because he knew he was gonna tell me. 'Least that's the way I got it figured. Once we got this ninja guy's squeeze staked out, you come back here and wait. I'll take care of the hardball part."

"Nuts. Just 'cause I'm a woman."

"You're not just any woman. You're my woman."

"Since when?"

"Since I told ya. Got any gripes about it?"

Andy smiled. "Nope."

Mulvaney smiled back.

The rain had stopped before Osgood awakened to receive the messenger from Tsukahira, but then started again when he had taken the Jaguar down into the city to the exclusive club where Ikuta Chie, Tsukiyama Koji's inamorata, was employed, presumably as a bar hostess. Aside from the rain and the lack of a physical description of the young lady in question, there were several disturbing elements. Tsukiyama Koji was supposedly very good. To capture a ninja and then somehow get him to talk might well be totally out of the question, but to follow such a man to his lair and hope to find Peter Ellermann might be even more difficult. And assuming all that could be accomplished,

Tsukiyama would have a band of followers, equally well-trained, who most assuredly would be averse to Ellerman's release.

Then there were his two charges, Oakwood, the military policewoman, and Mulvaney, the Chicago police sergeant. If they were still alive and the Yakusa hadn't gotten them, they were most likely well-established by now as thorns in the side of Mizutani Hideo and their days would be numbered. But it was the girl and Mulvaney who had led him to the Zen Buddhist shrine. That in turn had led him into the chain of events which he hoped would culminate in extricating Ellermann before he divulged everything he knew.

Mulvaney and Oakwood had been viewed as bait since the conception of the plan, as expendable commodities if it came to that, as a means of drawing attention and consequent reaction which could be capitalized upon in order to free Ellermann. If he could, Osgood had told himself from the outset, he would bring them in and keep them alive. But Ellermann's rescue was more important than human concerns. That had been implicit.

It was common practice in the books and films which chronicled the careers of the fictional counterparts of the men and women who shared his curious profession for the plot to involve something or other which would change forever the geopolitical balance of power. Which would, to use the cliché, mean "the end of civilization as we know it." Civilization as he knew it wasn't something he much revered. And he had often wondered over the years what, if any, difference human sacrifices made in the scheme of things. He had known men and women of courage on his side of the political fence and on the other side. Their lives and deaths were sometimes the stuff of fantastic adventure, their missions sometimes the stuff of heroic import, but in most cases these people themselves meant little except to those who knew them. It was increasingly harder these days to do the job right. Anything that might work well was usually legally prescribed or so religiously regulated that actual accomplishment was impossible. And those relatively rare times when all the stops were pulled and the only goal was to get the job done, no matter the cost, had to be undertaken with greater care for the scrutiny of the political opportunists in Washington than of the pervasive intelligence network of the KGB in Moscow.

And yet Ellermann's survival was a human concern of the greatest magnitude. Because if Ellermann were lost, it might mean something that no rational man wanted to consider but that no rational mind could ignore.

Osgood stopped the Jaguar beside a pay telephone and got out into the rain, the collar of his navy-blue trench coat turned up against it.

He placed the call.

He waited.

The line answered.

"This is Osgood. Copy this address." He read the address of the place where Ikuta Chie worked. "Meet me two blocks north of there in a half-hour. I'll be outside in a gunmetal-gray Jaguar sedan. There is a woman whose photo I must have." He gave her name. "Bring the photo for me. You'll have an umbrella and be crossing the street and have difficulty with the umbrella and I'll get out to assist you. Say in Japanese, 'You are a most welcome visitor to my country.' And I'll say, 'Any visitor to your country is very fortunate.'"

The female voice on the other end of the line asked, "What else?"

Osgood hesitated. To divulge the name Tsukiyama Koji would require that he trust the local contact. He didn't. "Nothing else. Thank you. Will you be able to get the picture?"

"I know several persons who may be able to help. A half-hour is very little time."

The rain seemed even heavier now. "Yes, well, I have less. I appreciate this. Sorry to have disturbed you so late in the evening. Until later, then."

He hung up, soaked to the bone below the trench coat. He climbed back into the Jaguar and fired up the engine, continuing on, a quick glance at his Rolex to concretize the designated meeting time.

Andy Oakwood, now changed into dark gray woolen slacks and an all-weather coat, a gray silk scarf tied over her hair, stood beside the pay phone. Mulvaney sheltered her

121

with his body against the rain as best he could, his clothes already soaked through for the second time this evening.

"Helen. This is Andy. . . . No, I didn't die. . . . Damn right I need a favor. How're your connections with vice? . . . Wonderful. Here's what I need. . . . No, not that." Andy laughed. "A girl named Ikuta Chie. Probably in her twenties. . . . 'Probably' is the best I've got, Helen. She works at the Garden of Blissful Beauty. A hostess, I think. . . . May not have an apartment in her name. Check vice in case she's been busted. . . . Don't check the National Police Agency. Just stick with the municipal cops. . . . I got my reasons, okay? But I need a picture. . . . Anything. . . . Yeah. I'll call you. I need it fast. Twenty minutes?"

Mulvaney started to laugh.

Oakwood hung up.

"Who's Helen?"

"Provost marshal's secretary. If she can't get it, nobody can."

They ran back toward the car to get out of the rain. He didn't want to risk going back to her place, so they drove, Andy at the wheel, rain drumming so hard on the roof it sounded like rocks.

Andy's second call to Helen was short. Mulvaney waited for her in the car this time, the engine running. He didn't like being in the same place twice, but it was the only pay phone they'd spotted.

He leaned across the seat and wrenched open the door as she slid in behind the wheel. She slammed the door shut against the icy rain, whisked the scarf from her head, shook her hair free. She looked wet and she looked pretty, he thought. He smiled: she looked pretty wet.

"Helen'll have the picture in fifteen minutes. She's got a Japanese boyfriend who owns a shop on Shinmonzen Street. She'll meet us there."

"You sure about Helen?"

"I'm sure about Helen."

"What's a shop doin' open this time of night?"

"She's got a key. We come around back."

"Good—I like alleys."

The car pulled away from the curb and into the all-but-deserted street.

122

The rain kept up.

She didn't have to tell him when they turned onto Shinmonzen Street. Parts of North Michigan Avenue were like this, each city having its Rodeo Drive. He'd seen that once when he'd gone out to L.A. as a technical consultant for a television movie about a Chicago cop. The only reason he'd been sent was that Hymie wanted to get rid of him. But three weeks on somebody else's money hadn't been bad, and in real small print when he'd freeze-frame the VCR, he could see his name there at the end of the movie. They hadn't wanted advice, he'd learned, just to put down somebody's name as an adviser. If the guy on TV had been a real cop, he woulda been dead ten minutes into the film.

He had her pilot the car around the block twice, then turn off Shinmonzen and onto a side street, parking near the mouth of an alley.

Mulvaney got out, Andy out on the driver's side, not waiting for his gentleman act. They started into the alley, Mulvaney reaching for his gun, Andy with her right hand inside her purse.

A light midway down the alley blinked on and off twice, then twice more. "We made a signal. Everything's okay."

Mulvaney's mouth was dry, the only part of his anatomy that could make that claim since it had started raining. He kept walking. "You sure you can trust Helen?"

"For the second time, yes."

He kept walking. He didn't trust Helen. He'd never met Helen. And if Helen was so trustworthy, why was the provost marshal supposedly the only guy who knew what kind of assignment Andy was working? Or didn't they count the secretary? And what about the setup at the airport with the neglected code phrase? And the setup at the love hotel with the Yakusa goons waiting to cut them down?

He could live with the fact that he'd intentionally been made hot. Nobody was paying his way just to be a tourist and to hop in the sack with Andy Oakwood. But there was a difference between that and the love-hotel ambush.

Was this the same thing?

Mulvaney kept walking.

Was Andy reporting to somebody? Aside from the fact he'd fallen in love with her, the setup at the love hotel had put her in just as much danger as he'd been in. "Who do you report to? The provost marshal directly or through Helen?"

Andy stopped walking.

"Come on, Andy—you've heard of crooked cops!"

"Not Helen!"

"Fine, then let's keep walkin'." He started up again, the Beretta tight in his fist. Sometimes people learned hard.

She was talking to him. "You're right—I told her about the love-hotel thing. I told her about Jill having some information for us, just before Jill was murdered."

He kept walking. "See? But maybe she's got the picture anyway. Play it by ear."

"That bitch."

"Yeah."

"Go back to the car," she told him.

"Fuck you—which'd be a pleasure." He kept walking. He glanced over at her. The gun was out of her purse.

"Go back to the car, damn you!"

"No. Shut up and be ready to use that Dick Special."

"How can you love somebody and hate his guts at the same time?"

He looked at her and laughed. "It's called being married. Maybe we can try it."

"You asking me to—"

"Yeah. Gonna make somethin' out of it?"

"The best I can," she told him.

"Keep walking." The light by the door was on now and it made a difused yellow cone that the rain kept cutting through. He stopped a few paces from the doorway. "Let me knock. If we're gonna get married, I gotta get to know your friends."

"Shut up. If you get killed after just asking me to marry you—"

"You'll never forgive me; I know."

He tried the door. The knob turned and the door opened inward. It was dark inside. "Hey, Helen!"

There wasn't an answer for a long second. He called out again. "Helen?"

"Hello?"

"Hey, look, Helen, I'm night blind, ya know. Got some lights you can hit inside there? Dark like it is, I'd probably fall flat on my face. Embarrass the hell out of Andy here."

Mulvaney waited. He'd never been night blind, but Helen wouldn't know that.

"Just a second. I'll see if I can find the switch."

"Sure thing. I like the rain myself," he told her.

He wanted a cigarette but wanted to hold on to his gun more, so he skipped the cigarette.

"I found the switch," the woman's voice called out of the darkness.

"Hey! Terrific!"

The lights came on. It was a trap. He'd already known that. And he'd set it up so he didn't have any choice but to walk right into it now.

He started into the doorway, Andy so close beside him he felt like half of a sandwich. He kept his eyes squinted as tight as he could and still see. If she had company—and he didn't figure she'd be doing this all by herself—they might count on the night-blind thing and knock out the lights before the play got made.

He was inside now.

Andy whispered, "This scares me to death."

"Me too," he told her honestly.

He almost pulled the trigger when a woman, tall, dark-haired, wearing a trench coat that was water-stained at the shoulders, stepped from behind some high-stacked packing crates, some of them marked in English "Product of the Republic of China."

"Helen! Hey! Andy told me so much about you!" Mulvaney shifted his gun into his left fist and walked forward fast, practically grabbing her by the right hand and pumping the arm hard as he drew her close to him, his left hand, which still held the gun, going over her right hand. Under his breath he whispered, "I know this is a setup. You can get outta this alive and have twenty-four hours before we pull your plug if you give me the picture of the Ikuta woman, Helen. Otherwise, when your little Yakusa buddies start shooting, you get it first. Gut-shot. The kind that takes a long time to die from and the doctors can't do shit to save you. Get my drift, kid?"

Her eyes were blue and they were so big with fear they reminded him of the blue-willow china dinner plates his mother had set the table with when he'd been a kid.

"You're . . . you're . . ."

"Crazy?" Mulvaney supplied.

"You . . . ahh . . ."

"You got the picture?"

"Yes . . ."

"Is it the real picture? The real girl?"

"Yes. But . . ."

"What?"

She was shaking badly. He held her hand more tightly. "You won't ever get out of here alive," she said.

Andy said, "Helen, stuff it up your ass."

"Is that your problem, Helen?" Mulvaney grinned.

Helen started to move her left hand. Mulvaney crushed her foot under his heel to get her attention. "The picture, Helen. And maybe you live. No picture, you die first."

She licked her pretty lips.

"Give him the picture, Helen. Your Yakusa friends aren't gonna wait forever," Andy hissed.

"All right." She reached into the left outside pocket of the raincoat and there was a photo in her hand when it came back out. It was a picture of a very pretty girl, very Japanese, very young, with the kind of dark eyes Mulvaney could see himself or any man drowning in.

"Ikuta Chie," Andy whispered.

Mulvaney almost felt sad as he pocketed the photograph. Now there was nothing left but the shooting. He didn't let go of Helen. "If I use you as a shield, will they shoot? Give me the straight dope, sweetheart."

"They'll shoot."

"Mizutani Hideo's guys?" His eyes found the bank of switches beside the loading-dock door off to his left.

"Yeah." She was starting to cry.

"Shit!" Mulvaney held her hand tight, then whipped her back and off her feet to the floor behind some more of the packing crates. He shoved Andy left, dove right.

Helen screamed as the bullets started coming and the lights went out. Automatic-weapons fire came in bright tongues of orange against the black of the darkness. Mulvaney shut his eyes for an instant.

More automatic-weapons fire. He opened his eyes, not looking directly toward the muzzle flashes, able to see better now. He started moving, shouting to Andy, "Stay down!" His left shoulder slammed into a stack of packing crates and they started to fall. He jogged right to avoid them, tripping over something and going down, rolling as bullets tore into the concrete floor beside him, sparks flying from the ricochets. He pumped the Beretta's trigger twice toward the flashes and rolled, hearing a curse and a scream of pain. The guns sounded like submachine guns, the reports too light for assault rifles. His ears rang with the noise nonetheless as he clambered to his feet, going back the way he had come, hoping none of the assailants would think he'd do that. He almost tripped over the same thing again, stepping over whatever it was, edging back along the sides of the packing crates, the Beretta tight in his fist.

He heard something shouted in Japanese and a second later Andy screamed, "They're splitting up, Ed!"

Mulvaney didn't answer her.

"Ed!"

There wasn't much time now. In another few seconds Andy would open fire and get cut to pieces. Mulvaney focused all his attention on his hearing. And he heard feet shuffling lightly over the floor from what sounded to be the other side of the stack of crates behind which he had taken cover. He shifted his weight hard, throwing his body against the stack of crates. They fell. He was moving, shouting to Andy, "Stay back and hold your fire!" He climbed over the packing crates as moans, unintelligible shouted curses and a burst of automatic-weapons fire filled his ears.

He bumped into somebody, a rush of air against his face. The breath smelled foul. He stabbed the pistol toward the shape and fired twice. Hands grabbed at him . . . a moan of pain. He shook free of the man, falling over one of the packing crates, something snatching at his leg. He hammered the butt of the pistol toward it, heard a groan.

He was up, tripped, fell against the wall, got to his feet, feeling along the wall with his gun hand. The switches. He hit them all, his eyes shut tight as he dove left.

He came out of the dive in a roll, his left elbow smacking into something, suddenly locked with pain, his right arm stabbing forward as he opened his eyes.

He had a split-second advantage—the darkness had been so total, the light was now so bright. He saw a man with an Uzi submachine gun and he fired twice. The man's neck was suddenly awash in blood and his body fell. Mulvaney swung the muzzle left—a man with a Beretta 93R machine pistol, the front grip folded down and the stock attached. Mulvaney fired twice, then twice again, the body of the man with the machine pistol spinning, going down. Mulvaney rolled, his elbow hurting still, pistol shots ringing in his ears, the wall beside where his head had been taking multiple impacts as he returned fire—a man in a gray suit and black fedora with a Browning High Power in his fist. Mulvaney's first double tap slammed the man into a stack of packing crates; the second double tap put him down, his arms flopping out from his sides and the pistol dropping, skating across the floor.

Mulvaney's body was half-crouched, his left arm starting to get the feeling back into it, his right arm extended, the pistol still tight in his fist. There wasn't any movement.

"I'm getting the guns," he heard Andy shout.

He looked toward her. Helen was kneeling beside some packing crates, face white as snow, her body visibly shaking. Mulvaney shrugged. His body was shaking too.

He rose to his full height, his voice hollow-sounding to him as he spoke, his ears still filled with the sounds of gunfire in the confined space. "Andy, don't let Helen slip away." He crossed the storage room. He wanted to see what it was that he'd tripped over. On the way to it, he found another of the Yakusa guys, a bloody gash along the side of his temple. Mulvaney felt for a pulse. There was none. He moved on, saw a fifth Yakusa triggerman, this one shot. Mulvaney assumed this was the one he'd shot at in the darkness. Like the others, he was dead.

Mulvaney clambered over toppled packing crates, contents spilled on the floor: vases, ornamental fans, Japanese dolls that were dressed like geisha girls. Beneath one of the crates he found what he had tripped over. A man, Japanese, about forty-five years old, his eyes wide open and glassy, a dark bruise beside the base of his skull.

Helen's voice—shaky—came to him from across the storage room. "You killed five men."

"They were trying to kill me. What was your excuse with this guy, Helen?"

"What?"

"Come and take a look. Mid-forties, well-dressed, diamond-studded wristwatch—"

"Toshiro!" Helen started scrambling over the packing crates, kicking off her high-heeled shoes, tripping, Mulvaney reaching to catch her. But she shrugged him away. She fell on her knees beside the dead man. She started to cry, shaking the body, hugging it to her.

Mulvaney heard Andy's voice. "This must be the boyfriend."

Cops would be coming in a minute or so, Mulvaney knew. But he had to talk with Helen. "Look. These guys you're playing with. This is what they do for a living. What do you know about Peter Ellermann?"

Helen stopped rocking her dead lover in her arms, looking up at him from her knees. "The KGB wants Ellermann too. And the Yakusa has him. I don't know anything else."

It was like saying you knew the cure for cancer but didn't know anything else. Mulvaney just stared at her.

Andy said it. "The KGB? The Russians?"

"Aww, shit," Mulvaney said finally. He grabbed Helen by the shoulders and got her to her feet. "Andy, wipe down the light switches and the doorknob and anything you might have touched. If I left recognizable prints on the empty brass from my gun, we're up the creek. Grab Helen's shoes."

Mulvaney started propelling the woman toward the door. He figured she'd been punished enough.

John Osgood cupped his hands around the flame from his lighter and lit a cigarette. He pocketed the lighter, inhaling the smoke deep into his lungs. He had never smoked out of habit, lighting up casually or unthinkingly. Rather, he smoked from enjoyment.

To sit outside an establishment such as the Garden of Blissful Beauty and wait for a girl you had to identify from a photograph—when it was dark and raining so heavily that anyone would be swathed in raingear and moving quickly— was a poor proposition at best. But it was the only proposition at hand. He told himself that there was always the possibility that the mere acquisition of Ikuta Chie's photograph had somehow alerted her ninja lover. If that were the case, Osgood knew that he ran the substantial risk of dying this evening—or in the predawn hours of the morning, to be more correct.

He smoked his cigarette, waiting as he had already waited for more than an hour. The drumming of the rain was incessant, the wind cold through the slightly lowered window; but without the window lowered, there would have been no way to observe.

As the thought crossed his mind, the front doors of the exclusive club opened quickly. Osgood snatched up the already focused vision-intensification binoculars and brought them to his eyes. A woman, scarf over her hair, trench coat belted tightly around her. But she was too heavily built to be Ikuta Chie—the body shape didn't go with the sculptured slenderness of the face in the photograph. A car was pulled up alongside the curb and as the woman was ushered into it by the club doorman, Osgood saw her face. It was not Ikuta Chie. He put down the glasses, took a last puff from his cigarette and stubbed it out in the Jaguar's dashboard ashtray.

A car drove up along the opposite side of the street, pulled to the curb about a half-block from the club entrance and the exhaust smoke cut out.

Osgood brought up the binoculars again, refocusing them for the further distance.

As the window on the driver's side rolled down, he caught sight of light-colored hair and the distinctively attractive features of Sergeant Oakwood.

Osgood observed for another minute or so, seeing the flare of a lighter or match to the left of his field of view. Mulvaney was with her.

Why were Oakwood and Mulvaney here too?

He smiled at the thought that he could have walked up to their car, introduced himself and merely asked them; but such action wasn't to be considered, of course. One of the ancillary objectives of his mission was that if Oakwood and Mulvaney did survive, they should never know of his presence.

He glanced at his Rolex and exhaled a deep sigh. He waited in the darkness.

A man left the club, accompanied by a woman whose hair, uncovered, seemed too short for Ikuta Chie. As she entered the car a valet had driven to the front entrance, a moment's closer examination showed all the wrong features. A half-hour went by and four men and six women left almost simultaneously. Osgood was concerned for a moment that the tallest of the women might be Ikuta Chie, but was satisfied finally, as she turned almost directly toward his binoculars, that she was not.

The club was clearly emptying out and if she were going to appear, it would be soon. The back of the photograph had her home address scribbled onto it, and if he failed to pick her out within a reasonable amount of time, he would go there. Periodically he focused the binoculars on Oakwood and Mulvaney. They were apparently waiting for the same thing he was. He wondered if somehow they too had the home address. And from whom had they learned about Ikuta Chie?

A black Mercedes sportster pulled up at the curb in front of the club entrance, a valet running toward it to catch the door, a tall man dressed in black fedora and black trench coat emerging from behind the wheel.

Osgood felt the thing in his bones. This was Tsukiyama Koji. Now, if only Osgood and Mulvaney wouldn't get in the way.

No sooner had the thought crossed his mind than he saw a brief flicker of the dome light in Oakwood and Mulvaney's car, the light gone, but Mulvaney stepping out of the car. "Good God, man," Osgood said under his breath. Was Mulvaney actually going to brace Tsukiyama Koji in the street?

The little black Mercedes wasn't moving, the attendant back under the protection of the awning, the car's lights full on, Mulvaney partially illuminated by them.

Tsukiyama was picking up his girl.

And now Tsukiyama Koji and a woman appeared in the entranceway, stopping under the awning. Osgood focused on the girl. It was Ikuta Chie. He shifted to the face of Tsukiyama Koji. It was the kind of face people often described as gaunt, the features drawn, the eyes moving as though they had a will of their own. Tsukiyama Koji was tall for a Japanese, a throwback to his grandfather, the ninja leader Tsukahira, perhaps. Osgood thought he detected a smile cross Tsukiyama's mouth and then go away.

Tsukiyama knew he was being watched. He was waiting to make certain his presence wasn't missed, that Ikuta Chie's gorgeous features were recognized.

Mulvaney was walking down the sidewalk toward Tsukiyama.

Tsukiyama stepped away from the woman, putting himself between her and Mulvaney. With astonishing grace he slipped out of the trench coat and hat, throwing them down onto the rain-puddled sidewalk, loose-fitting black pajamalike clothing revealed beneath. Tsukiyama's feet moved, his shoes flying from them into the gutter. He stood on the sidewalk barefoot. From beneath his garment came a flash like a streak of lightning in the night. A sword. Osgood looked to Mulvaney. Mulvaney had his gun in his right fist.

"Idiot!" Osgood hissed, reaching under his raincoat and the suit jacket beneath for his gun.

His eyes had left Tsukiyama Koji for the briefest second, but as Osgood looked back he now saw a dozen others dressed identically to Tsukiyama Koji except that they wore black footgear and black hoods, the hoods covering not only the heads but also much of the faces. Each man had his weapon or weapons bared. One had a sword in one hand, the short sword in the other. Still another of the black-clad men had something that looked like a sickle in each hand, the sickles silently slicing the night air as they scribed rapid arcs in the darkness. Another of the men had a short, recurved bow drawn, an arrow nocked; still another held a crossbow.

This was a trap, but only for Mulvaney and Oakwood.

An automobile horn sounded.

Osgood stepped from the Jaguar into the rain, his Walther 9mm in his right hand.

An archer in the semicircle of ninjas sprang to face him. He hadn't been expected, he realized.

Mulvaney shouted through the rain. "Hey! 'Scuse me. You that ninja who likes to chop off people's heads?"

Tsukiyama Koji's voice was deep, lifeless, as if from the grave. "You are the inquisitive Chicago policeman. You and your woman are dead."

Osgood brought up the Walther fast and fired, the man with the crossbow going down into the street, coming up in a roll, falling face-forward into a puddle. Osgood side-stepped right as he swung the muzzle toward the archer with the short recurved bow, the archer firing as Osgood fired, the arrow's tip clanging against the door of the Jaguar as Osgood fired again, the archer's body spinning with the impact. Three men were charging the Jaguar, swords flashing. Mulvaney shouted from across the street, "Who the hell are you?" Osgood threw himself behind the wheel, gunning the ignition and stomping the gas as he let up the clutch, cutting the wheel into a hard left away from the curb and straight toward the charging ninjas.

Sergeant Oakwood was out of the car, firing some sort of small revolver—he remembered her file: it was a Detective Special. A ninja vaulted over the hood of her car, his sword crashing down toward her, Oakwood stepping back and firing. Mulvaney was shooting. Incredibly, Tsukiyama Koji's sword was slicing through the air as he slowly advanced, sparks flying as bullets ricocheted off the blade. Here was indeed a man of considerable abilities.

Oakwood had dropped the first attacker, but a second sprang over the roof of her car, his foot catching her on the right shoulder, her revolver discharging into the street as she went down. The ninja's sword flashed. Osgood thrust the P-38 K through his now open window in his left fist, firing, in the blur to the right of his front sight seeing Mulvaney's weapon discharge simultaneously, the ninja's body spinning, his sword cleaving downward. Oakwood, to her knees now, her weapon apparently empty, fell back. Over the roar of the Jaguar's engine at high speed in first gear, Osgood heard a scream.

He cut the wheel hard right and hauled up on the emergency brake, sending the Jaguar into a controlled lateral skid, sweeping down two more of the ninjas. He stepped from the car, running toward Oakwood. He asked himself why he was doing this. He fleetingly tried reasons such as "We're all Americans on the same side" or "She's a woman and I can't let her die without trying to stop it" or "I'm an idiot." As he reached her, he considered the latter was his true motivation. Her raincoat was covered with blood. He grabbed up her revolver and dropped it into his raincoat pocket, grabbed up her purse and got her into his arms.

Osgood ran, despite the burden in his arms. Mulvaney was dodging a sword, the blade making sparks as it hacked against the wall of the club, Mulvaney's gun discharging again. Osgood shouted, "Mulvaney! Come on! My car! Move it!"

Osgood had her into the back seat, a ninja springing toward him as he started in behind the wheel. Osgood threw himself away from the vehicle, the sickles in the man's hands singing. There was no time for the Walther stuffed in the other pocket of his trench coat. Osgood feigned a shift to the left, then threw himself down, scissoring his legs into the ninja's legs as the man tried to step away. The man went down, coming up in a roll, Osgood to his feet first, pivoting half-right, his left foot snapping out toward the side of the ninja's head, a double Tae-Kwan-Do kick to the right temple. Osgood stumbled, lurched forward against the Jaguar, grabbed for his gun. He fired into the pavement at a sharply obtuse angle, skipping chunks of pavement and bullet fragments toward the rest of the ninjas. Mulvaney came up at the right side of his peripheral vision. The Walther was empty.

"Into the car, Mulvaney—quick!"

"Who the hell are you, man?"

"The cavalry!" Osgood was behind the wheel, the Jaguar's engine still running, more of the ninjas streaming out of the shadows toward them as Osgood popped the emergency brake and the clutch simultaneously, cutting the wheel sharp. The Jaguar fishtailed and there was a screech of rubber as he reached out and dragged the door shut, upshifted and accelerated, arrows and crossbow bolts pinging off the bodywork.

"Who are you?" Mulvaney asked him.

"I'm John Trench Osgood. You're Sergeant Ed Mulvaney of Chicago P.D. Central Division Tac Squad. She's Sergeant Andrea Oakwood, working undercover with the Army MPs. And she's also either dead or bleeding to death, so you'd better roll over into the back seat and see what you can do. There's an attaché case in back there with several items of interest in it, among which you'll find a rather rudimentary but adequate first-aid kit." Osgood upshifted, balanced the wheel with his left knee and changed magazines for his pistol.

Mulvaney was rolling into the back seat. "Holy God!"

"A *katana*—samurai sword—did it. She may have a

partially severed limb. Be careful as you examine her, Mulvaney. Your military training in Special Forces should allow you to keep her alive until we reach medical assistance."

"Special Forces? You know my shoe size?"

"Not off the top of my head, no. But if you've forgotten it, I'm sure I can look it up." Osgood turned off at the next major intersection, skating the Jaguar across as police cars entered the intersection and turned down in the direction from which he had just come. Gonroku-san's was the only place to go. If he recalled correctly, Tomiko was the Japanese equivalent of a registered nurse. "There's a trained nurse where we're going," Osgood volunteered by way of comforting Mulvaney.

"What kinda tricks does she do . . . Oh, shit—"

"What is it?" Osgood asked, unable to see into the back seat.

"The radial artery in her left arm . . . bleeding like—"

"If it's severed, she'll be dead in another thirty seconds. You'd better think fast."

"No shit." Mulvaney's voice seemed to sneer back from the darkness. "I'm making a compression bandage from your sweater, then elevating the arm. I'm gonna block the artery with pressure from my kneecap. When we get wherever it is, I'm not gonna be able to release the pressure until we have some help or else she'll bleed to death in seconds."

"Understood."

"CIA?"

"National Hockey League, actually."

"Yeah—my ass. What's Peter Ellermann and this ninja motherfucker got to do with the KGB?"

Osgood felt the expression on his face freeze. Quietly he asked, "KGB?"

"The world-class bad guys, huh? The Yakusa leader, Mizutani, is playing footsie with 'em. The provost marshal's secretary set us up with the Yakusa and apparently the Yakusa didn't figure their own boys could be counted on to ice us, so Mizutani called his boy Tsukiyama Koji for backup in case we made it as far as the nightclub. Are you the guy who set all this up?"

"Who mentioned the KGB?"

"Andy Oakwood tracked Mizutani to a meet where there

was a Soviet-embassy car. She tracked him to a meet with Tsukiyama Koji. Helen, the bimbo that set us up earlier tonight and just now, said she knew the KGB wanted Ellermann too. What the hell's goin' on?"

"How's Sergeant Oakwood doing?"

"Cold as ice, probably pale as a ghost, and even with the pressure, your sweater's soaked through with blood. That Tsukiyama motherfucker's a walking dead man."

"Commendable sentiments, Mulvaney, but easier said than done. If I'm not mistaken, he was using his sword to deflect the paths of your bullets."

"I saw it too, but I don't believe it."

"I believe it. There are men who can catch a slower-moving projectile, such as the 230-grain Full Metal Case bullet fired from a .45 automatic. Catch it in their bare hands. I've seen it done. Tsukiyama Koji must have phenomenal reflexes. Such ability is almost supernatural."

"Fine. You start him a damn fan club and I'll go find a wooden stake to pound into his heart."

"Tsukiyama Koji isn't the objective here, Mulvaney. It's Ellermann we want."

"We?"

"Much as the thought repulses me—and I mean nothing personal by this, actually—but logic seems to dictate we may have to work together. You're too hot to get out of the country now without blowing the entire operation, and it's possible you could be of some use."

"So what's our first move, 007?" Mulvaney snarled.

Osgood allowed himself to smile. "One of the prime skills of the ninja, Mulvaney, is Tonpo—the mastery of escaping. We practice it even now. Another attribute of the ninja, Mulvaney, is Inpo—the mastery of hiding. It's the wise man who is able to learn from his enemies."

7

On the Sly

MULVANEY'S RIGHT LEG was stiff and still cramped him when he moved it the wrong way. He had kept his knee wedged against Andy Oakwood's arm for the entire length of the drive to the picture-pretty Japanese house with the bookish-looking old man who had killer eyes and the pretty Japanese girl who was a nurse and couldn't seem to keep her eyes off this CIA guy, Osgood. There was no accounting for taste, Mulvaney thought when he first observed the girl watching Osgood.

Osgood had to be somewhere in his late forties, one of those lean guys, tall enough but not powerfully built, yet evidently tough enough. "Suave" was the word women used to describe men like Osgood, Mulvaney knew. The perfectly tailored clothes, the cigarette case, the haircut, all of it. Even the funny-looking gun, like something out of a movie. What kind of guy carried a Walther P-38 K these days? There was even a silencer for the thing in Osgood's attaché case. Mulvaney had spotted that when Osgood closed the case after replacing the medical kit. Did the attaché case turn into a motorcycle or a helicopter, or just a speedboat? Mulvaney had made a mental note to ask.

Mulvaney was chain-smoking through his cigarettes now, waiting for the doctor the old Japanese guy Gonroku-san had called to finish with Andy. And he realized he was terrified. For the first time in his life, he was actually in love with somebody and she was lying inside some silly house with paper walls with some guy who didn't even speak English trying to save her life.

"How are you doing, Mulvaney?"

Mulvaney looked up from where he sat on a small stone bench in the garden. The rain had stopped and the air smelled cool and fresh to him. "I'm okay. Thanks for asking. Any word from your Japanese friends on Andy?"

"Sergeant Oakwood is in competent hands. The gentleman attending her is a professor of surgery at the university here, and Gonroku-san's daughter is a highly trained professional as well. Rest easy."

"What the hell is goin' on?" Mulvaney looked into Osgood's gray eyes, watched the set of them.

Osgood lit a cigarette from his funny-looking cigarette case with his funny-looking lighter. "I'm afraid I'm not at liberty to divulge all the details. I imagine many of your criminal cases in Chicago have sensitive aspects which must be left unsaid. But suffice it to say, in answer to your question, that freeing Mr. Ellermann from his Yakusa or ninja captors is of paramount importance."

"Paramount—yeah, I know. Just like the movies."

"You mask your college background remarkably well, may I say, Mulvaney. For all intents and purposes, your mission hasn't changed. Mr. Ajaccio's nephew must be freed at all costs and gotten safely to the United States embassy. What more do you need to know?"

"Three little initials?"

"Ahh." Osgood smiled, exhaling smoke through his nostrils. His silk knit tie hung nonchalantly at half-mast, one of his black wingtip oxfords raised to rest on the edge of the stone bench. The hand that held the cigarette draped carelessly across his knee. "Wouldn't be the same initials that stand for Committee for State Security, would they?"

"The very ones. Gosh, you're smart!"

"True enough." Osgood smiled. He seemed to sigh, as if his patience were ebbing. Mulvaney's patience had already done that some time ago. "The opposition, as we sometimes euphemistically call our Soviet opposite numbers, do indeed have a definite interest in Mr. Ellermann. All I can say by way of amplifying on my remark is that their interest in

Mr. Ellermann is all the more reason that we should redouble our efforts to find him first. And as quickly as possible."

Mulvaney stood up. "What the hell kind of little superspy shit you playin', Ozzie?"

"Don't call me Ozzie, Mulvaney."

"Aww, gee. Sorry. So, what's the big picture, pal? Whip it on me. Go ahead. I can take it."

Osgood stubbed out his cigarette in the ashtray the old Japanese guy's houseboy had brought when Mulvaney had first lit up. "I can't tell you any more, Mulvaney. You of all people, with your background in Special Forces, should well know that intelligence information is disseminated on a strict 'need-to-know' basis, and that's it."

"You know everything about me. I don't get to know shit about you, right?"

"You may finally have captured the spirit of the thing, yes."

"You . . . you . . ." For once in his life, Mulvaney couldn't think of a good insult.

"I've been called 'smug' before. 'Sticks and stones,' as they say."

"Don't give me that Pee-Wee Herman routine!" Mulvaney snapped.

"Who is Pee-Wee Herman?"

"You live in the real world or what? You only stick your head outside your Park Avenue apartment every time February 29 rolls around?"

"It's not a Park Avenue apartment, but a rather charming A-frame which I designed myself on the shores of a secluded lake in Virginia. Does that satisfy your curiosity? No, of course it wouldn't. Let's see. I graduated magna cum laude from—"

"I don't care if you flunked kindergarten, Ozzie," Mulvaney said through his teeth, lighting up again.

"I know you're distraught over this dire turn of events concerning Sergeant Oakwood."

"What the hell you know about lovin' a woman? You're the kind of guy that loves himself so much—"

Mulvaney had to give Osgood credit, because Mulvaney never saw it coming, only felt Osgood's fist slamming into the left-side base of his jaw, felt his head snapping back and

139

his balance going. Mulvaney shook his head. He was sitting on the flagstones of the garden walkway, his palms flat on the stone, legs spread. His jaw hurt, but it didn't feel as if any teeth were loosened or damaged. "Long time since somebody got a sucker punch off on me like that."

"In answer to your unspoken question, Mulvaney: yes, you struck a nerve. Not that it's any of your business, but it will save your jaw the next time. My wife died, along with both our children. Say what you like about me. If I valued the opinions of louts like you—"

"Louts? You're calling me a lout?"

Osgood, rubbing his knuckles in the palm of his left hand, smiled. "It was the most charitable term that came to mind."

Mulvaney stood up, dusting off his pants.

"You're not going to try something ridiculous, are you?" Osgood asked him.

"Oh, gee, I don't know. It depends on whether you consider me kickin' the shit out of you ridiculous or not."

Osgood seemed annoyed. "Then let's get it over with quickly. I've got more pressing matters to consider. Give me your best shot."

Mulvaney just stared at Osgood. Old Dapper Dan didn't seem the least bit worried. "What? You one of these karate experts? I know all that stuff."

"I'm terribly impressed, and as you've no doubt detected, totally consumed with fear. Either commence your pitiful attack or shut up."

"Pitiful?" Mulvaney echoed.

"You do have familiarity with the word, do you not?"

"I was gonna let you slide. Now I'm gonna kick your ass."

"Then I suggest, Mulvaney, that you get about it quickly and stop wasting my time with your rather puerile school-yard vituperations."

Osgood stood squarely opposite him, appearing totally relaxed. Mulvaney made a show of snapping back his right, his left snaking forward in a short jab to Osgood's gut; but Osgood wasn't there anymore. Mulvaney's leading left foot swept out from under him, his balance going. Mulvaney caught himself, staggering back. Osgood didn't even look rumpled.

"Oh, you're a quick one," said Mulvaney.

140

"I'd appreciate the compliment more, but I'm compelled to consider the source. Meeting a man versed in all aspects of hand-to-hand combat face-to-face isn't like rousting a drunk from behind, I suppose. Perhaps you'd feel more comfortable with a blackjack?"

Mulvaney threw himself into a charge toward Osgood, but he'd already caught the pattern of Osgood's movement, so he veered right as Osgood veered left, colliding with him, Mulvaney's right fist hammering out, catching Osgood at the very tip of his jaw. Osgood fell back as Mulvaney threw the left hook; but Osgood's right caught his fist and there was a blur of motion, Mulvaney's feet leaving the ground, a momentary wave of nausea sweeping over him and the muscles in his left shoulder screaming at him: Fool! Mulvaney took the fall just as he'd been taught to take a judo throw and he rolled with it. He was up, shakily but quickly, to his feet.

Osgood was dabbing at his lower lip with a handkerchief. "You cut my lip. Does that satisfy your ego?"

Mulvaney moved into what he called his "kung-fu crouch" but it wasn't kung-fu. It was Tae Kwan Do, and he began circling Osgood.

"Ahh. Are you supposed to be Chuck Norris, Bruce Lee or Jackie Chan?"

"Shove it!" Mulvaney wheeled half-right, feigning the start of a roundhouse kick. Osgood reacted. Mulvaney dodged left, his left fist snapping out twice, catching Osgood in the face but not hard enough to put him down. Osgood was turning out to be a good counterpuncher, Mulvaney realized too late, catching a stiff shot in the jaw. Mulvaney's right straight-armed, the middle knuckles hitting Osgood's solar plexus, Osgood folding up and falling to his knees.

Mulvaney's left fist snapped outward and downward, Osgood dodging back from it, Mulvaney's hand connecting with the side of Osgood's neck rather than the jaw. Mulvaney felt his balance going suddenly, Osgood's fingers pressuring the backs of his knees. Mulvaney stumbled back, falling. Osgood was up. Mulvaney was up.

"Gentlemen!"

Mulvaney wheeled toward the voice. It was the bookish-looking guy, his hands lost inside the sleeves of a blue-and-black patterned kimono.

"This is my house."

"Forgive my unpardonable discourtesy, Gonroku-san." Osgood's voice sounded strained.

Mulvaney looked at Osgood. Osgood was bowing.

Mulvaney shrugged, made a quick bow and grunted, "Yeah—me too, Mr. Gonroku."

"The woman with red hair will live."

Mulvaney closed his eyes and bowed his head.

John Trench Osgood stepped from the very American shower and continued toweling himself dry. His jaw hurt only slightly, his pride more, he realized. There would perhaps be some slight discoloration, but there was no damage. Edgar Patrick Mulvaney had been the most challenging opponent Osgood had encountered for quite some time, and in a bizarre way the encounter had been quite refreshing.

Tomiko had left a fresh kimono folded and waiting for him, and Osgood slipped into it, coiling the sash around him and tying it at his back. He stepped from the shower room to the narrow hallway and walked along it, Gonroku-san waiting in the tatami-floored room at the corridor's far end, gesturing him inside.

Osgood dropped to his knees and then into a cross-legged sitting position.

"Your American friend is with the injured American woman."

"Your doctor's art is considerable. I had thought that certainly the girl would die, or at the least lose her arm."

Gonroku-san smiled fleetingly. "She is more Japanese than when she arrived, Osgood-san. I feel quite close to her. Since her blood type was neither yours nor that of your friend . . ." The smile came and went again.

"She is the richer for it, Gonroku-san."

Gonroku smiled again. "Mulvaney-san is quite enigmatic. My daughter confided the details of the transfusion to him. He shook my hand as though it were the handle of a pump, and then he said something about Sergeant Oakwood being destined to like raw fish. Then he ran off to be at her bedside."

Osgood smiled. "Love has found Andy Hardy, I believe." He knew Gonroku would understand the reference to the old American films because Gonroku's one vice, if indeed it could be called such, was a collection of videotaped American films that could be accurately described as vast.

Gonroku genuinely laughed. "I would not have detected a resemblance between Mulvaney-san and Mickey Rooney had you not alluded to it, Osgood-san." And then the laughter left his eyes and his voice returned to its more usual serious tone. "It is inexcusably rude of me, I know. But then, we are both men who have chosen a rude profession, are we not?"

Osgood didn't answer for a moment. But then he nodded, saying, "I suppose that is one way of putting it, yes."

"You appear to be in desperate circumstances, Osgood-san."

"As usual, Gonroku-san, your analysis is painfully accurate."

"It is not my wish as your friend to cause you pain; but perhaps through such unpleasantness can be found ease and comfort. You seek Tsukiyama Koji, do you not?"

"I seek someone whom Tsukiyama Koji presumably holds captive. An American of great importance to my country's security and to the security of your country and all free nations as well."

"And Mulvaney-san? He is an ordinary policeman, as I thought you mentioned?"

"Not too ordinary, really. But yes, you are correct. He and Sergeant Oakwood were at once to serve as a screen for my involvement and as bait to draw out the opposition so that I might more effectively be able to find the American whom I seek. What I am telling you, I shouldn't tell you. But circumstances dictate that I must. For some time, Sergeant Oakwood has been working undercover in your country to expose a highly placed figure in your government who is in league with the Yakusa. Someone who shields their operations and provides them with information. She has not conferred with Japanese authorities in the event that she might inadvertently alert the very person whom she seeks to expose. The object of her investigation, if it had proved successful, would of course have been to expose this unscrupulous official to the authorities and turn over all evidence that she had acquired so that it might in some way aid in his prosecution and conviction. The investigation began out of

143

a series of drug-related incidents involving controlled substances illegally being brought into Japan and sold to American service personnel here. It was later learned that these same Yakusa criminals were constructing a means by which greater quantities of these prohibited narcotics could be brought into Japan and shipped from your country to the United States. And then the Yakusa stumbled upon an American, the nephew of one of the most powerful figures in the Chicago Crime Syndicate. They endeavor even now to utilize this young man as a wedge against his uncle to force the man to deal with them. It could cause the greatest internecine gang warfare the United States has ever experienced. And, of course, would further exacerbate the drug problem in the United States and enhance the economic strength of the Yakusa in your country."

"Admittedly, Osgood-san, a grave situation. But not the sort of situation one might ordinarily anticipate would fall under the aegis of your principals, nor require the talents of one such as yourself."

Osgood wanted to smoke. He wanted to tell Gonroku the rest of the truth. He could do neither. His cigarettes were with his other things; the rest of the truth could be confided to no one. He spoke. "I can say no more specifically. But I can tell you, as I mentioned a moment ago, that the young man whom the Yakusa or the ninjas of Tsukiyama Koji hold prisoner is of vital importance to our nations. Far more so than this drug-related investigation might lead one to believe."

"You are a man of honor. You are my friend. Let the injured American woman stay here under the care of my daughter, a 'safe house' as it were. Allow me to initiate a line of discreet inquiry which may or may not prove to be of some minor aid in your quest."

"Gonroku-san, these men who—"

"Are dangerous? Of that I am aware, Osgood-san. Some say that I too am dangerous." Gonroku, whose hands had been finger-laced across his abdomen, swept his arms gently outward, palms upward.

Osgood very slightly bowed.

Mulvaney had fallen asleep at Andy's bedside. The Japanese girl, Tomiko, who was the old guy's daughter, had awakened him. After confirming that Andy was breathing well and seemed at least as alive as before, if not better, he had inquired if there were a place where he could grab a shower. When he had emerged from the shower, everything except his gun, his pants belt and the Milt Sparks carrier for the Beretta's two twenty-round extension magazines had been gone. A robe had been left for him and some kind of long wide belt for it.

He returned to the bedroom where he had originally been ushered, a bedroom he had been told he shared with John Osgood, and he stood now in front of the mirror tying the belt. When you tied a regular slip knot, the belt was so long that it trailed to the floor at both ends. He was afraid he would trip over it.

He heard Osgood's voice behind him. "Good morning. What are you doing?"

Mulvaney looked across to the far side of the room. Osgood was propped on his left elbow, reclining on one of the little mattresses the Japanese people used for sleeping on the floor.

"What the hell's it look like I'm doing?"

"I'm not sure. Playing dress-up, perhaps?"

Mulvaney ignored the remark. He wasn't about to start another fight, especially indoors. With the thin walls there wouldn't be a house left. He continued trying to tie the wide belt for the robe. Osgood was pretty good with his hands and feet. Mulvaney caught himself smiling. It was the best fight he'd been in for a long time.

"Mulvaney? Are you attempting to tie the kimono?"

"Yeah. I almost got it."

"Divide the sash into two essentially equal halves as you draw it forward, then wind both halves rearward so they meet at the small of your back, then tie a bow. That's the simplest advice I can give you."

"I was just gonna do that," Mulvaney laughed, following Osgood's instructions. He looked at himself in the mirror. "This looks stupid."

"They're amazingly comfortable, though. I frequently wear one for lounging about at home."

Mulvaney resisted the impulse to make a crack.

"How is Sergeant Oakwood?"

"I left her fifteen minutes ago and she was okay. Thanks."

"You're welcome." Mulvaney heard the sound of a lighter being worked, then Osgood continued. "Gonroku has volunteered his residence as a safe house for Sergeant Oakwood's recuperation. I think it advisable that his offer of hospitality be accepted. He's also volunteered to aid us in locating Peter Ellermann."

"What's the CIA doin' in a drug case?"

Osgood laughed.

Mulvaney turned around and asked him, "What's so funny?"

Osgood exhaled smoke through his nostrils as he spoke. "I'm only laughing because Gonroku asked me a very similar question."

"Great minds, like they say." Mulvaney grinned.

Osgood shrugged his bare shoulders as he stubbed out his cigarette in an ashtray beside the mattress. Then in one fluid motion he was out from beneath the quilt and closing a kimono around him. He tied his sash, then said, "I told you, I can't confide the exact details. Nor have I confided them to Gonroku, if that's any consolation. But we are running out of time. If Ajaccio doesn't shortly tell the Yakusa his intentions, Ellermann may well be killed. That would be disastrous. Every moment we tarry—"

"Tarry?"

"Linger."

"Naw—I knew what it meant. I just never heard anybody use it before."

"At any event," Osgood continued, lowering his voice, "the longer we . . . wait, the greater the possibility that the KGB, whom you seemed so interested in a few hours ago, will find Ellermann before we do. And you'll have to take my word for it, Mulvaney. Were the KGB to find Ellermann first, a disaster of considerable magnitude would ensue."

"Don't you ever use just regular words?"

"What?"

"I mean," Mulvaney said, "you always gotta find some fancy way of saying somethin' instead of just saying it plain. You know?"

Osgood paused, as if reflecting for a moment, then answered. "I have no wish to be evasive. But I might best answer your interrogative by posing still another. I have the distinct impression that you feel some compulsion to sound as if you had never completed third grade. Is this just your way of camouflaging yourself amid the denizens of the streets you prowl in the course of your policework?"

"Maybe." Mulvaney nodded.

"And now it's habit?"

"Yeah."

"I can accept that, regardless of how unfortunate it may be for you. I'll attempt to ignore the urban argot if you'll attempt to excuse my correct English. Fair enough?"

Mulvaney wasn't quite certain what he was agreeing to, but he agreed to it with a nod and a grunt. Osgood crossed the room and extended his right hand. "Shall we start afresh, then?"

"Right," Mulvaney agreed, taking Osgood's extended hand. The grip was solid without being a crusher.

"Excellent. Then I suggest we dress. It appears"—he gestured toward a small platform thing that was too short for a table, where two sets of clothes were stacked—"that our benevolent hostess has restored our habiliments with admirable dispatch." Mulvaney didn't say anything for a second. Osgood said, "She cleaned our clothes."

"Aww, shit, yeah," Mulvaney agreed.

Mulvaney hadn't asked what happened to the Jaguar Osgood had driven the previous evening. The car Osgood drove now was a 300ZX. Sporty and, unless the domestic versions were different from the ones in America, very fast; Mulvaney had given pursuit to a fleeing felon once who'd used a 300ZX for a getaway car after boosting a 'stop & rob.' Luckily the robber had been a world-class klutz behind the wheel.

"I doubt my contact betrayed the stakeout, and logic would substantiate that. Tsukiyama Koji was apparently looking for you, not for me, Mulvaney."

"The shoot-out at that importer's place? This girl named Helen set us up there, like I said. Tsukiyama could've been the Yakusa's backup."

"Interesting theory, and quite likely valid." Osgood nodded, downshifting as he took the car into a tight curve, upshifting out of it. "I told you about his grandfather, Tsukahira. I would assume—although Gonroku was rather closemouthed about it—that Tsukahira was the source of our current information. I doubt Tsukiyama Koji would be stupid enough to have his girlfriend return to her normal place of residence after what transpired last evening, but at least it may be a start."

"Let me ask you this," Mulvaney said, lighting a cigarette. "If this ninja guy—I mean the grandfather, the old dude—is so put out with his grandson, then why doesn't he . . . ?" Mulvaney didn't finish it.

"Kill him? I told you: the promise."

"Naw. I answered my own damn question. Even if he hadn't promised his daughter. I mean, all this family-honor stuff's fine, but it takes a lot to make you ice your own kid, any way you cut it. But I got a kicker for ya."

"Yes? And what's that?" Osgood smiled indulgently.

"What if our Yakusa buddy, Mizutani what's-his-name, doesn't have—"

"Mizutani Hideo."

"Right. What if Hideous doesn't really control Tsukiyama Koji, huh? What if the Yakusa's ultimate muscle went shopping?"

Osgood looked at him for an instant, then returned his eyes to the road. "What if Tsukiyama Koji is holding Ellermann for the highest bidder? Is that what you mean?"

Mulvaney opened the ashtray and got rid of the ashes he'd been collecting in the palm of his left hand. "We're playin' cops and robbers, right? Where I come from, there's always a chance that the old guy who's been the headman for a long time can get himself some real headaches from some Young Turk. So, what if the rackets in Japan aren't too different from the rackets back in Chicago? What if our little ninja buddy has bigger aspirations?"

"Aspirations? I'm impressed."

"I knew you would be, Ozzie. That's why I—"

"Don't call me Ozzie. 'John' is fine, or my last name."

"What do your . . . ? Naw . . ."

"What?"

Mulvaney made himself laugh. "I was gonna ask what your friends call ya, but then I realized it was a silly question. What would a guy like you be doin' with friends?"

"I sincerely hope, Mulvaney, that we bring this affair to a conclusion with all good dispatch. Then hopefully I'll never—" Osgood cut himself off. Mulvaney caught

Osgood's eyes, glued to the rearview mirror. Mulvaney twisted around in his seat. "The Mercedes," Osgood said calmly. "And the Volvo behind it."

A flood of thoughts filled Mulvaney's mind, things like: how did the Yakusa or whoever was in the car know what road they'd be driving along, and just what time to intercept them? Who was the informer? But there wasn't time to ask them. Mulvaney's right hand snaked back under his jacket, the Beretta filling his fist.

"What are you doing?"

Mulvaney looked at Osgood. "Just in case." He grinned, but not the kind of grin that came from any genuine emotion except the desire to cover up fear. He had learned, back in his Army days, that there were two kinds of people when it came to danger: those who were afraid and those who weren't. Those who were afraid could be broken down into two categories: those who were paralyzed by their fear and could do nothing and those who did what they had to do despite their fear. Those who were not afraid were more easily classifiable: nutballs.

The road was two lanes, well-paved, gravel shoulders on either side and, as it wound down toward the city, for long stretches bordered precipitous drops. They were entering such a stretch now, and as Mulvaney looked back again, the black Mercedes and the medium-blue Volvo behind it were speeding up.

"Fasten your seat belt, Mulvaney. And hold on," Osgood advised, downshifting, the engine roaring so loudly for an instant that Mulvaney thought they might be overrevving. The 300's rear end fishtailed as Osgood cut the wheel sharp, slipping them into the curve, upshifting, accelerating, upshifting again. Mulvaney unbuckled the seat belt he'd closed behind him and closed it over him, leaving his right arm and shoulder unfettered so he could shoot if he had to. In the passenger-side mirror he could see the Mercedes, coming fast, a glint of gray light on the dark-tinted passenger-side window. Suddenly there was no glass, just an opening with a man pushing something through. It looked like a shotgun.

"Guy's got a shotgun. Goes to prove what I always said."

"And what's that, pray tell, Mulvaney?"

"Gun-control laws don't do shit. All they do is screw the

man or woman who wants to defend himself. The bad guys ignore them."

Osgood laughed. Mulvaney looked at him sharply. *"Mirabile dictu!* Something we agree on!"

Mulvaney started to laugh, which was insane, he knew, because the guy with the shotgun would start using it in a minute. The rear-seat passenger window was rolling down now, another face in the window opening, no weapon visible yet.

"There's a particularly tricky stretch that runs approximately nine-point-five miles. We'll be entering it in seconds. That's when they'll strike. If you need it, take the P-38 I have in my attaché case."

"Thanks. I'm more worried what that guy in the back window's got. I don't see anything yet."

Osgood said nothing; then, "Look out—RPG!"

Mulvaney felt the acceleration before he heard it. His shoulders slammed into the 300ZX's seatback, his fist tightening on his gun, his eyes finding the sideview mirror. He could see it now, a Soviet rocket launcher being positioned to fire by the man from the rear seat of the Mercedes, the man halfway through the opening so he could operate the RPG.

Mulvaney hit the release for his seat belt, the little finger of his right hand working the power-window button down. He twisted his upper body through the opening as Osgood shouted, "He'll be firing in a second!"

"Not if I can take him out first!" Mulvaney shouted back. The Beretta was in both his fists, his forearms braced on the roofline.

Osgood shouted, "Do it now, Mulvaney!"

Mulvaney's right first finger pumped the trigger. The pursuing Mercedes swerved wildly, the shotgunner opening up. It looked like a SPAS-12 in the semiautomatic mode. Pellets of buckshot sprayed across the rear deck of the 300ZX. Mulvaney fired again—better trigger control, single action—and despite the swerving of the target vehicle, he made a hit, sparks flying as the 9mm jacketed hollow point skated across the hood of the Mercedes. The Mercedes veered into the oncoming lane. Mulvaney fired, the right-side headlight shattering, the Mercedes dropping back.

The Volvo was coming up fast, a submachine gun punching through the front passenger window, sparks flying as bullets tore across the rear deck of the 300ZX. Mulvaney almost lost his balance as he dodged, more bullets ricocheting off the roof. His left fist knotted into the shoulder belt just inside the open window, his knees all that held him as he swayed over the pavement, the 300ZX speeding on. He could hear Osgood shouting but couldn't make out the words. Mulvaney worked the safety on his pistol, almost surprised he still held on to it, then thrust the gun into the front of his pants, his right hand slapping upward, grabbing on to the shoulder belt. He started pulling himself up. More submachine-gun fire, the 300ZX swerving away from it.

He could hear Osgood now. "I can't help you! Hold on!"

But Mulvaney was already up, coughing, feeling like he wanted to vomit. But anger suppressed it. He held tight to the windowframe, Osgood shouting, "Thank God. I thought—"

"That asshole with the subgun's history!" Mulvaney had the Beretta bunched tight in his right fist, the safety wiping up and off, his right arm stabbing across the bullet-pocked roof of the sports car. The man in the blue Volvo with the subgun was leaning out to fire. Mulvaney emptied the Beretta toward him, the submachine gun spraying into the road surface, the Volvo looking like it was out of control, then zigzagging from one side of the road to the other, the front passenger door swinging open and the submachinegunner rolling out, the Mercedes trying to swerve so it would miss him, bouncing over the body, crushing it, speeding ahead. Mulvaney tucked back inside, the Beretta empty.

Osgood's face was a mask of concentration, the speedometer translating to nearly ninety miles per hour. The 300ZX fishtailed as they skidded into another curve, a mountain vista spreading out before them that at any other time Mulvaney would have considered breathtaking. But at these speeds, with the curves and the enemy still behind them, it was terrifying.

Mulvaney pocketed the empty magazine, ramming one of the twenty-round spares up the butt, working the slide release chamber the first round.

"Mulvaney—the RPG!"

Mulvaney was out the window again, the Mercedes about twenty yards back, matching their speed, the RPG coming into position, almost ready to launch, Mulvaney knew. He started to shoot. There was a puff of off-white smoke. He pulled inside. "They launched!"

"Brace yourself!" Osgood stomped the brake pedal and hauled up on the emergency. The 300ZX hesitated, then skidded rear end left. Mulvaney felt it as he braced his hands against the roof, the 300 starting to roll, the road surface ahead of them—where the car would have been if Osgood had taken what Mulvaney realized had been a desperate gamble—vaporizing as the Soviet rocket hit. A fireball—Mulvaney could see it as the car barrel-rolled past it, the windshield imploding, the rear window doing the same. Mulvaney's body hurtled against the interior of the roof, then all motion stopped.

"Out of the car," Mulvaney told himself. He tried to move. His legs and arms worked and he could still see. He looked for Osgood. Osgood's head lay against the steering wheel, blood trickling down from the right temple. There was a smell of gasoline. And if the car didn't explode, the guys in the Mercedes and the Volvo would be with them in a second, he knew.

He tried Osgood's seat belt. It wouldn't release.

The only knife he'd ever carried since Vietnam was in his blue-jeans pocket. He twisted around, to his knees now on the roof, getting the primary blade of the Swiss Army Champion pried out. He started cutting the tough seat-belt webbing.

Osgood was coming around. "Mulvaney?"

"Yeah—be cool. Don't move in case you busted yourself up."

"No, no, I'm fine. Save yourself. They'll be coming back."

"Shut up. I'm workin' on a life-saving merit badge, all right?"

Mulvaney could hear the sounds of brakes screeching. He knew the next instant he'd hear the sounds of high-speed reverses, or fast three-point turns. He was nearly through the lap portion of the seat restraint.

"Look, Mulvaney, I appreciate . . . appreciate your con-

152

cern. But if Ellermann falls into the hands of the KGB, the man in Hanoi will be compromised. And worse, the details of the prototype will be lost. And we can't afford that—do you hear me?"

Osgood was cool, but Mulvaney had seen hysteria before and Osgood was on the edge of it; oddly, though, Osgood seemed totally removed from his own imminent demise, Mulvaney realized. He had the belt cut, working now to get it away from Osgood.

"Take your gun and get out of here, Mulvaney. You did your good deed. I'll certify it with your scoutmaster later. Get out. Take my case. The extra gun and the ammunition will—"

"Shut up, man, huh? Tryin' to ruin my image?" He closed the knife, pocketed it, realized for the first time that he still had his gun, shoved into his trouser band. He started easing Osgood from behind the wheel. "Tell me if anything hurts."

"Everything hurts—but I'm all right. Get out of here, Ed."

"Look . . . John . . . we get out together or we don't get out at all. So shut the fuck up and start movin' your legs."

There was pain etched across Osgood's face, but he started moving, Mulvaney half-dragging him from behind the wheel, across the roof and toward the open passenger-side window.

"The case, Mulvaney. The case!"

"Tell me it's somethin' out of a James Bond movie and it turns into a helicopter or something, huh?"

"You're certifiable, Mulvaney."

"You're sweet too. Come on!" Mulvaney was out, the case in his right hand, Osgood's right hand in his left. He was dragging the man. The Mercedes was coming, the blue Volvo four-door right behind it. Mulvaney dropped the case and grabbed for his gun, wiping off the safety.

"I'm all right, Mulvaney. Get into the trees. I'll be right behind you."

"Right with me, man—I don't take wooden nickels." The gasoline odor was stronger now on the outside of the car and Mulvaney thought he smelled something burning, told himself he didn't.

"Damn you!" But Osgood had crawled from the car now,

was on his knees, his right hand disappearing beneath his leather sport coat, reappearing with his funny gun. "All right? What are we waiting for?" Osgood was up, lurching across the roadway, Mulvaney grabbing the case, running after him.

The Mercedes was bearing down fast, Osgood's right arm snapping out toward it, firing two shots with his funny pistol, the left headlight and the driver's-side mirror going. The shotgun fired from the front seat as the car swerved. Mulvaney threw the pistol up in both fists, the attaché case dropping to the road surface as he fired through the open window, a double tap, then another and another, the shotgunner just inside the door falling back, his weapon skittering across the road and onto the shoulder.

The shotgunner's face wasn't Japanese.

The shotgun was too far away, but it might be their only chance. Mulvaney grabbed up the attaché case and ran for it, the blue Volvo angling toward him. Osgood shouted from behind him, "Down, Mulvaney!"

Mulvaney hit the pavement, rolled, the shotgun less than a yard away on the gravel of the shoulder. Submachine-gun fire came from the front seat of the Volvo, the tarmac beside Mulvaney rippling with it, bursting upward in great chunks as he averted his eyes. He saw Osgood, the P-38 K in a "rock-the-baby" hold Mulvaney hadn't seen in years, Osgood's right fist resting over the crook of his left elbow, his left hand cupping his right elbow. The P-38 K bucked once, then once more. Mulvaney reached out for the shotgun, his eyes riveted to the Volvo. The right-front tire blew and the Volvo veered left and away from him. "Holy shit!" Mulvaney rasped. Osgood was better than he had thought.

Mulvaney had the shotgun and the handle of the attaché case in his left fist, the Beretta in his right as he ran toward the trees. Osgood waiting there, the funny—but deadly accurate, Mulvaney had learned—little pistol in his right hand, his shoulders slumped.

Mulvaney reached him.

"You all right, Mulvaney?"

"Pretty good. Yourself?"

"Shock, I think—I'm cold. Let's get out of here." Osgood started into the trees and stumbled to his knees. Mulvaney was beside him, the Beretta going into his trouser band, the shotgun and attaché case into his right hand. He hauled Osgood's left arm across his shoulders and got the man to his feet. "Get out of here. I'll hold them off, Mulvaney."

"Bullshit. I hate guys like you, always tryin' to grab all the commendations for themselves. Well, you zeroed on this one, babe." And Mulvaney was loping into the tree cover, Osgood hobbling along beside him still clutching his pistol, Mulvaney still clutching Osgood.

"Those guys," Mulvaney gasped, shock or delayed reaction starting to set in with him as well. "They were white. At least the guy I nailed who was usin' the shotgun."

"White?"

"Yeah. Who?"

"KGB. They're the only wild card in the deck—unless the crime-syndicate people have gotten into it."

"Chicago guys? Here?"

"You're a Chicagoan; you're here."

Mulvaney didn't say anything. Behind them, he heard voices. It sounded more like Chicago Lithuanian than Chicago English. As they moved up a defile, Mulvaney looked at Osgood. "That kinda solves that, doesn't it?"

"Indeed. Here! Stop here!"

They were parallel to some long, low rocks beyond which were the sounds of a stream rushing. Osgood shook free of him and started for the rocks, but Mulvaney was right behind him. Osgood scrambled over them, skidding down, his wingtips going into the water, but his gun clear of it. Mulvaney was more careful, the shotgun scraping along the rocks as he settled in beside Osgood.

"They'll come this way, Ed. What's the status on that shotgun?"

Mulvaney looked at it seriously for the first time. Unlike the gun he'd "made" earlier, this one was no automatic, but rather a Mossberg 500 police pump. Quickly he worked the slide release catch and edged the chamber open, a shell loaded. He tromboned the slide forward again, then set to working the shells out of the tubular magazine. Only four were left, plus the one in the chamber. "We got five." Mulvaney looked at Osgood.

"Envelopment of a sort? Hmm?"

"Gotcha—just don't shoot me, John," and Mulvaney was off, moving in a fast, low crouch paralleling the trail they had just taken, but heading back toward the road.

The face of his Rolex showed three minutes had elapsed. The sounds of Russian voices had stopped shortly after they had begun, but there had been telltale signs of movement in the woods around him, the snapping of a twig, the rustling of a pine bough.

Osgood had swapped magazines in his pistol, then reloaded the partially spent one from the dwindling supply of spare 9mms in his case. The full-size P-38 in his left fist, the P-38 K in his right, he waited.

If Mulvaney were any good at all in Special Forces, the woods sounds Osgood had heard were the KGB people. There would be no reason for them to have had Spetznas training. They were urban assassins dispatched from the Lubyanka, graduates of the school at Kuchino, working for the infamous Ninth Section, the Vodennaya Kontr Rozvedka.

And suddenly, his stomach still churning from the crash, cold still washing over him in waves of nausea, he saw one of them coming toward him, unseeing, from the edge of a bracken of pines.

Osgood tucked down, his mind racing. The silencer suggested itself as a solution. He possessed eight rounds of subsonic ammunition, but neither Walther was fitted with a slide lock. The silencer was for inconspicuous killing, one on one, not for taking out an adversary whose comrades were mere yards away in the woods.

He shook his head to clear it.

Osgood knew what he had to do.

He shoved the full-size P-38 into his trouser band, the smaller pistol into the outside pocket of his sport coat. He reached with his right hand to his shirt pocket, extracting the ball-point-pen-size B&D Grande. With his thumbnail he pried open the blade, slowly, so the click of the lock catching would be less likely to be heard. He told himself the rush of the water of the stream would mask such a tiny sound, would mask the sounds to come.

He pushed off his shoes, letting them fall into the sand beside the streambed. His socks were wet. Slowly he edged upward, peered over the top of the rocks. On the other side, the KGB hit man just stood there, turning his head right and left, his nostrils twitching as his lips exhaled steam. It was cold here, a wind rustling the trees as if to confirm the temperature to anyone who might doubt it.

Osgood edged across the rocks, his eyes focused tight on the Czech CZ-75 pistol in his adversary's right fist, the Grande in his own right fist.

Osgood was at the midpoint of the rocks now, drawing himself up into a crouch, a wave of nausea making him momentarily dizzy. He swayed, steadied himself. He shook his head, then edged forward again.

The man started to turn as Osgood hurtled himself forward, bringing the man down with a crunching of gravel, a gust of wind roaring through the pines at the same instant, masking the sound, he hoped. His left hand was over the man's mouth and nose as he hauled the head up and back, raking the edge of the Grande across the Russian's throat, slicing the carotid artery, blood spurting wildly into the wind, Osgood squinting against it, inside his head counting the seconds until unconsciousness. He reached five and slammed the head into the dirt. In another few seconds, death.

Osgood rolled from the body of his victim, wiping the knife blade clean on the tacky-looking cheap blue suit, searching the trees to see if he had been detected, the Grande closing in his hands, the P-38 K back in his right fist. With his left hand he took up the CZ-75, thrust it into his belt beside the full-size Walther, then hurriedly searched the man. A spare magazine for the CZ-75 loaded with 9mm solids. A package of French cigarettes, a book of matches stuffed carelessly inside. The matchbook was printed in both Japanese and English: "The Happiest Ladies." Osgood pocketed all of it, then looked about him once again and crawled back over the rocks, shivering, waiting. . . .

Mulvaney had almost reached the road before crossing over the path along which a few moments earlier he and Osgood had moved. He kept moving now, the shotgun at low port tight to his chest, five rounds loaded, the Beretta with fourteen rounds in it and one spare-loaded twenty left.

He had no idea of the number of men. Four at least was

his guess. Maybe more. The RPGs, if they had more than the one fired, would be useless in the dense woods. From a sufficiently safe firing distance, the target couldn't be seen. But the submachine guns were another matter entirely. He kept moving.

What had Osgood meant? The man in Hanoi? The prototype? And what were KGB killers doing roaming the roads in Japan armed to the teeth? And what did all of this have to do with Enrico Ajaccio's nephew with the Rambo complex? What did any of this have to do with running drugs out of Japan and into Chicago?

The wind was stiffening. Mulvaney was cold, still shaken, he realized, from the car accident. With his luck, he'd get whiplash, and his lawyer was thousands of miles away. And who could he sue? The KGB?

He kept going.

Barely audible over the wind, he heard the sound of a branch snapping. He froze, slowly shifting his eyes right and left, a subtle flash of movement to his right. There was the muted sound of human whispers. Mulvaney swung his left leg around, both feet planted square. He had the shotgun carried the way he always carried one when use was imminent, chamber loaded and safety off. It wasn't the safest way to carry a shotgun, and a sportsman would have been a perfect fool to carry one that way, but for a police officer, as he had been taught by his father years earlier, a shotgun was cold and ready or hot and readier, and fumbling a safety could get you killed because the shotgun only came out when things were already scary. Mulvaney shifted his right foot slightly rearward, bringing the weapon to his shoulder. At least the KGB had good taste; the Mossberg was as good a riot pump as anyone could ask for.

He sighted along the barrel toward where he had seen the flash of movement, heard the whisper. He heard it again. He touched the trigger, his right shoulder rocking with it, his left hand tromboning the pump, his finger touching the trigger again as he shifted the muzzle right and fired. There was a scream and a pine bough fell and a man fell after it. Another scream, somebody shouting something that was unmistakable as a curse despite the language barrier. Mulvaney was already running, looking back as the roar of the submachine guns came and pine trees and low bushes where he had been standing a second earlier were sawn and slivered. He kept running.

Osgood worked his way along the rocks, his sodden socks back in his not-much-drier shoes, the P-38 K in his fist, his second gun and the pistol he'd taken off the dead KGB man in the waistband of his trousers. He heard the shotgun fire, hoping it was Mulvaney, the submachine gun fire just after it, hoping it wasn't Mulvaney that was the target. Osgood had asked himself why Mulvaney had risked his own life and stayed with the car in order to cut him free of the seat belt and pull him to safety. And the reason was an uncomfortable realization for him. The brash and abrasive young Chicago police sergeant was one of the rare people Osgood had encountered in recent years who had struck him as, beneath it all, a decent man merely trying to cope in a world that was becoming progressively more distasteful. Although decency was an inarguably desirable trait, it was also a first-class means of dying young under certain circumstances.

Osgood stopped where the rocks sloped into the stream, protected on two sides at least, waiting.

There were thrashing sounds in the trees. He drew the second Walther and waited.

He would have to be certain Mulvaney was out of his field of fire.

The thrashing sounds became louder, then three men came into view, all of them in uniformly ill-tailored suits, two of them holding Uzi submachine guns, the third a SPAS-12 shotgun. Osgood stood to his full height. *"Tovarische!"*

The one with the shotgun spun toward him as Osgood opened fire with the pistols in both hands, the shotgunner going down, slamming back into one of the Uzi-armed men. Osgood took out the other man with an Uzi. The remaining man pushed his fallen comrade away, thrusting the submachine gun forward. Osgood placed a shot from the P-38 K between his eyes. The shotgunner was still moving, and Osgood put two shots into the back of his neck where the spinal column was. The body twitched. He looked to the first of the Uzi-armed men he had shot. Another bullet, this to the left temple.

Osgood stood there, the guns still raised in his extended arms.

And then he saw Mulvaney coming out of the trees, raising the shotgun as if to fire. "My God, man!" Osgood's mind raced. There had been nothing in Mulvaney's file to indicate that he carried with him emotional trauma from Vietnam that could have triggered this. "Mulvaney!"

"Down!"

It was a question of trust, something he never gambled on. But he threw himself forward and down, rolling onto his back as the shotgun belched over him, the roar of a submachine gun cutting across the rocks, the shotgun firing again, a man in a windbreaker with blue slacks and a turtleneck, Slavic features, thrown back from the far side of the stream and lost in the trees.

Osgood looked up.

Mulvaney smirked. "He almost nailed you, pal."

Osgood stood.

"I caught the Wyatt Earp act," Mulvaney continued. "It was pretty good, but with all the noise of your pistols, you couldn't hear number six coming up behind you."

"Seven," Osgood corrected, on his feet now, still shaky from the crash, chilled to the marrow. "I slit his throat."

"So you're one up on me this trip. Could I interest you in a used Volvo? If the price is right?"

"You're thinking what I'm thinking. Whether it's for vindication or retribution, we need to get back to Gonroku's rather quickly."

"We either save his life or kick his ass, I figure. Either somebody at his house set us up, or he's in deep shit. Andy's in deep caca too, maybe."

Mulvaney started to run. Osgood grabbed up weapons and I.D., shouting after him, "I'll be with you in a moment!" There were spare magazines for the Uzis and Osgood took them, stripping the men of anything useful, taking one of the dead men's jackets and using it like a sack for the handguns and magazines, the submachine guns slung from his shoulders. He crossed the stream, the shoes beyond help. He stopped at the dead man Mulvaney had gotten who had been about to kill him. He gathered up what was useful, then crossed the stream again, starting after

Mulvaney, not really able to run, the weight of the weapons he'd "liberated" bearing down on him. He caught up his attaché case as well.

Halfway along the track they had followed into the woods, Osgood stopped. There was another dead man, and just beyond him, still another. Again Osgood stripped them of what seemed useful. One of the two men wore what seemed to be a compatible shoe size, but Osgood rejected the idea. Better wet Florsheims than dry Bulgarian clodhoppers. He jogged on, hearing a horn sounding.

As he broke through the trees, he saw Mulvaney standing beside the Volvo, its engine running. "Come on!"

"Coming! Open the trunk."

Mulvaney apparently pushed a trunk release inside the car. Osgood reached the trunk of the Volvo. All the Uzis were in good condition. He kept out two.

"Hold on to just one of 'em," Mulvaney said. "I'll use the pump. There was a box of double-O buck in the car."

"Whatever. Shall we?" Osgood was pushing himself too far, he knew. But he kept pushing, starting for the driver's side.

"Let me," Mulvaney volunteered. "I mean, no cut on your driving, man, but I've seen stiffs on autopsy tables with better color."

"I can't argue with such insight. Drive on, Mulvaney." Osgood sank into the passenger seat, his attaché case going onto the back seat, his hands automatically starting to check the Uzi as Mulvaney popped the Volvo's clutch.

Mulvaney downshifted into second, cutting the wheel sharp left as he turned the KGB car into the driveway leading toward Gonroku's house at the top of the hill. Gravel sprayed up and audibly strafed the car's undercarriage. He stomped the clutch and upshifted, staying in third to get the maximal combination of speed and the torque necessary to climb the incline.

"You're a good man with a manual transmission, Mulvaney. What do you usually drive?"

"Got a bathtub Porsche I bought when I got back from Vietnam."

"Ahh—those are great automobiles."

"How about you, Osgood? What do you drive?" Mulvaney wanted to keep talking to avoid thinking about what might be in store once they reached Gonroku's house.

"I own a carefully selected battery, if you will, of vehicles. A Ferrari I bought about the same time you bought your Porsche, red of course—" Mulvaney laughed. So did Osgood. "I got it at a steal, you might say."

"With your job, I might believe that."

Osgood laughed again, but the laughter sounded hollow. "I also own a relatively new four-wheel-drive, a Jeep, actually. And then there's the motorcycle."

"You're a biker?"

"I'd hardly call myself that. But I own a rather stimulating—" Osgood never finished. The drawing back of the Uzi's bolt cut him off. Mulvaney downshifted rapidly, the driveway all but played out, the Volvo skidding along the gravel as Mulvaney braked. "What is it?"

"You tell me. Look at the wall just beyond the garden."

Mulvaney had seen it as they entered the last leg of the driveway, the house wall gone, as though bulldozed away. "Somebody burst through that wall. Out of the car!" Osgood moved quickly. Mulvaney stepped out and grabbed the shotgun he'd kept balanced between them, his left fist on the pump, snapping it, the action cycling as his right fist grasped the stock at the pistol grip.

"Right and left?" Mulvaney suggested.

"I've got the right," Osgood said emotionlessly.

Mulvaney didn't look at him, walking slowly ahead at first, then quickening his pace into a jog trot, the shotgun at high port as he neared the garden, snapping down into an assault position as he entered it.

The stone bench was overturned. Mulvaney dropped to one knee as he spotted a dark stain on the stone. He grasped the shotgun in his right fist, the fingers of his left hand touching at the stain. It was blood.

"Mulvaney! Over here! Quickly!"

Mulvaney licked his lips, rose to full height, ran, bursting through the already destroyed wall of the house, going for the sound of Osgood's voice. He ran along the hallway, into the large tatami room.

Osgood knelt over someone. For a moment Mulvaney

162

thought it was Gonroku. But it was the houseboy, or parts of him, his left arm and his right hand not attached anymore.

"Tsukiyama Koji," Mulvaney almost hissed.

"Yes, his handiwork."

Mulvaney ran across the room, using the butt stock of the shotgun to punch through the wall into the next room, the room where Andy Oakwood had been left to recuperate, the room . . . He stopped, the sounds of pieces of the wall falling behind him filling his ears as the pounding of his heart subsided.

There was no headless torso here.

There was no one at all.

"The motherfucker got her. Tell me what's going on, Osgood. Tell me now, dammit!"

Mulvaney heard Osgood's voice. "You have a right to know. Yes."

Mulvaney just looked at him.

Mulvaney had cleared the shotgun. Osgood loaded the magazines for his pistols. Years before, he had prevailed on Gonroku to store a modest quantity of ammunition at the house for him. He used that now.

"I'd be willing to bet the Ferrari that Tsukiyama Koji goes by another name."

Osgood lit a cigarette and held the Dunhill for Mulvaney.

"What do you mean?"

"Have you ever heard of an assassin, a contract killer, known as Dark?"

"What? Wait . . . uhh . . . shit, how long ago was it? Yeah . . . Vietnamese gangs. We had some heavy problems with them and then all of a sudden the leaders of one of the gangs all turned up dead. Throats slit, tongues cut out. We had one witness to one of the killings. All she could do was babble about something in black that had cut the dead men down. That it was an evil spirit. She was scared out of her mind. She died that night in the hospital. Suffocated."

"I doubt she suffocated. A killer who favors edged weapons and dark clothing has been popping up for the last five years or so. We see information from the FBI. He's been used to liquidate a number of Asian organized-crime figures. My own agency has encountered him, in Taiwan and as far off as South Korea. We code-named him Dark, borrowing it from the FBI. I think some things are starting to fall in place."

"What the hell's some damn Japanese assassin have to do with . . . ?"

Osgood exhaled, watching the smoke for a moment. "There have been some indicators pointing to a more-than-casual relationship between our mysterious assassin and the KGB. This Ellermann thing confirms it."

Mulvaney hesitated, and then all at once he seemed to spit out the words. "Who the hell is Ellermann?"

"During one of his forays into Southeast Asia, Peter Ellermann got as far as what used to be known as North Vietnam. By sheer accident, he contacted the most highly placed agent we have in Vietnam, a man in place ever since the days of the Vietnam war, an official these days of the Vietnamese government, a man of great influence, as loyal to the United States as either of us, a man of great courage. His name doesn't matter."

"That's a terrible thing to say," Mulvaney said, his voice low, sounding as if it were full of pain.

"Of course it matters. That's half the reason both of us are here."

"What do you mean? Maybe I'm dense, but you're gonna have to spell it out, Osgood."

Osgood did something he rarely did: he lit a cigarette with the one that was nearly burned out, inhaling the smoke deep into his lungs. "The man in Vietnam had just uncovered information that was of inestimable importance, but at the same time there was a purge of sorts going on. If our man had used his regular sources for getting information out, he would have endangered his entire network, one in existence for better than two decades. And he would have run the substantial risk of being discovered. I doubt seriously that he was all that concerned over his own life. He was perhaps more concerned over the possibility of the information pipeline, of which he was the head, being permanently shut down. He convinced Ellermann of his identity and utilized Ellermann as a courier, getting word out to us only with considerable difficulty through a man who was found nearly dead in Thailand. The courier provided us with all the information we have."

"Which is?" Mulvaney asked slowly.

"All right. Our man in Vietnam is very trusted, very well-respected, especially by the Russians.

"The greatest Soviet naval base in existence today—where would you say that is?"

Mulvaney considered the question, then answered, "Maybe that Archangel place up in the Arctic."

"Wrong, Mulvaney. It's Camranh Bay in Vietnam. It's the principal naval research station as well, once projects have reached the prototype stage."

"You mentioned prototype when I was getting you out of the car."

"I was delirious. And if anyone ever asks you, I was delirious when I told you all of this. The information is inside Ellermann's head, just as is the identity of our agent in Hanoi."

"What information?" Mulvaney asked quietly, lighting another cigarette.

"I don't mean to be annoying with this, but you'll appreciate the gravity of the situation more this way. How are Soviet submarines monitored? Their movements, I mean."

Mulvaney paused, then answered, "Infrared out of satellites, I guess. I read something in *Time* or *Newsweek* about it once."

"Very good—and for once I'm not trying to be patronizing. Satellites monitor Soviet submarine traffic by infrared emissions. And our vessels and those of our NATO and SEATO allies and some other friendly nations who entertain a certain amount of distrust for the Russians also monitor Soviet submarine traffic with sonar. Very sophisticated sonar, but sonar nonetheless. Do you have a solid understanding of the Stealth concept?"

"You mean like the bombers?"

"Like the bombers, yes. How does it work?"

"Some kind of paint, right?" Mulvaney snapped his cigarette into the garden, then apparently thought better of it. He stood up and reclaimed it, putting it into the ashtray Osgood himself used.

"Without getting into things neither of us could properly understand without a number of degrees in physics and chemistry, it appears the Russians are testing a prototype of one of their monstrously large nuclear submarines that is fabricated in a manner which renders it for all practical purposes invisible to both infrared and sonar sensing devices. If the prototype is successful, Mulvaney, it would be the harbinger of an entire fleet which would be immune from conventional detection systems utilized in our satellites, aircraft and naval vessels. Able to penetrate totally undetected to the very shores of the United States or any other free nation and fire its missile complement with total impunity, it would be the ultimate strategic advantage—perhaps enough of an advantage that the Soviets might well consider a first strike because so many of our missile installations and other strategic targets could be hit without warning. Their submarines could approach to within killing distance of our submarines and surface vessels and attack before any countermeasures could be initiated. That is why Peter Ellermann is so important, Mulvaney. I realize drugs are a problem of great magnitude, but if Ellermann is taken by the KGB, all hope of getting the information inside his head will be lost, and the man who originally obtained the information, our man in Hanoi, will be executed. The Russians will hold the upper hand. With the United States in possession of the information, they can't be certain we won't construct submarines similar to theirs, won't be certain of our abilities to creep in undetected to their shores and destroy them. Do you understand, Mulvaney, what I'm trying to tell you?"

Osgood watched Mulvaney's eyes.

Mulvaney said simply, "Yes." Then his eyes closed.

"I have no idea how close the KGB are to getting Ellermann, if Tsukiyama Koji has already closed a deal, or if he's still trying to play off against the Yakusa for some sort of confidence game. For all I know, it could be that Tsukiyama Koji is planning on retiring, that this will be his last gambit. If that is the case, he might be prolonging this to up the ante to as high a level as possible. There are too many variables."

"He's got Andy. He's got your buddy Gonroku and the old guy's daughter. And somebody Gonroku talked to turned us in to the KGB. Andy told me about following Mizutani Hideo to a meet where there was a government official she couldn't identify and a Soviet-embassy car. What if Tsukiyama Koji's better connected than we figured?"

"I don't know if I follow you, Mulvaney," Osgood told him.

"What if this government official who's been feeding information to the Yakusa also feeds information to the KGB? There'd be a lot of money in that. And what if he hired Tsukiyama Koji as his own muscle, just letting Mizutani Hideo and the Yakusa think they were working Tsukiyama? And what if he did the same thing with the KGB? That guy'd be able to get more money out of the Japanese mob and the Russians than Tsukiyama, even if Tsukiyama is this high-roller assassin you were talking about. It's the only way it makes sense."

"Then, if you're right, Mulvaney, we have to find the man in the government who's behind Tsukiyama Koji in order to find Ellermann and Sergeant Oakwood and Gonroku and his daughter. And we don't have any of what in your profession would be called leads."

Mulvaney seemed to be thinking out loud. "The place we were going when they ambushed us, where Tsukiyama's squeeze is supposed to live. If whoever tipped Gonroku to that set us up, as it figures he did, then on the off chance we got through the ambush, the address would have been a dead end anyway. You searched all those KGB guys we stiffed?"

"Nothing of consequence . . . Wait." Osgood began searching his own pockets. He found what he was looking for. "Here. What do you make of this?" He passed over the book of matches he'd taken from the man whose throat he had slit, the matches marked in Japanese and in English: "The Happiest Ladies."

"That's the place run by the white slaver Ajaccio tipped me to. I was there the other night. I muscled him a little bit. I was looking for whoever killed this girl Andy knew who worked for him, and also killed Andy's partner, Koswalski. The M.O. was the same, ya know? He's the guy that tipped me to Tsukiyama Koji being the hitter. This matchbook was on one of the guys that came after us?"

"Yes." Osgood nodded. "The gentleman who runs the

Happiest Ladies—I'd say he ought to be spoken with again. Perhaps by both of us."

"I'll kick his ass until he tells me who his fuckin' boss is."

"What's his name?"

"Right now it's Shinoda. Give me two minutes with him and his name's gonna be shit."

Osgood stood up, looked at his watch. Time was at once meaningless and vital, because there might be no time left at all.

The Happiest Ladies was more or less like all the gin joints Mulvaney had seen from Chicago to Saigon, when it wasn't in prime time. It smelled of alcohol and a few other things. Chairs were stacked on tables so the sweeper could get his work done. Glasses were stacked on the bar to be given a once-over and stacked behind the bar. Partially empty bottles were being filled and Mulvaney didn't want to know with what.

The guys from the other night—the doorman who spoke English and the bouncer with all the muscles—weren't in the main salon unless they were laid out behind the bar. Mulvaney considered that unlikely.

"Where to, Mulvaney?"

"The middle door in the back."

"What's behind the other two doors?"

"I didn't look. The two guys I told you about were outside and the main room was full of customers."

"Fair enough." Osgood nodded. Mulvaney had let them in, using the lock-pick set Osgood had sewn into the lining of the attaché case. It was the same kind Andy Oakwood had. There had been no security, no alarm tape. That it was what in Chicago would have been called a "protected operation" was obvious. Now Osgood drew his little gun from the shoulder holster Mulvaney had seen it in. Holding the gun almost as if he were holding a cigarette, Osgood announced something in Japanese and the bartender and the sweeper and the two busboys working in the salon all gave him their immediate attention, then started raising their hands.

"What the hell'd you tell 'em?"

"That life or death was their choice and the choice was

immediate," Osgood explained. The barman and the sweeper and the two busboys were all coming toward the center of the main floor with their hands up high over their heads. Mulvaney drew his gun, figuring he should get in on the act too. "Who speaks English here? Take a step forward. Now!" Osgood gestured again with the gun.

One of the busboys, about twenty or so and painfully skinny, stepped forward slowly. Osgood bowed toward Mulvaney, gesturing with his gun. Mulvaney walked closer to the busboy. "Where's Shinoda?"

"I don't know."

"You speak English real good?"

"Real good. You bet!"

"You're full of shit. Where's Shinoda?" Mulvaney thumbed back the Beretta's hammer and put the muzzle of the pistol at the tip of the busboy's nose. "I'm asking again. If I get tired of asking, my finger'll start twitching and you'll be dead. Where's Shinoda-san?"

"There!" The skinny kid nodded his head toward the three doors.

"The office?"

"No—the other place."

"Take me there. Now," Mulvaney whispered.

The busboy was trembling, but he started walking toward the door at the far right. He stopped in front of it, Mulvaney's pistol at the back of his neck.

Osgood's voice was low, full of menace. "What's behind the door?"

"I don't know how to say it in English!"

"Tell him in Japanese, boy," Mulvaney advised. The busboy began speaking, the words unintelligible, but their import readable on Osgood's face. The kid stopped talking. "What'd he say?"

"I don't know if I know the words for it in English either. There's a phrase that describes it in Egyptian Arabic."

"That'd do me a hell of a lot of good."

"You wait here," said Osgood. "Keep our friends company. How will I know Shinoda?"

"A scumbag."

"I'll know him then." Osgood stepped up to the door and opened it, then passed through, closing the door behind him. Mulvaney heard what he thought were animal sounds in the moment the door was open. It was thick, looked to be soundproof.

Mulvaney looked at the kid. "Get your friends over here. Now."

The busboy said something in Japanese. Mulvaney kept the pistol in the kid's field of vision just in case he tried anything cute. The barman, the sweeper and the other busboy moved closer, hands still raised. "Do they know what's behind the door?"

"Yes."

"Is it very bad?"

"Yes."

Mulvaney was silent for a moment, then told the busboy, "Tell the bartender to get me the club or whatever it is he keeps behind the bar. Just in case. Do it now."

The busboy spoke to the bartender, and the man, his hands still raised over his head, started moving toward the bar. Mulvaney herded the two busboys and the sweeper toward the bar as well.

The bartender crossed behind the bar and very slowly submerged, Mulvaney ready to shoot him if he came up with anything too interesting. But his hands rose first, still over his head, as he reappeared holding a policeman's nightstick. "Tell him to put it on the bar and then come around this side."

The kid translated and the bartender laid the nightstick on the bar and came around to the front. Mulvaney picked up the nightstick. "Tell everybody to turn around. You too."

The front of the busboy's gray washpants started staining dark. The kid said something in Japanese and one of the men started to his knees, but Mulvaney gestured him up with the gun.

They all turned around. "Now, boy, translate as we go. Tell them that a skilled police officer can use a nightstick like this in a number of ways—tell them!" The boy started translating. Mulvaney continued. "Such a skilled police officer can use a club to disarm an assailant, use it like an Australian boomerang to stop a fleeing suspect, even use it to inflict injury if necessary. A skilled man can tap someone on the head in just the right way so they go to sleep nice and peacefully and when they wake up all they have is a little headache. Or he can hurt 'em bad. Tell everyone to sit on the floor. Tell everyone that if they move or try to resist I might strike them in the wrong spot and severely injure them or kill them. You sit down too."

They started sitting, Mulvaney shifting the Beretta to his left hand, the club to his right. He'd never been ambidextrous when it came to use of the nightstick or a blackjack. When they all were seated, he hit the bilingual busboy on the head first, then walked behind the bartender, the second busboy and the sweeper, knocking each out in turn. He checked each of them. Pulse and respiration seemed more or less normal. He worked down the safety on his pistol, shoved it into his belt and tossed the nightstick across the room behind the bar, breaking some glasses.

He opened the door on the right and drew his gun again. And now he could hear the sounds.

They weren't animals. They were whimpering sounds. From people. Mulvaney started down the steps, the smell of disinfectant heavy, almost as heavy as the smell of human feces.

John Osgood's right fist tightened on the butt of his gun. He realized he was filled with fear. It wasn't fear for himself. He'd been up against far tougher men than Yakusa gangsters. But it was fear for what he might find in this subbasement beneath the Happiest Ladies.

The smell of hospital-strength disinfectant and the smell of human fecal material had assailed his nostrils as he first started down the steps. The stench had worsened as he reached the first basement, as had the sounds of women whimpering and crying.

In the first basement there had been shipping crates. Inside the shipping crates were various items of interest— chains, padlocks, dog collars, canned goods, cereal boxes and industrial-size containers of disinfectant. There had been one crate of M16 rifles with U.S. markings. Stacked in a corner there were marine batteries of the type used with boats and recreational vehicles, two of them hooked to chargers that were plugged into wall outlets.

He left the first basement and returned to the stairs, the sounds and smells of human misery stronger now, his fist tighter on his gun.

Shinoda, Mulvaney had said, was the man's name.

Osgood moved down the stairs, stopping dead as he heard footsteps across concrete below. He flattened himself against the wall, looking back up the stairwell, seeing nothing, starting quickly back up three steps at a time, reaching the first-basement level and then ducking back from the stairs, waiting.

He reached into his trouser pocket, debating whether he should load the solitary magazine of subsonic ammunition and attach the silencer. He did neither. Instead, he flattened himself still more against the wall, waiting.

The footfalls were loud on the steps now. He licked his lips.

The sounds grew louder.

He saw a bald head atop an almost neckless torso that was covered with an aloha shirt, muscles rippling beneath it. The figure attained the landing. Osgood stepped outward, but a board from the landing creaked and the bullet-headed man wheeled toward him. Osgood thrust the P-38 K forward, but not fast enough. The muscular man's body twisted left, his right foot connecting with Osgood's right fist. The Walther flew from his grasp and skittered across the floor. Osgood dove toward the man, his hands going for the neck that wasn't there, his right knee smashing upward. Osgood stifled a scream of pain as bone contacted what should have been testicles. The man's hands were on him, hammering at his shoulders. Osgood felt himself being picked up, the arms slipped around him at the small of his back for a bear hug that would snap his spine. Osgood's hands came free, and he slapped them both as hard as he could, cupped, over his opponent's ears. The bear hug weakened, the heel of Osgood's right hand slamming forward, missing the base of the nose as the man's bullet-shaped head snapped back and away. Osgood's hand connected instead with the base of the jaw. The bear hug loosened more and Osgood's left fist straight-armed into the man's Adam's apple, not hard enough to kill because he didn't have enough leverage. The grip released and Osgood fell back, sliding across the floor, but in the opposite direction from his gun.

The bullet-headed man's hands were at his throat and he let out a low moan like a wounded, angry animal.

Osgood was up, launching himself into a dropkick, his left foot impacting the big man in the chest, hammering him down. Osgood landed less than gracefully, the big man sprawled in the far corner of the landing.

Osgood looked to his right—his gun. He picked himself up and threw himself toward it, the big man already moving at the far left of his peripheral vision. Osgood skidded across the floor, his fingers reaching for the Walther, something grabbing his left ankle as tightly as if it were caught in a vise. He rolled, his right foot kicking out, the toe of his shoe contacting bone, the big man's grip on his ankle fading, Osgood's right hand finding the butt of the Walther.

He stabbed it toward his opponent, right first finger already drawing back.

Then the big man started to fall and Osgood's finger pressure eased. Mulvaney was standing there. Battery acid was puddling from a split-open battery case Mulvaney held. The crack in it was only marginally larger than the crack it had made in the bullet-headed man's skull, his eyes wide open in death.

"Lucky you happened along. If I'd shot him, it would have raised an alarm."

"That's Muscles from the other night." Mulvaney smiled. "Or that *was* Muscles."

Osgood was up, dusting himself off, inspecting his weapon. There was apparently no damage to it.

"What's Godzilla been hoardin' down here?" Mulvaney asked casually.

"Chains, padlocks, subsistence food, a case of M16s. Dog collars."

Mulvaney's face paled. "I take it you didn't get quite as far as the next basement?"

"You take it correctly. Let's go. There's a case of M16s here too, so watch yourself. But no ammo."

"I could go back to the car for one of the subguns or somethin'."

"No—although I may regret it. There isn't the time. What happened upstairs?" They were onto the landing and starting down the stairs, one on each side to minimize the possibility of creaks. "Put them to sleep, did we?"

"The bartender had a nightstick and I sort of couldn't resist. Talk about those feelings of déjà vu, ya know?"

"Right," Osgood whispered hoarsely.

Osgood, a tread below Mulvaney, reached the bottom of the stairs. In a second Mulvaney was beside him.

The sounds of misery were very loud here, and there were other sounds—the rattling of chains, occasional dull thuds. The smell was all but unbearable.

Osgood looked at Mulvaney. Mulvaney nodded. Osgood stepped into the open. He felt a wave of nausea washing over him. There were girls of virtually every physical description, their only common traits youth and, beneath the dirt and filth which splotched their skins, beautiful bodies. All of them were naked, collars around their necks, the collars fitted with large padlocks. Chains led from the collars to studs anchored into the concrete of the basement walls. There was straw, in pitifully meager quantities, beneath them. They squatted or crouched, huddled as close to one another as their chains would allow, eyes pinpoints of fear. There were roughly a dozen of them, and two men stood in the center of the floor, one short and stocky, the other thinner and slickly dressed. He spoke to them in stagy English. This would have to be Shinoda. "Some of you are being good. When you're *all* good, we'll clean you up a little bit. Let me ask ya. How many of you are tired of breakfast cereal twice a day, huh? Go for some chicken-noodle soup or some beans, maybe? How about something to cover up your body? How about a nice hot bath and a crapper to use?"

Mulvaney's voice boomed from beside Osgood. "How about I stick your face in one, motherfucker?"

Shinoda wheeled around, his stocky companion doing the same. Shinoda held a rubber truncheon in his right fist. The stocky man balled his fists at his sides.

"You . . ." Shinoda said the word as if it were a dying gasp.

"My name's Osgood. I'm afraid we haven't met. But I'm glad for the opportunity."

Mulvaney and Osgood started forward, as if of one mind, Osgood placing the P-38 K in its shoulder holster, glancing at Mulvaney, Mulvaney making his pistol disappear beneath his jacket.

The stocky man's right hand suddenly held a knife.

Shinoda and the stocky man—Osgood presumed him to be the doorman Mulvaney had mentioned—started forward.

"We need to know some details concerning your employer, Mr. Shinoda," Osgood said evenly. "We need to know who he is and how to get in touch with him. We need to know all that you really know about Tsukiyama Koji. But don't tell us yet. It will prove much more pleasant—for us at least—to make you tell us."

"I won't tell you shit," Shinoda hissed, snakelike.

"That's good. That's real good," Mulvaney whispered.

The stocky man with the knife—apparently some sort of switchblade—charged, Osgood snapping, "I've got him. Get Shinoda!"

Osgood dodged left as the man with the knife made his first lunge. Osgood reached to his shirt pocket, snapping open the little Grande knife. The stocky man started to laugh. "You're fucked now, man."

"I hardly think so," Osgood told him. The stocky man lunged, Osgood dodging, hacking downward with the comparatively tiny knife, slashing it across the back of his attacker's knife-hand wrist. The man screamed in pain, his knife falling to the floor. Osgood kicked it away toward the stairs.

The stocky man broke, running for it, Osgood after him. Osgood's left hand grabbed at the collar of his shirt, hauling him back. The knife in Osgood's right hand flicked downward across the back of the stocky man's right knee. The man shrieked in pain as he collapsed to the floor. Osgood's left foot snapped out, catching the man at the tip of the jaw, knocking him unconscious. Osgood turned away from him, drawing his gun.

Mulvaney and Shinoda stood less than six feet apart, Shinoda brandishing the rubber truncheon. Osgood wanted to watch.

Mulvaney spoke, his voice so low as to be almost unintelligible. Almost. "I'm gonna ram that thing up your ass. And I hope the girls enjoy watchin' it." Shinoda made to strike, Mulvaney letting him do it, back-stepping at the last moment. Mulvaney's left fist snaked outward, catching Shinoda on the right cheek, Shinoda's body seeming to vibrate with the hit. Mulvaney stepped in, his right crossing

Shinoda's jaw, then his left, then his left again and his right. Then another combination—a left jab, a right, then two left jabs. Shinoda's body fell back, the truncheon waving weakly, as if he could somehow force Mulvaney back. Mulvaney's left fist caught the truncheon in mid-swing, his right snapping forward, leaving a bloody pulp where Shinoda's nose had been the instant before. Mulvaney dropped the truncheon and grabbed Shinoda's expensive shirtfront. Mulvaney ripped, the shirt tearing partially away. Mulvaney's left slapped hard across Shinoda's mouth, blood coming from his lips now. Mulvaney's right grabbed another piece of the shirt, tearing it away.

Shinoda fell back against the far wall, Mulvaney's left jabbing at his face twice more. Mulvaney's right grabbed at Shinoda's left-front pants pocket and ripped, half of Shinoda's left pants leg tearing away. Mulvaney's left slapped at Shinoda's mouth, backhanding him, Shinoda's head slamming into the wall. Mulvaney's right closed over Shinoda's throat, his left grabbing the right-front pants pocket, ripping. Shinoda's pants were all but gone.

Mulvaney stepped back, turned half-away, then spun back, kicking Shinoda in the groin, Shinoda sprawling to the floor. Mulvaney was on him then, grabbing both his pants pockets and ripping out the seat of the garment. Shinoda was screaming unintelligibly.

Mulvaney took a step back from him and hammered the toe of his right foot into the center of Shinoda's rear end, Shinoda sprawling, screaming in pain.

Mulvaney picked up the truncheon from the floor. "Got a nice hard handle, Shinoda. Should feel real good to a scumbag like you."

"No . . . no . . . I'll tell you everything . . . please!"

"Not yet you won't," Mulvaney said quietly.

Under normal circumstances, Osgood would have stopped the thing. But he just watched.

Mulvaney leaned over Shinoda and tore the man's pink underpants away, then grabbed Shinoda by his hair and brought him up to his knees, then to his feet, slamming Shinoda's face into the basement wall.

"How's it feel, dogshit?" Mulvaney rammed the truncheon just exactly where he had said he would. Shinoda screamed, Mulvaney twisting. Shinoda slumped along the wall, Mulvaney keeping him standing, his right arm tensing and driving forward and upward, Shinoda bellowing in pain.

Mulvaney let him fall, Shinoda's hands over his buttocks. "No more . . . no—"

"Who do you work for, asshole? Or you want another ream job?"

"No . . . it's Tanaka Hideyoshi."

"Who the hell is he?"

Osgood answered. "He's a special public prosecutor designated by the national government to fight the Yakusa."

"Double dipper, huh, this Tanaka-san? Well, now tell me everything you know that I'd be interested in hearing, or I'll start again."

"Man, I need a doctor, a—"

"That's not what you'll get. Talk to me."

Shinoda, still holding himself, crying now, whimpering like the terrified women who watched from both sides of the aisle had whimpered, began to talk.

"Tanaka's been with the Yakusa for the last dozen years or so, feeding 'em stuff on investigations going on, like that, keeping 'em out of trouble. He almost owns Mizutani Hideo. He's the one that got Mizutani into drugs, 'cause before that the old guy never touched 'em, kept the Yakusa out of it. But Tanaka made the connections in Burma and Thailand and Mizutani Hideo's got the biggest dope business in the Orient now. But he's got too much product, so instead of just bein' a pipeline into Europe and America, Tanaka got him to start sellin' it here. Tanaka's been usin' Tsukiyama Koji as his hit man, using the ninjas to back him up. Made Mizutani afraid to try havin' Tanaka hit 'cause then he'd have this ninja freak after him and his family."

Osgood cleared his throat. "Tell us about Peter Ellermann and about the KGB people who were in your place the other day."

"KGB? I don't know shit about—"

"Too bad," Mulvaney said, looking at the truncheon in his right fist.

"No, man! No!" Shinoda started crawling away toward the nearest of the chained women. The girl kicked him in the face. Mulvaney hauled him back, starting to pull him to his feet, Shinoda screaming in pain. "All right. Mizutani put the bag on Ajaccio's nephew 'cause he was askin' tons of questions, ya know? Then he figured out who the kid was. And he got the kid talkin'. I don't know much more."

"The KGB men, Shinoda-san," Osgood reminded.

"Okay, okay, yeah. Mizutani uses this place sometimes during the days for meetings. He set me up here—it was his idea to keep the women like this, to do the whole thing, yeah. Yeah. It was his idea. I wouldn't do this kinda thing to no human being. He did it. If I didn't play along, he woulda had me wasted, man. Woulda wasted me bad! Mizutani had 'em in here."

"What did they talk about, Shinoda-san?" Osgood asked.

"I don't know."

Mulvaney smiled. "How about a little jog of the memory, hmm?"

Shinoda broke down into heavy tears now, on his knees, holding his behind, screaming instead of talking. "Mizutani promised the Russian guys five thousand M16s to pump into South America or wherever they wanted if they'd kill Tsukiyama Koji for him. Tsukiyama Koji put the bag on the Ellermann fella after Tanaka found out who he was. Word is Ellermann knows somethin' big and the Russians want him for it. The Russians agreed to ice Tsukiyama. Then Mizutani told 'em where Tsukiyama Koji was hidin' Ellermann."

Shinoda paused. Osgood rocked on his heels. He smiled. "And where was that, Mr. Shinoda?"

"I dunno! I swear to Buddha I dunno, man."

"Would Mr. Tanaka Hideyoshi know, perchance?" Osgood still made himself smile. It was a Mutt and Jeff routine, the sort of technique often used in interrogating difficult prisoners—the interrogator hard, the other man willing to ease the prisoner's woes if only he will cooperate, an ally against the harshness of the interrogator.

Shinoda said, "I dunno. I'm tellin' you the truth, man. But I figure he's gotta know."

"Is Tanaka dealing with the KGB as well?" Osgood asked quietly.

Shinoda's head fell. "I think he's a Russian agent or somethin'. I bring a lot of stuff into Japan and I get a lot of stuff out. Sometimes it's Russian, or sometimes it's goin' to

North Korea or places like that, or Vietnam. I asked Mizutani about it once and he near cut my head off and cursed about Tanaka bein' a son of a bitch."

"Sort of like the pot calling the kettle black, isn't it?" Mulvaney remarked. Then he looked at Osgood. "You through with him?"

"I think so. We can find Tanaka without him."

"Right." Mulvaney threw down the rubber truncheon and drew his pistol from the small of his back. "Good-bye." Osgood started to speak, but there wasn't time. Mulvaney pulled the trigger, Osgood's ears ringing with the gunshot as it echoed and reechoed off the concrete walls.

Shinoda was screaming. Mulvaney said, "Just figured you'd appreciate knowing what dying's about. Because you won't get it from me." One of the marine batteries, with cable leads coming from it and metal clips attached to the ends of the leads, was leaking acid onto the floor. "I figure Japanese prisons can't be too much different from U.S. prisons. Some crimes make even murderers and rapists pissed. They're gonna love you." Mulvaney left Shinoda whimpering on the floor, his arms and legs trembling uncontrollably.

Osgood swallowed.

Mulvaney walked over to the stocky man who'd had the knife, talking to the women as he moved. "We'll have you ladies out of here in a little bit. And just remember something. When you get a ticket home, use it. Don't ever be this stupid again, because a lot of girls like you never get a second chance."

Mulvaney pointed his gun at the stocky man. "Well, doorman. I have no special reason to keep you alive. Tell me where the keys are to unlock the little ladies from their dog collars. See, with this pistol cocked after that last shot I fired, all I gotta do is just wish and the hammer falls. Capeesh?"

"Yeah, okay."

"Go get the keys."

"I can't walk. He cut the back of my leg."

"Then crawl. Let's see you do it. And then you crawl through that slime and muck you've been keepin' the girls in and unleash every one of 'em. Then you drag your dirtbag boss Shinoda over there and leash him up good. Then do it to yourself. Move."

The stocky man began to crawl, Mulvaney meandering after him. Osgood began checking the women held prisoner to ascertain whether any of them needed immediate medical attention. They were all Americans, all of them scared to death, some of them too scared to talk or cry.

8

Alliance

OSGOOD HAD CALLED the English-language Japanese newspaper in Tokyo and spoken to them in Japanese, tipping them to what could be found in the subbasement of the Happiest Ladies. Then he called the U.S. embassy in Tokyo, and the Kyoto police about fifteen minutes later.

They had brought all of the girls into the upper-level salon and scavenged tablecloths and waiter's jackets and anything else that could conceivably be used as clothing. Osgood made the first call from Shinoda's office, then both of them left the women to use a public telephone on the next corner. They waited until the police and ambulance sirens came near, then drove off in the KGB blue Volvo.

"Turn here," Osgood told him, Mulvaney taking the left as the sirens started to fade in the distance. "Does it feel good avoiding the police?"

"A little. I saw your face. You really thought I was gonna shoot that bastard. Maybe I should have."

"I'll tell you something I've never told anyone," Osgood said slowly.

"You wear women's underwear?"

Osgood laughed. "No. I'm serious."

Mulvaney said, "What?"

"The principal thing to watch out for in my business—and the more I learn about you, I gather it's the same in

181

your chosen field—but the principal thing is that you don't become what you're fighting against. Does that make any sense?"

"Too much sense, maybe. Where are we going?"

"This is still the tail end of a business day. While I was waiting to make the second and third calls, I checked the address of the special prosecutor's office with the telephone listings, then called and confirmed that Tanaka Hideyoshi was in."

Mulvaney smiled. "Such a conscientious public servant. I think he deserves a visit so we can give him the kind of commendation he so richly deserves."

"We can't barge into a government building and use the same approach we used with Shinoda."

"Yeah, and anyway, I didn't bring the rubber billy."

Osgood just looked at him for an instant. "We'll have to follow Tanaka and wait until he makes it home."

"If he's into Shinoda's stuff, he might never go home. And by now he probably knows Shinoda's operation was busted."

"That's just what I'm counting on, Mulvaney."

Mulvaney took the next right when Osgood told him. Tanaka owned Shinoda and was using Tsukiyama against the Yakusa. And Tanaka was in the pocket of the Russians. Now the Yakusa was trying to use the Russians to take out Tsukiyama so Tanaka'd be naked enough the Yakusa could hit him without fear of reprisal. Tsukiyama, the renegade ninja, was the key to it all. International assassin, playing house with the Yakusa and Tanaka and at the same time trying to use Ellermann as leverage against the KGB. Mulvaney wondered if Ellermann knew just how important what he knew really was. Had he agreed to play courier knowingly? Or was he carrying the information somehow without knowing it?

The Volvo handled well, and despite the heaviness of the traffic, they were making good time. "If Ellermann had this information in his head, and knew it, Osgood, then why—"

"He was told he'd be contacted. He was told not to go to the embassy. A man like Ellermann, illegally entering Southeast Asian nations for military purposes—the embassy would be the last place he'd go. The idea, of course, was that Ellermann's information would be passed to us and the Russians wouldn't be any the wiser."

"Then their potential strategic advantage would have been even less," Mulvaney said, finding a cigarette.

"Exactly." Osgood lighted Mulvaney's cigarette and his own. "With any luck—and our scientists could still pull it off—a means of defeating their infrared and sonar invisibility could be discovered. Then if the Russians did creep in for an attack, we'd have them with their pants down. That's still possible. But now that they know we're aware of the system, even if we don't obtain Ellermann's information, their scientists will have to work on the same thing, in case we are able to come up with a similar system to make our undersea vessels immune to their detection."

"Why don't we just all declare war right away and be done with it?" Mulvaney suggested.

"Sometimes it seems that way, I agree. But with each day that passes, the potential for global suicide in the event of war becomes ever more apparent. I don't think anyone wants to push the button unless they can be assured of a first-strike victory. This new process could do that for the Russians. They already have it. It might take our best scientific minds years to duplicate it or develop a means to defeat it. If we have it, at least it should nullify their advantage. We hope." Osgood tapped on the dashboard. "Turn at this next corner. Right. Tanaka's offices are on the far corner."

"How we gonna pick one Japanese guy out of a whole street full of 'em?"

"Mr. Tanaka and I have met in the past. What part of Chicago do you usually work?"

"Central Division Tac. You travel a lot, but usually the South Side and the West Side. Why?" Mulvaney's cigarette was between his lips as he made the turn. There was a huge blue-tinted-glass-and-chrome office building on the far corner, an unintelligible sign running from the center of the building down toward the ground floors. "What kind of building is that?"

"Insurance. The reason I asked about your beat . . . well, the Orient had been my beat for the last ten years or so. Before Tanaka was appointed special prosecutor, he was a liaison man between friendly-nation secret services and his country's own. He was in a position to know of most major operations before they ever came off. He was, doubtless, invaluable to his Russian friends."

"That why you guys picked me and set up this whole deal with Andy Oakwood for us to be the bait while you held back?"

"Not entirely. If Tanaka's involvement in this thing and his involvement with the Russians was known to anyone, the information wasn't relayed to me. No; Tanaka was a trusted man. The reasoning behind my entering the country quietly was that we were carrying out an intelligence operation on friendly shores, and whenever that is done, you don't exactly go in with a brass band. Tanaka would have known I was in the country. I'm sure their customs and immigration people have lists they monitor. No; trying to keep my presence secret from Tanaka would have been the wrong way to manage things. It could well have been Tanaka that Gonroku approached for information concerning Tsukiyama Koji. And with what resulted, I wouldn't doubt that it was. Go around the corner and find a place to park. We'll walk back."

Mulvaney nodded, taking the next right. He found a parking place that he could glide into, then backed up to straighten out and give them room to make a hasty departure when Tanaka surfaced.

They got out of the car, Mulvaney running his hands back through his hair to get it out of his eyes, zipping the horsehide jacket against the wind. Osgood joined him, his coat collar turned up, his shoulders hunched against the wind. "This way. There's a McDonald's across the street from United Northern Casualty and Liability. You look like you could use a hamburger. And we can watch the entrance from there."

"What if Tanaka tries slipping out the back?"

"He wouldn't. He'll know about Shinoda's operation being destroyed by now, but he won't upset his daily routine. He may abridge it somewhat, but he won't radically alter it. His car will pick him up at the front entrance."

The Golden Arches loomed ahead, signs of civilization in a strange land. Mulvaney felt like kissing them. Osgood

184

went inside, Mulvaney following. Osgood pushed his hair back from his forehead. "So? What's good at McDonald's?"

"You gotta be jivin' me!"

"I've stopped in one before, of course, and I must say their coffee is generally quite satisfactory. I'm just not into fast food."

Mulvaney approached the counter. A pretty Japanese girl in the familiar McDonald's uniform smiled at him, saying in nice-sounding English, "Welcome to McDonald's. May I take your order?"

"You sure can, lady." He ordered two quarter-pound cheeseburgers, a large order of fries, a chocolate shake and a box of chocolate-chip cookies.

"You recommend the cheeseburgers—these quarter-pound ones?" Osgood asked.

"Yeah."

"Excellent. One of those for me, miss. Rare please."

Mulvaney looked at him. "Rare? They only come one way."

"Odd," Osgood said thoughtfully. "However, then. And french-fried potatoes as well, and a cup of coffee. Large, I believe."

She asked if they wanted it to go and Mulvaney told her no. Osgood vanished, sticking Mulvaney with the tab. Mulvaney saw him staring out the windows toward the insurance building across the street.

Mulvaney took the tray, balancing it as he got napkins and a straw for himself. He joined Osgood at a table overlooking the street. "Apologies for leaving you with the check, old man. What do I owe you?"

"I don't know. I just held out a handful of money and she took some of it and gave me back some change."

"My treat next time, then."

"Right. Eat your fries while they're hot. They taste better that way."

"When in Rome, eh?" Osgood smiled. It was clear that he had never opened a ketchup packet in his life. Mulvaney opened it for him. "Er, thank you. You eat in such establishments often?"

"Yeah. Beats eatin' in the car. I wonder if anybody sells pizza in this town?"

"I'm certain you could locate pizza, but I don't think we'll have the time now." Osgood nibbled at his fries, sipped at his coffee. Mulvaney was wolfing down the last of his first burger.

"What if Tanaka's already split?"

"Dubious. It would have been too much of a break with routine for him, would have drawn suspicion. As it stands now, no matter what Shinoda told anyone, his word would hardly be taken against a man of such rank and prestige as Tanaka Hideyoshi. He's in little danger from the authorities. But if he is aware of the fact that I'm in Japan and associates me with the Shinoda affair, then he'll realize he must take some drastic action. If you had a fellow such as Tsukiyama Koji available to you, what sort of action would you take?"

"Have him ice you."

"Precisely. Which means he has to contact Tsukiyama Koji. We follow Tanaka and catch him at the pregnant moment if possible. If nothing else, we confront him with the situation and get his cooperation, however unwillingly."

"You mean we beat the crap out of him?" Mulvaney asked through a mouthful of fries.

"Good God, no. For one thing, he'd die before talking. For another, he's very heavily guarded because of his role in combating the Yakusa."

"Right. So we just go up and knock on his door and hope he asks us in for tea?"

"Essentially. And he will if he knows we know he's there."

"You're puttin' me on," Mulvaney said through the first bite of his second burger.

Osgood gestured with a french fry. "You'll see anon."

"Anon?"

"Yes."

"Right." Mulvaney kept eating, working on the milk shake a little. Inside himself, he knew this was why one American could take on any ten foreign bad guys: American food. Selling cheeseburgers, fries and shakes overseas was possibly more dangerous than disseminating defense secrets.

"Here he comes," Osgood said casually.

"Great." Mulvaney nodded, looking out the window as

he stuffed the last half of the burger into his mouth. He gathered up his leavings, the shake in his right hand, the cookies down the inside of his jacket. As he approached the trashcan, he stuffed the last of his fries in with the hamburger and took a draw on his shake. He kept the shake with him as Osgood disposed of his food, downing the last of his coffee.

"What a novel if somewhat unsavory idea—busing one's own table."

"Yeah." Mulvaney was through the doorway and onto the street, sipping on the shake as he started back toward the car, looking over his shoulder toward the towering insurance building across the street. There was a glowingly polished gray-blue Mercedes limousine parked there. A distinguished-looking man with steel-gray hair and Barry Goldwater glasses stood beside it, conversing with a younger man, some kind of assistant maybe.

"The good-looking gentleman in the blue suit," Osgood remarked.

"I made his action. Let's get to the car."

"I'll drive this time." Osgood slipped behind the wheel, Mulvaney beside him, working on his shake. "All told, a hasty but satisfying repast. Thanks for recommending the cheeseburger. I gather that's their specialty."

"Aww, gimme a break, will ya?" Tanaka had vanished into the limousine, which was pulling into traffic, taking the same corner Mulvaney had turned. The Volvo fired up, Osgood ducking, Mulvaney doing the same, almost dropping his shake for his trouble.

"We're rolling," Osgood announced, the Volvo peeling into traffic, Mulvaney thrown against the seatback. The Mercedes moved through traffic as if the guy driving it was a frustrated jet pilot who had never heard of speeding tickets. The Volvo went right after it, through a traffic light, a policeman waving frantically at them. "The worst that can happen is the KGB getting a ticket," Osgood remarked casually.

The Mercedes took a left, the Volvo following. "Aren't you bein' a little damn obvious, Osgood?"

"That we're following him? I certainly hope so."

"He's speedin' up."

"So are we—rest easy." Mulvaney slammed into the

passenger-side door as Osgood took a tight turn onto an access ramp, the Mercedes about two hundred yards ahead and burning rubber.

The traffic was heavy here, the Mercedes weaving in and out precariously, the Volvo right behind it. Mulvaney braced the shake between his knees and went for the box of cookies inside his jacket. He got the cookies open. "Chocolate-chip?"

"Thank you, yes."

Mulvaney passed him the box, Osgood poking inside it, his right hand emerging with a cookie.

"Mmm, quite tasty."

"That's what I always say," Mulvaney agreed, taking a fistful and starting to munch. The KGB guys were going to have crumbs all over their upholstery if they ever got the car back, but it didn't really bother him much.

Traffic was mellowing out ahead, the Mercedes speeding up, the Volvo's engine roaring. Osgood upshifted into fourth after nearly sideswiping a truck. "Could I possibly have another cookie?"

"Sure thing. These things are addictive." Mulvaney passed over the box. "Try 'em with a cigarette. Makes the smoke taste good."

"Hmm, good thought, Mulvaney." Osgood lit up, Mulvaney doing the same.

"What kinda places you eat lunch?"

"I'll confide one of my favorite places. You may have tried it if you've been to New York. Oscar's—it's the coffee shop in the Waldorf. Delectable chocolate mousse."

"I don't like wild game much." Mulvaney grinned.

"Touché. The club sandwiches are good there too."

"I'll make a mental note." Mulvaney nodded. The Mercedes was accelerating now, the Volvo's engine sounding as if it were cutting out. "What happened?"

"Overdrive. The limousine's pushing eighty. So are we. You just might want to buckle up."

"Safety first—right," Mulvaney said through his cookies. If the drive kept up much longer, he told himself, he'd be seeing his cookies for a return visit.

"He's passed the proper exit—I don't know where he's going."

"Wonderful," Mulvaney said. "Maybe he figures the jig is up and he's makin' a break for it."

"Of course! Mulvaney, you're a genius!"

"What the hell you talkin' about, Osgood?" Mulvaney just stared at the man. Osgood was actually laughing. "You all right?"

"I'm fine, Mulvaney! Thank you. You're exactly right, though. He knows this car. He thinks we're the KGB and that we're pursuing him for some nefarious purpose or other."

"Took the words right out of my mouth, yeah." Mulvaney offered Osgood another cookie, but Osgood declined. He inspected the glove compartment to see if the previous users had left anything incriminating. He doubted they had. Aside from a few road maps with nothing marked on them and the car's owner's manual and a Japanese phrase book, he found nothing. He looked back to the road, feeling the motion more now that he had looked up. The Mercedes was still the same distance ahead of them, zigzagging between cars and trucks, making time. "How fast we goin'?"

"Ninety. I don't think the Mercedes has much more to give, Mulvaney. Not that size."

"What about this heap?"

"Another five or ten miles per hour will be hitting the limit."

"That's a comfort. Don't do anything exciting. I'm gonna pull up that rear seat and get that Uzi subgun and the riot shotgun just in case Tanaka's guys are really nervous."

"Good idea," Osgood agreed.

The rest of the pirated weapons had been locked in the Volvo's trunk, but after discovering the invasion of Gonroku's house, Mulvaney had opted for stashing what might prove immediately useful under the rear seat. He was over the seatback now, feeling the sway more as he half-knelt, half-crouched on the floor, pulling out the seat cushion. He had the Uzi and three extra magazines, the Mossberg riot pump and a box of shells. He rammed the seat cushion back, then clambered over the seat again, sliding down beside Osgood, grabbing the Uzi and the shotgun before bothering to belt himself in.

"Look ahead, Mulvaney!"

Mulvaney didn't want to, but he looked. The Mercedes was starting into an off ramp, but the ramp was closed, under construction, the Mercedes starting into it anyway. "He's nuts. That's no Jeep."

"When one finds apparent madness, there frequently is a method to it, Mulvaney. Be ready."

"You bet." Mulvaney checked the magazine tube. Loaded. He left the chamber empty, made certain the safety wasn't on. "I'll check the squirtgun for ya."

"Thank you."

Mulvaney checked the Uzi's condition of readiness, feeling it as the Volvo left the finished road surface and started along the under-construction off ramp, the Volvo bumping and jarring, Mulvaney beginning to regret the chocolate shake. He had thrown the cup into the back after finishing the last drop. The Uzi was ready to go. "Bolt closed over a full stick."

"Thank you. Look there."

Mulvaney had been trying to avoid looking at the pursuit, but he did now. The Mercedes was almost lost in a cloud of dust along an unpaved roadbed. The Volvo turned in behind it, Osgood activating the windshield wipers and washers, mud sloshing across the windshield as he upshifted, the Volvo fishtailing a little. "He can't go on much longer."

"Good thing. Neither can my stomach."

"Carsick? Just breathe deeply."

"If I breathe too deeply you're gonna need wipers for the inside of the windshield, Osgood." The dust clouds were starting to part. Mulvaney heard something overhead. He powered down the window, choking on the dust for a second, then shouting to Osgood, "Chopper!"

"What I feared, Mulvaney. He wouldn't have had this arranged in advance, in all likelihood. There's a helipad on the roof of the building. He must have called up the helicopter from a car phone after he realized he was being followed. How can a police officer get carsick?"

"What?" Mulvaney looked at him.

"I said—"

"Yeah. I'm fine if I'm doin' the driving. No offense. It happened with my partner, Lew Fields, once. After we pulled the bad guy over and made the collar, I puked."

"Ahh! Something to look forward to."

Mulvaney didn't say anything. The Volvo slowed, the Mercedes a hundred yards ahead, slowing as well. The helicopter became clearly visible as the waves of dust from the roadbed parted. A conventional Bell Long Ranger, the kind sometimes used as traffic copters, often for policework. It was green and white. And it was starting to descend.

"Stop the damn car!" Mulvaney had the riot shotgun in his left fist, his right hand on the door handle, punching it as the Volvo skidded, almost stopped. Mulvaney was out, the riot shotgun in both fists, his left hand pumping the slide. He threw the gun to his shoulder, firing, wishing he had slug loads instead of just buckshot. The helicopter was hit, backing off, slipping left and rising, Mulvaney tromboning the shotgun again, firing, the helicopter sweeping far out over the highway now.

A man with a submachine gun came out the rear of the Mercedes, firing. Mulvaney ran toward the Volvo, throwing himself down into the dirt behind it. Osgood fired the Uzi, the submachine-gunner from the Mercedes dodging behind the car. Mulvaney pumped the shotgun and pulled, peppering the left-rear quarter of the Mercedes.

Osgood was shouting something and Mulvaney realized he couldn't hear him because of the sound overhead. The helicopter was coming back. Mulvaney pumped the shotgun, shouldered it, but tucked back. The door in front of the fuselage was open, assault-rifle fire coming through the opening, bullets glancing off the rear of the Volvo.

Osgood fired back. Mulvaney peeked up, loosing a round of buckshot, then pumping the shotgun again, firing another round. The helicopter spun, assault-rifle fire plowing a furrow across the ground between the cars.

Mulvaney coughed, the dust so thick now he could hardly breathe or see. He was feeding more rounds into the riot shotgun's magazine tube, Osgood less than a yard from him ramming a fresh magazine into the Uzi. "He'll be making his break for it. You cover me. Keep that helicopter busy. I'm going after Tanaka when he makes a run for it to the chopper. All right?"

"Gotcha!"

Mulvaney stroked the pump, chambering a fresh round, waiting.

Osgood shouted, "Now!" Mulvaney threw the shotgun's

muzzle up over the rear deck of the Volvo and fired for the helicopter's chin bubble. There would be instrument packages near it, dangerously near if he could penetrate it. He worked the pump, fired again, assault-rifle fire coming at him, the rear window of the Volvo shattering, Mulvaney averting his eyes as he tucked back.

He looked to his right along the side of the car. Osgood, one hand over his eyes, protecting them from the dust, the other holding the Uzi, was running at a tangent between the Volvo and the Mercedes. The submachine-gunner and the classy guy in the blue suit were running for the chopper. It was starting to settle. Mulvaney stroked the pump again. As he started to look away, he saw movement beside the Mercedes. "The driver!" He threw the pump to his shoulder, the driver of the limo leveling an automatic pistol toward Osgood. Mulvaney fired, and the driver's body hurtled back as his pistol discharged into the air. Mulvaney was up, working the pump, running as he fired up toward the chopper.

As he fed more rounds into the tube, he could just see Osgood and the submachine-gunner bracing each other, an instant of silent appraisal. Then both guns opened up. Mulvaney threw himself to the ground, firing for the chopper again. It swerved away.

Mulvaney looked around. The submachine-gunner was down in the dirt. For an instant he didn't see Osgood, but then he did—hurtling into Tanaka in a body slam. Tanaka was down and so was Osgood. Then both of them were up, Tanaka in a classic martial-arts stance, Osgood going into the same. Tanaka charged, Osgood sidestepping, going into a roundhouse kick, missing, but driving Tanaka back. Tanaka's hands moved fast, Osgood rocking with a jab to the midsection, Tanaka's right knee smashing up. But Osgood rolled onto his side, leg sweeping Tanaka, the man in the blue suit down. And Osgood was on him, straddling him, fists hammering down at him.

Mulvaney worked the pump, throwing it to his shoulder as the chopper made one more pass, firing, pumping, firing, pumping, firing, pumping, firing. The chopper slipped left, heading for the horizon.

Mulvaney fed more rounds into the Mossberg's magazine tube, running toward Osgood and Tanaka. Osgood was hauling Tanaka up to his knees, backhanding the Japanese across the mouth. And then Osgood's pistol was in his fist.

As the roar of the chopper died, the menace in Osgood's voice grew. "You're the worst kind of traitor, Tanaka! Pious on the outside, a crusader for law and order, for Japan's rightful place in the world. And when everyone's back is turned, you sell out your own nation for profit." Osgood had Tanaka by the hair, the man's head bent back unnaturally. Osgood thumbed back the hammer of the P-38 K, putting the muzzle against Tanaka's forehead. "I want Peter Ellermann, and to get him I'm going to have to kill Tsukiyama Koji. Where are they? Talk, damn you!"

"It will do you no good, Osgood-san! You can never get him."

"Why? Because your rotten KGB friends told you so?"

"There is no hope."

"Then I had just as well kill you now, correct?" Osgood threw Tanaka to the ground and took a step toward him, the pistol at maximum extension at the end of his right arm, aimed at Tanaka's head.

"Wait, Osgood-san!"

"Then talk! Now!"

Tanaka's face fell. "All right, Osgood-san. Tsukiyama Koji holds Peter Ellermann. For me! If any force attempts to penetrate Tsukiyama's stronghold, Ellermann will be killed. And so will the lovely Sergeant Oakwood, as will be Gonroku-san and his beautiful daughter. You are not powerful enough to beat me! You can kill me. But you cannot beat me!"

"Where are they?"

"It is a small island on the northwest edge of the Musahi Banks. It is impenetrable!"

Mulvaney walked up to Osgood. "You through with him for now?"

Osgood only nodded. Mulvaney took a step forward and stroked Tanaka's jaw with the butt of the shotgun and put his lights out for a while. . . .

"The northwesternmost edge of the Musahi Banks is approximately a hundred and fifty statute miles off the Soviet coast, if my geography serves."

"Gee whiz," Mulvaney said noncommittally.

"Yes. It would be painfully simple for the KGB to mount some sort of operation to penetrate the island. Severe cold this time of year. Subarctic conditions, really."

"Sounds better and better all the time. Surprised I never won a vacation there. Thanks for lettin' me drive," Mulvaney added. Tanaka was stirring in the back seat and Mulvaney shouted to him, "Hey, Tanaka! Thanks for the loan of the limo, babe. Drives a little weird, but the seats are great."

Tanaka passed out again.

"Where are we goin', by the way?" Mulvaney asked.

"The only place we can go. Take that right and head for the mountains."

"Ahh—goin' for a Busch beer, huh?" Mulvaney took the right.

Tsukahira stood rigidly straight, his black skirts tossing in the wind. Osgood stood alone before him, Mulvaney back at the limousine. Tanaka had awakened as they started up into the mountains.

Tsukahira said softly, "Osgood-san asks that Tsukiyama Koji be killed. Tsukiyama Koji is already dead to me."

"Tsukahira-san. Your grandson is an assassin in the very worst sense of the word. He murders helpless women. He performs the bidding of anyone who will pay him. He aided Tanaka Hideyoshi in subverting the government of your nation. He engineered the kidnapping, the murder perhaps, of Gonroku-san and two helpless women. One of these two women was nearly killed the night before, by one of Tsukiyama's men—a man who masquerades is the guise of a true ninja. The other of the women is Gonroku-san's young daughter, Tomiko. During the war between your nation and mine, I am given to understand that you fought bravely."

"It was my duty as a Japanese!"

"It is your duty as a Japanese now to aid me in penetrating the island where your grandson holds his prisoners."

"We will walk together." Tsukahira turned on his heel and started through the niche in the wall, toward the tòrii gateway and the pond beyond it. Tsukahira's stride was long, yet carefully measured, as if at once combining

194

impatience with discretion. "He serves the evil of Tanaka, which you have spoken of, and the Russians as well?"

"Yes, as I have said, Tsukahira-san."

"Why is this man Ellermann so important? This I must know."

At the moment, Osgood felt he had everything to gain and absolutely nothing to lose, so as they circled the pond several times, he told Tsukahira all of it: Ellermann's accidental encounter with the highly placed agent in Hanoi, the agent's use of Ellermann as a courier for what was perhaps the most important defense information since the dawning of the hydrogen-bomb era. All of it.

When Osgood had concluded, Tsukahira stopped abruptly. "You may smoke if this pleases you, Osgood-san."

"Thank you, Tsukahira-san." Osgood lit a cigarette, noticing Tsukahira's eyes narrowing. "Would you care for one?"

"I have tried cigarettes occasionally. I will try one again. Yes."

Osgood extended his case to the man. The hand which reached out for the cigarette, despite Tsukahira's age, was without tremor. He took the cigarette and Osgood held his lighter for him.

"I know the island of which you speak. It is a rocky place, and very cold. The castle was built centuries ago by the Chinese. The castle dominates the island in all directions. The coastline is accessible only in certain places, which of course will be watched. But I will not arrange to get you there, you and your friend Mulvaney."

Osgood's heart sank.

"I will take you there myself. There is only one way in which to penetrate the castle, if you wish to do so before Tanaka's threat of death against the hostages can be carried out. One can only enter the castle as a ninja. Tsukiyama Koji's skills are great. He will have taught these skills to the dishonorable men who surround him. It will be very difficult and many will die. You and Mulvaney would be best advised to remain here under the guard of my ninjas."

"I must be there. I think I speak for Mulvaney as well. He is in love with Sergeant Oakwood."

"Then he is doubly foolish to participate in her attempted

rescue. His judgment will be clouded and he will become his own worst enemy."

"That may be so, Tsukahira-san."

"It will take at least twenty-four hours to prepare. Boats must be prepared, weapons readied. I will warn you: guns will be of little use. Those men of Tsukiyama Koji whom you have encountered were his best men. His best men will present themselves not at all as targets. You may never see them until it is too late. You and Mulvaney must cleanse yourselves."

Osgood was startled at the remark—then he smiled as the realization of its mundaneness struck him when Tsukahira continued. "You are covered with dust! And mud! Then you must eat and sleep. Then you must give yourselves over to me to learn the most basic of things which will keep you alive long enough, perhaps, to reach your target. I cannot make either of you ninja. But I can teach you how to move silently, how to see with all your senses. But I doubt that will be enough. I have no encouragement for you."

"I understand, Tsukahira-san." Osgood bowed slightly.

Mulvaney threw down the small towel and stepped into the hot tub. Osgood and the old man named Tsukahira were already seated. Osgood had told Mulvaney it would be a great honor to share the bath with this man. Mulvaney liked sharing baths and showers with women occasionally, but sliding into the tub with two other guys wasn't his usual idea of a good time.

The water was scalding hot, but Mulvaney eased himself into it quickly enough, his body shivering slightly. His eyes focused on Tsukahira. The man had to be into his eighties, but seemed as fit and physically imposing as a man half his age in good physical condition.

"So, Mulvaney-san. You find the water warm?"

"Just a shade, sir."

"Then cherish the memory. The island where we will go? The water through which we will travel is, at this time of year, colder than anything you will have experienced. If you do not die because your heart stops from the cold, then you will reach the beach. There the winds will tear at your cold skin and the clothing you wore in the water will begin to stiffen with ice. And so you must change that clothing quickly. But before that, you must hide in the surf until the sentries which Tsukiyama Koji will have put in place have been killed. Then! We will storm across the beach, up from the surf. You will find a place secluded from view from the castle above and you will strip to the skin and change into the warm clothing you will have carried with you. If you are fortunate, the water will not have penetrated the sack in which you carried the clothes. If you are not fortunate, then the clothing will be wet and again the chill of the wind will cut through you. Then we shall fly into the rocks, where the snow is drifted several feet deep at this time of year, moving cautiously through the crevices and silently approaching the outer walls of the castle. There will be traps for the unwary. There will be guards waiting for an excuse to kill. And all the time, the cold wind will blow down from the Arctic along the Sea of Okhotsk. And inside, you will be colder with the fear of death because death will be everywhere you turn and you will survive only by becoming death yourself."

"Sounds like a cheerful spot," Mulvaney said softly.

Tsukahira only laughed.

9

Invasion

"MOVEMENT IS WHAT BETRAYS. So! You must not move."

Mulvaney just stared at Tsukahira. An eighty-some-year-old man wearing an ankle-length pleated black skirt with a samurai sword and a killing knife stuffed through his black sash was telling him not to move.

"You must not move until you are ready to strike. The key is in the mind, to control the breathing and to control the muscles. There is a man in this room. If you do not find him, he will kill you perhaps. Perhaps"—he looked now at Osgood—"both of you!"

Mulvaney looked around the dójo. There were four walls, and there was an entranceway in two of them, the entranceways opposing each other. The other two walls held two windows each, panes of rice paper making them opaque, propped open though against the morning light. Suits of medieval-looking Japanese armor were ranked along the walls on both sides of the entranceways, swords, *sais,* edged tools that looked like primitive farm equipment, spears with trident heads decorating the walls. Bows, crossbows, knives of all descriptions.

Mulvaney saw no man. "I don't see him, Tsukahira-san."

"Ahh."

Mulvaney wasn't certain what that meant. He started to move about the room, looking behind the suits of armor, gingerly putting a finger inside one of them. He looked over his head into the rafters. He saw no one. "So help me, look already, Osgood," Mulvaney said.

Osgood began searching as well. Mulvaney glanced at his watch. If the key to invisibility, or Inpo, as Tsukahira had called it, was holding your breath, if he took long enough the ninja hiding in the room would have to breathe. Either that or there was no ninja at all and Tsukahira was giving them some other sort of test.

Seven minutes had elapsed and finally Mulvaney tired of the game. "I give up."

"In real life, you cannot give up, Mulvaney. Stand at the center of the room and look very carefully."

Osgood joined Mulvaney, who dropped into a crouch and looked along the floor in all directions, beyond where Tsukahira stood in the corner between the far entrance and the wall with the windows.

"Let him try to kill me," Mulvaney announced.

"Ed!" Osgood exclaimed under his breath.

From behind Tsukahira there jumped a man, clad in black as was Tsukahira, but in loose-fitting pants and tunic and hood, his sword drawn. "As you wish, Mulvaney," Tsukahira said.

"Tsukahira-san—" Osgood began.

"Let him come," Mulvaney said. The ninja approached in long, graceful strides, as though he were a dancer performing some musicless ballet. Mulvaney had gotten the point of the invisibility lesson, but felt that he too had to make a point. He reached to the wall, his hand moving blindly, his eyes on the ninja as he approached. Mulvaney's hand touched a sword, and he drew it away. He kept his hand moving, finding one of the spears. He pulled it from the wall. The trident, or *sai*, at the tip gleamed dully in the gray morning sunlight that passed through the open entryways and windows.

Mulvaney began moving the spear in his hands, twirling it, the *sai* at its tip slicing heavily through the air, whistling as it rotated under his hands.

The ninja slowed his advance, drawing the killing knife now, one edged weapon in each hand, both of them moving as though they had lives of their own, independent wills that had nothing to do with the man in whose fingers they flew.

Mulvaney stopped the movement of the spear, thrusting the tip of the *sai* into the wood of a support beam and pushing himself up, the *sai* breaking from the shaft of the spear as Mulvaney threw his body weight down. Only the shaft in his hands now, he began moving again.

"Mulvaney, you don't know what . . . how far this man—"

"It won't be far enough anyway," Mulvaney hissed.

The ninja flew up, the samurai sword pointed toward Mulvaney's throat, the killing knife in a guard position, the left leg extended. Mulvaney sidestepped left, then wheeled right, twirling the spear shaft, catching the killing knife at the blade flat and knocking it from the ninja's hand. The ninja sprang toward him again, Mulvaney kicking away the killing knife, moving the spear shaft in a lazy, wide circle in his fingers.

The ninja edged forward, thrusting with his sword, the steel singing on the air. Mulvaney went clockwise, the spear shaft still moving.

The ninja thrust, Mulvaney tossing the shaft hard right. The ninja hacked the shaft in half with the sword. Mulvaney threw himself into a body block against the ninja's legs and the ninja fell back, the sword skating across the polished wood of the floor.

Mulvaney was up, the ninja up.

Mulvaney bowed low. The ninja bowed.

Mulvaney heard Osgood breathe.

Tsukahira laughed.

Tsukahira raised three fingers, the middle three of his left hand. "Advance with caution to the left," Osgood said.

"Hai." Tsukahira raised the thumb of his right hand with a jerking motion to the right and looked at Mulvaney.

"Maneuver element follows its own Chunin, who'll receive a facial signal immediately prior to that at a tangent to the main body of the force."

"Hai!" Tsukahira held up his left thumb, with a jerk away from his body, looking at Osgood.

"The main force follows the Jonin ahead quickly because there is a dangerous area ahead which must be passed through rapidly."

"Hai." Tsukahira held up the first finger of his right hand

and made a circular motion with it forward. He looked at Mulvaney.

"The Jonin wishes the man designated as his personal Genin to move ahead alone and take out a target, then return or send word via his black cord."

"Hai." Tsukahira raised his right thumb, jerking it first right and left, then looked at Osgood.

"The Jonin wishes his two flanking Chunin to move off at tangents right and left for a flanking maneuver."

"Hai!"

Tsukahira looked at Mulvaney. He made what Mulvaney recognized as the universal gesture of a blade being drawn across a throat, drawing his first finger from left to right, ear to ear, over his own throat. Mulvaney said nothing. Tsukahira looked at him again, made the gesture again. "We both know what it means," Mulvaney said, standing, bowing. He turned and walked away toward the doorway behind him, passing through and stepping into his shoes.

He kept walking, the cold air feeling good on his bare arms, his sleeves rolled up past the elbows, his lungs filling with the cold air. He heard the sounds of gravel crunching behind him and turned around.

"What the hell is the matter with you, Mulvaney?"

"Profanity? Tsk-tsk, Osgood-san." Mulvaney found his cigarettes in his pocket and kept walking.

"Mulvaney!"

Mulvaney stopped. He didn't turn around. He heard his own voice but it didn't sound to him like his own voice. "Leave it alone, Ozzie."

"Getting me angry won't help you evade my question."

"Then I'll answer it. None of your business. Now, fuck off!" Mulvaney started walking again, down the hill toward the wall of the original enclosure, the practice-field garden between him and the wall and beyond the wall the pond or lagoon or whatever it was called. He could feel the anger rising in him. He'd told Osgood what to do, but Osgood wasn't the focal point of his anger.

He was the focal point of his anger. He kept walking, hammering the heels of his untied track shoes into the dirt and gravel, reaching the immaculately raked practice field, circumventing it as he aimed himself toward the opening in the wall.

"Mulvaney-san!"

It was Tsukahira's voice.

Mulvaney stopped. He turned around. He bowed slightly. *"Sensei."*

"Mulvaney calls me *'sensei'* and yet disobeys?"

"If you don't believe me, ask Osgood. I'm as good a man as you'll see in a fight. It's not bullshit. It's a statement of fact."

"I do not question that. I question this: Why did you break the *sai* from the shaft of the spear?"

Mulvaney answered him quickly, looking down at his untied track shoes as he did. "It was just a practice thing. I knew he was more used to that kind of thing than I am and I didn't want to see—"

"Mulvaney will not lie to me!"

Mulvaney looked him in the eye.

Tsukahira lowered his voice, his words slow and deliberate. "You wish to go to the island to find Sergeant Oakwood. You will not go unless you speak the truth to me now."

Mulvaney found his cigarettes, realized he was still smoking one, put them away, not knowing what to do with the nearly burned-out butt. To throw it to the floor of the walkway around the practice field would be a disgracing thing in the eyes of Tsukahira. He held it instead, the cigarette nearly burned down to his fingers.

Tsukahira looked at him, eyes unwavering, unblinking.

The cigarette was burning his fingers. Mulvaney held it.

Tsukahira still looked at him.

Mulvaney's flesh felt the searing heat. His skin was burning. He held the cigarette.

Tsukahira still looked at him.

"I won't kill with a knife or anything like it. I did all that once. I won't do it again. And if you don't want me to go with you, then you'd better be ready to kill me to stop me."

His fingers were burning.

Tsukahira walked up to him, reached down and crossed his hand over Mulvaney's left hand, taking the glowing tip of the cigarette between his second finger and thumb, holding it, then snapping his fingers, the cigarette crushed but still between his fingers, the burning tip dead.

"Did it all where?"

"Vietnam."

"How?"

"I, ahh . . . I was captured. Almost captured. They had me. I was out of ammo, away from my guys. My pistol—I lost that getting out of the firefight with all the guys that could still walk or be carried. I had a knife. A big Randall bowie. There were three of 'em. Either they were out of ammo or they wanted to play. They came at me with their bayonets. That started the whole thing. I killed one of 'em, cut the second one up badly, and he went for his rifle. And just then a bunch of their buddies came over the rise, started opening fire. I ran. They pursued me. Chased me around. It wound up ten days in the jungle. I got a gun after a while, killing to get it. An AK and plenty of ammo. But if I'd used the AK, I woulda brought 'em all down on me. So I hadda use the knife. You've done it, right? During World War II?"

"Before and since, Mulvaney."

"Then you know how it is."

"And the gun you carry? It is not that way?"

"No. It is not that way."

"To kill is acceptable, but only in certain ways."

"That's not what I mean."

"What happened to your knife?"

"I gave it away to a guy to take home as a souvenir."

"Do you think that he spoke of your bravery with this knife, or that he manufactured his own?"

"I don't know. I don't care," Mulvaney told Tsukahira.

"Why does use of the blade not affect me?"

Mulvaney thought for a moment, then said, "You grew up with it. Fighting with a knife or a sword was a way of life. It wasn't to me. Until then."

"But you fought well, unless the three men who attacked you were blind or crippled. Were they?"

"They weren't."

"Where did you learn this, then? I saw you with the spear, as you called it. Where did you learn this? Even the son of a ninja is not born knowing this."

"I studdied the martial arts when I was in high school and college and I worked with a tactical group in the Special Forces that had advanced training in hand-to-hand combat, so you could instruct indigenous forces in special sentry-removal techniques. If you grew up on the South Side like I did—"

"South Side?"

"Of Chicago. You learned how to use a knife. I was always good with one."

The wind was blowing harder and Mulvaney was freezing cold suddenly in just his shirt. Tsukahira seemed unaffected by it, unnoticing it. He spoke. "The problem you have will force you to solve it or die, I think. I think you will not die."

Tsukahira turned and walked away.

Mulvaney, despite the cold, stood there and watched him.

They didn't look like ninjas. No black clothing. Simply ordinary workclothes, gym bags and haversacks in their hands. The only odd thing about their appearance Osgood could detect was that not a one of the hundred or so of them seemed to have an ounce of fat on his body. And each of them carried himself as if he were more than human.

Perhaps they were.

Osgood stood, Mulvaney beside him, listening as Tsukahira addressed his troops. Osgood tried, as best he could, to translate for Mulvaney. The wind, which had gone unabated for the last several days, blew even more intensely. Osgood, in the same lightweight clothing he had worn the first day, shivered slightly. He whispered Tsukahira's charge to Mulvaney's left ear. "'I sought the path of honor, and found that the path was divided in two. So I stood at the joining of the two paths . . .'—something, I don't know the words—' . . . the path I took was that of a coward. I allowed an evil to grow and to consume much good. And so now we go. But I promise death to the man who takes the life of Tsukiyama Koji, for his life is mine to deal with. You know the rendezvous, my Chunin. Leave now.'"

The men, ranked before Tsukahira and filling the garden practice field to near-overflowing, bowed to him as if they were one man rather than over a hundred. Tsukahira returned the gesture, turned and walked silently away.

Tanaka Hideyoshi's right ankle was shackled to a stone weight that had taken four powerfully built young men to move into position. But beyond the chain of his confinement, he sat in comfort on a tatami mat in the corner of a comfortable, clean, well-lit room, a container of some liquid beside him, along with a cup and a bowl of fresh fruit. There was a dark bruise along the side of Tanaka's jawline where Mulvaney had struck him with the butt of the shotgun.

Mulvaney stared at him.

"It's finished for you now," Osgood said softly to Tanaka. "The papers are full of stories about the Happiest Ladies. Your man Shinoda is talking his head off because he knows he has no choice. What he's already said signed his death warrant with the Yakusa. His only chance is full-time government protection."

Tanaka smiled enigmatically.

Osgood spoke again. "If you cooperate, I can get the U.S. government to formally request that you be shown leniency at your trial."

"I will never stand trial. I am dead; that is true. But you and the other American have lost, Osgood-san. What Ellermann knows will be extracted and Ellermann will die, and your agent in Hanoi will die. And the nation I have served for fifty years will be closer to triumph. I will die an honorable death. You will either die in futile battle for a childish ideal or survive to live as a slave. There can be no victory for your stupid democracy."

"You used the Yakusa," Mulvaney began slowly, "the same way you used the Japanese government, as a tool for advancing your beliefs. That's all."

"Of course, stupid man."

"And what the hell was the Happiest Ladies for, then?"

"Money, Mulvaney. To defeat the capitalist system, one must use capital." Tanaka held to his smile.

"You couldn't have made that much dough off an operation like that," Mulvaney insisted, incredulous.

"It was all the rest of what went through there," Osgood said softly. "Wasn't it, Tanaka? Drugs. Guns. And the women brought you favors, brought you power when you sold them further east, didn't they? Some rich man with power who wanted a special order filled, and you filled it for him, put him in your debt."

"It had to be done," Tanaka said easily. "For the greater good. You, Osgood-san, and he . . ." Tanaka cast his eyes for a moment toward Mulvaney's eyes and Mulvaney met them. There was more hatred in Tanaka's eyes than Mulvaney had ever seen. "You are doomed. I will tell you nothing except this: you will find more than you seek." He laughed.

Mulvaney balled his fists. Osgood turned and walked from the room, Mulvaney walking after him, not looking back. Mulvaney found Osgood waiting outside, his shoes not on yet, lighting a cigarette. Mulvaney squatted on his haunches and started putting on his track shoes.

"When you meet one of them like that, it always makes you feel very strange," Osgood said, stepping into his shoes, standing on each foot in turn as he tied the laces. "The first of the old hard-liners I met was an American, oddly enough. He'd been an Army officer for twenty years, a decorated combat veteran. He was feeding information on surface-to-air missile sites in NATO countries to the East Germans. He said he'd joined the party in college and decided then and there that whatever it took to advance his beliefs was right and necessary and he would do it. That was why he had joined the Army, gone through OCS, devoted his entire life to being a good soldier. Simply so he could get into a position of trust and serve the cause he believed in."

"That's scary shit," Mulvaney said, lighting up. "I've seen movies like that. The old World War II movies with the Nazis who would do anything just to . . . Aww hell." He exhaled the smoke, listening to himself and hearing it more as a sigh.

"They can't be rooted out en masse. McCarthyism was an attempt at that and it almost destroyed the nation it was trying to purify, a cure at least as bad as the illness, perhaps worse. But each time you find one, you don't sleep well afterward for a very long time. Because you ask yourself about everyone you know, maybe even about yourself."

"Yourself?"

Osgood looked at him oddly for a moment, exhaling smoke from his nostrils. The air was cold, but Mulvaney was only aware of the temperature at one level of his consciousness, watching Osgood's face. "We formed an elite unit once. Seven years ago. I can't tell you the purpose. I shouldn't even be telling you that it ever existed. These were the best of the best. Every man who was chosen for the unit knew he was considered the best of the best. I'm not saying this to brag, but I was its tactical leader. I thought there were other men more qualified than myself and I said so, but they gave me the assignment. We trained, planned, trained some more. Finally it was time to execute the mission, and suddenly everything started going very badly very quickly. It traced back to a man I'd known for longer than I cared to remember. The mission had to be scrubbed and the man had to be killed. I was the leader. It was the only way to get the rest of the team out alive. Because as long as the man who had betrayed us lived, what was in his brain could destroy us. So I executed him, took my gun and put it to his head and pulled the trigger. We got out.

"Afterward, there were investigations, inquiries," Osgood went on. The cigarette snapped away, his hands thrust into his trouser pockets. "It was discovered that he was a mole. You're familiar with the term?"

Mulvaney only nodded.

"He'd been planted on us at the end of the Korean War. He'd been born in the Ukraine, been trained by the KGB, was substituted for an American POW. With the help of another Soviet agent, fingerprints on file in the Pentagon had been exchanged with his prints. He volunteered for the CIA. Passed every background test, became one of the Company's top case officers, moved into training. He trained me."

Mulvaney didn't know what to say.

The island of Changling at the edge of the Musahi Banks had been settled first by the Chinese, a warlord building the castle as a bastion from which he could defend the pirate ships he controlled, the pirates preying on the shipping within the Sea of Japan. The pirate warlord died when he was poisoned by his mistress. The story went that somewhere hidden beneath the castle was buried a vast trove of unthinkable wealth, the accumulated master's share of more than a dozen years of ill-gotten gains. Japanese samurai twice in those twelve years attempted to seize the castle by force, but never succeeded, the castle's defenses impregnable. The island was ceded by the Chinese to the Imperial Russian monarchy, under whose aegis it remained until the Russo-Japanese War of 1905. The peace then was mediated by Theodore Roosevelt, Japan having won the war with a resounding victory at the Strait of Tsushima— but losing the peace.

But Japan was given Changling. For services performed against the forces of the Czar, Changling was given in perpetuity to the grandfather of Tsukahira Ryoichi, himself one in the long familial line of ninja leaders. During World War I, it served as Tsukahira Ryoichi's grandfather's training base and as an early-warning post against possible treachery by Russia, which never came to pass. It was indicative of the low esteem held for this island that its name had never been changed to something Japanese.

During World War II, a young Tsukahira Ryoichi practiced his skills there under his own father, leaving and returning as missions for his nation demanded. It was on Changling that Tsukahira's wife died in childbirth. The child was a girl, and she would become the mother of Tsukiyama Koji.

Mulvaney sat between Tsukahira's son and John Osgood. Considering the similarity of the two men's English vocabularies, he felt like a Donald Duck comic book between two copies of *Roget's Thesaurus.* Tsukahira Nobunaga had been away on family business and been recalled by his father so he could participate as chief among Tsukahira's Chunin, almost himself a "deputy Jonin," were such a position possible titularly. When the young man—perhaps nineteen —had arrived and been introduced by his beaming father, Osgood had explained that Tsukahira's son bore the name of one of Japan's three greatest warriors. Mulvaney had contented himself with studying the young man's face and eyes and hands, the hands long-fingered, bony but strong, the face lean and high-cheekboned. The eyes combined amusement with lethality in a way few men Mulvaney knew could. Mulvaney had decided on the spot that if this son of Tsukahira's second marriage had been born in Chicago, the kid would have been either a cop or a hit man.

They shared a bench-type seat in a black van of American manufacture, Mulvaney happy to see that at least someone was still buying American vehicles. Mulvaney and Osgood had been designated as attached to Nobunaga's force,

Osgood having whispered to Mulvaney that this was a great honor.

"It will be almost exactly twenty-four hours before the force under my father's command is in position to strike. The nearest island to Changling is only five hundred yards off its western shore and it is to be assumed that Tsukiyama Koji will have posted men there to alert him to any possible invasion. But since the smaller island is so mountainous, if our approach is cautious, our vessels will not be detected from even the highest pinnacle of the castle battlements. The five-hundred-yard swim can then be accomplished in dead of night, considerably enhancing our chances for surprise."

"How large is this second island?" Mulvaney asked.

"Changling, Mulvaney-san, is almost perfectly oval in shape, the castle dominating the exact center, high atop a dormant volcanic cone. The rock is black, perhaps what first suggested that the island be given over to my illustrious great-grandfather. The unnamed island which will serve as our intermediate objective and which is vital to the success of our mission is less than two kilometers square, whereas Changling is five times this. Does this answer your question?"

Mulvaney nodded. "You ever get out of the ninja business, you'd have a natural talent for pitching resort property."

Nobunaga laughed heartily. "I like your sense of humor, Mulvaney-san. Perhaps one day if the fates are willing, I shall visit you in Chicago. It should be much like Kyoto."

"Only in some ways, Nobunaga," Mulvaney answered.

"Is our force the one which will be sent against the intermediate objective?" Osgood asked.

"Yes. But you, Osgood-san, and you as well, Mulvaney-san, need not risk yourselves in this endeavor."

"We're gonna do it, we're gonna do it. No sense farting around," Mulvaney said.

Osgood, after a second, added, "I would have couched it differently, perhaps, but Mulvaney's sentiment is inarguable. We got you and your father and the rest of the force into this. We won't hold back while others risk their lives to shield us."

"You could both be ninjas, I think."

Mulvaney shook his head. "Nice idea, but Chicago's got so many martial-arts schools now, the competition'd be murder."

Nobunaga laughed again and then it was as if he turned off, because he lowered his head, chin to his chest, and closed his eyes. Osgood raised his eyebrows and shrugged, Mulvaney shrugging as well. Mulvaney closed his eyes. He had been told the first stage of the journey to the island—the van ride—would take approximately four hours, and less than an hour of that had passed. Mulvaney told himself to sleep. He scrunched his eyes closed like he used to do when he was a kid, trying to will himself to sleep. Was Andy Oakwood alive? And if by some miracle he got her out and he got out as well, what would happen to them after that? He had told her he loved her. She had said the same to him.

The same words had been exchanged before. He had told Stella that and gotten into her pants because of it. She had told him that as a way of letting him in. But it wasn't only words this time, he felt.

Ajaccio. Ellermann. Tsukiyama. Tanaka. But there was one name missing. One name. He had to find that name, and thinking about it, he felt sleep starting to come and let it wash over him, hoping it would stay, because the longer he thought about it, the more he thought he knew that other name. . . .

At Himi, on the Toyama Wan, Osgood exited the black van. It was already appreciably colder. To his left, beyond the peninsula of land which rose like a serpent's head from the center of Honshu into the Sea of Japan, the sun was starting its rapid winter decline. There had been little heat in the van, but it had been warm enough that Osgood had removed the navy-blue seaman's coat he had been given. In this isolated spot there had been no need to don it again in order to conceal his shoulder holster, but he slipped into it now against the wind and the coming of the night chill.

Mulvaney jumped out of the van to the ground beside him.

It was a gravel pit, the sides gently sloping to form the dish, the gravel crunching under their boots they walked, each man lighting a cigarette, Osgood saying to Mulvaney jokingly, "It appears Tsukahira-san's son is quite taken with your humor. To the good, I think."

"You tell jokes or you get to thinkin' how you're gonna get killed and you go nutso."

"I suppose you're right. Gallows humor."

"Yeah, call it that."

"No jokes then for a moment, all right?"

"All right. Gonna whip somethin' serious on me?" Mulvaney said straight-faced.

"No jokes. Remember?"

"No jokes."

Osgood hesitated. "I hope you and Sergeant Oakwood are able to get out of this together alive. Real things in life—friendship, respect—they're difficult to come by and too easy to lose. Or ignore, for that matter. So. I wanted to tell you this. The business with my old trainer, about me having to kill him. Since that time . . . Hell."

"What?" Mulvaney asked.

"Since that time, I've never worked with a partner of any sort. I wouldn't place my trust in anyone. But I wanted to tell you, before we go and get ourselves killed, that for some insane reason I can't even begin to fathom, I trust you. So there, Mulvaney. Now laugh."

"I'm not laughing," Mulvaney said, extending his hand. Osgood took it.

"I've got a partner back in Chicago. Lew Fields. He's my best friend and the only guy I'd trust with my life. Used to be the only guy I trusted that way, anyway."

They still clasped hands, Osgood saying after a moment, his voice tight-sounding to him, "So. That's said."

"Right. That's said."

They released hands. Osgood took the cigarette case from the pocket of his borrowed coat. "Cigarette, Ed?"

"Thank you, John." Mulvaney took one, offering his lighter, Osgood taking a light from it, then Mulvaney doing the same. "You're a damn good shot with that little gun of yours. First time I saw it, I thought it was a kinda weird choice. Goes to show, you live and learn."

"I like that Beretta of yours. I think the U.S. military made a wise choice shifting to it."

Osgood stopped talking and so did Mulvaney.

Osgood turned toward the sunset and watched it, realizing after a few seconds that Ed Mulvaney had done the same. In the distance, Osgood heard the beating of helicopter rotor blades on cold air, a helicopter that would take them to the far side of Okujiri to where the boats would meet them. But he didn't turn to face the helicopter, instead enjoying his cigarette and a rare feeling for him—camaraderie. . . .

The helicopter touched down, Mulvaney first out the door after the pilot, Osgood and Tsukahira Nobunaga following, Mulvaney shouldering his knapsack and running from beneath the blades as the chopper went airborne again, another pickup scheduled. Portable generators were everywhere, powering arc lamps that made the beach as bright as if a full moon shone. Breakers crashed over the seawall some two hundred yards out, the seawall coated with huge dollops of white crystalline ice which drizzled from the gray stones like frosting on a birthday cake, catching the light of the arc lamps and the headlights of the vehicles.

It was bitter cold. Mulvaney was grateful for the borrowed gloves and the borrowed sweater beneath his horsehide jacket. Powerboats, their outboard engines turned up to spare the propellers, were beached in the wild surf, men in yellow slickers attending to them, moving equipment from the pickup trucks and vans which would park at the boundary of the surf, their contents then disgorged. Then the trucks would move along the beach and up toward another landing site where material already stacked and waiting was shifted aboard.

"This is quite an extensive operation, Nobunaga!" Osgood shouted over the roar of the surf.

The young man nodded, huddling his neck deeper into the fur collar of his leather jacket. He shouted back, "The family owns many businesses which are modestly profitable. The helicopters are utilized by the businesses. The rolling stock was negotiated locally. Some of the additional boats needed to be purchased. Moving one hundred men and their equipment into battle requires a considerable logistics effort. Fortunately, ninjas travel light." He grinned and gestured for them to accompany him.

Mulvaney lighted a cigarette after pulling off his gloves,

then pulled them back on. There was a large lean-to set up at the rear of a vehicle that looked for all the world like a U.S. Army 2½-ton truck. A roaring fire blazed a few yards from that. Some of the ninjas were there dispensing hot drinks. Mulvaney quickened his pace.

They reached the lean-to, the shelter providing little break from the wind. The scene reminded him of something from a Japanese monster movie, the men and equipment busily moving into position, unintelligible orders shouted. All that was missing was some kid running around talking about how the flying radioactive turtle shouldn't be destroyed.

Mulvaney took a Styrofoam cup—it smelled like tea— and raised it to his lips, toasting, "Here's to 'Gamara' and 'Godzilla,' gentlemen."

Osgood started to laugh, nearly spilling his tea. Nobunaga downed the liquid in a single gulp, as if it weren't hot at all, saying, "We will board the vessel which will transport us to within striking distance of the island in"—he consulted a Rolex with black face and stainless-steel case and band— "in exactly fifteen minutes. It is not one of these on the beach, but a larger craft. We will utilize rafts after we leave the craft to get us nearer to the coast of the small island, then into the water. You are strong swimmers? The seas will be heavy, the latest weather information indicates."

"How about the temperatures?" Osgood asked, lighting a cigarette.

"In degrees Fahrenheit, the surface temperature on the land should be in the lower thirties until well after midnight, when of course it will drop to the predawn low. Somewhere in the upper teens. Colder weather is expected tomorrow, and the temperature is anticipated to rise only slightly if at all. And, of course, there is a wind-chill factor to be considered."

"You have scuba gear, then, to get us in?" Osgood asked.

"The ninja invented scuba gear, gentlemen." Nobunaga smiled. "It is my turn for jocularity!" He laughed, then turned away and gestured them after him. Mulvaney fell in, Osgood beside him, Nobunaga leaving the modest shelter of the lean-to and going around toward the front of the truck. There was a Toyota Land Cruiser parked there and he climbed aboard, Mulvaney dropping into the back seat,

Osgood sitting beside Nobunaga. The vehicle started across the beach and down into the surf toward where the material being loaded aboard the boats was stacked just after off-loading from the trucks and vans.

Nobunaga edged the Land Cruiser back up from the surf and hopped out, Osgood after him, Mulvaney following. Nobunaga made his way toward where a smallish man was inspecting crates the size of children's coffins.

Mulvaney looked inside the crates. Edged weapons, full-size *katanas* and the smaller *shutos*, or killing knives, each pair wrapped in a sash of red, strikingly blood-red in color against the black of the sheaths for the blades. Japanese characters were scrawled in black ink on white paper, the paper tied to the sash with thread. Nobunaga was apparently looking for a special pair. He found them and took them from one of the crates.

"This may look like a samurai sword, but it is really a special ninja sword," Nobunaga said, not drawing the blade, but holding the tied-together sheathed blades in both upraised palms. "The scabbard is specially constructed to be longer than the actual blade, and made of the finest materials so it too can be utilized as a weapon if needed. The *tsuba*, as you can see clearly, is devoid of decoration and is larger and rectangular in shape, allowing its use as a foothold. The cord attached to the haft has many potential uses. But you gentlemen will find the double open-endedness most interesting of all."

"Like a hollow reed," Osgood said, as if thinking aloud.

"Bravo, Osgood-san! A snorkel. We do not need scuba gear!"

"Aww, wonderful." Mulvaney nodded.

Nobunaga handed over the sheathed blades to Mulvaney. Mulvaney inspected them, handed them back. . . .

They walked through the icy surf now, toward the launch, the larger vessel perhaps five hundred yards out to sea, perhaps the size of a Florida sport fisherman. The wind whipped at them, icy spray drenching Mulvaney before he was halfway out to the launch. He had told himself that he would take one of the ninja swords when it was given to him, use the sheath like a snorkel as the others would, carry the blasted sword and the killing knife to avoid the explanations and the arguments. But he wouldn't use them. And that would be that. Two men already stood beside the launch, soaked to the skin, holding the craft steady as Mulvaney clambered aboard, Osgood after him and Nobunaga last, flipping over the side and into the craft like Douglas Fairbanks skimming a fence.

Nobunaga shouted something over the roar of the surf. The two men let loose of the craft and it started arcing out to sea, Mulvaney squeezing the water from his gloves, shoving them in his pockets. The larger vessel was turning from a darker shadow against the horizon to something more well-defined in the running lights of the smaller craft. It seemed to have an enclosed cabin, for which he was grateful. He did not envy the rest of the strike force, which would be moving toward their objective in the smaller, open boats throughout the night.

The launch docked alongside the larger vessel. There was a ladder already down, and Nobunaga sprang to it, Osgood after him, Mulvaney last. Mulvaney reached the deck and saw Tsukahira-san, who was in his customary black, greeting Osgood.

"Ahh! Mulvaney-san. All is well?"

"Cold but well, Tsukahira-san." Mulvaney bowed, the older man returning the bow.

"Come. This way." Mulvaney followed after him, beside Nobunaga, looking back once. Osgood was right behind them as they started down the ladder into the companionway below. They walked its length into a luxuriously Western-looking cabin, its greatest asset its warmth. "The rest of Nobunaga's force which will strike at the small island will come in the other boat. We shall set out immediately, as I have instructed the captain, but we will hold back our speed until the second boat is in sight. I know little of the sea, but should anything engage your intellects, Mulvaney-san, Osgood-san, feel at ease to discourse with the captain. My son can translate for you, Mulvaney-san."

"Thank you."

A man in blue jeans and blue workshirt entered the cabin and bowed low. Tsukahira instructed him in rapid Japanese. The man bowed again, Tsukahira merely nodding as the man left.

"Sake will arrive shortly. To warm us. Then, to sleep.

Each of you will be awakened one hour before the vessels will be in position for the assault on the small island. Sleep well."

The man in workclothes returned, with him another man, carrying four little bottles of sake and shallow cups, just as Mulvaney had so often seen in Japanese and Chinese restaurants. Before each of them was set one bottle and one glass.

When all were served, Tsukahira poured out his first glass and raised it. Mulvaney, Osgood and Nobunaga did the same. "Westerners enjoy toasting to good fortune. But I toast to ability and then to the fates."

He tossed back the glass. His son, Osgood and Mulvaney did the same. It was warm in the throat and stomach.

Osgood reminded himself, as he fell asleep with the warm feeling of sake still in his belly, that someone would tap him on the shoulder to awaken him. He programmed his body not to react automatically. He then closed his fist over his gun and slept. When the tap on his shoulder came, Osgood opened his eyes immediately, his fist tightening on the butt of his pistol. But the gun never came out from beneath the Western-style pillow. One of the men who had served sake bowed and smiled.

Osgood nodded in return and said his thanks for being awakened, then sat up as the man left the cabin. Mulvaney was already sitting up. Osgood felt slightly chilled and hurried into his sweater.

"So, this is it," Mulvaney said.

"Yes. Be glad when it's over."

"Me too."

Mulvaney lit a cigarette.

Osgood set to a last-minute check of his pistols, unloading and field-stripping both of the Walthers, inspecting them carefully, reassembling them. There was to be only ten minutes after being awakened until they and the others of Nobunaga's team were to assemble in the salon of Tsukahira's vessel. Osgood wondered absently how crowded it would be. There was no way to tell how many guards Tsukiyama Koji would have stationed on the island, nor what their rotations would be. It was a hit-or-miss operation out of necessity, the sort of operation that got people killed.

He had noticed in himself recently an alarming tendency toward fatalism.

The cabin he shared with Mulvaney had its own head and Mulvaney disappeared inside it. Osgood stuffed his feet into his shoes, tying them, then stood, slipping into the shoulder holster, placing the P-38 K inside it securely. He took his little B&D Grande from the nightstand beside the berth and placed it in the pocket of his shirt beneath the sweater. There was the sound of a flush, Mulvaney exiting the head, Osgood going inside. Unlike what was obvious from the slight odor, Osgood had defecated before sleeping. He merely urinated now, flushing, exiting and taking up the flap holster for his full-size P-38. He threaded it onto the borrowed belt and cinched it below his waist, the holster suspended slightly forward at his right hip. Mulvaney was stuffing the Beretta under his sweater. Osgood waited beside the door for him. "Ready, Ed?"

"You bet, John." Mulvaney nodded. Osgood stepped through the doorway and into the companionway, then started forward, taking the ladder up to the salon of the deceptively designed vessel. It extended far further below the waterline than he would have thought at first impression, far more capacious than the average vessel of its length.

Tsukahira and his son were already in the salon. Osgood wondered if they had ever left it. Maps and charts were laid out on the central table around which earlier they had drunk their sake. Osgood smelled coffee, fresh and hot. He assumed it was a concession to Mulvaney and himself and he searched it out, pouring a cup for himself, offering one to Mulvaney. Tsukahira and his son were drinking out of classic Western teacups and, as Osgood neared the table, the smell confirmed the contents to be exactly what the cups indicated—tea.

"Tsukahira-san." Osgood bowed.

"Osgood-san. Mulvaney-san. You have rested well?"

"Speaking for myself, yes."

"Me too." Mulvaney nodded over his coffee. He fired up another cigarette.

Osgood lit one for himself.

Others were filtering into the salon, some of the men dressed in wetsuits, some only wearing the tops or bottoms with conventional attire otherwise evident. Osgood inwardly sighed relief. The thought of a swim in the ocean in this weather without at least some protection was not something he relished.

No word was spoken, but silence instantly fell as Tsukahira-san looked up from the table.

He began to speak, but too rapidly for Osgood to interpret for Mulvaney, Nobunaga slipping beside Mulvaney, whispering the translation.

"The weather is our ally. There is fog. The fog will further enhance the invisibility of our vessels and of our movement. It has been impossible to detect the positions of the guards on the small island, but it is known they are present. No number is known. In the fog and darkness, each of us will wear the red headband over the hood as the means to know who is friend and who is foe. In exactly one hour after the anticipated arrival on the small island, these vessels and the smaller vessels closing on our position will move toward the sanctuary of the small island. Your work must be finished then." He looked at his son. "Nobunaga! Do you wish to add to my words?"

"Your words have included all, Father." Nobunaga bowed.

Tsukahira nodded and his eyes gleamed. "Go."

Tsukahira exited the salon down the same companionway ladder Osgood and Mulvaney had used to enter.

Osgood looked to Nobunaga, the young man leaving the salon for the upper deck. The others started after him, Osgood slipping in, starting up the ladder into the cold and the darkness. The ninjas were donning the rest of their wetsuit gear, one of them handing Osgood the pants, jacket, hood and boots. Osgood did as the rest of the men, stripping down to his underpants there on the deck and redressing, Mulvaney doing the same. By the time he was completely suited up, Osgood was freezing.

A few of the ninjas would carry firearms in the event greater numbers were encountered than anticipated, but it was implicit that to fire shots would doom the operation. There were air-cushioned waterproof bags and Osgood was given one, placing his guns, holsters and spare magazines inside it, the little penknife as well.

Nobunaga approached him, bowing slightly as he offered a sword and *shuto*. Osgood bowed as he accepted them, placing them between his weight belt and his suit, as the others were doing. He eyed Mulvaney, who was taking the weapons, bowing, belting them too.

Nobunaga was consulting his watch. Then he looked up, signaling Osgood and Mulvaney in turn to join him. "I know the route. I swam it earlier this evening, placing markers."

"You what?"

"It will only be necessary to follow me. I am first. You two are second and third. Carry the *katana* in the right hand ready for use, holding the scabbard in your teeth and supporting it with the left hand as necessary. Continue to follow me when we reach the surf."

Osgood nodded his understanding, Mulvaney grunting something. There was a ramp set beyond the aft rail and Nobunaga clambered over it easily, Osgood following not quite so easily but easily enough. He looked back. Mulvaney was coming, the ninjas lining up to follow. Osgood checked that the waterproof container was secure on its strap.

Nobunaga drew on the line, the rubber raft coming in. He got into it, Osgood followed him, then Mulvaney, then three more of the ninjas. Two of the ninjas paddled, cutouts in the paddles to minimize noise. The fog was cold on the skin and dense enough that after several seconds, when he looked back, Osgood could barely make out the shape of the vessel he had left.

No one spoke, silence implicit in the operation. Sound carried great distances over water.

The men at the paddles worked in perfect rhythm, both with each other and, Osgood realized, in perfect synchronicity with time—one stroke every two seconds, thirty strokes per minute.

Nobunaga was holding a Mini-Maglite cupped over his watch so only the watch face would be illuminated. The light went out. Nobunaga tapped each of the paddlers instantly on the shoulder. They kept their paddles in the water, the movement of the inflatable stopping, rocking only in the mildly pitching sea.

Nobunaga closed his waterproof bag.

The paddler on the port side of the raft slid into the center of the thwart, taking both paddles as the starboard-side paddler withdrew his sword and sheath from his weight belt.

Nobunaga stood up, pulling goggles down over his eyes. Osgood looked into the fog. Not a hint of the small island's outline was visible. This would be quite a lap, he told himself.

Nobunaga drew his sheathed *katana* from his weight belt, the scabbard in the left hand, the sword hilt in the right, separating them in one fluid motion, steel gleaming. He turned his back to the starboard side of the raft, then rolled back into the water.

Osgood realized everyone was looking at him. He pulled down his goggles and performed the same motion with sword and scabbard, less gracefully he knew. He held the sword as Nobunaga had held his, the unsharpened spine of the blade against his forehead. He spread his arms back like a child about to make an angel in a snowdrift and let himself go, into the water, suddenly more chilled than he had ever thought possible and still live. He rolled over in the water, faintly able to see close to the surface the human shape he knew must be Nobunaga. Osgood started up, thrusting the scabbard through the whitecaps above him, blowing out water and taking his first breath through the sheath that was now his snorkel. It worked, he was happy to realize.

Others were entering the water. To Mulvaney's credit as a swimmer, Osgood was unable to tell which was he. Osgood returned his eyes to Nobunaga, starting forward through the water now, just a foot or so beneath the surface. Osgood stayed less than a yard behind Nobunaga's heels. To become lost here with the fog and no compass to aid him would have meant death from exposure or drowning. And even a compass would have been of little avail, because the "small island" was so small that even the slightest error could have taken him past it and back to the open sea.

It was necessary every thirty seconds or so to readjust the position of the scabbard, his left hand doing it as he had been directed; but it broke his stroke and made the swim even more arduous.

His body was no longer truly aware of the cold, the

numbness alleviated only by a fading warmth at his center and the exertion of the swim itself. On a logical, rational basis, he had calculated a rough duration for the swim, but he no longer even attempted to look at his Rolex. It was too much added exertion.

The haft of the *katana* in his right fist was something of which he was no longer aware, except that his fingers were numbing over something and it was necessary to keep them closed tight.

He kept swimming, the distance between himself and Nobunaga widening almost imperceptibly, but Nobunaga still faintly in sight.

He wanted to look back, to ascertain that everyone else was still behind him and that he was not just swimming on and on following some phantom that was only in his mind. He kept swimming.

Nobunaga—for an instant John Osgood could no longer see him and he was seized with a cold that was colder than he had known, that radiated from within him. It was panic. And then he felt the bottom shoaling up beneath him and he quickened his pace, feeling returning to the hand that held the *katana*. His head broke the surface and he drew the scabbard down and swam with both arms fully in motion, breaststroking until his arms were stirring sediment, to his hands and knees then, raising his head higher above the water. He stripped down his goggles, blinking against the cold of the air, rivulets of seawater draining from his hair. He saw a blacker shape against the blackness of the night as it moved through the silver luminescence of the surf. Nobunaga. Osgood kept his sword unsheathed, starting laterally across the surfline as Nobunaga did. The leader disappeared into rocks that seemed as dark as the wetsuits and the night, and Osgood followed him, feeling Nobunaga's touch at his shoulder, beckoning him down. Osgood dropped into a low crouch, Nobunaga making hand signals, not those for unit movement, which Tsukahira Ryoichi had shown him and Mulvaney, but simple gestures. Osgood understood, tapping Nobunaga twice on the shoulder.

There was a solitary guard on either side of the expanse of beach which they had penetrated. Nobunaga moved right, Osgood left, darting through the surf again and across the sand, hugging to the rocks. Osgood knew that these guards could not see him, told himself that they were not true ninjas and to keep going.

Where was Mulvaney?

Osgood pledged to himself that if somehow Mulvaney had not survived the swim, he would find Andy Oakwood—if she lived—and save her even if it cost his life.

He reached the end of the rock wall which angled upward from the surface, catching his breath.

The rocks here were slick, polished from centuries, millennia of seawater crashing over them. There was no handhold, but the guard was up there somewhere.

Osgood thrust the empty sheath through his weight belt. He stabbed his *katana* into the sand, unwinding the cord at its hilt, his right foot going to the *katana*'s oversize rectangular guard, boosting himself up.

His hands groped for purchase, the cord that was his lifeline to the *katana* wound several times around his right thumb.

He found a slight handhold, pulled himself up with great exertion, his fingers screaming at him with pain, his left foot finding a crack, his body thrusting upward onto the smooth surface of the rocks above.

The problem was to get the *katana* up without its scratching along the rocks. No one had told him that technique.

He assumed it was speed and fluidity, the hallmarks of these ninjas, from what little he had seen. He snapped his right hand abruptly upward, realizing as he reached for the *katana* that it was sharp enough to sever his fingers if he grabbed it incorrectly.

He felt the steel at the tips of his fingers and held it, drawing the blade slowly in to him, careful lest he scratch it over the rock surface.

He sheathed the *katana* slowly, silently, moving ahead along the slick surface of the black rock. He saw nothing, no one.

What was he to do to find a ghost?

Osgood waited, held his breath.

Movement betrays, he had been told. He began to regulate his breathing as his eyes shifted and his head slowly turned.

In his mind, he ticked off the seconds.

Movement. Betrayal. A darker blackness against the blackness of the night, fifty yards to his right. Osgood slowly drew himself up, edging left in a low crouch along the rocky smoothness, sand suddenly beneath his right foot. He kept going.

There would be no second chance. Now he could not even see his adversary. He kept moving, blindly forward, his right hand at the hilt of his *katana,* pushed hard against the rectangular *tsuba.*

Movement. Betrayal. Ten yards.

Osgood ran forward, unsheathing the *katana,* a flash of silver from steel ahead of him, his *katana* locking against the parrying blade of the Tsukiyama ninja. The man shifted right, Osgood stepping back to keep his opponent from rolling out of his thrust and countering with his own.

Their blades were locked for an instant; then the pressure was gone and Osgood dodged back, the whistle of steel across the air centimeters from his throat, his blood turning to ice.

The Tsukiyama ninja wheeled, thrust, Osgood parrying, turning a full 360 degrees as he held the ninja's blade, then hacking outward and downward, steel against steel.

Osgood stepped back, their swords touching at the very tips. The ninja vaulted into the air, Osgood throwing his body right because all his movements had been left-oriented, the ninja crashing down to the sand less than a yard from him, Osgood realizing this was the best chance, the only chance he would have. The *katana* was at shoulder height, edge toward the sky, Osgood's wrists twisting as his arms swung and his body spun, the blade catching momentarily, sweeping through. The body of the ninja sagged to the sand. Osgood stepped forward, his wrists twisting again, back-swinging downward across the neck and chest.

His opponent was dead.

He felt nauseated, not from what he had done, but because he had been breathing shallowly. He stabbed his *katana* into the sand and rested his weight against it for an instant, the cold suddenly returning to him, not the cold of fear but the cold of his surroundings, his wet skin.

He shook with it as he drew the *katana* from the sand,

wheeling toward the darkness behind him as he felt a finger tap at his shoulder. But he heard Nobunaga's whisper. "Well done, Osgood-san!"

Osgood followed Nobunaga through the darkness until they reached a depression in the rocks, two of the ninjas still clad in their wetsuits holding a black drape, the other ninjas changing behind it, the drape not for modesty, but to prevent the lightness of their skin from betraying their presence. Osgood stepped behind the drape, freezing even more as he stripped away his wetsuit and toweled himself as dry as he could. Then he drew his sweater over his head, pulled on the loose but somehow form-fitting black pants, and slipped the tunic top over his arms and up to his shoulders, belting it at his waist with the sash. He gave his hair another quick brush with the towel, pulling on the hood and winding it over his face as he had been taught, his feet going into the tabby boots. He took the smaller red sash and, like the others were doing, bound it over his forehead, tying it behind his head. He picked up his *shuto,* slipping it between the sash and his abdomen. And then his *katana,* with a feeling for it that he had not had the last time he donned it.

He stepped from behind the curtain.

Osgood heard a familiar whisper. "I understand you've already had a busy evening, ninja."

He looked at Mulvaney, in the darkness barely able to see what little of Mulvaney's face was uncovered within the folds of the headpiece. Osgood was slipping into his shoulder holster, then the belt holster.

"How was the swim, Ed?"

"It wasn't as much fun as the Y pool, but it was okay. You cool?"

"Yes. I think so. Shall we?"

Nobunaga was already moving out. Osgood quickened his pace, Mulvaney jogging beside him. Nobunaga used the unit signals now, calling a halt, then utilizing the signals again. Osgood went off to the left, Mulvaney to the right.

If Mulvaney would not use a blade, Osgood asked himself, then how could the man perform his mission here?

The two ninjas with him passed him, Osgood letting it happen so he could follow their lead, the two dashing across the rocks, Osgood after them, once feeling his footing slip, running his way out of it, realizing he was climbing the mountain which would shield the armada Tsukahira would be drawing toward shore soon—how soon? Osgood had forgotten to check his watch.

He was warmer now, the head and face covering at once comforting and stifling to someone unused to it. He remembered as a little boy the knit aviator-style helmet he had worn. All the little boys wore them, and when the first warm breeze would come they would turn the earflaps brazenly up toward it. He kept running, the two in front of him stopping, crouching, Osgood joining them, one on either side of him.

There was a hut, a relatively permanent-looking affair of what seemed to be cinder-block construction or perhaps natural rock. The roof was uneven, light visible in a thin line beneath a crack in the door.

The other two ninjas—he told himself he was starting to think of himself as one, and that was insanity—moved forward soundlessly, Osgood with them. As they crouched, he crouched; as they spurted ahead, so did he.

They stopped and so did he.

They remained motionless.

So did he.

And then they ran for the doorway where the thin line of yellow light showed, one on either side of the doorway.

Suddenly Osgood realized he was the man who would enter first. He felt the coldness again, wanted to feel the familiar shape of the P-38 K's butt in his fist.

He looked at his two companions. One of them nodded toward the doorway. Osgood held his right hand to the haft of his *katana,* taking a half-step back and kicking outward with his left foot. The door swung inward, Osgood unsheathing the *katana* as he charged through.

There were three men in the guard hut, two of them playing some sort of dice game at a small low wooden table beside which they sat on their hams. A third man rolled from the floor mat and swung his sword upward. Osgood hacked downward, catching the crown of the man's skull, splitting the top of the head, half the nose falling away. He wheeled left, blocking the thrust of another *katana,* wheeling right, parrying the blade again, seeing the sleeping mat on which the Tsukiyama ninja stood, hacking wildly toward the man. The man drew back, Osgood swiftly reaching down with his left hand, jerking the mat away, the Tsukiyama ninja losing his balance. Osgood charged forward, the *shuto* almost magically in his left hand, his right arm moving, his opponent's blade clattering away against the wall. Osgood's left arm arced toward the man's throat, brilliant red there and the eyes suddenly wide as the body slumped back. Osgood wheeled 180 degrees around.

The fight was over, each of the two Tsukahira ninjas sheathing their swords. There was the sound of suppressed laughter, one of them giving him a thumbs-up signal, the other saying, *"Hai, Osgood-san!"*

The two ninjas ran from the hut, Osgood after them, almost losing the blackness of them in the blackness of the night, running, his *katana* and *shuto* sheathed, hands at his sides, running.

They stopped at a height of black rock, and for a moment Osgood thought they had gotten turned around, but he realized that what lay below and before them was just another part of the coastline.

The two ninjas ran left, Osgood with them, behind them, running, feeling an exhilaration of battle that he had not known since his youth.

The rocks sloped downward and the ninjas he ran after followed the terrain, Osgood running full-tilt now, feeling younger inside himself than he had for a decade.

The two ninjas stopped at the base of a sinkline, then moved off slowly but determinedly left, Osgood with them, the rocks rising somewhat, then dropping steeply just beyond where the two ninjas stopped.

Osgood looked below. Four black-clad ninjas in the rocks there, but none of them wore the red sash tied over his headpiece.

Osgood looked at his compatriots.

The one who had said *"Hai"* before nodded.

Again Osgood was in the middle. It was a game, an insanely dangerous game that at once terrified and thrilled him.

Osgood jumped, feeling an instant's freedom of weightlessness, taking the shock with his knees as he flexed and the ninjas turned toward him, his *katana* unsheathing without his mind consciously thinking of it. And it was *his*.

He parried one of the men, lunging for another as the two ninja compatriots were suddenly behind the four enemies. The four men formed a defensive inner wheel, Osgood and the two Tsukahira ninjas an offensive wheel around them. The four in the inner circle were like a single living organism, multiheaded with fangs seeking prey. Osgood eyed his two companions, holding his *katana* as they held theirs, charging the instant after they charged, hacking with his steel, hearing grunted curses and shouts and threats in a Japanese so guttural it was impossible for him to understand.

Osgood realized instantly that he had been picked as the poorest fighter of the three attackers, two of the enemy ninjas coming at him. He fell back, the circle breaking as they rushed him. Osgood was barely able to parry their thrusts, counterattack impossible. He had nothing to lose so he drew the *shuto* with his left hand, crossing both blades as he dodged back, then charged toward his opponents. He screamed the best curse he could muster in Japanese, one of the men falling back, the other holding his ground. A *katana* hacked down toward him, Osgood blocking the blow with his own blade, then doing something that he thought might be insane but was his only recourse. He snaked his left arm forward in a sharp, fast-stopping arc, the *shuto* leaving his palm underhand, the enemy ninja taking the blade in his abdomen. There was a scream of pain, the man wrenching the *shuto* from his body, his *katana* hacking outward as he fell.

Osgood picked up the second *katana,* barely able to get it before his second opponent screamed and charged. With both *katanas* now, he had a reach advantage. But the other man was by far more skillful, Osgood just holding him off. Osgood's compatriots were fighting their ninja opponents one on one—no aid was immediately forthcoming from that quarter.

Osgood was backing away still, the *katana* in his opponent's hand moving as if it were alive, then suddenly the man's left hand filling with his *shuto*. The ninja charged, Osgood pressed back against the rock wall, the *katana* spinning, cutting the night air inches from his face.

Osgood raised both *katanas* to defend himself. Attack was impossible. So far, he had survived by guile, not skill. And he told himself this was his only hope now. As the enemy ninja's blade crashed down upon his blades, Osgood let both blades fall to his left. He dodged right, drawing his gun as he fell to his knees, his left hand cupping sand. The ninja wheeled, hesitated as he saw the gun. Osgood hurled the sand into his opponent's eyes. The man coughed, raising both swords to protect himself. Osgood's right hand with the gun went down for balance, his left leg sweeping out, catching the ninja at the knees, sweeping him down. Osgood was up, kicking more sand into the ninja's face, grabbing his *shuto* from where the dead ninja had dropped it, then hurtling himself on the ninja's back as the man rolled away from the sand to protect his eyes. Osgood's left hand drove the *shuto* down hard between the ninja's shoulder blades, crashing the butt of his pistol down hard against the back of the skull.

Osgood was up, ramming the gun into the leather, grabbing up the *katanas,* charging the rear of one of the enemy ninjas still fighting his compatriots. As the enemy ninja turned to fend him off, the Tsukahira ninja struck, the enemy ninja falling back off Osgood's compatriot's blade. Together Osgood and the Tsukahira ninja attacked the last remaining enemy. The man fought well, holding Osgood and both his compatriots back for several seconds. Then Osgood feigned a thrust, the ninja blocking with his *shuto,* one of Osgood's compatriots locking *katanas* with him, the second of Osgood's compatriots thrusting and running the man through.

Osgood stood for a moment.

Both the men he had fought beside looked at him. Both bowed.

Osgood bowed in return, taking his *shuto* from the hands of one of them, who offered it like a gift.

Mulvaney ran, the ninja furthest ahead silently signaling a halt.

One of the enemy, the hand signals said. The two Tsukahira ninjas looked at Mulvaney. One of them, the man to Mulvaney's right, gestured to the hilt of his *katana,* then gestured toward Mulvaney's.

The pit of Mulvaney's stomach was ice.

He nodded, then moved slowly forward, the black-clad

target some fifty yards away at the edge of an outcropping of rock, almost invisible in the darkness. But of course, he told himself, that was what ninjas were supposed to be. The thing to do was to come up on the man and crush the larynx with one hand as you drove the *shuto* into the spine with the other hand. There were myriad variations on the same theme, and he knew them all, had used most of them.

His mouth was dry and his hands were trembling. He stopped when he had halved the distance. He closed his eyes. . . .

The sun was strong and the jungle smelled like garbage. As the sun would rise to its zenith, the garbage smell grew worse and the flies buzzed in thicker swarms. It was an ordinary V.C., in his funny straw hat and his rubber-tire sandals and his black pajamas, an AK-47 in the crook of his right elbow, held like somebody in a British movie would carry a shotgun when he walked through a hunting field and didn't expect game to flush. Mulvaney remained perfectly still, sweat dripping through his matted hair and down his forehead into his eyes, the Randall bowie vised in his right fist. The V.C. was passing under him. Mulvaney tumbled out of the tree and onto his back, the AK tossed into the jungle mat, Mulvaney's right arm arcing down for the back of the neck, the V.C.'s face pushed against the ground. But the V.C. jerked and the knife impacted only the top of the right shoulder. Mulvaney grabbed the face and his fingers slipped on the sweat and spit as he hauled the head up and back, his hand going over the mouth, the bowie's primary edge swiping across the throat. He stabbed it back, into the chest, burying it diagonally almost to the hilt. Mulvaney fell back on his haunches and rolled the dead man over so he could get his knife free. But it wasn't a man. The straw hat fell away, black hair like silk cascading into the bloody throat. . . .

Mulvaney felt the cold intensely. The ninja who was his target hadn't moved. Mulvaney drew his *katana,* but with the sheath, starting forward again.

He focused his mind on the rock, keeping the Tsukiyama ninja at the far-right edge of his peripheral vision. There was gravel here and Mulvaney picked his steps, moving so slowly at times that his legs and back were beginning to cramp. He kept moving, the sword and scabbard tight in his fists. He was nearly on the man. He would use the scabbard and break the enemy ninja's neck, crushing the larynx so there would be no sound.

The ninja turned, *katana* flashing in his right hand, *shuto* in his left. The *katana* arced toward him, Mulvaney blocking, the steel crashing against his scabbard. Mulvaney abandoned it, wheeling half-right and roundhouse-kicking into the abdomen, the ninja doubling over. Mulvaney was on him, his left knee smashing into the left temple, his hands closing over the throat. He lurched over the body and got his face mask pulled away in time as he vomited.

The other two Tsukahira ninjas were beside him. He looked up at them. They ran on. Wiping his mouth with the back of his left hand, he grabbed up the useless steel they had given him and followed them into the darkness.

They stood on the promontory of the small island, Osgood and the two men he was with, reporting to Nobunaga that their portion of the quartering of the small island was complete, a final search conducted as the end of the hour after landing approached.

As Nobunaga issued his directives, Osgood drifted off, Mulvaney standing at the periphery of the knot of men. Not a single one of Tsukahira's men had been lost, and only one was slightly injured. The attack was a glowing success, the sort of thing that could build dangerous overconfidence.

"Ed. You all right?"

"Fuckin' wonderful. No."

"It must be worse for you—I mean, not understanding the language. But I gather you got by."

"No, I didn't. When we get to the big island—"

"Changling." Osgood nodded, stripping away his headgear.

"We'll use guns, won't we?"

"Not in the initial stages, I understand. You know yourself, we have to penetrate the castle and get as close as possible to where Tsukiyama Koji is holding the hostages before there's any alert. Otherwise . . . Well, you know."

Mulvaney nodded. "Not a damn tree on this island, you know that?"

"A tree?"

"I need to make a staff."

"Ohh . . . ahh. Why?"

230

"This." Mulvaney held out his *katana*, still in its scabbard. "I can't use this."

"Listen, Ed. We haven't known each other that long. But I count you a friend. Tell me what's wrong."

"This is what's wrong."

"I don't under . . . Back in the dojo . . . You won't use a blade."

"No, I won't use some damned blade. I'm not some cockamamie Roman soldier or some barbarian."

"So you'll make a staff for beating people over the head, like a long nightstick, and that's okay. Cavemen used clubs. What's bothering you?"

"Fine," Mulvaney said with an air of desperation bordering on something Osgood didn't even want to consider. "You wanna know? Fine. Fuckin' fine. In Vietnam I knifed this V.C. But this V.C. was a woman."

Osgood looked down at his tabby boots, closing his eyes for an instant. "It was a war like that. I was in Vietnam. Women were just as much to be feared, children. It was insanity. I shot a woman once. She was trying to kill me. And I realized I was insane because I'd fired back after hesitating long enough so I'd only wound her. It unnerved me. I know—"

"You don't know shit."

"All right. Then I don't. But if you had to kill a woman in defense of your life, what were you supposed to do? Let her kill you?"

"I jumped out of a friggin' tree onto her back and slit her damn throat. All right?"

"Ed, for God's sake, you can't—"

"Oh, I can't, huh?" Mulvaney stalked off into the night. Osgood stared after him.

10

Death

IT WAS A BOAT HOOK. He had asked Tsukahira's permission before cutting it into a stout staff of some six feet in length. He'd used the *shuto* for the cutting, chopping with it. The *shuto* balanced well in the hand. . . .

His right fist still vised the bowie and he fell forward over her, the exertion and the heat and his meager diet of the past nine days bringing a wave of nausea over him. But he fought it, because he had eaten nothing in two days since the diarrhea had started and his heaves would be dry and already his abdomen was consumed with pain. His left hand felt something, and he realized it was pressed against her abdomen—

"Ed. I see you found your tree."

Mulvaney took his eyes from the blade of the *shuto* and turned around. Osgood, in his black ninja gear except for the headpiece and swords, lounged against the port-side rail, his left palm flat against the low overhead for the superstructure which jutted out over the upper section of the main salon. In his right hand was a cigarette. "It was pure hell gettin' the leaves and bark off it," Mulvaney said, forcing the smile more than he'd forced the attempt at humor.

Osgood smiled. "I may have a solution for the situation. So hear me out."

"I'll hear you out."

"Good. Good. All right. There's a residual force that Tsukahira-san's holding back until the castle has been penetrated. They'll be armed with automatic weapons and sweep in over the castle wall or through the front gate over the old moat, if we're lucky enough."

"Make your point."

Osgood nodded. "All right. You're the ideal man to lead them. Tsukahira agrees. It's just the sort of hit-hard small-unit tactic you were trained for in Special Forces."

"And I don't have to worry about bruising my sensibilities and sticking somebody, right? And nobody has to worry about me not doing it when I'm supposed to and blowing the whole thing or getting somebody killed. Right?"

"I wouldn't have put it that way, Ed. But I suppose that's a point in favor of it as well."

Mulvaney lit a cigarette, cupping his hands over the lighter. The fog was still thick here and there was no danger of being spotted from shore anyway, since the small island lay between them and any watchers on Changling. "This . . ." He grasped the staff he had cut. "This'll do me fine. Somebody's just as dead with his skull cracked as with one of these"—with the toes of his tabby boots he kicked at the *shuto* he'd laid on the deck.

"Then I can't change your mind."

"Or stop me either, John. I mean, Tsukahira and his son and all their ninja buddies can stop me, but you can't. We can put ourselves both in the hospital, but I'm gettin' onto that island with the first wave. I'm goin' in and gettin' Andy out. Your intentions'd be good and everything, but your first job's gotta be Ellermann. I know that. And Tsukahira's first orders will be to make certain that Gonroku and Tomiko are safe. And if everybody's held in the same place, that makes it all neat and nice and everything. But if Tsukiyama Koji's half the hard-ass I think he is, he'll have stashed each of them separately, at best putting the two women together. Which means Andy's low lady on the totem pole. I'll take care of myself and I'll take care of anything else I need to. And once the fighting starts, one of those Uzis we grabbed off our Russian buddies is gonna be in my fist. You can bank on it."

It seemed that Osgood was either formulating a speech or

considering a well-chosen reply; he waited that long to speak. "Perhaps, in the few moments remaining before we get under way again, it would help if you . . ."

"What?" Mulvaney snapped.

"Talked about it."

"What's there to say? I mean . . . all the grisly details? No thanks, man."

"Scars somehow seem less deep if they're brought into the light."

"Aww, gee, that's real profound."

Osgood exhaled smoke from his cigarette, his voice low. "I'm not certain how profound it is, but it might help. If you'd been a bomber pilot, you couldn't say that your bombs would kill only male soldiers, never harm a woman or a—"

"Shut up, will ya, John?"

"A child."

"Shut up, I said."

Osgood snapped his cigarette over the side into the fog that surrounded them, walking nearer to Mulvaney. "My God."

"Forget it."

"The woman you killed. If she'd been a girl, you wouldn't have used the word 'woman' to describe her. But I distinctly remember that you did use the word. But the way you reacted when I started to say 'child,' you—"

"Shut the fuck up, will ya?" Mulvaney snapped his cigarette away and dropped the staff, starting away.

"Pregnant."

Mulvaney didn't turn around. . . .

The wave of nausea was just starting to pass and his left hand moved across her abdomen and he felt the swelling there. He dropped his knife to the jungle floor. His hands pushed up the loose-fitting pajama top, pulled down the front of her pants just enough that he could see. Six months, maybe. And then the nausea conquered him and he pushed himself away from her and on his knees he hugged his own abdomen and his stomach muscles churned and knotted and he coughed up nothing but liquid and his eyes filled—

"Ed!"

Mulvaney felt Osgood's hand at his shoulder. He turned

around and looked at him. Mulvaney felt the tears in his eyes. "You're a terrific detective, man."

"I didn't . . . That . . . that wasn't my intent."

"Go away." Mulvaney shoved past Osgood and picked up his staff and the *shuto,* hacking at the staff where he had been working when Osgood interrupted him. "I buried them. I killed a baby before it was born, man. Let me the hell alone!"

It was easier this time, somehow, Osgood swimming more rapidly despite the previous exertions of the night, at Nobunaga's heels again, the scabbard/snorkel more easily used as well. They swam in a wedge this time, Osgood's suggestion, Tsukahira-san and Tsukahira Nobunaga endorsing it instantly as they had assembled once again in the salon. This time only the Chunin and Mulvaney and Osgood himself were included, the word to be disseminated to the individual Genin by each man's respective Chunin.

And the word was the plan of attack, held back until after the assault on the small island in the event that somehow word would reach the enemy if a man were captured and were unable somehow to take his own life. "It is the wise man who anticipates treachery. So it was with my grandfather when he and his most trusted Chunin discovered what shall now be revealed to you. For generations, there were whisperings of vast treasure beneath the castle erected by the evil warlord of the pirates. And when Changling was given to my grandfather, he fell to exploring it. His heart leapt, he told my father years afterward. He found a secret passageway within a wall, and the passageway led far beneath, into the bowels of the mountain on which the castle was built. My grandfather realized that the passageway was merely a means by which the castle could be entered or evacuated in total secrecy. There was no treasure beyond a modest quantity of antique arms from the period of the warlord's reign. Eventually the series of natural tunnels led to a distant beach. Wisely, my grandfather swore his Chunin to secrecy, and when the Chunin died, only my grandfather knew of the secret way of entering and leaving the castle. He told no one else but my father and swore my father to divulging this secret to me only when I attained twenty years. He did so, and swore me to tell my son only when he had attained twenty years. I had no son at first, and to tell a daughter was not something I wished, for it would violate my oath. But when my daughter's son was born, I felt that at last I could honor the oath I had sworn for my grandfather and reveal the secret of the castle to a grandson —Tsukiyama Koji. Tsukiyama Koji has attained his thirty-eighth year; Tsukahira Nobunaga his nineteenth. I break my oath now by revealing the secret to my son before he has attained twenty years, and by revealing it before you assembled here. But when Tsukahira Nobunaga was given me by his mother, I chose then not to reveal the castle's secret to Tsukiyama Koji. It is the wise man who anticipates treachery, and the man of good fortune who is spared from contributing innocence to abet it." Tsukahira Ryoichi had then, from memory, executed in charcoal on white paper, drawn the route of the passageway, then required each man in the salon to swear his own personal oath never to reveal the existence of the passageway or its route to any other man.

Nobunaga's force would penetrate the castle by means of the tunnel network, enter through the secret passageway and locate the hostages, then—its modernity had struck him as anachronistic—utilize a state-of-the-art H&K flare pistol to signal the main body of the attack force to swarm into the castle. Secondarily, if circumstances allowed, one of the force was to reach the castle drawbridge and lower it, thus opening the gate to facilitate the success of Tsukahira's force. And before they were dismissed, Tsukahira had enjoined each man against taking the life of Tsukiyama Koji. Through his loins, the old man in the black skirts had said, had come the mother who had borne Tsukiyama Koji, and from his hands only would Tsukiyama Koji be given death.

Osgood swam on, the bottom shoaling rapidly beneath him now, his face at last breaking the surface, the cold air thrilling his body and at once making him tremble. The fog had dissipated and it was almost as if, Osgood thought, he could smell the death of which Tsukahira Ryoichi had spoken, traveling on the night wind.

Strapped to his sides now were two waterproof bags, one

carrying his own weapons and one carrying one of the Uzi submachine guns confiscated from the KGB assassins.

Osgood saw Mulvaney now, lying in the surf, not moving at all. Tsukahira Nobunaga moved laterally in a dead run for the rocks. Others moved around Mulvaney, one other shadowy form moving with Nobunaga. Whoever he was, he would be the best of Nobunaga's Genin. Were a sentry to witness their landing—and live to speak of it—all would be lost.

Osgood waited, his mouth and nose barely above the surface of the water, his *katana* ready in his balled-tight right fist. The wind whipped over the surf, chilling him even more than the thoughts he tried to push from his mind.

Keeping his left wrist just in the water, he glanced at his Rolex to open a time frame for Nobunaga's removal of any nearby sentries. Soon it would be dawn. To have waited another twenty-four hours would have pushed beyond hope the possibility that Tsukiyama Koji was still here himself and that Ellermann was his living hostage.

Five minutes.

Mulvaney. Osgood wondered about Mulvaney. The young Chicago police sergeant was a man whose bravery he would never question. But it was doubtful Mulvaney could survive this without violating his self-imposed prohibition against use of an edged weapon. He had offered Mulvaney the easy way out, in collaboration with Tsukahira, but Mulvaney hadn't taken it. To his moral credit, certainly, but perhaps to the detriment of the operation and all those involved. Men who made their own private Geneva Conventions in battle were dangerous to themselves and to others.

That Mulvaney could pursue his violent work at all and hadn't ended up in some institution for the disturbed was a tribute to the young man's strengths or a testament to his precarious mental condition. To kill a pregnant woman and her child, regardless of the circumstances, would be more than most men could bear and retain their sanity. Had Mulvaney retained his?

Twelve minutes.

And now there was a shadow darker against the darkness, gesturing toward the surf. The Genin on either side of Osgood rose and darted forward. Osgood rose with them, running beside Mulvaney and the other ninjas. He looked back once as the ninjas with the waterproof equipment boxes ran more slowly after them.

Osgood reached the rocks. Nobunaga was already changing behind a curtain held up by the second ninja. Other ninjas, Osgood joining them, got behind the curtain and changed to the more traditional garb. He moved quickly with the cold, leaving off the sweater because he had found in his last sortie that it inhibited movement. A pit had been dug in the sand with *katanas,* and Osgood placed his wetsuit and waterproof pouches inside it, as had the others, the cases which had brought the heavier equipment through the water already buried below the wetsuits. A man, already changed, was assembling a Barnett Commando Crossbow, tightening the bolt against the prod, another ninja, as soon as he finished, helping to flex the prod so it could be strung. Another ninja was assembling the two limbs of a black longbow at least seven feet in length. The bow was bent, strung, the ninja archer slipping a black quiver of black arrows across his back. Swords and killing knives were being wiped dry, sheathed, stuffed in waist sashes. And each man had already tied or was tying a red band over his forehead.

In less than five minutes the first strike team under Nobunaga's leadership was redressed and ready. Nobunaga glanced over his commandos and nodded toward the night. Running, Osgood joined the men around him, his submachine gun slung tight against his side, the sling swivels and mounts taped so the weapon would not cause a betraying sound.

Mulvaney was beside him, running abreast of him. The boat-hook staff was in his fists, an Uzi slung at his side. His pistol was nowhere in sight, perhaps hidden under his black ninja garb.

The lead of the files stopped, and Osgood, panting for breath, stopped as well. A boulder was rolled back by several of the ninjas. Osgood shouldered forward to assist, throwing his weight against it. Mulvaney and some of the others joined him.

The boulder rolled away. There was a stone door, overgrown with dead husks of climbing vines. They tore the vines away, Nobunaga's hands going to the massive cleat built into the stone. He tugged it back, no one helping him. It moved with great effort, but—surprisingly to Osgood—almost soundlessly.

Nobunaga passed through. Osgood, Mulvaney and the rest of the ninjas, except for two, followed him. Nobunaga waited just inside the doorway beneath the stone lintel. As the last ninja passed through, Nobunaga reached out—the massive stone was already being rolled back—and closed the door.

There was a faint sound of stone against stone. Osgood felt a new coldness in his stomach. They were sealed in.

There was total darkness for an instant, then a scratching sound he thought at first might be a rat. But there was light and he realized it was merely a match being struck.

There was one comfort here, considering the cold of the climate. No bats would live in this cave. A torch was lit and then another and another. The torchlight flickered as Osgood felt a cold whistle of draft against the exposed portion of his face. The passage was not tight and the sounds of the wind might mask telltale noises.

Nobunaga stepped past him. Mulvaney was still wearing his swords but clutching his staff tightly—too tightly?

Nobunaga gestured with his head into the darkness beyond the haloes of light from the hissing torches. He took a torch and struck it to one of those already lit. He gestured two of his Genin ahead, the men running blindly and soundlessly into the darkness and disappearing. And then he followed, the others falling in after him in a column of two.

By chance, Osgood found himself beside Mulvaney. Mulvaney's skin was tinged orange in the torchlight, his face—what little Osgood could see beneath the enshrouding ninja headcloth—tight set.

They moved ahead in silence, the passageway narrow. The rock glistened black with wetness on either side of them. Darkness was total and absolute both ahead of them and behind them. Osgood ducked as the others ahead of him had, a stalactite growing downward at the center of his path. The rock surface over which he walked was slick and made him constantly aware of his balance. The cold here was only heightened, despite the absence of real wind. The dampness moved through him from the soles of his feet.

Osgood kept walking. He looked again at Mulvaney, wondering what fears moved through the younger man's mind. And inside himself, he didn't want to know.

A halt was signaled ahead. He realized the others were stopping, getting their interval again with almost military precision. But after a moment there was movement again.

This would be the portion Tsukahira had drawn with even greater care back in the salon of his vessel. There was a natural rock bridge which traversed a chasm several hundred feet deep. A stream ran beneath that, the island's natural water supply. The rock bridge disjointed at the center, where a several-foot-wide gap of airspace would have to be crossed with utmost care.

It was Osgood's turn to move out now, but Mulvaney shoved past him, Osgood falling in after the younger man.

Ahead, Osgood could see the glowing of two torches, bright in the blackness. He stepped onto the shadow that he knew was the rock bridge, just behind Mulvaney. Mulvaney slowed his pace.

Osgood looked down. In the torchlight glow which extended well beneath the narrowness of the rock bridge, he could not see the stream. But he could hear it now, rushing wildly downward. So far, at least, he could not detect any inclination to their path, so the climbing still lay ahead.

Mulvaney was near one of the torches. On the far side of the gap—just under five feet, as best Osgood could gauge it—stood Nobunaga.

Nobunaga, beside the second torch-holder, gestured to Mulvaney. Mulvaney sailed the staff toward him. Nobunaga caught it against his palms and shoved it away into the blackness. Gone.

Mulvaney stood where he had been, unmoving.

Nobunaga's eyes held a light in them Osgood had never seen before. Was this Nobunaga's idea alone, or his father's too?

Mulvaney still stood, Osgood unable to see his face.

And then Mulvaney jumped, crossing the gap easily. But he stood there, not moving on, toe to toe with Nobunaga for what seemed an interminable length of time. Then Mulvaney moved on and Osgood approached the open space. It looked wider than five feet from here. He told himself it wasn't. He stepped back a pace and ran, jumping toward the opposite side. His right foot caught the opposite side's surface, then slipped, his balance going. Nobunaga's hands reached out, Osgood catching Nobunaga's wrist in his hand. Then their wrists completely locked as Osgood felt himself being pulled back on balance.

He stood, feeling himself trembling slightly, his face inches from Nobunaga's. If Nobunaga had been willing to risk the noise of the staff falling away beneath them, he could risk a word. "Why?"

Nobunaga offered no answer, and after a moment Osgood moved on, Mulvaney just ahead of him again. He wanted to say something, could think of nothing to say.

They reached the end of the rock bridge, forming up again in twos and walking on after the torchlight for what seemed at least a mile. The tunnel walls grew further apart here and the air slightly warmer.

Suddenly they were in the tunnel no longer, but in a room of incredibly vast proportions. On one side, barely visible in the yellow fringes of torchlight, was a wall of natural rock rising into blackness. But beside Osgood and the others was a wall of stone blocks as old and solid-looking as the term "wall" could encompass.

The torches were pitched so they stood in wall brackets. A whispered command was ushered back. Osgood relayed it to the men behind him, then turned to Mulvaney to relay it once again in English. But Mulvaney only nodded as Osgood explained that they were to rest themselves and consume the balls of rice and cooked fish they carried with them.

They sat down, Osgood realizing suddenly that he was starved. He removed the first of his two rice balls from the black cloth sack that he had been given to carry cross-body under his right arm. He bit into it, the fish slightly salty but good. The rice ball was dry on the outside but moist inside.

Mulvaney wasn't eating.

Osgood wanted to ask him why. But silence was the order here. Instead he tapped Mulvaney on the shoulder, took another bite of his rice ball and nodded approvingly. Mulvaney shrugged and looked away.

Osgood consumed his second rice ball, grateful for the

small black flask carried on the opposite side from the bag. The flask was made of wood and filled with water. He drank from it now, noticing that at least Mulvaney was responding to thirst.

Osgood watched the others. Each man scoured himself and the stone on which he hunched for stray grains of rice, picking them up with great delicacy and placing them in an outer pouch on the bag. Osgood did the same. The idea, of course, was to leave no evidence.

Nobunaga stood. The rest of the ninjas sprang to their feet. Osgood rose. Mulvaney didn't move.

Osgood just looked at him. There was a look in Mulvaney's eyes, one he had seen only once before—when Mulvaney had wreaked vengeance on the white slaver Shinoda.

Nobunaga, a torch in his left hand (Osgood thought that use of the left hand, since Nobunaga was right-handed, was somehow significant), slowly walked toward Mulvaney, moving with the ease of a natural athlete or a cat. Osgood looked at Mulvaney. He looked at Nobunaga, who had stopped six feet from Mulvaney, but now drew closer, bringing himself in range.

Mulvaney's voice was a rasping whisper, with the insistence of steel being drawn over a file. "You can't make noise down here because they'll hear you upstairs, so I don't have to worry about you drawing your damn sword because you don't know if I just might draw mine. That deal with the staff I made. I know why you knocked it down into the stream below the bridge there. Well, you mess with me again, I'll blow your fuckin' brains out first chance I get when this is over. Got it?"

Osgood was watching Nobunaga, the young ninja's body like a coiled spring. "Mulvaney-san. When this is finished, I will fight you however you wish."

"Fine with me, squint-eye."

Nobunaga was a man of infinite self-control, Osgood realized in that instant. Ignoring Mulvaney's insult, Nobunaga, his voice tension-filled, snapped a tight-lipped, whispered command in Japanese. He turned and walked away, the other ninjas ranking up.

Mulvaney stood, taking the sheathed *katana* and *shuto*

242

from the rock beside him, thrusting them beneath his sash. He walked past Osgood, standing there as the torchlight began to fade.

They marched on, the room of such vast proportions that it took several minutes before they reached the far wall. Inset into the wall was a system of stone steps running laterally at opposing angles, rising upward into a blackness beyond which Osgood could not see.

Nobunaga, torch in hand, waited at the base of the first set of steps. He glanced at his wristwatch, continued to wait.

Osgood looked at his own watch.

After several minutes the Genin who had accompanied Nobunaga onto the beach approached him. They conferred for several seconds. Osgood shrugged, walked toward them. In Japanese he asked, "The two whom you sent ahead were to rendezvous with the main force here?"

"Yes, Osgood-san. It does not seem well that they have not arrived."

"Should some of us go ahead and see what might have happened to them?"

"We cannot, Osgood-san, further divide our forces. If they have encountered difficulties, all our strength may be needed to overcome what has deterred them."

"Yes, Nobunaga. You think wisely. May I volunteer to walk after you?"

"Yes, Osgood-san. It is a great honor that you should. It is regrettable concerning Mulvaney-san. But he has left me no choice."

"May I speak with you alone, Nobunaga?"

The Japanese's face hardened a moment; then he dismissed his Genin. "I trust the man I have just dismissed."

"It concerns Mulvaney and why he said what he said. He did so intentionally, Nobunaga. He fought bravely in Vietnam. He was on his own in the jungle for many days and could not use a firearm. It would have meant his death or capture. And so he used only his knife. Mulvaney confided to me something of which I would not otherwise speak were it not for this situation."

"Do not betray a confidence, Osgood-san!"

"It was not given me as a confidence. Mulvaney threw himself down on a Vietcong beneath him on the jungle floor and killed the Vietcong with his knife. It was after he had taken the life that he discovered that the Vietcong was a woman and that she was carrying a child in her womb."

Nobunaga's eyes hardened. His whisper deepened. "Mulvaney-san bears this on his spirit?"

"Yes. That is why he will not fight with a blade. I have fought with him. He is a man of supreme courage and daring. He intentionally endangered his own life in order to save mine. But the use of an edged weapon brings his mind back to the moment when he discovered what he had done; it saps his courage and his will. He has reacted against the decision you made when you discarded the staff with which he had hoped to fight and thus avoid using his *katana* or *shuto*. You have placed him in a position where he must tear down a wall—like this wall before which we stand. It is a wall he has erected so that he may hide behind it and save his sanity. If you have never done something that can never be undone, you are indeed fortunate, but you are also young."

Nobunaga's eyes smiled. What Osgood could see of Nobunaga's face did not smile. "Osgood-san should be Japanese." And then the younger man shook his head. "Perhaps Mulvaney-san or I shall die. Mulvaney-san has made this something of honor. Such a thing cannot be ignored, Osgood-san."

Osgood nodded, saying, "But at least you know."

"Yes, Osgood-san. Come." And Nobunaga gestured toward the steps, starting up, Osgood after him. Osgood looked below as he reached the first landing. It was a block of stone perhaps eighteen inches wide and two feet long. Mulvaney was already starting up the steps.

Osgood cautiously continued upward. The system of stone steps and landings seemed endless, dissolving into the blackness above and below. There was a feeling of isolation there such as Osgood had never known in his life.

He had checked his watch as they started, and when he heard the laughter, he had just checked it again. They had climbed several hundred feet and been at it for some fifteen minutes.

The laughter was from the darkness above.

Nobunaga froze. The laughter died; then after a moment a voice replaced it. Osgood did not have to be told that it was the voice of Tsukiyama Koji, somewhere above them in the darkness. "Age has conquered the mind of my grandfather as no sword could have conquered his body!"

"Tsukiyama!" Nobunaga shouted the name like a curse. "Uncle!"

"Killer of the helpless!"

"Believer in dreams!"

"My two Genin! What have you done with them?"

"Here!"

Osgood pressed himself close against the damp, cold stone. The first body brushed against him as it fell, the body no longer human-looking. The skin was gone from it, flailed away. Osgood averted his eyes as the second dead ninja fell from the blackness above.

And then Osgood looked up.

There was nothing to see. He heard the sound of an arrow hastily withdrawn from its sheath, the soft clicking as the crossbow was broken open to be cocked. He looked down. The ninja with the seven-foot-long bow had an arrow nocked, pointed above them toward the darkness. The other ninja crouched low, the weapon shouldered, a three-bladed hunting broadhead nocked, the scope mounted atop the crossbow catching a glint of torchlight.

"Prepare to die, Tsukahira Nobunaga, unworthy one!" The laughter came again.

Osgood heard the click of a submachine-gun bolt being drawn back. He looked to Mulvaney below him. Osgood snatched his P-38 K from the Lawrence shoulder holster.

The laughter stopped.

Osgood heard a whistling sound and looked up. Black-shafted arrows rained down on them, clattering against the rock wall and steps. He heard stifled moans as arrows struck flesh of men who would not cry out.

"Torches out!" Nobunaga commanded.

The torches were struck, but not discarded. For now all was in total blackness. Osgood hugged closer to the wall. The sounds of arrows persisted. Osgood felt one brush against the back of his right hand, almost causing him to drop his gun. But he tightened his grip, flattening himself still more against the wall.

Nobunaga shouted in Japanese again. "Return fire!"

Osgood thrust his 9mm pistol toward the blackness above

and fired, the crack of his two shots washed over in the roar of a full auto burst from an Uzi—Mulvaney. There were twanging sounds and whistling sounds, arrows being fired into the darkness above.

The laughter came again. And Tsukiyama Koji's voice. "This ceases to amuse me!"

There was flame high above them at the other end of the darkness, and a hissing roar such as Osgood had never heard before. Then he saw it. Tongues of flaming liquid licking down toward them. He smelled burning oil. Osgood shielded his face, shouting in Japanese, then in English for Mulvaney, "Burning oil! Look out!"

Osgood felt something searing his flesh. He looked to his right thigh, his trousers burning. His pistol went to his right fist, his gloved right hand swatting at the flames, his flesh afire beneath it. But he smothered it. The man below him and further out toward the center—his body was a living torch. More oil plummeted downward. Osgood tucked back, a piece of burning cloth from above floating past him. In the glow of the flaming oil that cascaded down he could see Nobunaga. His clothing was aflame, his hands beating at it.

The man below Osgood who had been consumed dove away into the blackness. There was no scream. Osgood pressed against the wall as he moved upward, holstering his pistol. He tore away his head covering, using it to beat at the flames that consumed the lower half of Nobunaga's body. Osgood pressed the younger man's body against the wall, trying to smother the flames against the rock.

The fall of burning oil stopped, but oil was still burning far beneath them. In the dim orange light cast upward, Osgood was able to see his surroundings. Several of the ninjas from their company had vanished. For a moment he couldn't see Mulvaney. Then he saw the younger man clambering over the body of an arrow-shot ninja balanced precariously on a step. Mulvaney was checking the body. "Dead," he shouted upward to Osgood.

The flames were out. Nobunaga collapsed insensate against Osgood. Osgood was sickened momentarily by the smell of burnt flesh. No one was taking command.

Osgood heard shouting in Japanese. "More burning oil!" He repeated it in English for Mulvaney. Osgood shielded

Nobunaga's body beneath his own, dragging the son of the ninja master downward along the steps to get away from the center of the wall, where the greatest concentration of burning oil flowed.

The steps were so narrow that Osgood almost lost his footing. There was a rattle of submachine-gun fire from below him, into the blackness above. Then there was a solitary wail, and as Osgood looked upward, a black-clad ninja plummeted from the darkness above him. There was a shouted cheer from the ninjas below, a slaughtered "Mur-va-ni" following it. Osgood knew it could have been nothing more than a lucky shot, but the men there on the wall needed all the encouragement they could get.

The oil kept coming, followed by more gunshots from below. Osgood was still moving, working his way downward with Nobunaga. The young man jerked around suddenly and Osgood lost his footing. Nobunaga slipped from his grasp, falling. Osgood's head snapped after him. Below, in the hellish glare of the burning oil, Osgood saw Nobunaga hanging by his wrist. The hand clasped around that wrist was Mulvaney's.

"John! Get me some help!"

Osgood barked a command in Japanese and ran downward. He reached the far edge of the wall and started outward again as the steps moved downward. Ninjas clambered up from below, reaching for Nobunaga's legs. Osgood was beside Mulvaney, the flaming oil still pouring down from above. The smell of burning flesh and oil was suffocating, smoke rising from the pit below in clouds of noxious vapor. Osgood's left hand reached out, closing over Mulvaney's hand, then slipping below it to Nobunaga's forearm.

The ninjas below were pulling their Chunin back toward them, Osgood and Mulvaney guiding his body back.

One of the ninjas shouted that they had him. Osgood let go, shouting to Mulvaney, "It's all right; release him!"

The cascade of burning oil subsided. In the glow from the fires below, Osgood again assessed their losses. More of the ninjas were gone. Besides Nobunaga, only a dozen remained.

Osgood clambered past Mulvaney and onto the step above where Nobunaga had been rested.

There was no escape above or below. Above lay the enemy, below the burning oil, the flames licking ever higher. Nobunaga was still conscious. Osgood spoke to him hurriedly in English. "Nobunaga. Listen to me. We're trapped here. You must put someone in command."

In Japanese, his eyes rolling back, Nobunaga shouted, "Osgood-san will lead you!" His head rolled toward his left shoulder, his eyelids shut. Osgood reached out for a pulse. It was there, weak but stronger than he would have thought. But Nobunaga was of tough stock.

The ninjas on the steps above and below looked at him. Osgood licked his lips. In a few moments there would be more burning oil, or maybe something worse. Before he could speak, another volley of arrows was fired down. Osgood pulled himself back, shouting in Japanese, "The words of your Chunin must be obeyed! You . . . and you, with the automatic weapons, open fire. Conserve ammunition, but keep them back from the edge. Try to judge the arc of the arrows to find your targets."

There was a moment's hesitation from the two ninjas with submachine guns strapped to their backs.

Osgood stared at them hard. Another volley of arrows came, ricocheting off the stone wall and steps.

One rasped something unintelligible to the other and their weapons were unslung. They began firing intermittent three-round bursts into the darkness above. "Get back toward the edges of the rows of steps. The burning oil for some reason only comes down the center! Hurry!"

And then he remembered Mulvaney. "He told me to take command."

"So, what's your command?"

"Glad you asked." Osgood smiled. He turned to the ninjas near him, asking in Japanese, "Climbing claws—do you have them?"

"Yes," one answered.

"Enough for all of us?"

"Each of us has the claws. You do not."

"How about the men firing the submachine guns?"

"Yes."

"I will get theirs. Then show Mulvaney and me how to use them. We can't go down and we can't stay here." Osgood edged closer to the submachine-gunners, signaling them to cease fire, telling them, "Give me your climbing claws. You two must care for Tsukahira Nobunaga. Take turns while the other returns fire into the darkness above us. We are climbing up the wall using claws. The amount of time this will consume is impossible to estimate. Conserve ammunition. When the top has been reached, an arrow that is lit like a torch will be fired into the darkness above you. This is understood? You must stop shooting then so none of us will be hit."

"Yes, Osgood-san."

"Then, good luck." Osgood started back up, the climbing claws in his hands. They were to be attached to the feet and hands, he knew, having seen them used more than a dozen years ago. He handed a pair to Mulvaney. "Put them on, Mulvaney. And when we get up top, you can shoot anybody you like as often as you like."

Osgood looked away, strapping the claws to his feet, closing the safety strap on his shoulder holster and checking the slinging of his submachine gun.

"Why'd you save Nobunaga? . . . Forget I asked. You're a living, glaring contradiction, Mulvaney. I think it's about time you got to know yourself a little better." He had the claws on the palms of his hands, then looked at Mulvaney, who had been silent all the while. Mulvaney was securing the last claw to his hand. "No jokes? No threats?"

"No jokes. No threats."

"No shit?" Osgood snapped.

He stood, another volley of arrows starting. It had to be at least a hundred feet to the top, perhaps twice that distance. To use a light would have made them easier prey than they already were. He spoke in Japanese. "The wall must be climbed far out from the steps. Otherwise, if the oil is used again, our fate will be sealed. Understood?"

There were nods and "*Hais*."

"Good." He looked at Mulvaney. "We cross out laterally until we're out of the light from below as much as possible, then we climb until we get to the top. When we get up there—"

"I know." Mulvaney slung his submachine gun behind his back. Osgood noticed that, curiously, Mulvaney had not discarded his swords.

Osgood looked at the ten ninjas. They were waiting for

him. He reached out one clawed hand, hammering his open palm against the rock, then a foot, doing the same. Then another hand, his right foot still touching the security of the step. His weight held. A wave of fear swept across him and he forced his will against it, moving his right foot away. The claw on his left foot slipped; for a moment he hung only by his hands. Then he rammed the right-foot climbing claw against the rock. He had it. He rammed his left foot into the rock wall, raising his left knee as he did. He pulled himself up, his right hand snapping upward, the claw slipping, catching, the fear still consuming him. But certain death was the only alternative. He moved his left foot up, pulling with his right hand and pushing up with his left, his feet doing the reverse of the process. Then his left hand and right leg moved up, pulling with his left hand and pushing with his right. His body was flat against the cold surface of the rock. He looked downward. The ninjas, Mulvaney with them, were following.

Osgood kept going.

There was another volley of arrows.

The oil began to dribble, then pour downward. Flames rolled across the center of the rock surface and plummeted into the already raging inferno below. He heard Mulvaney's voice from beneath him, breathless. "If we had some hamburgers or some hot dogs—"

"—we could have one hell of a cookout," Osgood finished. He started to laugh. He felt insane for laughing, then thought perhaps he was, clinging to a sheer rock face hundreds of feet above a flaming pit, with only steel claws on his palms and his feet to keep him from falling to his death.

He kept climbing, averting his eyes as a river of oil washed down the rock face mere feet from where he moved.

"Look out!" Osgood shouted in English, then Japanese. He kept moving, the rock surface radiating cold, the river of burning oil near him generating heat, his body bathed in the cold sweat of terror. More submachine-gun fire from below him. Another volley of arrows from above. The arrows whistled past his head, sometimes only inches off. He kept moving.

The oil slowed to a trickle. Osgood looked below. The

flames in the pit were rising higher now, the black cloth of his gloves tinged red with the glow.

His left hand reached up and he froze. There was either a shelf within the rock or he had reached the top. Osgood gestured behind him, using Tsukahira's hand signals. Slowly, more cautiously than he had ever moved in his life, Osgood pushed himself upward. He had reached the top. As many as two dozen men in black clothes and hoods, each man armed with *katana* and *shuto*, at least a dozen armed with bows, were stoking a massive bonfire with pieces of timber the size of railroad ties. The flames roared higher. In the glow of them the black-clad men looked like devils. They were lean, muscles rippling when they moved beneath their black garb. One was taller than the rest, the *tsuba* of his *katana* seeming to pulse with the bright red reflected light of four rubies, one set in each corner.

Tsukiyama Koji.

Suspended above the flames were three caldrons. The smell of them was so nauseating that the image of a hell manned by heavily armed devils would be burned into his memory forever—if he lived that long.

At the far edge of the flat expanse at the top of the wall was a line of fifty-gallon-size drums. Oil.

Osgood swung downward, signaling to Mulvaney and the other men below him that they had reached their destination, found their enemy. He told them of the number of men. No faces of the Tsukahira ninjas could be seen, Osgood's the only head and face that remained uncovered.

Mulvaney crept along the wall to be beside him, ripping away his head covering as well. His face was red-tinged in the glow of fire above and below.

Their eyes met.

Osgood nodded.

For once Mulvaney didn't grin.

Osgood pushed himself up and started over the top. He cast away his right-palm climbing claw, ripping the P-38 K from the leather as he contacted the flat surface above. His legs were bent, the Walther extended in his right fist like a wand against an evil demon. "Tsukiyama Koji!"

Osgood fired. The man with the ruby-*tsuba*-ed *katana* wheeled, both blades flashing. Tsukiyama Koji dodged left

and down. Osgood saw the evil ninja Jonin's body twitch as
he rolled, his men forming a wall in front of him. Osgood
fired as two of them charged. He emptied the P-38 K into
one of the ninjas as he fell less than a yard from him, the
second man's *katana* raised to strike. There was a burst of
automatic-weapons fire from behind him—Mulvaney. The
second ninja went down. Osgood rammed the P-38 K into
his belt, grabbing for the second loaded pistol at his belt. An
arrow with black shaft and fletching struck the pistol from
his hand, the second Walther clattering to the rock floor
beneath him.

Automatic-weapons fire from below.

Osgood shouted in Japanese as he drew his *katana,* "Fire
the flaming arrow!"

There was just time to dodge as one of the ninjas lunged
toward him, Osgood feebly blocking, slipping away and
back. The ninja wheeled. Osgood hacked outward and
downward, striking flesh, the ninja's *katana* falling from his
right hand, his left hand holding a *shuto,* the steel flashing
inches from Osgood's throat.

More submachine-gun fire now, Mulvaney mowing down
three of the ninjas, forced back as a fourth hurtled his body
against him, driving Mulvaney down to the stone floor.

For an instant Osgood's eyes flashed toward the edge. One
of the Tsukahira ninjas was firing the flaming arrow, but as
the arrow flew, a hail of arrows from the Tsukiyama ninjas
brought him down.

Osgood edged back, the *shuto*-armed ninja pressing him
toward the flames of the bonfire. The fighting was general
now, ninjas with and without the identifying red headband
locked in personal combat. Osgood heard another volley of
arrows loosed. He looked quickly to his right: more
Tsukiyama ninjas joining the battle. Osgood searched for
Mulvaney as he heard pistol shots. Mulvaney's Beretta spit
tongues of yellow fire in the half-light beside the bonfire.
Two of the enemy ninjas went down, another still charging
as Mulvaney fired two double taps, wheeling, kicking his
attacker in the face to put him finally down.

More arrows fired, some of them passing through the
bonfire, aflame. More of the Tsukahira ninjas went down.

Osgood dodged left as his opponent struck, taking
Mulvaney's lead, wheeling, double-kicking to the already

wounded ninja's right rib cage, then falling on him with his sword. He slit the throat, wheeled as arrows fell to the stone, ricocheting off the stone as if fired again.

Osgood saw Mulvaney fire two shots, the slide of his pistol locked open, then sidestep and use the empty Beretta as a bludgeon to crush the skull of the man he'd shot who wouldn't fall down.

Osgood had his submachine gun, shouting in Japanese, "Tsukahira ninjas—down!" Then, "Ed, hit the floor." Osgood opened fire, no time to place his shots if someone had failed to follow his order, spraying across the surface of the rock floor and walls, bullets whistling as they ricocheted maddeningly, Tsukiyama ninjas going down dead.

The Uzi was empty, the cyclic rate one of the fastest of any submachine gun, sometimes too fast. A Tsukiyama ninja charged, Osgood beating the man back with the automatic weapon, no time to reload it.

At the edge of his vision, near to the fire now, he could see Mulvaney, backing into it as three Tsukiyama ninjas with *katanas* and *shutos* drawn pressed toward him. There was nothing Osgood could do, drawing his own *katana*, fending away his attacker, still no chance to reload. "Ed! Your swords, man! Use them!"

As Osgood wheeled away from his attacker, he saw Mulvaney again, trying to grab up one of the flaming railroad-tie-size pieces of timber, the wood already half-consumed by flame. Mulvaney had it, hurtling it, driving one of his attackers down, the man's clothes aflame. A living torch, the Tsukiyama ninja ran off the edge and fell away into the abyss.

"Ed! Use your swords!"

Osgood parried a thrust, sidestepped, hacked outward, the ninja backing away, another man joining him, Osgood realizing his already slim chances were more than halved now.

He backed away toward the fire, a third ninja joining the other two, this one armed with a black seven-foot bow, using it like a staff. Osgood looked right and left. The few Tsukahira ninjas who remained were locked in combats of their own, fighting to the death with multiple opponents.

"Mulvaney!" Osgood screamed the younger man's name. "No private Geneva Convention, remember! Ed!" Osgood's three opponents were closing for the kill, Osgood feeling the heat of the flames from the bonfire more intensely now, hacking wildly with his sword just to hold them back. "Ed!"

Osgood felt it like a rush of wind, felt it that way before he felt the impact and the pain, the seven-foot-long black bow crashing down against his upper forearm, his body swept left by it, the *katana* falling from his grip. He skidded across the rock surface of the floor as two ninjas with swords drawn rushed him.

Osgood's right arm was numb below the elbow, aching like a toothache above the elbow. With his left hand he drew the *shuto,* clambering to his feet.

"Ed!"

"Damn you!" It was Mulvaney's voice, a cry of pain unlike anything Osgood had ever heard before, as if somehow Mulvaney's soul were being torn from his body.

Osgood saw twin flashes of steel in the light from the bonfire, the swords of both his attackers wielding downward, Osgood's *shuto* striking upward to deflect the blows, locking against one of the swords at its *tsuba,* the other coming. And suddenly it was gone, something round and . . . It was a human head flying past his eyes.

Osgood had been forced to his knees and he looked up. Mulvaney, the firelight in his eyes and on his bloodied steel, stood over him.

And then Mulvaney wheeled away, the ninja bowman attacking, Mulvaney's *katana* stopping the bow, cutting it in half, Mulvaney twisting his upper body, the *katana* moving in his hands as though it were alive, biting deep between the bowman's neck and right shoulder.

Osgood was up, the *shuto* in his teeth, fumbling one-handed to reload the Uzi with a fresh magazine.

But his eyes couldn't move from Edgar Patrick Mulvaney.

It was a ballet when Mulvaney moved, the subtle turn of the head, the flick of a hand, the blade moving, an opponent struck down again, Mulvaney's entire body moving now with a grace and precision Osgood had never seen in any fighting man in all his years and knew somehow he would never see again.

Three of the Tsukiyama ninjas closed with Mulvaney, their movements stylized, as if performing a *kata* rather than doing battle. Mulvaney edged laterally, the blood-dripping *katana* in Mulvaney's hands held at shoulder height. Mulvaney's left hand flashed forward, palm outward, the *katana* in only his right hand now, edge upward, point aimed at the throat of the central of his three opponents. Almost faster than Osgood could see, the motion a blur, Mulvaney's left hand snapped back, both fists gripping the *katana* as it arced outward, the ninja at Mulvaney's far right stumbling back. And then Osgood saw the face, sawn almost in two, where upper jaw and lower jaw met, the skull demandibulating as the body sagged to the stone floor.

Mulvaney's left palm was extended outward again, the *katana* high over his head, point left, edge upward. The right arm moved, both fists on the *katana*'s haft now, a full presentment of the blade. His two opponents charged, their *katanas* flashing.

Mulvaney's right hand snapped back, the arm hooking outward as the blade found the throat of one of the two ninjas, the *shuto* suddenly in Mulvaney's left hand, parrying the third ninja's sword. Mulvaney's right arm twisted and snapped upward as Mulvaney dropped to his right knee, his *katana* flashing upward, severing the third ninja's right arm at the shoulder, the arm falling away, the ninja falling back.

Mulvaney blinded himself to the man intentionally as he wheeled to his feet, his sword swinging outward in a perfect arc. For a moment Osgood thought Mulvaney had missed— the sword never contacted the third ninja's throat. But suddenly it was raised over Mulvaney's head, then crashed forward and downward, hacking through the forehead of the already dying man. Then all movement stopped and Mulvaney let the dead man fall from his steel.

Osgood had the submachine gun loaded.

Mulvaney turned slowly.

There was an instant's lull in the killing.

Osgood told Mulvaney, "I didn't understand."

"Neither did I." And for less than a second Mulvaney closed his eyes and seemed to draw in breath.

The eyelids opened and Mulvaney turned 180 degrees around, his sword blocking a downward-hacking blade from still another of the Tsukiyama ninjas, Mulvaney dodging left, letting the man's own charge carry him past. Osgood stabbed the Uzi toward the ninja and fired a short burst.

Feeling was returning slowly to his right arm, and with it terrible pain. He forced his fist to flex.

As the pain came, his reason returned. "I shot Tsukiyama Koji. I think I creased him along the top of the right shoulder. But he's not here."

The *katana* spun deftly in Mulvaney's right hand, the *shuto* in his left, both weapons simultaneously sheathed. From beneath his wide-open black top, sweat glistening on his abdomen and his forearms, Mulvaney drew his pistol, the slide still locked back empty. Mulvaney's left hand drew a twenty-round extension magazine of the type used with the 93R machine pistols, ramming it up the butt of the weapon, his right thumb working the slide release down. "Then let's go find him, John."

"Yes." Osgood tossed Mulvaney his P-38 K, saying, "Here, load this for me. Hard one-handed." The submachine gun still hung on its sling from his left shoulder. He gave Mulvaney a spare eight-round magazine. "Thank you." Mulvaney gave him back the pistol and Osgood twisted his left hand to holster it, looking around him as he did.

Three of the Tsukahira ninjas had survived unscathed. Two others were wounded, the others dead. Osgood gave them orders. "You two—guard the entryway to this chamber. Here." He walked to the nearest of the men and offered him the submachine gun. "You have the skills with which to use this?"

The man, sweat glistening on his face, his left cheek dripping blood from what looked to be a superficial wound, nodded. Osgood handed him the submachine gun, then fished out the remaining magazines and handed them over. He looked at the third man. "Help Tsukahira Nobunaga and the two men below to reach this chamber safely. Leave two men here to stay with Tsukahira Nobunaga and also to guard this chamber against further attack. The other two will follow after us. Gather up any useful weapons and be ready to pour oil down the wall in the event the ninjas of Tsukiyama Koji should attempt to circle behind you and attack at your backs."

The other man nodded.

Osgood looked for Mulvaney. But Mulvaney was already gone. Osgood found his second Walther protruding halfway from beneath a dead man, then his *katana*. With the P-38 K in his left fist, barely able to hold the torch in his trembling right hand, he chased after Mulvaney into the darkness beyond the chamber. . . .

His gun was wet with his sweat, more sweat running down his forehead and between his eyebrows and stinging his eyes as he walked through the black-velvet darkness, the torch whistling and hissing and providing so little light beyond a few feet on all sides of him that shadows looked like men. Would a man look like a shadow until it was too late?

Andy Oakwood was probably dead. And Ellermann also, although there was a better chance that Ellermann would be spared as a potential bargaining chip.

Andy . . .

Mulvaney kept walking, his right fist balled tight on the butt of the Beretta, the 9mm close at his right side lest it should be struck out of his hand by some sudden blow from the darkness. And as he thought of Andy Oakwood, tears filled his eyes. Alone in the darkness, Mulvaney let them come.

His entire body trembled. His arms and neck and the small of his back ached. He had always kept himself fit, but this predawn morning he had used muscles he had not used for a decade and a half, the last time he had touched a sword or a blade of any kind for something even remotely like this. And after he had left Osgood and found himself alone in the darkness, he had felt like vomiting. When his hand would touch the haft of the *katana* in the darkness here, the feeling of revulsion returned to him.

And as he walked, just beyond the light, he could see the plain, very young face and the black eyes staring deadly upward into the full sunlight.

Stella had bitched at him that he would wake up during the night covered in sweat and babbling about how he was sorry. She had told him to "go find a damn shrink so I can sleep at night" and rolled over and after a while started to snore. In the darkness in their bedroom he had seen what he saw in the darkness now. A dead girl barely old enough to conceive and a dead baby inside her that he had killed.

Had it been a boy? Or a girl? Would it have been a loyal party member who fought for the proletarian revolution just as she had done? Who fought for people who used her just to build their own power, who took advantage of her ignorance and filled her head with lies about communism and democracy? There were thousands of kids with no parents there. Would it have been that way for this kid? Would somebody else have iced Mommy and the kid grown up an orphan? Or when the kid was five, would somebody have given it a shoeshine box wired with a booby trap and sent it into some bar to singsong, "Hey, G.I. Want shiny boots?" And then the box would open up but nobody, not even the kid, would see it or hear it. Or see or hear anything else again.

Mulvaney kept walking.

And he heard something ahead of him. He threw the torch behind him into the darkness and waited, not daring to move.

He wouldn't have heard ninjas.

So what was it that he heard? . . . again now?

A voice, an unintelligible whisper in the darkness and a clicking sound.

He waited, controlling his breathing as Tsukahira Ryoichi had told him, to aid in achieving invisibility. He felt the gun in his hand. In such absolute darkness, were he to fire it the muzzle flash would blind him. A cold feeling washed over him, settled in the pit of his stomach, stayed there as an unwelcome guest. As slowly as he could, Mulvaney lowered the Beretta's thumb safety, sliding the pistol into the sash at his waist. It would have to be the sword. And his right hand settled over it, ready to withdraw it, his palm sweating within his glove.

He heard a shuffled footstep and a muted curse—in English.

Mulvaney's fist tightened on the haft of his *katana*.

The darkness moved to his left and Mulvaney's right hand was moving, the steel of his *katana* against the wooden sheath rattling slightly as his right knee flexed and the sword was at full extension in his right hand, then contacting flesh with the leading inches of the blade, drawing it back as there was a death scream.

"What the fuck's goin' on, Tsukiyama?" A voice from the darkness, an American voice, Chicago. A match was struck as Mulvaney sidestepped through the darkness, his sword

258

poised, unmoving. He heard the scratch, smelled the sulfur over his own sweat, heard the rising and falling hissing wave of flame. He looked toward it with the edge of his peripheral vision only. He saw a white shirt cuff and an expensive ring. Mulvaney lunged forward, his left leg extended, right leg bent, the *katana* moving, the hand severing, the match extinguishing, another scream. "Holy shit—my hand!"

Mulvaney could see the extinguished match's image still in his eyes. Silently he moved right, heard the whistle of steel through flesh. "No!" It was the Chicago voice, the shrieked word a death cry. But he hadn't bled to death yet.

"So. Who are you? Is it Tsukahira Nobunaga? I think it is one of the Americans."

The voice was Tsukiyama Koji's voice, and suddenly the blender had gone on in Mulvaney's stomach. If Tsukiyama Koji was speaking in English, it was obvious that he thought it was someone other than his grandfather's son.

Mulvaney said nothing.

There was a faint rustling sound of fabric to his right and he dodged left, raising his *katana* in a series of blocking motions. He could see nothing except the faint glow from the tip of the match on the ground near his feet, presumably still gripped in the severed hand with Chicago-style American English. A mob man? Here?

There was the sound of steel slicing air to his left and Mulvaney started to dodge right, but back-stepped, unsheathing his *shuto*. As he raised it, it vibrated with the impact of a full strike from a *katana*. Mulvaney edged back.

"Your *sensei* taught you well, American. Put down your weapons and I shall make the strike bold and quick and merciful."

"Fuck off and die," Mulvaney hissed, moving left, then back-stepping, moving right and forward as there was the whistle of steel again.

"Very good. I killed the American woman. Did she matter to you? I cut off her breasts first and then her feet and then her hands and then her ears so she could no longer hear herself screaming. And then her tongue and—"

Mulvaney reacted the way he knew Tsukiyama Koji wanted him to react. He moved toward the voice, the *katana* twirling in his right hand, the sound of steel through air, his *shuto* driving downward and forward, steel locking against steel with both blades. Tsukiyama Koji had eaten onions; Mulvaney could smell them on his breath.

"You are dead."

"You're full of shit!"

"The American girl is not dead. But after I leave you, she will be, as I described." Mulvaney felt a shift in pressure. He twisted the lower half of his body left, felt the impact of the knee smash against his right hip, his right foot hammering down, Tsukiyama Koji's breath coming in a rush as heel contacted bone. Their blades were still locked. "Try this, American!" Mulvaney felt the pressure shift again, Tsukiyama Koji snapping back, Mulvaney's blades still locked with his, Tsukiyama Koji dropping, Mulvaney rolling over Tsukiyama's knees and feet. As Mulvaney slammed into the ground, he rolled, still holding to his blades, rolling left, to his knees, his swords up, catching a thrust from Tsukiyama's *katana*. Mulvaney dodged left to avoid the *shuto* that he knew was coming, felt it grazing along his right bicep, but not deeply. He was to his feet. "You are really very good, American."

"What you doin' with the scumbag outta Chicago, squint-eye?" The racial slur had angered Tsukahira Nobunaga, but he had stifled that anger. Would it work now? For Nobunaga, Mulvaney felt great respect. For this man, he felt only loathing—and fear.

"I promised a fast death. I think you will die slowly, now."

Mulvaney kept moving, unable to see his opponent at all, unable to hear him except when he spoke. "You tied in with the Chicago Crime Syndicate or the Mafia?"

"The information will serve you little. What you call the Crime Syndicate. They wish Mr. Ajaccio's nephew to die. They pay me. The Russians and Tanaka Hideyoshi wish Mr. Ajaccio's nephew to tell them his secrets, the name of his contact in Vietnam. And they pay me. The Yakusa and Mizutani Hideo wish Mr. Ajaccio's nephew to be their hostage, and they pay me. I will leave this place forever, possessed of wealth a man such as you could not even imagine."

"Change your name. Change your face. If you take Ikuta Chie, change her face too. You'll have to, because everybody's gonna want your ass in a meat grinder."

"I have spoken enough—"

"Wait. One thing. Who's your contact in Chicago with the mob there?"

There was no answer.

Mulvaney stood still, controlling his breathing.

Tsukiyama Koji would come now.

Slowly, his legs wide apart to prevent even the slightest rustle of fabric from his trousers, he edged forward and right, then again, both blades held in guard positions.

Nothing would see him through this, short of a miracle or phenomenal luck, he knew. His luck had been nothing but bad lately; and God probably had other things on His mind.

John Osgood wasn't God and looked not a bit like lady luck, but Mulvaney heard Osgood's voice. "Tsukiyama Koji!"

Osgood's little flashlight—the one Mulvaney had seen in his briefcase—in the total darkness here was a bright beacon, a lighthouse burning bright. Mulvaney averted his eyes, dodged right as he saw the shadow of Tsukiyama Koji's blade coming down. His ears rang with the sound of Osgood's pistol. There was a flash of gold and the whine of a ricochet as Tsukiyama Koji's blade caught the bullet and deflected it, then again and again. Mulvaney rose with his *katana* and struck as Tsukiyama Koji's *katana* deflected another bullet. He felt something hitting his right thigh— the deflected bullet? His blade crashed downward. Tsukiyama Koji, seeing it, swung his *katana* with the ruby-studded *tsuba* in a broad arc, catching Mulvaney's blade.

"Don't shoot, John! And keep the light on us!"

Mulvaney, his *katana* still locked with Tsukiyama Koji's blade, rammed the *shuto* forward, catching Tsukiyama's *shuto,* the shorter blades locked between them at groin level, the *katanas* locked over their heads.

Mulvaney cleared his throat and spit into the middle of Tsukiyama Koji's face where the head covering didn't reach. Tsukiyama's eyes squinted tight against it. Mulvaney rocked his body in a tight right, his left elbow smashing against Tsukiyama Koji's sternum, his left knee hitting Tsukiyama's right hip near the joint. The ninja Jonin's balance was gone for an instant.

Mulvaney sidestepped, freeing his *katana* and his *shuto*

simultaneously, the *shuto* in a diagonal guard position near his groin, left leg fully extended, right leg back and flexed, *katana* held high over his head.

Mulvaney moved.

The *katana* in his right hand swiped outward and into a lateral arc for Tsukiyama Koji's neck. The *shuto* twisted upward and outward backhanded. Tsukiyama Koji's blades rose rapidly to parry, but not rapidly enough. The tip of the *shuto* caught at the tip of his jaw, ripping away the head covering, Tsukiyama Koji's right cheek ripping open with it, the first six inches of Mulvaney's *katana* hacking off Tsukiyama Koji's left ear and still biting downward, glancing off the jawbone and finding soft flesh. Mulvaney wheeled ninety degrees left, dragging the *katana* with him.

Mulvaney stopped moving. Something dripped onto his left cheek and he squinted upward into the shaft from Osgood's flashlight. The lower-right quarter of Tsukiyama Koji's face was impaled on the tip of his *shuto*, and what dripped onto Mulvaney's cheek was blood.

Mulvaney heard Tsukiyama Koji's body fall, the clatter of steel on the rock floor, but he didn't watch it.

11

Cold Warfare

IT PUZZLED OSGOOD that Tsukiyama Koji had been alone except for the man Mulvaney had branded "an ambassador for the Chicago Crime Syndicate." But approximately a thousand yards further ahead along the tunnel there was another huge room, partially natural and partially man-made, the ceiling lower and not lost in darkness as in the previous room. And assembled in the room were what Osgood estimated as one hundred ninjas. The absence of guards beyond the perimeter of the room and the solo journey into the darkness with the Crime Syndicate man were now abundantly clear to him. Tsukiyama Koji had taken the man off to assassinate him, which would mean his money had arrived.

The tunnels served as natural shields against sound, rather than a whispering gallery where sound was magnified. Osgood had learned that when he had nearly stumbled upon Mulvaney and Tsukiyama Koji locked in combat. He had heard no sound of voices, no sound of battle. The tunnels were, in fact, just that—not a single tunnel, but a series of interlacing tunnels with narrow openings between them, as though blasted or hammered out. Osgood wondered how many lives had been lost while the process of connecting them had gone on. When he had found Mulvaney and Tsukiyama Koji, he had just left one tunnel and was entering the next. Only then had the sound alerted him.

They waited now at the end of the tunnel that fed into the room where the ninjas were assembled. Beyond the small groups of men passing from one knot of hushed conversation to another, was visible what Osgood recognized as the entryway into the castle proper. He gestured toward it to Mulvaney, who nodded his understanding.

Osgood reached beneath his tunic, extracting two ninja head coverings he had taken from dead Tsukiyama ninjas, offering one to Mulvaney, inclining his head toward the hundred or so men in the room beyond.

Mulvaney's eyes lit with a smile.

Osgood donned the head covering, wrapping it especially tightly to better mask his face, Mulvaney doing the same. Mulvaney gestured to Osgood's left. Osgood looked at the shoulder hoslter there, then at his right hip. He slipped the sheathed swords from his sash and gave them to Mulvaney to hold, then hurriedly undid the sash, stripping away his tunic. Mulvaney watched the room. Quickly Osgood pulled the shoulder holster on over his bare skin, donning the tunic again, securing it with his sash. Slowly, as silently as he could to avoid the scratching sound of steel against gun leather, Osgood drew the full-size P-38 from the flap holster and positioned the weapon beneath his tunic, stripping off the belt and holster and carefully placing both in a niche of rock, to be handily located should he be able to return.

He took back his swords, waiting beside Mulvaney now until one of the nearer groups of ninjas would be turned away and they could drift from the tunnel mouth and into the room.

Their chance came. Osgood elbowed Mulvaney, but he was already starting ahead in a long-strided walk, his left hand balanced easily on the haft of his *katana,* his face turning neither right nor left but aimed straight ahead. Osgood did the same, staying close at Mulvaney's side, since Mulvaney's total ignorance of Japanese language and culture and the potential for inadvertent betrayal represented by these inabilities was not to be ignored. Osgood did not delude himself, either. His Japanese was more than satisfactory, but not good enough to convince a Japanese that he was one.

A head turned toward them, then another and another. From a distance, Mulvaney could have passed for Tsukiyama Koji, the height, the bearing being similar. But to have taken Tsukiyama Koji's *katana* with the jewel-studded *tsuba* would have been inviting disaster.

A remark. "Where is the Jonin?"

Osgood answered while clearing his throat, "The Jonin is with the foreigner still."

This seemed to satisfy the questioner. Osgood and Mulvaney walked on, nearing the center of the room, the greatest concentration of the ninjas there, the greatest danger of being detected as impostors as well. But they were halfway to the castle entryway.

Mulvaney paused, stopped, turned around, stared at Osgood, who mumbled something to him in guttural Japanese. Mulvaney spoke barely moving his lips, his voice a harsh whisper. "We get through the door into the castle and lock 'em out. There'll be more guys inside. One of us gets to the drawbridge."

"Agreed. Now?"

"Slow and easy or fast and tough—which?"

"Try slow and easy first and then we'll always have something to fall back on." Osgood added something about the great fighting prowess of Tsukiyama Koji in Japanese as a head turned their way and eyes stared. Osgood started walking toward the entryway into the castle.

A hand reached out and touched his shoulder. He tensed, but didn't draw his *katana*. Narrow-slitted dark eyes stared at him, the ninja as tall as he. The ninja spoke to him in Japanese. "What is wrong with his leg?" The ninja gestured to Mulvaney with a nod of his head.

Osgood looked to Mulvaney's right thigh, the pants torn in a thin ragged line, bloodstained.

"Who are you?" the ninja asked in English.

Osgood held himself ready. Once the man had seen his face from so close, the game had been up.

Mulvaney spoke. "We're from the Katana Quality Control Commission. Here to make certain your blades are nice and sharp and also rust-free."

The ninja just stared.

Osgood started to turn to Mulvaney. "He's probably got a rusty blade. He looks the type, Doctor."

"Yes, Doctor. I agree."

Osgood turned back to the ninja. "Well? Do you have a rusted and pitted blade? You realize, of course, that a hand-crafted *katana* is a national treasure. Think of the difficulties you can get into by abusing a national treasure."

The ninja's eyes narrowed still more.

Osgood turned to Mulvaney. "Should we, Doctor?"

"I think so, Doctor—yes."

Osgood nodded solemnly, started turning back toward the ninja, his left knee smashing up to the groin, his right fist straight-arming outward square to the center of the ninja's face.

As the body fell back, Osgood shouted in Japanese, "An intruder is among us!" As he spoke, he unsheathed his *katana*, leaping away, running, Mulvaney drawing his *katana* and doing the same, both of them breaking into a dead run for the entryway to the castle, ninjas closing in on them from both sides. Mulvaney leapt into the air, twisting around a full 180 degrees, his *katana* bloodied twice before his feet touched the ground. Osgood reached under his tunic, tearing the P-38 K from the leather. A pack of three ninjas was descending upon him, and as he fired, he hoped Tsukiyama Koji hadn't taught them his bullet-deflecting trick. A double tap to the chest of the nearest man, the body spinning, twisting, the legs crumpling under it. The second man—Osgood shot him once in the neck. He dodged the third man's *katana* and fired a single shot into the left temple, the body rolling away.

He started running again, looking for Mulvaney, not seeing him. Then suddenly there was a shout in English, "Fuck off and die!" Mulvaney! Two Tsukiyama ninjas fell, Mulvaney bursting through a half-dozen more, his *katana* flashing wildly, a hand severed as the blade touched an opponent, an arm cut off from another, Mulvaney running, his pistol coming into his left hand, firing into a knot of men about to close with him.

Osgood stabbed the P-38 K toward the knot, fired once, then again, bringing down two more of them. By quick reckoning, by now they were outnumbered only forty-five or so to one. He kept running, a ninja lunging toward him with a *sai* mounted at the head of a spear shaft, Osgood firing, the ninja's left eye exploding inward, the body slamming down. One shot left, Osgood drew the second pistol, working the safety off, stabbing it toward the ninjas behind him, firing two-shot bursts, bringing the odds down still more.

He heard Mulvaney shouting, "John! The entrance! Hurry!"

Osgood wheeled toward the sound, Mulvaney's pistol discharging twice, then twice again, three ninjas down, Mulvaney's sword flashing as still a fourth died.

Osgood ran.

He was about fourty-five feet from the entrance to the castle now, about the same distance from Mulvaney. A ninja bowman was nocking an arrow into a seven-foot black longbow. Osgood saw the target. "Ed! Down!" Mulvaney threw himself down, Osgood punching the P-38 K forward for its last shot, firing, the ninja bowman struck in the left side of the neck, the body toppling, the arrow loosed, hitting the wall beside the entryway into the castle, the ninja's body skidding across the floor toward it.

Osgood ran, jumping the dead body, beside the doorway now, the full-size P-38 in his left fist emptying toward a phalanx of ninjas rushing him. He stepped back through the doorway, thrusting the empty full-size 9mm under his tunic, finding a spare magazine, working the spent one free, ramming the full one up the well and working the slide release. For the first time he noticed his surroundings. In spring it would be a place of considerable beauty, heavily snow-laden pines, terraced where flowerbeds would bloom, the entryway through which he had just passed a garden wall. Osgood stepped back into the entryway, a ninja with *katana* and *shuto* drawn less than a yard from him. He fired twice into the ninja's neck and face, the body flopping back.

Mulvaney was edging nearer, his pistol apparently empty. "Ed! Run for it!"

Mulvaney took him at his word, breaking into a dead run.

Osgood braced the P-38 K over his left forearm, firing, killing, firing again, bringing still another ninja down, Mulvaney skidding on his heels through the entryway, Osgood stepping back, four shots left. "Find something to block the door—hurry!"

Osgood swung his little pistol right, belly-shooting one man, swinging the muzzle right, a chest shot for another. Only two shots left.

"John! Inside! Hurry!"

Osgood glanced back once, sprinting back through the entryway, Mulvaney slamming the massive steel-banded wooden door, Osgood firing out the P-38 K, throwing his weight against the door.

There was weight pressing back, more than he could hold even with Mulvaney. But Mulvaney was moving at his right, doing something. Osgood twisted around to see exactly what. The younger man was holding a wooden tie approximately six feet long and several inches thick. Osgood looked to right and left. There were metal slots to hold the bar. "Out of the way and down—but keep your weight on the door! Now!" Osgood dropped to his knees in the snow, throwing his full body weight to the door, Mulvaney dropping the bar into position as the door bucked against him, the bar stuck out of the notch on the left. Mulvaney threw his weight to the door, Osgood to his feet again, doing the same.

"Together! Now!" Osgood shouted. He hammered his right shoulder to the door, Mulvaney doing the same, the bar dropping into the notch at last.

Osgood sank back, drenched with sweat. His left hand moved to the ninja headgear he wore and pulled it away from his face and hair, a wash of cool air flooding over him as he glanced around the garden, his breath steaming, his palms steaming as he pulled off his gloves.

Osgood sagged against the door.

"Wouldn't do that, John. Those *katanas* could slide through a crack between the beams in the door and—"

Osgood stepped away quickly, loading a fresh magazine into the P-38 K, then wiping the sweat from his face with the black head covering. "One of us has to reach the drawbridge. One of us has to find Sergeant Oakwood, Peter Ellermann and the other hostages. Doubtless there are more ninjas in the castle and in the courtyard." He thumped a full magazine into his second pistol. Mulvaney was loading his Beretta. "That's your last full magazine, correct?"

"Yeah."

"I'm down to just two more myself. Here." He handed

Mulvaney the full-size pistol. "Use it in good health for backup. You've got the drawbridge because you're the best man with a blade I've ever seen, and between us there might not be enough ammunition to get you there. I may find other weapons available in the castle."

"I know you're going after Ellermann, but—"

"I have no choice."

"I know, but—"

"I'll do my best. If your Sergeant Oakwood's life can be saved, you know I'll give it my all."

Mulvaney pulled off his ninja headgear and nodded solemnly. "I couldn't ask for anything better."

"Thank you. Be seeing you, then!" Osgood shot Mulvaney a wave, stuffing away his ninja headgear beneath his tunic just in case it might prove useful again, the P-38 K tight in his fist as he ran. He was trying to remember the charcoal drawing Tsukahira Ryoichi had made aboard the command vessel. The garden entryway from the network of tunnels was at the far rear of the house. The room they had just left, where they had locked the ninjas, was a hollow segment of the interior redoubt, guard walkways atop its low-ceilinged surface outside. The walkways and the redoubt itself formed a distorted octagon, the furthest forward portion fronting to a ground-level passageway accessible from the interior courtyard just beyond the drawbridge. The passageway was blinded with positions on both sides and at the rear from which arrows or something worse could be shot or spilled to kill intruders who had somehow gotten that far.

But the castle grounds and castle wall were Mulvaney's concern now. Osgood's battleground was the castle itself. It was a single floor, in some areas the ceilings thirty feet tall.

At last, at the edge of the garden, the building wall was before him. He stopped, standing there in the snow, catching his breath, the light gray with dawn. His fist balled tighter on his pistol. There was a double doorway leading to what would be the equivalent of the master suite, just beyond. He started for the doors. . . .

Ed Mulvaney had nearly reached the top of the interior redoubt, the wall some twenty feet high, connecting here at the garden wall on both sides to the exterior wall by means of tunnels. As he finally attained the top of the wall, before he swung up onto it, he looked right and left. No guards were in evidence. It was hard to imagine Tsukiyama Koji leaving his castle walls all but unguarded unless somehow he assumed the main invasion to be coming through the secret-tunnel system.

Mulvaney flipped onto the wall, on hands and feet in a low crouch, waiting for something to happen.

Nothing did.

He drew his *katana,* nearer to the wall on his left than the wall on his right, breaking into a long-strided run along the parapet, his eyes scanning the freshly fallen snow for signs of human trespass, seeing none. He kept running.

At his right now was the courtyard or training yard, where the ninjas housed here would work to keep their fighting skills in top form, Tsukahira Ryoichi had recounted. To his left was the main wall of the house, the garden area an arc scribed into the rear wall of the house or castle. It was both and neither. Tall, sweeping horned arches were cast outward in four directions from a central pinnacle, each arch up-sweeping into still a smaller arch and smaller pinnacle, these dominating the four primary corners of the building, the building actually eight-sided, more regularly octagonal than the castle walls that surrounded it, their octagon so stylized that Mulvaney recalled, as Tsukahira Ryoichi had drawn it, it somehow gave the appearance of a mask, the drawbridge a grotesquely distended tongue.

Mulvaney slowed his pace as he reached the passageway between the house wall and the exterior parapet. If there were a trap, it would be waiting for him here or just beyond in the area between the weaponry rooms.

The interior redoubt broke left at a forty-five-degree angle, like a covered bridge or tunnel, the interior in the gray postdawn half-light murky, black. He left his pistols hidden and, both fists knotted to the haft of his *katana,* pressured tight against the *tsuba* to take the strongest blow and hold it, he walked forward.

He started to smile. If the pushers and pimps of Chicago could see him now, gotten up in black pajamas and boots with compartmentalized toe pockets and carrying swords, they'd take a petition to have him committed.

And then he felt the smile fade from his lips.

Two men, black-clad, stepped from the blackness at the sides of the passageway and into the gray light.

Mulvaney guessed he should try to converse with them, although he knew his accent would be unpardonable. "Nissan Panasonic Mitsubishi. Kawasaki Honda Subaru. Sanyo Tempura Sake. Toshiro Mifune. Akira Kurosawa. Fujifilm." They did not respond and he presumed they were in no mood for intelligent conversation.

Mulvaney shrugged, moved into a fighting stance, whispering, *"Sayonara."* When the talking broke down, there was nothing left but violence. He held his *katana* at shoulder height, edge forward, waiting.

Both men drew, Mulvaney back-stepping, the *katana* wheeling in his hand, steel whistling through frigid air. The man on Mulvaney's right—Mulvaney edged right, parrying the *katana* as soon as it was drawn, locking blades, drawing back, parrying again, then swiping downward and inward as his opponent made to parry his blade, the leading edge of Mulvaney's *katana* severing all four fingers of the ninja's sword hand, the ninja's *katana* falling away as Mulvaney sidestepped right and wheeled left, his steel contacting the ninja's neck beneath the left ear, laying flesh open half across the throat, Mulvaney's eyes squinting against the spray of arterial blood.

He back-stepped as the second ninja attacked, both sword and *shuto* arcing toward him, Mulvaney unsheathing his *shuto,* catching the *katana* against it, his own *katana* hacking inward across his opponent's left bicep and down to the bone, the *shuto* falling from the man's grasp as Mulvaney edged off. The second ninja's left arm hung useless at his side, his legs moving awkwardly, stumblingly as he lunged, Mulvaney parrying the thrust easily, wheeling his *katana* clear and backhanding the edge of his *shuto* across the second man's neck below the left ear, still moving, swiping the *katana* across the same spot in the neck, the blade hesitating for an instant, passing between vertebrae, the head falling away as the lifeless body collapsed at his feet.

Mulvaney's left hand wheeled his *shuto* into its sheath, and with *katana* at shoulder height, he slowly advanced on the darkness of the passageway between the interior redoubt and the parapet.

The ceiling of the master bedroom was vaulted, the plane of the interior wall intersecting it at a height Osgood estimated as better than twenty feet.

The bedding moved and he leveled the P-38 K toward it.

He walked toward the massive modern-looking bed, gently leaning toward it, prodding at the foot of the mattress with the muzzle of the Walther. "Hello?" He used English.

There was no answer and the movement stopped.

Osgood felt a smile cross his lips and he shifted the Walther to his left hand. He flexed his still-sore right fist and drew his *katana,* then arced it outward and horizontally, right to left, across the mattress. He stepped back as water sprayed from it.

There was a squeal, almost animal, very feminine. "Ikuta Chie?"

The voice came back in English as the raven hair and the upper half of a pale, very pretty almond-eyed face emerged from beneath the covering of a robin's-egg-blue silk sheet. "Tsukiyama Koji'll bust your ass."

"My, my—such talk from a lady indeed! But as a matter of fact, Tsukiyama Koji won't be doing much of anything, unless of course you count decomposing as an activity."

"You—"

"Actually not. You might put me down for an assist on the goal, however. Detective Sergeant Edgar Patrick Mulvaney had the honor." Osgood sheathed his *katana,* shifting the Walther into his right hand, balancing it there for an instant, then gesturing toward her. "Out of bed. Help me find the hostages or I'll grant your fondest wish to join your lover in the grave. If he ever gets that far, of course. Now!"

He leveled the Walther P-38 K at her pretty head and smiled.

"Fuck you!"

"Some other time, madam. Out of bed."

Ikuta Chie sat up on the rapidly shrinking water bed with all the elegance of a slightly abused queen. "I'm not tellin' you nothin'."

"I can see that your self-vaunted knowledge of English is

merely a bold front. Get your ass out of bed before I move your nose over a few inches!"

Osgood had found over the years that persons responded in their own way to their own stimulus or set of stimuli. Apparently a threat to her physical beauty, however hollow, was just the thing.

Ikuta Chie slunk out from under the covers, stark naked, with little upswept breasts, the nipples large and fully erect, her waist incredibly small. She grabbed up a floor-length pink silk robe and cocooned it around her, belting it tight.

Osgood made his voice as menacing as he could. "Take me to where the hostages are being held. And remember: if anything goes wrong, you die first. If you cooperate, you'll get out of this in one piece if any of us do. Understand?"

She grunted something, her pretty face a hard mask. He assumed it was a reluctant agreement to cooperate. She started for the door, Osgood keeping several feet back from her lest she be tempted to try something that would get her shot.

Beyond the iron-banded wooden door, quite medieval in appearance, as was the exterior of the castle, lay a room much smaller than the master bedroom, and equally as modern in its decoration. It was a sitting room, a Western-looking conversation-pit couch and several end tables and a large-screen television, complete with remote speakers, videocassette recorder and stacks of videotapes. These latter, Osgood reflected clinically, were stored in the improper horizontal position. Ikuta Chie paused and Osgood allowed himself another look at the tapes. They were all English-language films, some of which were possessed of bizarre erotic titles. "I imagine television reception on the island is rather limited."

She didn't answer, walked on toward the double doors at the opposite side of the room. "His ninjas are out there. They'll burn your ass."

"Your concern is touching."

"Hell, I just don't wanna get it."

"My bubble is burst. Open the doors. And remember, try anything stupid and you die."

Ikuta Chie laid both tiny hands on the rings near where the two doors met, jerked at them and—he could see her coming—kicked her right leg up and back, the foot missing his gun hand by inches just as he had calculated it would. She wrenched open the doors and ran into whatever lay beyond the doors—a corridor, he presumed, unless Tsukiyama Koji had altered the internal plan of the castle since Tsukahira Ryoichi had seen it last.

As he started after her, he heard a scream. Osgood went through in a low dive, Ikuta Chie's body falling back, a black crossbow bolt in her throat, red spraying onto the pink robe, a black-clad ninja at the opposite end of a rough-hewn stone corridor cocking his crossbow with a goat's-foot stirrup. Osgood came out of the roll on his knees, the P-38 K in both fists, firing once. The ninja was still bent over his crossbow. Osgood's bullet struck the man in the crown of the skull, the body collapsing onto its knees, dead. Osgood was up, a quick glance at Ikuta Chie's lifelessly staring eyes showing she was beyond help.

The corridor and the guard post that lay at the southern end were exactly as depicted in Tsukahira's drawing. Servants' quarters were behind him and he had no interests there. He turned his back on the dead crossbowman and jumped Ikuta Chie's body as he ran along the corridor to its extreme northern end, where it took a sharp bend left.

He stopped, waited an instant, hearing no sounds of running feet, no sounds at all except his own heavy breathing.

Osgood reached under his tunic, extracting the ninja head covering, tossing it quickly into the corridor. A crossbow bolt caught it in mid-flight, impaling it against the stone in a niche between the rocks. Osgood threw himself into the corridor and fired as he identified his target, a crossbowman frantically cocking the prod of his weapon, left foot into a goat's-foot. Osgood's bullet struck the face, the ninja's body slamming against the corridor wall and collapsing. Osgood ran forward, past the north wall of the servants' quarters, jumping over the dead ninja, reaching the large rectangular reentrant from the corridor which abutted the north wall of the kitchen and the east wall of the guards' quarters. There were no kitchen smells, nor were there sounds of hastily taken-up weapons. He kept running, the north wall of the guards' quarters to his left, the corridor wall to his right. He had nearly reached the far edge of the guards' quarters when he saw three ninjas rounding the corner from the opposite direction in a dead run, one of them with a crossbow. Osgood snapped the Walther up to eye level and fired once, then again, downing the crossbowman first because he was potentially the most dangerous.

One of the other two threw a knife. Osgood sidestepped, firing. The second man went down, the third ninja disappearing around the corner.

Osgood pressed himself against the guards'-quarters wall, removing the P-38 K's magazine, inserting one of the two remaining filled magazines, pocketing the nearly empty one. Its one round might be needed. He advanced along the wall. He anticipated one of two things, each as bad as the other: the guard was waiting for him with a *katana* or some other deadly weapon; the guard had run off to alert those who were guarding the hostages to carry out the orders for execution Osgood was certain they had been given.

He kept moving forward, bending over as he passed the body of the dead crossbowman, catching up the weapon, his pistol shifted to his left fist. It seemed straightforward enough. There was a quiver of bolts on the dead man's left side. Osgood shoved his pistol into his sash, took up a bolt, put it in his teeth. He slipped his right foot into the goat's-foot, bracing his back and shoulder muscles as he pulled back on the string to cock the prod. He estimated the draw weight at somewhere between 150 and 175 pounds, the string clicking under the retaining piece. It was a simple trigger release and he kept his fingers clear of it, nocking the bolt.

He edged forward, trying to sense the uncertain enemy presence around the corner, unable to. He carefully set down the crossbow, drew his pistol and removed the fresh magazine as silently as he could, exchanging it for the magazine with only one round remaining.

He edged forward to the very corner of the corridor, stepping back to avoid a sudden attack from the opposite side of the corner, firing his pistol down the corridor once, seeing a fleeting flash of black, firing again, purposely waiting an instant, the slide of his pistol locked back, empty for all the world to see.

He dodged back to cover, making muffled grunting

sounds as he replaced the spent magazine with the fresh one, not even daring the noise of the slide releasing, leaving it open, his left thumb twisted behind the weapon's backstrap to work the slide release.

Osgood edged to the corner again, stepped away and fired the crossbow, swearing loudly in English as he ducked back behind the shelter of the wall.

If the ninja had bought it, he would take advantage of the reloading time for the crossbow and charge.

Osgood held his breath as he edged back.

The ninja rounded the corner, screaming a curse, his *katana* raised high over his head in both hands, crashing downward. Osgood's left thumb worked down the slide stop, the thumb sweeping back around the pistol butt as the slide slammed forward. Osgood's right arm went up in what he knew was a useless defense, his left first finger touching the trigger. The Walther rocked gently in his hand, the ninja's face suddenly frozen in a rictus of pain, a 9mm hole between his eyes just at the depression where the nose began. The body swayed for an instant, the *katana* falling from limp hands, Osgood stepping back. The ninja fell face-forward onto the corridor floor.

Osgood sprang over the man and into the corridor beyond the corner, the P-38 K back in his right fist.

No guards were visible and he ran diagonally across the pie-shaped entry hall, the dining hall visible beyond through open doors.

And beyond that, he knew, was the torture chamber.

There were seven guard/weaponry rooms on the exterior wall, one dominating the entire rear portion, one flanking that on each side, then two more just forward of those at the centers of the north and south walls. There were two more at the furthest forward corners where the north and south walls abutted the west wall, which overlooked the sea toward Russia and through which was cut the niche for the massive drawbridge.

The icy wind tore at him as he ran along the exterior of the wedge-shaped northeast guardroom, making for the drawbridge controls.

Mulvaney's face, hands and body sweated beneath the

ninja gear he wore, and under the sting of the wind his body shivered. He could see over the wall now to the west, the sea choppy, high whitecaps crashing off the black rocks which dotted the coastline in massive, erratically assembled aggregates. But no sign of Tsukahira Ryoichi's ninja attack force.

He sprinted along the west wall now, trying to envision the diagram Tsukahira Ryoichi had drawn, to know precisely where the drawbridge controls were.

But he couldn't see them, his mind focusing instead on Andy Oakwood, the paleness of her blood-drawn face when he had last seen her. Even if she had not been murdered, if she hadn't been given the proper care she could have died from natural causes. And there was no vengeance he could wreak, Tsukiyama Koji already dead at his hands. And who was the missing piece? Who tied Tsukiyama Koji in with the Chicago mob, who was playing the mob against Tsukiyama, and Tsukiyama against the mob, all for himself?

He reached a narrow flight of stone steps, something he had seen in Tsukahira's diagram falling into place for him now.

He took the steps down, the Beretta tight in his right fist.

Mulvaney reached the bottom of the steps, a guardroom ahead. He closed his eyes for an instant. The small guardroom was for the purpose of keeping anyone from reaching the drawbridge.

He opened his eyes, starting ahead into a narrow, arched passageway, only gray light and black shadow here, the guardroom on the other side.

One of the shadows came alive—a *katana* crashing downward. Mulvaney stepped back, a second shadow coming at him as he fired. The pistol was struck from his hand as it discharged. Mulvaney's left hand drew the *shuto* and thrust it toward the second shadow. A scream punctuated the reverberation of the pistol shot. Mulvaney fell left, the *katana* from the first figure coming for him again. There was no time for his own *katana* and no room to draw it in the confined space. His right hand reached under his tunic— Osgood's full-size P-38. His right thumb swept the safety up as his right first finger jerked the trigger. The Walther bucked in his hand, his ears ringing with the concussion.

His finger worked again and again and again, the body staggering, the *katana* falling and clattering across the stone. The body fell.

Mulvaney ripped his *shuto* from the other dead man's chest and sheathed it. His eyes scanned the ground. The Beretta. He picked it up. Aside from a bright gouge over the exposed midsection of the barrel, it seemed undamaged. There was one way to know for sure. Both pistols cocked in his fists, he ran straight for the guardroom. Men came from the shadows as he dodged, fell, both pistols firing. A body collapsed over him, a *katana* cleaving into the stone of the wall inches from his face. The Walther was empty in his left hand, the Beretta still firing at everything that moved.

And nothing moved anymore.

He judged that four or five shots remained in the Beretta. He worked the Walther's slide release, stuffed the empty pistol under his tunic, shifting the Beretta to his left fist, drawing his *katana*.

Mulvaney crossed the guardroom, another narrow passageway on its other side.

Into the passageway, running.

In the gray light he saw a huge wooden crank, and surrounding it, a system of massive pulleys, ropes leading from them, disappearing into the wall. Through a niche in the wall near the clustered pulleys was visible a segment of the enormous wooden drawbridge.

He stood before the controls, trying to make out how they worked.

A footfall behind him.

He wheeled toward it and fired. A black-garbed ninja dropped in his tracks, a second right behind him. Mulvaney fired again, the second man collapsing against his gun as Mulvaney's hand reflexed and the Beretta fired again. A third ninja sprang at him. Mulvaney's *katana* rose, blocking the thrust as Mulvaney was thrown back against the pulleys by the force. His left kidney hit the crank handle and his knees sagged as he rolled away, the *katana* in his opponent's fists hacking toward him, missing his throat by inches.

To his knees. He threw himself right as the enemy ninja charged, the blades of their *katanas* touching for an instant. Mulvaney was up, sagging against the wall, his breath coming in gulps. The ninja wheeled, Mulvaney launching himself away from the wall, turning half-away, his *katana* parrying the ninja's weapon, Mulvaney's left hand drawing the *shuto*. Mulvaney wheeled right, under his opponent's *katana,* the *shuto* slicing outward, catching cloth and flesh. The ninja fell back.

Mulvaney stormed toward him, both blades ready, the ninja grasping for his *shuto,* Mulvaney's attention drawn to it for an instant—as his gaze shifted, his mind screaming to him that he was a fool.

He barely felt it the instant it came, and then the next instant tears welled up in his eyes and he screamed a curse as he fell back, his *shuto* clattering to the floor. His left forearm seemed on fire. He felt his left glove instantly saturate. He backed to the wall, drawing his body across it. Where his arm brushed, the wall streaked crimson with blood. He had taken it along the outer side of the forearm, not immediately life-threatening from blood loss, but already a wave of nausea was sweeping over him.

The ninja's gloved left hand was clasped to his side where Mulvaney's *shuto* had sliced him open, blood dribbling between his fingers.

The ninja hissed something through the folds of his head covering, Mulvaney not understanding a word, saying to him almost under his breath, "You're damn good, man. But I'll get that fuckin' drawbridge down, and not you or anybody else is gonna stop me."

They stared at each other for a moment, and then the wounded ninja hurtled his body toward Mulvaney, shrieking a battle cry, *katana* and *shuto* flailing. Mulvaney threw himself down, body slamming into the ninja's feet at the very last moment, the body tumbling over him, Mulvaney rolling, cleaving down for the ninja's head and neck, the *katana* vibrating in his hand as steel struck bone. A cry like that of a dying animal came and died, and the body went limp, never moving.

Mulvaney was on his knees.

He looked at the wall, his eyes struggling to focus, the pain in his arm worsening. The largest of the pulleys served a rope that appeared several inches in diameter. Mulvaney stabbed his *katana* downward and used it to push himself to his feet. He stared at the rope.

"Hell . . ." Mulvaney grasped his sword, pain welling up

279

in him as he moved his left hand. The *katana* rose, his body wrenching around, both arms arcing forward in rhythm with his torso. The *katana* hit the rope, Mulvaney's left forearm feeling as if it were a separate entity, screaming at him to cease its brutalization. The rope and *katana* were one for an instant, and then the rope snapped.

Mulvaney fell to his knees.

The pulley spun insanely, the rope snaking through it with a loud rasping sound, fiber shearing from the rope, floating like motes of dust on the air as a shaft of sunlight penetrated the passageway, a grinding noise starting as though it were rising from the very bowels of the island on which the castle was set. And through the niche in the wall, the wood of the massive drawbridge seemed to pulse and shudder. There was a crack louder than any gunshot Mulvaney had ever heard and the drawbridge fell.

He staggered to the niche and stared out. The drawbridge slammed down over the interior moat, across the expanse of snow-covered ground, snow surging upward in waves around it, across the second moat, the rock beneath Mulvaney's feet shuddering as it hit.

From out of the snow on both sides of the drawbridge, black shapes appeared, ninjas with red headbands, their *katanas* unsheathing, snow blowing from their heads and shoulders and arms and legs as they ran onto the drawbridge and across, steel flashing, voices shrieking. And at their center, as though the years had never touched him, ran Tsukahira Ryoichi, *katana* and *shuto* unsheathed.

The castle was at once Oriental and yet hauntingly Western, the pirate warlord who had built it, Osgood conjectured, having been widely traveled. The dining table that dominated the center of the vast thirty-foot-ceilinged room he had passed was claw-footed and massive, like something that might have been found in the mead hall that was Grendl's charnel house until Beowulf successfully challenged the creature.

Osgood stood at the open doorway, thrust his body through into the torture chamber.

Devices Western and Oriental for the inflicting of pain and extraction of information were everywhere—along the walls, suspended on chains from the ceiling over a huge brazier pit, embedded in the floor. But there were no people.

At the far end of the room to his left, there was an arched opening. Osgood ran for it.

He reached it, stopped.

The P-38 K tight in his fist, seven rounds loaded, eight more in the one remaining spare magazine, he started down the steps, a rush of cold wind and dampness flowing upward along the shaft the steps traversed, torches mounted in cast-iron niches on both sides of the downward-leading passage, the steps circling, worn slick and in places worn away by the footfalls of abusers and abused over the centuries since the castle was built.

Halfway down, as Osgood judged it, he heard a scream.

He ran, slipping, catching himself with his left hand on one of the torch holders, grabbing up the torch from its rack, starting down again, watching his footing more closely but running just the same.

The scream he had heard was a woman's, the word she had shouted Japanese for "mercy."

Osgood jumped the last five steps, skidding onto his knees, a tableau like something out of a nightmare unfolding before him, his mind racing so fast he forgot to call out in Japanese, just saying in English, "Drop that brand!"

The shirtless, hooded man wheeled toward him, the flaming poker that had been about to be thrust into Gonroku Umi's bruised and bleeding face stabbing outward. Osgood dodged, came to his feet, double-actioning the Walther's trigger, firing point-blank into the torturer's heart.

The body spun once and fell. Osgood stepped over it as three ninjas who had been standing guard over Gonroku drew their *katanas*, coming at him in a rush. Osgood fired, a double tap to the nearest of them, sidestepping left as the already dead body's momentum carried it forward, carried the *katana* down.

He fired again, then again, the second ninja's body twirling around, collapsing in a heap less than a yard from his feet. Osgood wheeled left on the third man. As he fired, the *katana* swept toward him, just missing. One shot. The ninja's *katana* sliced air toward him, Osgood firing, gut-shooting the man, but the man still coming. Osgood backed off, the ninja cursing him and his ancestors. No time to reload the Walther.

Osgood shifted the pistol to his left hand and drew his *katana,* the ninja's blade and his locking for an instant, the ninja's body twisting, their blades still locked, the *katana* ripping from Osgood's hand, sailing across the subterranean torture chamber and clattering against the opposite steps. Osgood's left foot snapped up and out, catching the ninja in the testicles, the man's body doubling over, Osgood seeing the fallen poker. He threw himself toward it. His right hand gripped it at the leather-bound wooden handle. As the ninja lunged, Osgood rolled, stabbing the still-glowing tip of the poker straight up into the already battered testicles. As the ninja shrieked in pain, Osgood rolled, scissor-kicking the ninja about the ankles and bringing him down, falling on him, his right hand grasping the haft of his *shuto,* hacking it savagely across the back of the ninja's neck. The body shuddered in death as the blade stalled in the spinal column.

Osgood sheathed the *shuto,* found his last spare magazine and reloaded the Walther, working the slide stop.

Gonroku was already talking as Osgood raced to him. Osgood tried to control his breathing, visually inspecting the knotted leather straps that held Gonroku fast to the rough-hewn wooden flat propped against the stone wall. "The women, Osgood-san."

"What about Ellermann, Gonroku-san?"

Osgood ripped the *shuto* from its sheath and sliced away the bonds at Gonroku's ankles.

"The women and Ellermann. We were all kept together. It was most unseemly."

"Speak in Japanese if you like."

"*Hai.*" The old man sagged against him as Osgood cut the last of his bonds. Then Gonroku told him how they had been kept beyond the torture room at the center of the castle between the servants' quarters and the dining hall, in a vast windowless room, an open chimney in the ceiling and a fire for which they were responsible burning in the center of the room's floor. Wood was brought to them once every twenty-four hours and it was up to them to ration it. Otherwise, they would freeze. The Oakwood woman was doing poorly, was near death.

"Are there more ninjas with them now?" Osgood asked, fighting to order his thoughts into Japanese.

"Yes, Osgood-san. They were ordered by Tsukiyama Koji to despoil the woman and kill all."

"Woman—only one? I heard a woman scream here."

"There is a well. My daughter. They . . . they did the unspeakable act. She begged for my life, but I am not dishonored. And then they . . . they threw her down." The old man, tears filling his eyes, gestured toward a wooden pallet about six feet square at the far end of the room. "She is dead, Osgood-san!"

The pallet covered a hole leading down, he surmised, to the sea.

Osgood fell back on English. "All right, Gonroku-san. Please take my pistol. Just pull the trigger. It has a passive safety. Wait until Mulvaney or Tsukahira Ryoichi's men come for you. How do I get into the room?"

"Beneath a tapestry on the east wall of the dining hall. You will need your gun."

"You may need it more. And the rest of these vile, cowardly bastards will pay with their lives. You have my oath on that, Gonroku-san." Tomiko had been lovely, full of life and promise. She had deserved vastly better of fate.

Osgood embraced the old man, then got to his feet. He ran for the steps, snatching up his *katana,* taking the steps up three at a time, the torch he had dropped when he'd shot the first ninja in his left hand now.

He reached the head of the steps, running across the stone-floored upper-level torture chamber, back through the opening and into the dining hall.

He saw the tapestry, so aged and dusty that all that could be clearly discerned was that it bore some design, but the design itself was impossible to fathom.

Osgood ran for it, tearing down the tapestry, behind which hung another of the iron-banded wooden doors, a massive modern padlock and hasp, both open, swinging from it as he wrenched the door open, bursting into the room.

Three ninjas.

Sergeant Oakwood was lying inertly near the fire, a blanket half-covering her, one of the ninjas starting to drop his pants.

A tall, skinny, sickly-looking young man with shackled wrists struggled against the other two ninjas, trying to defend the helpless woman.

"Gentlemen!" Osgood shouted the word in English as though it were a challenge. And it was.

He drew his *katana* and his *shuto*.

The two ninjas who had been playing with carrot-haired Peter Ellermann threw him to the stone floor, one of them kicking him in the face.

The one with his pants partway down pulled them up. The other two, then the third, drew their *katanas*.

He heard laughter. They mocked him. And Osgood knew he had no prayer, but he would give the best account of himself that he could. He struck his blades together as though impatient for the fight. He owed the memory of Gonroku Tomiko and her proud father's grief no less.

They started toward him.

Osgood stood his ground. His father had been an American Ranger during World War II and lost the use of his right arm while defending a bridgehead covering the withdrawal of a mixed force of Rangers and Royal Commandos. His older brother, who had come through Korea unscathed, had died in battle in the very early days of Vietnam. Honor was his tradition.

And then he heard a voice. "I had two shots left anyway, John." There was a pistol shot, and one of the two ninjas who had wrestled with Ellermann fell. There was a second shot, the other ninja tumbling back, the effect of a shot to an area instantly vital, Osgood knew clinically.

"You get number three if you want him," Mulvaney drawled.

Osgood didn't look back at his friend. He realized Mulvaney understood honor as well.

"Yes. I want him."

The third ninja sheathed his *shuto* with great flourish. Osgood sheathed his as well.

They advanced on each other.

The ninja raised his *katana* to shoulder height, beginning what Osgood had begun mentally naming the death circle, moving clockwise, edging toward him. Osgood raised his *katana* to shoulder height as well, moving clockwise also, the circle drawing tighter, tighter. The ninja lunged, Osgood parrying the blade downward and wheeling a full 360 degrees, his *katana* arcing outward, feeling the drag as steel met bone beneath flesh.

Osgood stood there, the acrid smoke of the fire beside which Sergeant Oakwood lay bringing tears into his eyes. That was it, he told himself. The ninja's head seemed to loll left, the eyes showing only whites, the sword that had been raised to strike him falling from suddenly limp fingers, making a rattling sound as it struck the stone floor and bounced once. It was as if, then, all bones in the ninja's body had somehow turned to liquid, for the body seemed to melt to the floor.

Osgood still held his *katana*, blinking back the tears.

He looked toward the fire, the source of his tears, he tried again to tell himself. Ed Mulvaney was on his knees rocking Andy Oakwood in his arms. Beyond the fire, Tsukahira Ryoichi was picking the locks on the shackles that bound Peter Ellermann.

Osgood squatted on the floor between the fire and the partially decapitated ninja. His fist was still welded to the haft of his *katana*.

Mulvaney looked at Osgood. Osgood nodded.

Tsukahira Ryoichi shouted a command Mulvaney could not understand, but he knew its meaning nonetheless. He drew back the bolt of the Uzi as Osgood did the same.

The garden air was cold, but where the sun touched his face, he was warm.

Mulvaney told himself one didn't arrest ninjas.

The brace was lifted from the doorway where Mulvaney had dropped it in place as Osgood had fought to keep the door closed enough.

It was assumed that the ninjas beyond the door would be waiting, that Tsukiyama Koji would not have shared with them the secret interlacings of the tunnels.

And the condition of the door verified that.

The elapsed time had been perhaps twenty-five minutes or a half-hour. Sections of the door fell away as it was torn open, the work of edged devices against it clear.

A knot of perhaps twelve of the Tsukiyama ninjas was visible just beyond the door.

Tsukahira Ryoichi walked calmly through the doorway, his stride wide and firm, his right hand resting gently on the hilt of his *katana*. There was a slight movement to his right, and Tsukahira Ryoichi moved in time with it, hand tighter to the haft of the *katana,* his bare head turned, eyes staring down the one who would have drawn on him.

He kept walking, Mulvaney's palms sweating as he watched through the open doorway.

The forces of Tsukahira Ryoichi's grandson parted like a wave before the old man. As he reached the approximate center of the room, the enemy surrounding him in ragged groups, he began to speak with a voice like thunder. For the first time since he had arrived in Japan, Mulvaney felt genuine regret at being totally ignorant of the language. But he didn't need to know the words to know their meaning.

Tsukahira Ryoichi was telling these men they had committed an ultimate crime, for which they would pay an ultimate penalty.

When he concluded speaking, several of the ninjas broke away from their companions, walked resignedly to places along the walls and drew their *shutos,* removing their head coverings, tying bands around their heads as they folded the head coverings around their *shutos.*

Randomly heard voices took up a disjointed, cacophonous litany, punctuated periodically with muted whispers of pain and dying.

Mulvaney forced himself to watch.

Osgood's face dripped sweat despite the cold as Mulvaney glanced at him for an instant.

After several minutes, about one hundred of the ninjas still stood.

Tsukahira Ryoichi nodded.

The ninjas of his dead grandson bowed low before him.

Tsukahira Ryoichi unsheathed his *katana,* and in the next second his body was a whirlwind of motion, the enemy ninjas closing around him, the sounds of steel against steel.

Mulvaney, Osgood and the others ran through the doorway.

Osgood stopped. So did Mulvaney. Mulvaney's left arm

felt like a toothache but had been bandaged expertly by one of the Tsukahira ninjas.

"I feel wrong using this," Mulvaney said, gesturing at the submachine gun.

"I know." Osgood nodded.

Almost as one, both men removed the magazines of their weapons, let the bolts fly forward, remagazined and slung the weapons away.

Osgood drew his *katana,* fisting it with both hands. Mulvaney could use only one hand well, and he drew his *katana* with it. They looked at each other.

Mulvaney raised his *katana,* both of them running forward into battle.

The Tsukiyama ninjas were outnumbered, but only marginally, the fighting like something Mulvaney had never experienced before, medieval combat where enemies stood shoulder to shoulder, each locked in combat and too concerned with survival to contemplate the greater concept of victory, the pace too frenetic to turn aside for the briefest instant and attempt to kill the enemy whose breath and body you could smell, whose arm would perhaps rub against your own. And when the individual combat was done, you would turn on him and then fight him, and the intimacy of the battlefield was at once forgotten yet intensified.

Mulvaney's face was sticky with the blood of his adversaries and perhaps his own blood; there was no time to be sure; you fought while you could stand, and kept fighting until you fell or the battle was done. His good right arm ached with movement, his right shoulder and neck aflame each time he would lunge or parry the blades of his enemy.

He lost sight of Osgood after the first few moments, but as he fought his way toward the center—it was important to him that this fine old man Tsukahira Ryoichi should not die—he caught sight of Osgood again, fighting toward the center as well.

And then, without knowing how it had happened, Mulvaney was back to back with Osgood, each of them fending off the blades of multiple opponents, the battle more frantic here than at its perimeter, each of the Tsukiyama ninjas fighting his way toward Tsukahira

Ryoichi for the ultimate honor of killing him or dying under his blade.

Mulvaney's opponent lunged, Mulvaney parrying the blade, sweeping it aside, backhanding the *katana* across his enemy's throat, averting his eyes as the blood sprayed. Mulvaney turned and saw three of the Tsukiyama ninjas closing with Osgood. Mulvaney was shoulder to shoulder with his friend now—his friend, he realized with a depth of understanding he had never realized existed.

Together they fought—as Osgood parried a thrust, Mulvaney made his . . . and then Mulvaney parried, Osgood finding the opening and running their enemy through.

Osgood lunged, hacking with his blade like someone out of a pirate movie, advancing, advancing, parrying, lunging, advancing, feinting, thrusting, the steel coming back slicked red with the blood of an enemy.

Mulvaney ran one man through, shoved the body off his *katana* into the body of the ninja beside him, and as the lunge started, Mulvaney was already making his, the blade tip finding the mating of head to throat and penetrating through it.

Mulvaney wheeled, searching for an opponent.

And he heard Tsukahira Ryoichi's voice, the old man standing atop three bodies of the Tsukiyama ninja dead. He was speaking in Japanese, but Mulvaney heard Osgood's voice behind him: "Tsukahira Ryoichi is saying it is finished. The last of the enemy are being executed."

Mulvaney rolled the *katana's* haft in his fingers and sheathed his blade. "Come with me." He walked around the bodies, enemy and ally. Osgood fell in beside him. He looked at himself, at Osgood, their clothes torn and ripped and bloodstained, splotches of blood on hands and face. Mulvaney wasn't yet certain if he had sustained any fresh wounds.

He approached Tsukahira Ryoichi.

The old man turned to him, a glow of youth in his eyes. "Translate, John," Mulvaney instructed.

"What?"

"Just translate."

"All right."

"Tell Tsukahira-san that I became angry at his son and called him a despicable name—"

"Mulvaney!"

"Translate, dammit!"

Osgood began translating, Mulvaney beginning again when Osgood paused. "Tell him that I hope that his son will recover from the injuries I described and that if his son's honor dictates that I—"

Tsukahira Ryoichi stepped a long pace forward. "The honor you display, Mulvaney-san, even to having your friend speak to me in my own language, is not lost on me. As soon as the battle began, a party of ninjas under command of a trusted Chunin was dispatched to assist Nobunaga. The final decision is his, but I should greatly regret that a fight should ensue."

"I killed your grandson, against your orders, but there was no way in which I could do otherwise."

"Osgood-san spoke with me of this in the hidden room where your woman and this Ellermann person were found. Were a trusted friend to come to me and speak of some dishonorable deed he swore to have witnessed committed by you"—Tsukahira's other hand touched Osgood's right forearm—"or by you, Osgood-san, I would be forced to unsheath my steel and cut off the head of a liar."

There was a shout from the far end of the room. Tsukahira Nobunaga, arms across the shoulders of two other ninjas, was coming from the tunnel mouth.

Tsukahira Ryoichi clapped Mulvaney on the shoulder and started toward Nobunaga, taking Mulvaney in tow beside him. Nobunaga's face was drawn and pale, pain-etched lines at his eyes and mouth. The young son of Tsukahira Ryoichi shifted his arms from the shoulders of his companions, wavered—Mulvaney started to reach for him, but kept back—and bowed to his father. And then promptly collapsed.

Mulvaney caught the boy. Tsukahira Ryoichi dropped to his knees beside his son. Nobunaga looked up into Mulvaney's face and smiled. "You saved my life, plain-eyes!" His eyes closed.

Mulvaney felt for a pulse. It was there but weak. "Whoever did that number on my arm should see to him fast."

"*Hai!*" Tsukahira Ryoichi called out a command in Japanese, and a group of ninjas closed about them. Then Tsukahira, his right hand touching his son's face gently for the briefest instant, spoke to Mulvaney. "I think there will be no fight between you."

Mulvaney looked at Tsukahira, saying, "*Hai, Tsukahira-san!*"

There was a shout from the doorway leading back to the garden, Tsukahira rising immediately, Osgood saying to Mulvaney, "There's something wrong. Come on."

Mulvaney shifted Nobunaga to the arms of one of the ninjas and got to his feet, sprinting after Tsukahira and Osgood, holding his left arm, which ached more pronouncedly than before.

As Mulvaney joined them by the garden entrance, Osgood translated: "Inflatables off the westward side of the island, armed men in them, and the mast of a submarine."

"Shit—"

"Quite possibly." Osgood nodded.

Tsukahira ran off again, Mulvaney and Osgood and some four dozen of the Tsukahira ninjas at his heels.

They crossed into the garden toward the wall, two of the ninjas sprinting ahead of him as Tsukahira shouted a command. The two ninjas drove spikes into the wall with small hammers, climbed atop them, drove in more spikes, climbed again, driving in more, Tsukahira waiting at the base of the wall until the two ninjas had reached the top, then springing up after them, his hands and feet barely touching the spikes. Osgood was right behind him, Mulvaney, his arm protesting as he used it, climbing after Osgood, ninjas behind him and on the other spike track.

Mulvaney reached the top of the wall and took off in a dead run after Tsukahira and Osgood toward the west wall of the castle.

The wind was high and cold. Mulvaney felt the chill to his bones, sweat running down his back and matting the hair on his chest, his right hand going to his tunic to pull it tighter about him.

On the wall overlooking the drawbridge, Tsukahira stopped. "Look!"

Mulvaney sagged against the wall beside Tsukahira and

Osgood. He heard Osgood's voice: "That's a Soviet Typhoon-class submarine offshore. And if it's gotten in this close, I'd wager I know where it's from and how it got here."

"Explain, Osgood-san."

"The Russians wanted Peter Ellermann to keep the United States and her allies from learning the secrets of their new process which renders their submarines sonar- and infrared-undetectable. And to learn the identity of Ellermann's contact in Hanoi. The only submarine they could have risked getting this close without allied detection would have to be the prototype. We understand they have only one. That, gentlemen, is it. And those men in the rubber boats are Naval Spetznas, Special Forces."

Mulvaney could see the inflatables, some of them already beaching, men heavy-laden with equipment jumping from them into the surf below. He guessed it would take fifteen minutes at best until they were at the drawbridge, perhaps as little as ten.

"The drawbridge cannot be raised," Tsukahira stated flatly.

"We have one chance," Osgood said. "They want Ellermann alive, so they must intend to penetrate the castle in order to get him, not just blow it down around our ears. Could we take the tunnel system out?"

"What about that submarine?" Mulvaney said, finding his cigarettes, lighting one against the wind, his hands cupped over the flame. "We can't sit in the tunnels. We can't fight it out on the beach. Looks like maybe fifty men with automatic weapons and God knows what else."

The wind was higher now. Mulvaney shivered.

"Tsukahira-san," Osgood began, not looking at the ninja Jonin, but toward the beach, where part of the invasion force was still assembling, part of it already moving up. "Of all the survivors here, could you find a half-dozen volunteers?"

"Of course. I can give you ten times that."

"Explosives—are there any here in the castle or on your vessels?"

Tsukahira's eyes smiled. "Yes." The old man started to laugh.

* * *

John Osgood waited in the garden, the litter with Andrea Oakwood carried between four ninjas, blankets mounded over her, but more color in her face than there had been when he first entered the hidden room and thought that she was perhaps dead. Mulvaney made the litter bearers stop, looked down at her, bent over her and kissed her forehead, then waved them on.

Mulvaney looked at Osgood. "This arm wouldn't be that much in the way."

"Certainly not." Osgood nodded, firing a cigarette as the litter disappeared through the doorway leading to the room beneath the wall and the ever-descending tunnels beyond. "But when Sergeant Oakwood awakens, I think it will do almost as much good for her health to see you beside her as Tsukahira's medic has done for her. She'll make it, I'm sure. And anyway, somebody has to get Peter Ellermann to the embassy without the Russians or the Yakusa getting at him. Just on the off-chance, of course—"

"You can't lie for shit," Mulvaney interrupted, taking out a crumpled package of cigarettes. It was empty and he balled it up and put it inside his tunic.

Osgood handed over his Dunhill lighter and the cigarette case. "You hold on to those. I'd only get them wet. I'll see you in Tokyo at the embassy or in Kyoto if you're really serious about bracing Mizutani Hideo to see who the contact is in Chicago."

"I've gotta know. You know how it is."

"I know how it is. And just in case I don't make it there, well, I'll catch you along the way sometime. Just don't lose the cigarette case and the lighter."

"I won't. Here." Mulvaney drew the full-size P-38 K from under his clothes and handed it to Osgood. "Loaded it up with hardball from the submachine guns. Best I could do."

"I loaded this one the same way." Osgood patted the P-38 K in his shoulder holster. "So . . . until later, then."

"Right."

Gonroku Umi was being carried past, a chair seat made for him in the arms of two of the ninjas. Tsukahira Nobunaga had already gone on, as had Peter Ellermann.

Mulvaney extended his hand.

Osgood took it.

* * *

Mulvaney moved along by torchlight, his right fist bunched on his brand-X loaded pistol, Tsukahira Ryoichi beside him, both of them at the approximate center of the column, darkness ahead and behind. Mulvaney had shifted his Rolex to his right arm so he could see his watch without causing a spasm of pain. He judged that by now the Soviet Naval Spetznas would have found a way across the moat. The drawbridge had been burned at Tsukahira Ryoichi's order. Even corpses had assisted in the overall scheme of the delaying tactics which were their only hope: the dead of both sides were propped in the battlements of the outer and inner walls so the Soviet attackers would have to slow their advance for fear of sustaining enemy fire.

There had been no hope of disguising the entrance through the garden into the tunnel network, the snow hopelessly trodden down, but Tsukahira had dispatched some of his trusted Genin to leave signs of obvious travel along blind passageways through the side tunnels, diverting and further delaying any pursuit once the secret passageway through the garden wall behind the fir trees was discovered.

Tsukahira had sent runners ahead to secure the exit point where they would leave the tunnels. If the vessels used by Tsukahira, secreted in an inlet on the far side of the small island, had not been discovered, Osgood would soon be having them readied to move in on Changling once the submarine was otherwise occupied.

Osgood. Mulvaney felt the cigarette case and lighter beneath the fabric of his tunic. . . .

The sail of the Typhoon-class Soviet submarine rose like a black monolith above the whitecaps as Osgood's head broke the surface. His eyes squinted against the spray, the wooden sheath of his *katana* still in his mouth for breathing. Four guards were visible on the missile deck, and one, possibly two men in the sail. He tucked down beneath the surface, using the hand signals taught him by Tsukahira Ryoichi to alert the twelve ninjas just below the surface, waiting for him.

He had theorized that with so many men being sent ashore, the submarine itself would have only a skeleton crew, its housing capacity vastly less than infinite despite its size. But a skeleton crew in this case could mean well over two hundred officers and men. But the majority of these would not be trained fighters, but trained submariners instead.

Four of the ninjas swam off, to cross the stern of the vessel and attack from the port side. He dispatched four others to swim for the forward section, these the four who carried the explosives taken from Tsukahira's vessel—one hundred pounds of plastique, looking suspiciously American. If he survived this, he would never question the ninja leader about its origins.

Osgood, his face barely below the water, began swimming toward his target amid ships where the ladder had been dropped to facilitate reaching the rubber rafts that had taken the men ashore.

He had theorized also that a small group of men with a bare minimum of metallic equipment swimming close to the surface would remain undetected by the submarine's sensing equipment—he hoped.

Osgood took the sheath from his mouth and touched it against the base of the ladder. No sparks, although a silent alarm system could have been triggered. There was no choice but to follow through, regardless.

He attained the bottom rung of the steps, pushing his body out of the water, another ninja beside him, a knife going into the man's teeth as he sprinted along the steps toward the missile deck.

Osgood's fingers moved across the skin of the vessel—it had a rough-textured, rubbery feel to it. Was he touching the secret? There was no time for a sample scraping—not yet. He started up the steps, taking the P-38 K from beneath his tunic, stripping the plastic away from it, the silencer already attached, the subsonic ammunition loaded.

The ninja crouched just below the level of the deck, looked to Osgood, who nodded.

The ninja rose, the knife coming from his teeth into his right hand as another knife appeared from beneath his clothes in his left hand, the first knife snapping outward across the missile deck, into the neck of one of the guards, the second knife shifted to the right hand, thrown, a second guard taking a knife in the chest as he turned.

There was a thudding sound as one of the bodies slapped the deck. Osgood looked up to the sail. A man in what looked to be an officer's cap was peering over the edge of the sail. Osgood stabbed the silenced P-38 K toward the man and fired: a loud but indistinct pop, the sound of the pistol's action cycling. Osgood fired again and the Soviet officer plummeted over the sail rail and hit the missile deck like a falling rock.

The game was up.

The remaining guards on the missile deck were moving into action. A third knife was thrown. Ninjas swarmed over the port-side rail and under it, bulldogging the deck guards down, blades flashing for an instant, then disappearing.

Osgood was running, skipping the missile hatches as he crossed the deck toward the ladder leading up to the sail, looking for the four men carrying the explosives. They were running toward him, unlimbering the packs.

Osgood took the rungs of the ladder as fast as he could, a face appearing over the sail rail, a vodka bottle the size of a hip flask thrown down at him, Osgood swinging away on the ladder vertically, punching the P-38 K upward and firing twice into the man's face, the body falling back.

A Klaxon sounded now, and a voice that sounded prerecorded and tinny was calling in Russian for battle stations, warning that it was not a drill, calling for the closure of all watertight doors.

Osgood reached the height of the sail and came over the rail in a low fast roll, hands reaching up to the central hatch to secure it. He fired down the hatch, emptying the P-38 K, throwing the hatch back, automatic-weapons fire answering his shots as he tucked back, bullets ricocheting insanely around him, his left side struck, his body thrown against the bulkhead.

Osgood rammed a fresh magazine into his pistol, not the subsonic ammo this time, working the slide, not bothering to discard the silencer. He fired as a Soviet ordinary seaman with an AKS-74 assault rifle came up through the hatchway, dumping four shots into the sailor's chest, the 9mm earsplittingly loud by subconscious comparison with the subsonic rounds he had fired before.

The sailor's body crashed to the deck at Osgood's feet. Osgood grabbed up the assault rifle, to his knees now, firing as another sailor followed the first man.

The Tsukahira ninjas were swarming up onto the sail

now, their *katanas* flashing, blood spraying in the icy wind. Osgood struggled to his feet.

"Follow me!" He fired out his assault rifle, the P-38 K going into his sash, his hands grabbing up another rifle, one of the ninjas and then another and another diving through the hatchway ahead of him, the screams of battle from below, the sounds of automatic weapons. Osgood shouldered past another of the ninjas and was into the hatchway.

Below him, a half-dozen Soviet seamen were gunning down the ninjas. Osgood opened fire, spraying the entire area below him, the ninjas already dead, the Soviet seamen joining them.

He half-dropped, half-fell to the deck, to his knees, leaning forward, tremors of pain moving through his side where the bullet or bullets had struck.

To his feet. He grabbed up another assault rifle, discarding the emptied one, firing it into the access beneath the hatch here—a scream, a shouted curse, no answering shots. He fired again, throwing down the weapon, too tired suddenly to hold it.

He started down, the P-38 K back in his fist, a face appearing at the base of the ladder, Osgood firing a double tap into it, the face gone just as suddenly.

He reached the base of this new ladder. The con would be below. He had gone far enough.

He shouted up as ninja fighters joined him. "Explosives! Down here! Hurry!"

The ninjas bearing the explosives dropped like cats through the hatchway, Osgood stabbing his pistol into his tunic sash again. "Open the packs." He shouted to the other ninjas who had made it, "The Russian rifles—fire them down the hatchway! Just keep firing so they can't close the hatch!"

The four ninjas who were the explosive bearers positioned themselves like points of a compass, just as he had told them beforehand, opening the flaps on the packs, drawing out the waterproof-packaged explosives, Osgood stumbling toward the nearest of the men, helping to align the shaped charge against the bulkhead. "Like this—mold it into position so the shock wave can be directed," he ordered.

He set the first detonator, glancing at his Rolex. Time had

run out. He set the detonator to sixty seconds. "Set each of them to sixty seconds! Do not activate the timer switch until I say to."

Osgood forced himself to stand. "You . . . give me that rifle. Find me another one. Hurry."

He leaned against the bulkhead between two of the twenty-five-pound charges. Soviet hull construction was tough, but the combined outward and upward force of the explosives would rip the sail away from the missile deck as though it had been cut away with a can opener.

He had the second rifle.

"Everybody out except you four! Hurry! Back to the small island."

The Tsukahira ninjas, except the four who comprised the impromptu demolitions team, disappeared up the hatchway.

Osgood gave them thirty seconds, watching the sweep of the second hand on his watch. "When I nod my head, activate the timer switches and get out of here. I will be right behind you."

One of the four looked at him, nodded. He could see it in the eyes that the man understood the words he had not said.

Osgood nodded and the four men activated the switches and vaulted to the ladder, disappearing through the hatchway.

There was motion beneath him that he saw through the hatch leading into the con, the Klaxons still sounding. If they would only dive, the explosion would have even more spectacular results.

Osgood opened fire through the hatchway, emptying one of the rifles, throwing the other one down and through.

He looked at the charges surrounding him. "What the hell!" He lurched toward the ladder, started up, his side paining him more than anything had ever pained him in his life, a light-headedness washing over him, his hands and feet still moving, the seconds still ticking away for him mentally.

He verbalized the count as he reached the sail. "Forty-nine . . . fifty . . ." Osgood rolled over the rail, reaching out, grasping for a rung, sliding down half the length of the ladder before he caught one, breaking his fall, letting go, dropping to the missile deck.

"Fifty-seven . . . fifty-eight . . ." Osgood lurched toward the opening in the missile-deck rail, realized he wouldn't make it, told himself, "Run!" and threw the last of his strength into a dash for the nearest segment of rail, falling over it as the rumbling started and the deck began to tremble. Russian bulkheads were tough.

12

The Night Before Christmas

ANDY OAKWOOD HAD given him the number on the third day after her hospitalization, when the doctors had said she was strong enough to be spoken with, but only briefly.

He had kissed her and left, telling her he would be back and that after that he would never leave her again.

He slipped the rented Honda Accord into gear and pulled into traffic, following the Mercedes as it sped just under the limit along the tree-lined drive. He checked the odometer, juggling miles and kilometers as the Mercedes flicked on a turn signal.

Mulvaney pulled the Japanese baseball cap lower over his eyes as the Mercedes turned off and he kept going straight, his right hand reaching for the microphone. "Old One, this is Windy City Boy. Subject turned right three and a half miles from pickup point. I couldn't read the fuckin' street sign. Over."

Gonroku's voice came back. "Windy City Boy. This is Old One. I copy. Stand by, please. Old One out."

Mulvaney pulled over, waited for a break in traffic, made an illegal—he was certain—U-turn and started back, going left down the road where Mizutani Hideo's Mercedes had turned, cutting his speed now so he wouldn't blow the tail. Gonroku Umi's voice came back. "Windy City Boy. We have him. Take the same road onto which the subject turned and go to the corner past the Buddhist shrine and turn left. Black One has just transferred to Black Two. Subject is in sight. Old One over."

"I copy, Old One. Windy City Boy standing by. Out." He threw the microphone down on the seat and stomped the gas pedal to the floor. Black One and Black Two were Tsukahira ninjas, as were the drivers of three other cars set up for the tail if needed. He had gotten the license plate from Andy Oakwood rather than having Gonroku Umi or Tsukahira Ryoichi obtain it, in the almost certain event that despite the arrest of Tanaka Hideyoshi on charges running the gamut from white slavery to suspicion of espionage, the Yakusa still had powerful connections in government.

Mulvaney saw the Buddhist shrine and took the first left. It was a business district, towering modern office buildings ranked on either side of the street, but the early-morning traffic was light enough. He hit the radio. "Old One. This is Windy City Boy. Come in. Over."

"Windy City Boy. This is Old One. Subject has turned right five blocks after where you were told to turn. There is a building with a sign in both Japanese and English reading 'Sushi Delight.' Turn right just after—hold on!"

They were working on separate frequencies in the event Mizutani Hideo's car was equipped with a scanning monitor.

"This is Old One. After the right turn, drive three blocks and turn left at the forested corner. Subject vehicle has turned in at Location Five."

"Gotcha, Old One. Windy City Boy out!" Mulvaney saw the sushi sign and took the right, flipping open the marked map, making Location Five, then keeping one eye on traffic, one eye on the Polaroids he shook out of the envelope onto the seat beside him.

Location Five was the Japanese-American Friendship Society.

Mulvaney upshifted and stomped the gas pedal, taking the left at the "forested corner" so fast the tires screeched, seeing Black Two and Black One just past the driveway, in the rearview seeing another of the Tsukahira cars turning the corner.

Mulvaney downshifted, turning too fast again, up the concrete driveway between the manicured lawns, the

Mercedes already stopped at the end of the horseshoe-shaped driveway. Mulvaney upshifted, accelerated, bounced out of the driveway onto the curb and let the Honda clip down some ornamental shrubbery, the door of the black Mercedes already opening, a liveried chauffeur reaching under his coat. Mulvaney stomped the gas pedal, cut the wheel hard right and rammed the Mercedes, hitting the chauffeur and throwing him up into the air and over the hood of the Mercedes, ripping the door away, the Honda slamming to a halt, Mulvaney almost thrown through the windshield.

He was out of the car. A bodyguard lunged out of the rear compartment, a pistol in his right fist. Mulvaney fired first, emptying three rounds from the Beretta into the man's nice white shirt, the body slapping down over the trunk of the Honda.

Mulvaney stepped inside the Mercedes.

The little old man sitting in the middle of the seat had Coke-bottle glasses and was so skinny that even though his body trembled, his suit coat remained almost motionless. Mulvaney pushed the muzzle of the Beretta against the old guy's nose. And then he said the sentence he had memorized in Japanese: "Tell me one thing: the name of the man in Chicago who is your man."

Mizutani Hideo hesitated. Mulvaney twisted the pistol away and fired once into the seat beside the old man's left shoulder.

The old man's eyes started to roll.

Mulvaney repeated his one sentence in Japanese. "Tell me one thing: the name of the man in Chicago who is your man."

When Mizutani Hideo gurgled up the name, then sank back grasping at his throat, Mulvaney realized he'd already known the name.

He looked at the old man a second longer. He'd seen heart attacks. Mizutani Hideo was having one. "Have a nice death, huh?" And as Mizutani Hideo's arms twitched, Mulvaney saw something when a miles-too-big shirt cuff slipped back. It was an ornamental tattoo.

He ran from the car along the driveway, police sirens sounding, the photos and map in the Honda, nothing with his fingerprints or anyone else's on it, one of Tsukahira

Ryoichi's ninjas blocking the driveway, the rear door of the car open and waiting for him.

Japanese hell was about to get a new permanent resident. . . .

The snow was soft, soundless, almost warm-feeling on his face.

A CTA bus passed and he stepped back into the doorway a little deeper, a little more out of the yellow of the high-crime-area streetlight.

When he'd gotten out of Tokyo and reached Hawaii, he had called Dern from the hotel in Honolulu and Dern had asked how his vacation had been and Mulvaney had just outright asked him, "What happened to Osgood, motherfucker?"

"Who?"

"John Osgood. One of your guys."

"I . . . ahh . . . I never heard of anybody named Osborne."

"Osgood. He's a CIA agent just like—"

"Fuck off!" The phone clicked dead. Mulvaney had taken the next flight to Chicago.

Gonroku Umi knew nothing. The ninjas who had accompanied Osgood in the successful raid against the submarine had told Tsukahira Ryoichi that they had seen the sail of the Russian submarine blow outward all over the surface of the sea around them, but there had been no sign of the American. He had been seriously wounded, stayed behind until the very last to ensure the escape of the others with him. He had died bravely.

Mulvaney hadn't bought that. Guys like Osgood were too good at what they did to die like that, he had told himself, then proceeded to try to find out what he hoped was the truth. Did the Russians have him? Was he in some hospital somewhere, worse than dead?

He had called Andy Oakwood at the hospital in Kyoto.

She told him she had heard nothing except that Mizutani Hideo's car had been attacked by a man in a leather jacket and a baseball cap, tall, the police guessing the assassin was Chinese. But Mizutani had cheated death like he had cheated life, dying of a heart attack, no wounds on his body.

302

Mulvaney had told her that was nice and that he'd call again soon, then hung up.

He'd gone to see Dern. The other would keep awhile. Dern had closed the office door. "Look. If there were some guy named Osgood or whatever, I wouldn't know anything about him, and if I did, I sure as shit couldn't tell you."

"You know that little gun you have your suits tailored to hide? You'll never reach it." It was his own Beretta that he'd had in his fist that time, pointing it at Timothy Dern's head, his thumb jacking back the hammer.

"You're nuts!"

"Right." Mulvaney had smiled.

"I'm just the Company's damned employment counselor for the Chicago metropolitan area—what the hell you expect from me?"

"Whatever I can get. Otherwise I'll kill you. That trip to the Orient. It broadened my horizons, Dern."

"I . . . I'll try, huh?"

Mulvaney had put his gun away. "You do that. And if you say a word about me, this gun, and you, it's on the street you're dealin'."

"What? Drugs! You realize—"

"Yeah—kiss off the old security clearance, huh?" Mulvaney had lit a cigarette. "Have a nice day, Timmy. And say hi to Lassie too, huh?"

He'd gotten more out of Dern in the next few days, but only that CIA headquarters at Langley, Virginia, hadn't heard anything from Osgood and was presuming him dead.

Mulvaney had told Dern to keep his ear to the ground, then decided it was time to take care of the other thing.

Andy Oakwood was coming in the morning of Christmas Eve, permanently separated from the United States Army. He'd stopped at a jeweler's on State Street and bought her a diamond with the walk-around money Ajaccio had conspired to have put into accounts under his name. He'd found the key for the safe-deposit box with the hundred grand in it that Ajaccio had promised for delivering Peter Ellermann safe and sound. The key and the location of the box had been on the shelf at the top of his locker at Chicago police headquarters at Eleventh and State.

He hadn't called to thank Ajaccio, but he'd decided to keep the money.

When he pulled the plug and took over the security business for his dying Vietnam buddy, the money might make the difference. He'd asked Lew Fields. "Come to my Christmas Eve party at the house. You and your wife. I'm quittin' after I get a few things attended to. Why don't you come into it with me?"

"You shittin' me?"

"No. I'm dead serious."

"I gotta think."

"Thinkin's cool. It's open when you want it."

He'd called Dern. Nothing different on Osgood. Maybe he *was* dead.

He'd driven to the airport and used a blue-and-white so he could park in the passenger-loading zone without getting towed, then flashed his badge to get through security with three guns and a knife. The knife was one of the Cold Steel Tantos. He'd bought it when he got off the plane in Chicago.

She came in on the E concourse and he'd waited just inside the gate.

Her red hair was up. She was wearing the same silly poncho, and the huge purse was still there. She had tried to run, but it hadn't looked like she was making it and he had run to her and folded her into his arms. "You're marrying me, right?"

"Right."

"Good. I don't like punchin' out women in airports." And he'd kissed her harder than he'd ever kissed anybody and walked with her slowly—she was still pale—toward the baggage claim, gotten her three suitcases and her dress bag and carried them all, looking at her eye-to-eye sometimes as they walked to the car.

He'd driven her home, given her his sister's number in case she couldn't find anything, then told her about the party. She had wanted a bath and he'd pulled the L-frame Smith out of the Bianchi leather under his arm and given her the speedloaders. "This is Chicago. A nice town. Best museums in the world. Some of the nicest people. Anybody doesn't tell you who they are when they come to the door and sound damn convincing, blow 'em the hell away. Right?"

"Right."

She'd kissed him hard, taken the gun. He had given her a guest list.

He drove the borrowed blue-and-white to the little pie-wedge-shaped bank at Forty-seventh and Ashland where he still kept the safe-deposit box his father and mother had kept. He parked the car by the old People's Theater, walked east and crossed the street.

Inside the box had been what he held in his hand inside the pocket of the old tweed overcoat now, the snow crunching under his track shoes when he shuffled his feet against the dampness.

His father had told him, "An honest cop can make an ass outta himself with a drop gun. 'Cause you never know who dropped it. Maybe the gun you get nailed with was used in some damn B&E murder in Cincinnati ten years ago, right? So you keep this and never use it unless you gotta, right, Eddie? And don't shoot somebody with it who's more'n six, eight feet away 'cause the barrel's all smooth on the inside."

It was a Colt Official Police, a five-inch-barreled gun with a lot of blue gone from holster wear or something, the same frame size as the Python, but only a .38 Special. And the funny thing about it was there were no serial numbers anywhere on the gun. There never had been. His father had told him, "Back in the old days—they couldn't do it now—people'd maybe steal parts, ya know? Like the funny story 'bout the guy who stole all the parts from the car plant and built himself a damn Cadillac or somethin' in his garage? This is one of those. Wear gloves when you touch it, Eddie."

His hands had never touched it.

It was a wise man who listened to his father, his mother had always said. He stood in the snow and decided he'd been a wise man all the time.

He'd left the blue-and-white parked in front of his house, telling Andy that if anybody called he was in the shower, then left by the back steps. The snow was falling heavily enough that his tracks would get covered up if anybody bothered to look. He had walked over into Oak Park and met Lew Fields. When he'd driven out to the airport for Andy, he'd dropped Lew off and Lew had stolen a car for him out of the parking lot. Lew had volunteered, Mulvaney trying to talk him out of getting involved after he'd told him what he'd planned to do in the first place. He had dropped Lew back in his own neighborhood on Lake Shore Drive so Lew could drive back with his wife and be alibied while the thing was going down.

The party was still going on inside, but the man he waited for had a family so he'd have to put in an appearance at home on Christmas Eve. The man Mulvaney waited for had cheated on his wife for so many years that everybody who knew him knew it, but the wife was politically connected so they stayed married. She cheated on him too, so it evened out and the kids were grown anyway.

There was always the danger he'd leave with some half-stiff bimbo on his arm and try to lay her in the back seat of the car. But it was a pretty cold night for that.

Mulvaney looked at his watch, his right fist sweating with the rubber glove and the dime-store woolen glove over it.

And then the door to Halpern's Club 18 opened and Mulvaney's right arm stiffened. His left arm still hurt a little, but the bandages had been gone for a couple of days.

Mulvaney watched.

Edward Hilliard pulled his black fedora low over his eyes against the snow and snapped a butt away into the street, then started for the unmarked black Chicago P.D. Ford Crown Victoria. He was pulling his gloves on.

That was good.

With his gloved right hand, the deputy superintendent started brushing the accumulated fresh snow off his front windshield.

Mulvaney stepped out of the doorway, Hilliard less than twelve feet away.

"Hilliard."

Hilliard looked up at him across the hood of the car. "Mulvaney. So . . . Merry Christmas."

"It's the holiday season in Japan too." Mulvaney slowly began closing the gap until he could reach the desired six or eight feet. There was no law that could touch Hilliard, and the man who had fingered Hilliard as playing middleman between the Chicago Crime Syndicate and the Yakusa had died of a heart attack.

"I heard you got back. Go okay?"

"Yeah. Real good. Bunch of good men died. But then,

so'd the little shit who ran the Yakusa. Had a heart attack. But he told me to say hi to his Chicago contact just before he croaked."

Hilliard's body froze and for the first time Mulvaney saw that the left hand was inside the overcoat pocket. "That a fact? What's the name of the guy?" Hilliard always carried a little Smith & Wesson Bodyguard Airweight in the left coat pocket and Mulvaney knew Hilliard didn't think he knew it. You could fire the gun through your pocket without any hammer spur to catch on the lining.

"In Japan, when they toss ya in the slam, they tattoo you. Good way to keep track if somebody goes south."

"Barbaric."

"Yeah, maybe. But when they let ya go, they cover up the tattoo with some design or other, ya know?"

"Didn't know."

"So it won't be some kinda social stigma."

"Awful white of 'em, huh?" Deputy Superintendent Hilliard laughed at his little joke. "You get it? White?"

"Yeah. You should have a tattoo."

"I've never been in the slam, you drunken asshole."

"The tattoo brands you for what you are, Hilliard. You're the one Mizutani Hideo sent his regards to."

Hilliard looked Mulvaney square in the eye. "You can wind up dead or you can wind up makin' out a little better each week."

"Gee."

Hilliard's face softened a little, but the eyes didn't. "There's plenty of money in this. Ajaccio isn't as big shit as he thinks. There's other guys. You can get in on it too. If you're smart."

"I was never smart, Hilliard—not that way."

Mulvaney dodged right when the shape in Hilliard's left pocket started to move, because the gun could turret right but not left with the overcoat buttoned like it was. The shot split the night as it creased across the top of the car hood. Mulvaney had the old .38 out in his gloved fist and stabbed it toward Hilliard's face and fired once, missing. Hilliard was hauling the gun out of his coat pocket. Mulvaney took a step closer. He fired. Hilliard stared at him, eyes wide, the left arm no longer moving. Mulvaney fired again, Hilliard's body started to tumble back into the street.

Mulvaney stepped down into the street as Hilliard hit the snow.

"Remember how you threatened me with a murder rap? At that meet we all had with you and the rest of the big shots that sent me off to get killed in Japan? Well, I guess you were right after all, Hilliard. I *am* capable of murder."

Hilliard looked up at him. Mulvaney extended the revolver at the end of his arm until the muzzle was four feet or so from Hilliard's face. He fired, a red hole just above Hilliard's right eye. Snow was already making little wet white speckles all over Hilliard's black overcoat.

Mulvaney put the old revolver back in his pocket, took the beat-up navy watch cap from his other pocket and pulled it over his head and down over his ears.

He turned and walked away, the snow starting to fall a little heavier now, as if it had something to cover up. . . .

Lew Fields's wife had brought sweet-and-sour meatballs and shrimp dip, Lew had brought two quarts of Seagram's Seven, Mulvaney supplied the house. Andy Oakwood, while he had been gone, had cleaned up the place and thrown together some onion soup and sour cream into another dip. Nobody had brought potato chips, so Andy and Lew's wife were in the kitchen making toast in the oven and cutting it up into little pieces.

As soon as he'd gotten back into the house, he'd called for a couple of pizzas, from the same place he'd gotten pizza the night Vincent Washington had come calling and left in a body bag.

"Your girl Andy and my wife—they get along pretty well with one another."

"Be tough if they didn't, you and me best friends and everything and Andy marrying me."

"You do it?" Fields poured a drink for himself, neat with no ice.

Mulvaney leaned back in the couch and looked at the new TV he'd gotten. He was running a tape of an old Bing Crosby Christmas special. "You guys didn't have to—"

"You were here all evening with us. I told the women. We all agreed."

"I shouldn't've told ya in the first place."

"Maybe. You always talked too much anyway. Gimme one of your cigarettes."

"You quit, remember?"

"Gimme one anyway, white boy."

Mulvaney laughed. He took the cigarette case from the coffee table and then the Dunhill lighter, offered one from the case to Lew, then lit up both of them.

"You gonna quit the department and join me in that security company?"

"I still haven't decided. You ditch the thing like I told ya?"

Mulvaney had dropped off the stolen car after checking it thoroughly, left it on the West Side about a mile from his house. There would be nothing to tie it to the killing. But he knew what Lew was asking about. "Yeah." He had dropped the gun into a dumpster about six blocks away from where he'd made the hit, left the gloves in a garbage can on the Oak Park side of North Avenue, come back in up the alley and through the back door, snow still falling, more gently now, but enough to fill up his footprints.

Mulvaney set down the cigarette case. "You woulda liked him. I mean, WASP City, right? But a hell of a good guy, Lew. Woulda talked him into the security company too. Three of us, man, we coulda done some neat shit."

"Maybe the two of us can, buddy," Lew said.

The doorbell rang.

"Somebody get the door—must be the pizza!" Andy called from the kitchen.

"Not even married, and she's tellin' ya what to do," Fields gibed.

Mulvaney stood up, took the Beretta and shoved it into his pants in the small of his back. "Safety first," he laughed.

He opened the door with his left hand, his right hand hanging loose.

It wasn't the pizza.

"Rather hard to ring the bell and hold these at the same time—with this." The left arm was in a black silk sling, an expensively cut trench coat draped over the shoulders like a cape, snow wet on the trench coat's shoulders. "I met this fellow when I was coming up the steps. He started babbling about never going into this house again and just handed these to me and wished me Merry Christmas."

The CIA resident, Dern, would have given him the address.

"You're alive!"

"Apparently." John Osgood smiled. "I believe you have my cigarette case and lighter. Would you consider them an even trade for two pizzas?"